The Complete Crown & Daggers Series

By: Andi Lawrencovna

CHARMING

THE COMPLETE CROWN & DAGGERS SERIES

BY: ANDI LAWRENCOVNA

Front Cover art from: Julie Nicholls at JMN Art (www.JulieNicholls.com).

First Edition: June, 2018
ISBN-13: 978-1719587624
ISBN-10: 1719587620
BISAC: Fiction / Fantasy / Romance / General

10 9 8 7 6 5 4 3 2 1

WORKS BY ANDI LAWRENCOVNA

THE NEVER LANDS SAGA:

THE CROWN & DAGGERS NOVELS

Charming: *Book One*

The Captain: *Book Two*

The Prince: *Book Three*

BREATH OF FYRE SERIES

The Dragon's Sacrifice
Originally published in the **Stoking the Flames** *Anthology*

The Dragon's Storm
Originally published in the **Stoking the Flames II** *Anthology*

STAND ALONE TITLES:

So Sweet: *A Tale as Old as Time*

SHORT STORIES:

The First Ball: *A Charming Short Story*

Out of the Woods: *A Mother Goose Legend*

ForeverMore*: A Once and Future Legend*

Once Upon a Yuletide*: A Charming Holiday Collection*

The Pastry Prince: *A Sugar & Spice Short Story*
Originally published in the **Sinfully Delicious** *Anthology*

A Thief in the Night: *A Tale of Grimm Portent*
Originally published in **The Fountain** *Anthology*

COMING SOON

The Snake Charmer's Song: *A Tale of Grimm Portent*

Dedication

To our Princes, the ones we love, and we raise, and we remember and long for. Be charming and be brave and be more than what fairy tales say you are.

TABLE OF CONTENTS

AUTHOR'S NOTE

DEAR READER,

In the immortal words of most fairy tales: Once upon a time…

Even an author's note should start that way when the story demands it, no? Well, this one does. And once upon a time, I read the story of a scullery maid turned princess, and wondered what else was there, unwritten, between the lines of that fairy tale. So much went unsaid, was left to the imagination, and needed to be told, so, I figured, what the hell?

When you look at the Grimm Brothers and their original narrative, there's a whole lot of darkness between the beginning and happily ever after. Darkness that the characters have to face to grow and find true love in the end. But that story was for children and didn't have a chance to touch on all the darker elements it embodied.

Not so here.

Don't be afraid. The prince is still charming, and the princess is, well, isn't quite an orphan, but she could use the love of a good man to fall for, to sweep her away from the life she knows, and maybe he could use the same too.

Besides, isn't that what's most important? That story that hasn't been told before? The truth you've been missing?

Here it is.

I hope you enjoy!

Andi

ACKNOWLEDGMENTS

TO KAREN AND DARLENE. You two have been so amazing and have always been with me, my support, my friends, and my sisters. I cannot tell you how very grateful I am to have you with me on this journey.

TO MY FAMILY, for always believing in me, even when you don't know what I've been writing lately.

CHARMING

BOOK ONE

CHAPTER ONE

I
The One Hundredth Ball

"GODS TAKE IT, woman. Halt!"

She could barely hear his yelled order over the rushing of the wind from her galloped flight. It was easy enough escaping from the palace courtyard, making the forest road. That he chased her wasn't part of the plan, wasn't unexpected either.

She shook her head free of the thought.

"For all the hell- Stop, damnit!"

She did not obey the command hurled at her from the pounding of chasing hooves at her back.

And all this because she'd lost a blasted slipper and the bastard had decided to follow her from the ball. It wasn't enough to have danced every single waltz with the brat. No, now he was following her without a thought for himself during the middle of the night in a dark forest where bandits were rather routine, and she wasn't even armed in case the wretches did show up.

A snake slithered into the moonlight cutting the path before her.

Her horse reared and her grip on its mane faltered. The folds of her gown caught around her legs, loosening her thighs' hold on the horse's flanks. When she fell, it was with little grace, arms tucked around her head to protect herself while she tumbled to the ground, landing on her knee and rolling as quickly as she could away from the stamping hooves above her.

His horse reared in response, a motion of its owner's demands rather than being startled. While her beast bolted, he slid from his mount's saddle before rushing to her side.

"Hades—are you alright?" He reached for her, his fingers wrapping around her flailing wrists as she struggled to right herself from the ground.

"Get off of me."

She wasn't shocked that he didn't listen to her demand, continuing to help her back to her feet, even dropping to his own knee to settle her skirts around her legs more demurely.

For three days, she had ridden to the courtyard of the palace, slipped easily from the back of her horse and walked with confidence through the front doors to attend the royal ball thrown for the prince to find a bride. Said prince stood now before her, his face hidden in shadow from the moonlight though the glow no doubt highlighted her own olive complexion.

This was the prince's hundredth ball.

At one hundred and thirty, he was a young man, not yet even having reached his majority. A long-lived race, like her people, he wouldn't be considered an adult until his hundred and fiftieth year. He was so young to have such yearning, such shadows in his eyes.

He was handsome enough, she supposed.

Ah hell.

He was stunning. Hair black as night, eyes silver, glinting like steel freshly forged; he was a soldier trained from birth to lead and defend and it was evident in the definition of his shoulders, the way he stood before her. He loved his people, and that too was something to admire. Sharp nose, square jaw, cheekbones slightly less angular, softening his visage into something beyond classically handsome, something more charming than stately when he smiled.

Would he know a battle if he had to draw the ceremonial sword at his hip? It would be easier if this repost between them was one of steel and speed.

This was not a battle, not for him.

For her…

It was one of wits and words and hearts, damn it.

She pushed away from him, denying herself the opportunity to feel the strength of him beneath her palms a last time. Three nights were too much already. She had known better than to go to the ball, but forbidden the chance, told to stay away, she had had to.

Too dangerous, her council had said, to attempt a coup at the ball amidst all of his people. But she wasn't attempting a coup, just an assassination, which was much easier, all considered. So, she'd danced with him, and it hadn't been enough to dance only the one night. Engaging him in practice in the early hours of the morning, testing his strength and his skill in a sword fight, had been an even greater pleasure for her, had been another chance to strike, another failure. Honestly, the second night of the ball should have been an end to things, but he'd whisked her from the ballroom, walked with her in his gardens, spoke of his people the way she spoke of hers. She was born to fight, not talk, not dance. And yet it was the talking, the dancing she remembered most.

Not that she would think on that now.

"Why do you insist on running from me?"

"Why do you insist on chasing after?" She heard the petulance in her voice and would have blushed at the sound if she were not so well trained to hold her emotions in check.

Though she would not admit it, she enjoyed the bickering between them, the spirit he displayed. Pampered he may be, but there was a strength to him that reminded her of her people, called out to her as kin. And she could not and would not call him kin, no matter the desire swirling within her, reflected in his gaze. "I do not like you, prince. We have had our fun these past nights. Let it be enough between us."

"Never." He reached for her, pulling her close to him, bending his head to her own though his lips did not touch hers. They never touched hers, though she did not doubt he wanted to. "Never enough between us; you feel it too. I know you do."

No man's breath should smell so fresh, not after a night of champagne and wine and sweets and a jaunt through the woods. He should smell of horse and sweat and look put upon, not as though he were just now remade for the day. She must look a disgrace compared to him, her russet hair a mess around her shoulders, dress stained from her tumble from her horse.

She did not care for customs or norms, finding more comfort in breeches than the tulle of a skirt, and yet for him she had found a gown and now it was ruined and that was quite fine. She stomped her foot. Perhaps a bit more petulance, simpering condescension might make the male rethink his desire for her. "Foolish boy, I feel nothing for you." Her finger extended to poke at his chest, push him to her desires, make space between his heat that warmed her through. "You know nothing of me. Three days does not a knowledge grant. We have danced and wined but little else. If there were words spoken between us, I do not recall them."

"Liar. I was there too, my lady. We shared many words." He leaned into her finger, forcing her to retreat or bow to his advance, yield to his physicality pressing into her. "I am not blind. I know the expression in your eyes. Why run from me when you know my heart? I have told you—"

"You have spoken with the passion of a moment upon you, nothing more. Any feeling you profess is that of close encounters late at night when heads were full of drink and eyes upon the stars. What you feel is a lie, despite your words." The argument tasted of ash against her tongue. Lies upon lies and all starting the moment she was introduced at the opening of the ball and descended the stairs to the main dance floor.

She did not fall in love. Love was a thing for simpering toffs, not soldiers and assassins and princes and priests. Her people needed her return. No doubt they were already searching after her leaving.

Yet she stared at him, waiting for his words to deny her denial. Curse him.

Damn her.

"Why are you saying this? Why are you denying us?" His hands gripped her shoulders, hauling her close once more where she had let the small space between them build. "You spoke the words back to me, Ella."

"That is not my name."

He stared at her and her heart ached at the pain in his gaze. Damn him, she should not feel for him and his integrity, his humor, his compassion. This prince who was barely a man and had stolen her thoughts for three days' time and would steal her from the world she could not leave behind. No, and that was worse, that he wanted to keep her with him and she was weak enough to desire it. If he learned her name, he would hate her, hate who and what she was and yet she wanted nothing more than to tell him and see what response he would have.

Her fingers spread over the crisp feel of his doublet, the velvet brocade stitched with golden thread to set off the deep red umber, pressing for the beat of his heart beneath her hand. He'd met her at the bottom of the stairs and extended his hand. She was a silly girl, Sweet Darkness, was it really only two nights' past, to not know the man who stood before her was a prince, to ignore the tittering around her when she obliged her partner and slid gracefully into a quadrille struck by the orchestra.

"Another lie." He cupped her cheek, and even knowing the road was clear at her back, that she was free to run if she but turned away, she could not move, denied the desire to, holding his gaze which so easily captured hers.

She was soft towards him.

She should not yield.

It would be so easy to take the sword at his hip and finish what her people had long sought but been denied. Who would have thought to enchant the prince in a dance? It was trickery and not the way of the woods that were subtle and swift.

"What is your name then, if not that which you have so easily said to me these past nights?"

The name was there on her tongue, waiting to sound in the air between them, hiding for a desperate moment more.

Leaves shivered with the breeze, broke across the moonlight filtering through their canopy, showing his face within the darkness. He didn't think her name would matter. Surely an Abigail or a Tabitha or even a Rebecca would not change his mind towards her? But her name was none of those. Her name was a title, and he would loathe the title once he heard it.

To have his hatred felt a worse fate than to slip a knife between his ribs and end him quickly.

"Please do not ask this of me." It was the only plea she had ever made in her life, would ever make in her life. Yes, she'd started the damn conversation, opened herself to the questioning, but she didn't want to answer him. She wasn't ashamed of who she was. But there was a niggling prayer deep in her gut, a wish to the Night to let her carry on the charade of these three days rather than go back to what she was. "Stop this." If he heard the emotion in her voice, perhaps he would take it to heart and leave her be before she was required to spout harsher realities to him. Let this memory be sweet. Do not taint it with the truth.

"I am your prince."

She looked away, fingers digging into his jacket. Her words came out a shrill laugh. "You are nothing to me."

He could not be.

She wanted to tell him to look at where he was. Ask him why he thought a noble woman would run to the forest when not a single city dweller dared venture so close to the wood's edge without a full contingent of soldiers to guard them? Had he not realized where they were, where she led them?

Her voice hardened into a growl, casting aside the airy lightness his courtiers so easily used, the lilting accent that each word rang with, to allow him a glimpse of who she was, why he should run. Her people's tongue was harsher than his, the tone distinguishable. "You are a spoiled brat barely out of his leading strings. An infant thinking himself in love. It is easy enough to spout silken promises that innocents will believe.

Why would I want a whelp when I could have a wolf of the forest to wed?"

He jerked away from her, the venom of her words.

A lifetime of animosity built between their peoples, an animosity she had never herself felt, and yet could imitate without trial, sounded in her words. "A city dweller, protected by his walls." She spat on the ground between them. He stepped back another foot to avoid the assault. "You are weak; your people are weak. Your king is an old man and his son an imbecile who is easy to tempt, too trusting by far, a walking corpse without the sense to die like prophecy demands."

Anger sparked in his eyes, the mounting fury giving his softer edges the strength of steel, unyielding, unbending. Sweet Darkness, but this was no boy before her. She knew that but couldn't help tempting him, watching the spark of temper rise. How many times had she seen the same strength enter his face, straighten his spine on the dance floor, surrounded by simpering idiots who spoke thinking their prince was a simpleton and wouldn't listen to their words?

She watched his anger flare.

He would push her away now, cast her aside as he should.

His jaw clenched tightly closed and he said nothing.

"Would you deny the truth of my words, boy?"

He snorted, a sound undignified from the man she'd come to know so well these past nights. If he smiled, she rarely saw it, and if his lips did turn up, the emotion did not reach his eyes. His face was as much a show for the world as the gown swirling around her ankles, making her a woman in his eyes rather than the warrior she was and could not change from. He would hate her when he learned who she was, an enemy on his doorstep, taken into his confidence. She'd grown on mother's milk tainted with stories of how this prince was his father's despair, a boy marked by the gods yet worshipped by none, the death of his country if he would but lay down and die.

"I am no boy."

No, he was not.

Her lungs froze when he wrapped her in his arms once more. She gripped his elbows to steady the unseemly trembling in her limbs.

She was an assassin. He should not have this power to overwhelm her the way he did.

"Tell me you do not love me."

"I do not love you." There was no conviction to her words.

"Say it again, for I do not believe you."

"Foolish boy," was barely a breath of air between them, meant more for her than him.

He bent his head to her, and she nearly gave into the desire, nearly let his lips touch hers, brand her in a way she dared not know, that he most certainly was not meant to know. She was a core of iron. There was no love inside her. She closed her eyes, blocking her mind from the thought of the sweetness of his lips, the longing to reciprocate. He pulled back without touching her, pulled back to stare into her gaze, saved her from reaching out herself.

"There is no other who compares to you." He cupped her cheek in one hand, brushing his thumb across her mouth, his expression a mix of awe and consternation. She knew that look, imagined it similar to the one on her own face. "Is it that you run from me? Is it the chase that goads me so?"

"Yes."

He smiled. "Lying again."

Truly she wasn't. That she ran from him, rebuffed him, wanted him, was part of the appeal. Merciful Night, if she'd just remained at his side until the last chime of midnight and told him no, she would be free.

Her fingers smoothed over the rumple of his sleeve.

"Tell me what it is about you that I cannot resist." He caught her stare, this prince cursed by his gods, feared by his people for the destruction his death foretold, desired for his place beside a throne. "Tell me it is a spell or a curse that you have cast upon me and I will let you go." The spell was not of her making. His eyes dropped to her lips when she made to respond that she knew darker magics than a simple enchantment of a heart. "Tell me, and make me believe, that you feel nothing for me."

She could not make the lie sound in her own head. How could she convince him that she felt nothing beyond what any of his nobles felt, was nothing but another lass out to bed a prince when she was meant to kill him, and found herself equally enthralled? She could not love a man like this. And she could not lie convincingly enough that she didn't.

Very well.

She released her hold on his arms, trailed her hands over his chest to his hips, her right hand settling over the hilt of his sword, the filigreed steel fitting neatly in her grasp. "Do you know how easy it would be to kill you, Prince?"

His eyebrows rose, questioning her meaning, her intent.

She slapped the hilt against his side, forced the scabbard to sway against the length of his leg. "Is this truly the first you've worried about it? You rode out here with no guard at your back, no weapons in your hands. The sword at your hip is for ceremony and you've no dagger to block with. It would be so easy to steal your blade and run you through. A thousand and one dreams of your death would be easily accomplished and you look at me as though I am innocent in my thoughts and deeds. You're a fool to think I could feel aught for you."

She watched the doubt tighten his eyes as he stared at her. What type of woman would speak so forthright about death or the dealing of it? "You would not harm me." She heard the hesitation, the question of his next words. "You, a woman, could not do so even if you tried. What do you know of sword and shield?" He removed his hand from her face, covering hers atop his sword hilt. "Why are you running from me? Why are you pushing me away?"

Because you cannot love me, Prince. Not and know who I am. And I cannot love you.

And love was not a thing of three night's invention, no matter what fairy tales the children told.

She could not say that though. He would take hope like a bone, bury the feeling deep within his chest so he could dig it out some day like a dog. Hope would only hurt him more when she denied it again and slit his throat.

So why couldn't she say the words to him? Why couldn't she kill him like she should? "I have no desire to be a princess."

"I have no desire to be prince." He shrugged off her words, his fingers tracing whorls over hers beneath his grip on his sword.

"You don't understand, city-man. I have no desire to be a princess. No *Dienobolos* would."

She felt the stutter of his heart despite the distance between them.

His gaze sharpened on the angular planes of her face, her leaner build compared to his people's stauncher heights. Her hair was uncommon to the city, but norm enough within the trees. The olive of her skin was more suited to hiding within branches than working ploughed fields.

He shook his head, and his hand clenched hers, the threat of danger pulsing from him in waves. "A child of the Woods would not come to the Capital. Not for any call. Not even for a chance at killing me. They would have tried it before now if they dared."

The last assassin king had forbidden the attempt.

But she was queen, and her word was now law, even when council spoke in opposition.

She buried the tears beneath a growl. "Then ask me my name, prince, and hear my answer."

Darkness, but he had not pulled away from her, and she wanted him closer for a moment longer, just a moment longer before reality returned, reality that she had ignored for the past three nights of bliss at his side.

"*Gaindi ni prolestul, Elichi*?"

She had not heard her peoples approach, had not thought them daring enough to risk the roads this near the morning, this near the end of the ball and the emergence of the partiers on their way home. Even drunk, the city folk outnumbered her people and were equally vicious. But she had not expected to find her brethren so near the road, had not expected them to be looking for her.

His gaze snapped from hers to the tree line and she turned her head to look at the group of warriors emerging from the woods.

"There's nothing here for you, Beracsh. We're not to leave the woods—"

"And yet here you are, Elichisolos. And I see much worth my while."

Her hand tightened on the prince's sword as the leader of her mother's guard, the Priestosolos' guard, the High Priestess' guard, stepped onto the path and clear of the last row of leaves protecting the forest dwellers. The three men with him spread out at his back, seeking to ring her and the prince in the middle of the road.

"Stay behind me."

She looked quickly to the man at her side, the way he stepped in front of her, dismissing her hand on his sword to draw the blade in her defense. Had he not heard the name Beracsh gave her? Did he not know who she was? What she was? Did he really think that just because she was a woman she could not hold the title of Assassin Queen? Mistress of the Final Midnight?

He, they would kill without issue.

She, they could not come through when she fought.

He pushed her away from him, never taking his eyes from the priest who pulled two knives from his belt and advanced.

"We kill him now."

The sound of hooves rang in the distance, too far away to depend on. Her brethren wouldn't care. The sacrifice of their lives for the life of the male before her would be worth it in their minds, should be worth it in hers but still she hesitated. With the prince dead, his kingdom would fall. His father was an old man, easy enough to strike a mourning king from this world. But she did not strike at his back, turned instead to face her brethren in his defense.

Demetes smiled when she looked at him.

She would not let this prince who was honorable despite his title, wise despite his youth, die to treachery she herself had brought about. Her stupidity had led to this. She put him in harm's way when she allowed them to stop so near the threat of her people. She would not let him die for her mistake.

Her lips curled in a sneer.

Beracsh laughed behind her, his knives hissing through the air met with the cold ring of the prince's sword.

She struck too.

Elichi waited for Demetes to draw close, using the speed with which he attacked to pull him around her, taking his blade for herself before pinching the vein on the side of his throat and letting him drop to the ground.

Trao grabbed her from behind, knocking her liberated sword from her grip. The man was a master of hand to hand, had taught her all that she knew of the same, and she'd learned her lessons well. She struggled against him, drawing him closer to her, fighting to keep his attention pinned to her flailing arms and legs and away from the final man's stalking approach. He would lunge, thinking her an easy prize, but she would not die.

"You would betray your Mother for this boy?"

The Pristosolos, who had given Elichi to soldiers to raise at birth? She would that her answer could be anything but yes, but she there was no love lost between mother and child.

Her mother was the High Priest of the Darkness, and Elichi was Its sword. They did not always see in tandem. In this, apparently, they would be at odds.

But the Darkness that sang within her veins made no complaint at Elichi's actions to save the prince. She could claim it was no betrayal, even knowing that her disavowal would not mitigate her guilt.

"He is no boy."

Her weight went slack in her captor's grasp, dropping her to her knees and bending him over her at the waist. She flipped him, throwing him at the man who was too close to stop his approach, whose sword was too high to lower without damage. Trao fell on the blade, tackling the other male in the process. She retrieved her sword, slipping the sharpened steel through the leather breastplate her once weapons master wore, through his chest and out his back and into the body beneath him. They both died, the young one with a scream of pain, dishonoring the Darkness that his service was dedicated to.

The cry drew the prince's attention from Beracsh, turning him towards her in a moment of inattention, allowing his attacker to raise a knife to strike.

The dead one's scream did not pull her gaze from the battle.

Her sword flew, tumbling end over end.

She watched her uncle's knees buckle, the hilt of her blade clutched by one bloody hand where it sprouted from his chest. His gaze sought hers, and she honored him by meeting it.

"*Si onemi galastis, die aran.*" *You learned well, little fox.*

The prince turned his gaze to the dead man at his back, to her. Back and forth he looked until he was certain all the men were downed and she was safe, he was safe. She watched his stare rake over her fallen brethren, saw the question of her betrayal flare in his eyes.

The ground shook around them.

His guards rode to a halt.

She refused to look away from his eyes when he turned his gray metal glare to her.

"Your Highness?"

Prince Christophe de L'Avigne.

The Prince of the Walled City.

The Prince of the Ball.

And she saved him, this prince who prophecy said must die for her forest to thrive, spared by the hand of the deadliest elf to walk the land.

She bowed her head. "Your Highness."

II

THE GENERAL DISMOUNTED, drawing his sword, she assumed, for a precaution against future attack, only then looking at her, down at the blood staining her hands and gown and the prince standing pristine in his doublet. The soldier advanced, and she scanned the earth for the discarded weapons of their dead foes, her dead kin. She didn't need them, but one unarmed assassin against one armed guard was different than one unarmed assassin against a cohort of armed soldiers.

"She's not the enemy, Marius."

The towering giant of a man froze though his gaze remained on her. Smart soldier, to know the true threat and not dismiss it despite her lack of a cock.

"Then what is she, sir?"

"Your new Captain, General."

The prince's words succeeded in breaking the stalemate between her and the soldier's stare, drawing their gazes to the man who they both, apparently, now served.

"You would make a woman Captain, Highness? An elf?"

That her sex was the first issue he named amused her. To think, so burly a man afraid that she was to lead part of his guard. Or was it that he was afraid he would have to fight her? She was the more vicious of the two, of that she was sure. Unpredictable. Besides, elves were known warriors, even the gatherers within the woods knew how to kill a man.

"No, Marius, *this* woman, this elf."

The prince held her gaze. She couldn't look aware, unsure of what to do if she did.

He turned to his commander, dismissing her as another soldier of little import. It was so quickly done, so easily done, that his adamant avowal of deeper emotion seemed an affectation, his words the lie over hers.

She should not feel shattered by the rebuff.

Her mouth opened to respond, but what could she say? How dare he treat her as she had tried to treat him? How dare he push her away?

"Her horse fled when they attacked. See it found and returned to the city. She'll ride with me to the palace."

Unsaid was that they had much to discuss out of earshot of his men. She wondered if, perhaps, he would return to the debate from before her brethren attacked. She doubted it. That he was so easy to read even as he hid behind his name and his position meant little when she read the beginnings of hate and fear in his face.

The prince whistled, and his horse answered, trotting from the tree line to paw the ground at his feet before settling on the road.

The general signaled one of his men to dismount, hand over the reins of his horse so that she could ride the beast while others searched for her lost mount. The unseated soldier held the lead for her, but neither he nor the commander nor the prince offered her a hand to mount, not that she expected otherwise.

It had been hard enough mounting from the palace courtyard in her dress. She wasn't going to embarrass herself with the same difficulties in front of these new men.

A moment to locate her uncle's corpse, another to walk to the body and pull the sword from his chest. She passed behind the prince on her way to the blade. He flinched at her presence behind him but didn't turn. He flinched again when the wet suck of the sword pulled from the chest cavity.

She laid the blade along the ground, letting the blood glint bright red in the rising morning sun, dirt blowing in the gentle breeze, picked up and strewn over the steel, a macabre reminder of the massacre that she perpetrated here.

She pulled a knife from rigid dead fingers, the steel more maneuverable than the sword would have been for her purposes.

With a twist of the knife, she made a slit in her skirt, the fabric parting from mid-hip to hem, baring the layers of petticoats and tulle beneath. She made the same slash on the other side. It took some effort, but she managed to cut the stays on her undergarments, let the wash of white fluff and silk slip from beneath the heavy brocade over-gown and fall unheeded to the dirt covered road. Someone hissed when she stepped from the mess and her leg showed through the seams of the fabric. Another hushed the first soldier, though the horses shuffled with their riders' unease.

Freed of the restricting gown, Elichi returned to the waiting sword, knife shoved through the waist of her gown, dangerously close to the flesh of her hip as she bent to retrieve the weapon.

She glared over her shoulder when the brute called for her to stop.

It was the prince's hand that stopped Marius' advance, letting her finish whatever it was she was about.

Careful not to disturb the blood any further, she stepped to the edge of the forest, the edge of her homeland, no more. She pressed both hands together over the hilt of the sword, raised them into the air so that the flat of the blade stood between her and the wood, a barrier she could not cross. One hundred years for each life she'd taken. One hundred years for each man of the woods who would return to the Darkness and know light no more.

She didn't hesitate in burying the blade in the earth, letting her strength carry the metal deep into the ground so that the blood would nourish the grass, a last homage to the men who once walked the forest paths. Her hands slipped past the hilt guard, palms sliding along the edge of the blade, cutting deep into her skin, letting her blood wash with her kin's.

They were not the only to die this day.

The woman she was, was no more.

She cut a lock of her hair with the knife at her waist, knotted the bright length around the hilt of the sword, and walked away.

There were words, questions from the general, from the soldiers, men unhorsed to see to the blood dripping from her clenched fists into the dust.

He wrapped her hands in the remains of her tulle skirts.

She met the prince's gaze when he pressed her fingers into her palms, forcing pressure on the wounds. "They'll heal quickly."

"They're not healed yet."

He led her to a mount, and she stepped into the stirrups without aid, settling the ripped skirt around her legs as best she could. His hand hovered over her calf, ensuring she was steady, waiting until she met his eye before mounting his own steed, the flash of emotion there and gone, a fantasy forgotten in death and blood and soldiers and steel.

"What the hell was that?" "Is she insane?" "Why would he bring an elf into our midst?"

Words circled around her, whispered though the silence of the road did not hide them from her ears. She did not respond, staring instead at the reins tied round the pommel, wondering how she would hold them with the pain in her hands.

Yes, she would heal, and heal quickly, once she had a chance to tend the wounds, but for now she didn't know how she was going to manage to ride, and yet didn't regret her actions in the slightest.

She honored her homeland, her people, and said goodbye to them. She claimed her misdeeds, accepted her exile.

Now she would live with the choice.

"With me."

The prince settled into his seat and kicked his horse into a gallop, not looking back to see if she followed or not.

Her horse decided without her insight, racing to catch its mate far ahead. She didn't need the reins, her mount trained to follow its leader without a rider's direction.

She followed after the man, knees hugging tight to the horse's withers, flying at the prince's side. His guards did not rush to join them, apparently remaining to investigate the scene, give her time to speak with the man whose life she'd saved, discuss her actions without the commander as witness, the confusion of her rituals.

The prince slowed on the coastal road, keeping to an easy trot now out of earshot of the soldiers who finally fell into line behind them.

"Elichisolos, Elichi, is not a name but a title." His gaze turned to hers, quickly back to the road. "The elves call their greatest warrior such. No other would claim the title for fear of death by the hands of the one who it belonged to."

"You know of my culture."

"The *Dienobolos.* The Children of the Woods. A myth but to any who roam too close to your boarders and learn the skill with which you hide your presence."

"Not so much a myth to you, it would seem."

"I am a prince. You declared war against my kingdom when the walls first rose. I've learned your history from the moment I could speak." His shoulders stiffened, spine straightening though he didn't look at her again. "Was it your kin who said my death would fell the walls? Would give you back the land your forests once ruled?"

"I don't know."

His was a question for the priests.

She was a soldier.

He was silent after her answer. She took the moment to study his proud face, the eyes dulled behind an emotionless mask, the man of only an hour before hidden beneath the face of the prince. This face she knew, heard stories of, remote, aloof, unyielding and yet somehow, she knew he would be kind if he could. That kindness called to her; that kindness would get him killed.

Or perhaps it was not kindness that she sensed. Something more, deeper. Loyalty, honor. She'd threatened his life and the lives of his people if he died. Yet he'd spared her, claimed her despite it all.

"You cut your hands; you cut your hair. Ritual, yes? Ritual of the hunt?" He did not try to hide the suspicion in his voice.

"Of death."

A flash, only a flash of emotion in those gray eyes of his staring back at her.

"I killed my kin to save your life. I am as dead to my people as the ones who lie motionless back there." She raised her bandaged hands, the white cloth stained red as her palms seeped blood. "I accept my fate, and they will know that."

"And hunt you for it?"

She nudged her horse until it stepped closer to his, the motion subtle, unnoticed. "We hunt those the Darkness deems must die. We hunt those whose lives are bartered to the woods for something else."

"Assassins."

"You feed your people with crops in the fields. We have no fields."

He snarled, but truth was truth.

"We might be assassins; some of us might be assassins—"

"The ones who worship Echi, the Final Midnight."

That he knew her religion even that much shocked her. She blinked, hoping he did not notice the widening of her eyes. "But even the Echi has rules to follow, Kit."

He reined his horse in quickly, drawing his mount to a harsh stop, hers following his command. "Let us be very clear, elf. You will address me as 'Your Highness, Your Majesty, or Lord.' You have no right to call me by name." The flame of anger in his eyes was a harsher, crueler flame than the spark on the road before. There was true hate there now, distrust.

She ached to see it. "Apologies, your Highness."

He clicked his tongue, urging his horse forward.

She did not expect him to speak to her again.

The fresh breeze off the sea lifted her hair from her neck. The heavy strands had fallen from the delicate curls she wore for the ball. Now the mass hung heavy down her back, all but the hank she left behind at the sight of the battle. Moist air clung to her face, weighed down her eye lashes. The Elichisolos did not cry. She would not now, even when the position was dead to her.

"You're young to be your peoples' Elichisolos?"

"Elichi is fine," she hesitated, not liking the feel of 'your highness' on her tongue. She gave him no name, ignored the inelegance of her speech to continue beyond the thought. "Does age make any difference in the taking of a life?"

Even in the light, the Dark finds ways to cast shadow.

There is no hiding from the Blackness of Night, for even the sun falls to its cover at the end of the day.

She shook her head though he was not looking at her. "I am not the Elichi any longer."

"The title is yours unto your death."

Another tenant an outsider of the woods should not know, and she was unsurprised to find he did. "I am dead to the woods, my Prince."

He turned to look at her now, she saw it from the corner of her eye while she stared ahead, though he did not correct her choice of address.

"In saving your life against the threat of my people, I betrayed the greatest vow we take. I killed my brethren to save a foreigner, whose death they have long sought."

"They, but not you?"

She didn't answer. "Do you deserve to die, Prince?" She met his stare. "The Darkness has long spoken to me. I am its servant; I obey its commands. You were not meant to die by my hand, by my brethren's hands. A god may say something to one person that another will not hear. I believe myself right in my actions, as they will believe in theirs."

"You were never going to kill me?"

She could lie, tell him his life had always been safe in her hands. But it was his smile, the smile he showed her that no one else seemed to see amidst the swirl of gowns at the ball, that spared him. "Sometimes it is blind luck that we follow our god's commands when the order is yet unclear." She felt no pull to end his life now, had not felt it then upon their first meeting either, but it was her choice not to end his life, and the Darkness' allowance that kept him breathing.

They stared at each other in silence, and he did not ask if his life was safe again.

His mount sidestepped, his leg pressing to hers in the momentary brush.

She closed her eyes, so he wouldn't see how very much she enjoyed the accidental touch. With her eyes closed, she wouldn't have to see if he flinched away from her, scowled and increased the distance between them, growing since the moment her people stepped from the trees.

She leaned back on her mount, laying against the saddle and the horse's spine to stare at the stars shining despite the sun's waking light. "You pray to the gods for your salvation. They are your protectors, and healers, and avengers. We do not have that in the woods. We believe in the Darkness, the Great Unifier, the Place from Which We Came and Will Return. The woods hold the heart of darkness, shade of the trees, pitch of the night. There are no stars to see through the leaves, no sunlight that is not filtered through the branches. I am a child of those shadows, cast into the light. I've betrayed the bosom that is my family and been rejected because of it, all for a man my head tells me deserves a chance at life, whose death would not be the salvation my brothers would have it." She turned her head resting on the horse's rump, uncaring of her precarious position on her mount. "Are you worth it, prince? Are you worth the destruction of my life for the safety of yours?"

"Are you truly the Elichi?"

She snorted. "If I'd wanted you dead, you would not have felt the blow, never seen my face."

He held her stare, something comforting in knowing he saw her even in the blankness of his gaze. “I don’t know if I’m worth it.”

She straightened, her mount shuffling beneath her. “Which perhaps makes you the worthiest of salvation.” She hesitated, staring ahead at the walls beginning to peak in the distance, the palace topping the rise. “You would give me a home, within your walls, a place in your guard?”

“I would keep you close.”

Close as an enemy could be kept.

He did not need to say the words for her to know their truth. What trust was between them was shattered, what love he professed buried beneath the earth with the bodies left to rot upon the road.

“I accept, Prince.”

He nodded, waved a hand overhead and his soldiers rode hard to flank them, placing the prince in the center of their tight ring as they moved ever closer to the city before them.

They rode in silence, only stares passed between them, between the soldiers staring at her.

The prince never looked back.

III

SHE SETTLED IN a room off the barracks typically used as overflow servants' quarters for the ball. Now that the festivities were over, the quarters were empty, and she had the run of the small three chamber area.

It took her most of the day to clear out the three other beds from her newly assigned quarters, but she wasn't going to be sharing, no matter what the guards or the prince thought of her. The front space was the living area, a kitchen and small storage box if she desired to cook her own meals. She supposed she would have to ask if meals were provided to the soldiers, or if she was on her own, but that was a thought for a later time. There was no door between the walled off kitchen and the sleeping chambers, not that the arrangement concerned her much.

The second two rooms had a thin curtain rod separating them, likely to provide privacy for those changing and those sleeping on different shifts in the palace. She pulled the thin fabric back, opening the space for herself, enlarging the room.

A bed, of course, in the middle, something bigger than the damnable cots she'd already removed. A small table that could serve as her desk, a chair or two to relax in. The small closet was big enough for her meager belongings, and her trunk could fit against the wall without notice. She'd have to find a lamp, some candles. She probably wouldn't light them often and they might be an expense she could live without.

But most humans were afraid of the dark.

She was human now, wasn't she? One of the city's own? A Tornaldian. Or did they call themselves Spinichians? She didn't want to be associated with a vegetable grown in the fields. And she couldn't call herself an elf if she wanted these people to accept her.

She pushed the thought aside, sneezed at the dust in the air blown about in her passing. There was a bathing chamber off the farthest corner, a door discreetly tucked into the wooden wall. It was a luxury she'd never known in the woods where the most she hoped for was a private pool for a bath, heated by the earth's core if she was lucky, usually frigid beneath a leafy canopy of trees. When she turned the spigot for the bath, hot water flowed out. She didn't even need to use magic to heat the stream.

If she allowed herself, she could become quite comfortable in this new world, complacent.

She was human.

She was not an elf.

Human.

Less than one day exiled from her woods, and already she missed the shadowed groves that once soothed her.

A shake of her head, a slam of the bathroom door, her fingers glancing over the familiar and yet foreign feel of wood beneath her hand, and she walked away. There was no bark to scrape at her palms, rub against her feet when she walked across the ground. Everything sanded smooth, whitewashed, falsely bright to her eyes. She missed the dark grains of maple trees, poplars, the scent of pine and majesty of oak. Without a candle, at least she wouldn't have to see how the city dwellers had banished nature from their world.

Plants.

She'd buy plants and trees that could survive in her muted prison to make it feel more like home. Ivy to cover the disfigured walls; vines to form a canopy over her bed for the night. Green blankets, not leaves, but fabric, so at least she could pretend she was surrounded by the forest even as she was so far away.

Decided, she looked once more around the room, empty now of beds and dressers and everything that didn't belong to her, empty as she had nothing of her own.

She—

Darkness, she didn't even have a name anymore. She wasn't the Elichi. She wasn't "girl" as her father named her as a child, the name she bore until she claimed the position of highest worshipper of Echi.

She had no name, no bed, no clothes but the ripped gown covering her until she retrieved her things from the inn. Nothing but a job unwillingly given and a room she'd rather set fire to than sleep within.

Easier to start with the basics. The inn where her belongings for the ball were housed. She'd gather them together, move them to her rooms, find the prince who stranded her in this hellhole and she'd think of the rest when the time came.

THREE GUARDS RANGED before her door, a quick look to one another before they bowed their heads to her presence. Accepting their accompaniment seemed intrusive to her already chaotic life. Denying their accompaniment suggested that she had some nefarious purpose. No doubt they would report the same to their general, since she doubted the prince would stick her with a spy since he was against the same himself.

She nodded at the men, unsmiling since she was their "captain," whatever that implied, and snapped her fingers for them to follow in her wake. Asking their directions would have made the trip through the city a quicker journey, but she had an empty room to return to, despair at her current situation, lack of anything resembling companionship in her future, so she took her time journeying to the inn.

When she left the lodgings, she whistled loud enough to attract the attention of her poor shadows and the general populace around her. One of her guards answered her motioned summons, and she patted him on the back, forcing him to bend over and grab the handle of her trunk while she winked at the other two uniformed men and wound her way back to the palace via the central square and the vendors whose shops closed at the advent of night. It would have been nice to have found something other than her now modified dress to wear for the next day, something suitable for a lady, but she wasn't really a lady in the human sense of the word.

She would make do with what she had brought with her from the forest.

Her mother would likely hold a bonfire someday soon, the smoke rising within the woods for the surrounding towns to wonder at. Exiled, she was no longer part of the clan, her belongings must be destroyed, all reminder of her person annulled.

Four hundred years.

Four hundred years would see her exile pardoned and her feet allowed tread on the forest paths once more. A hundred years for every life she'd taken against the Dienobolos. It was a long time, even for a person whose lifespan was nearly quadruple that. She was young enough that four hundred years was both an eternity and not long at all considering her life span. Three millennium and she was not even two hundred years into it. The elves would still consider her barely an adult by the time she could to return to their fold. And she'd lived her life for them, for all they asked of her. She'd killed and saved and sacrificed and in two hundred years, the only moment she'd taken for herself had been the one moment that stripped her from the forest for what wasn't nearly an eternity but felt damn sure close to it.

And now she had nothing.

No food, no money, no friends to acclimate the change in her circumstances with. She was as dead to those who she once knew as the men lying on the forest road.

Would she be allotted a stipend for her services in the guard?

The thought sprang to mind as she passed a seamstress' shop, the window displaying a rather florid gown that looked like it must weigh a good amount and couldn't be all that pleasant to don.

Yes, think about money, about distractions. There was no place for self-pity in her life, not before, certainly not now.

Surely the men who served the prince were paid some sort of pittance?

She could pick a few pockets. No one would know she was there. It would be easy enough to touch the Darkness in their minds and wipe the memories from their—

No, she mustn't think like that. She was not of the woods and so had no right to the magic within her soul that was so connected to her riven home. A clean break was what she must envision. It was harder than she thought it would be, starting over as nothing. And she didn't know why she'd made the choice she had, been driven by the Darkness in her heart to protect the prince even against her own hard felt beliefs.

Do not think on it.

Damnit no! Think about money. About soldiers. Anything!

The barracks were not nearly large enough to accommodate all the guards and some of the men must be living within the town itself. That would imply they were paid for their services and that she too could insist upon some compensation.

Safe, that was a safe thought to have. Yes, the soldiers and whether they slept in the barracks or beyond the castle walls. What would she do with a stipend? She'd never truly needed money before coming to the city. Was begging to be paid in court dances and noble smiles a reasonable fee, or should she beg for coin and ignore the frown on his face?

HER TREK THROUGH the city took her past a baker. The sign on the door listed to one side. A display window housed old baguettes, the edges greening with mold though noticeable only if one looked closely. Yeast filled the air, almond bread, if she had to guess though the old loaves had no nuts atop them. Still, the scent was enough to draw her nearer, hoping to catch a glimpse of the proprietor within the darkened shop, beg a roll or two. Shadows moved within the room, but no one came to the door at her knock.

"M'lady, there is a tavern a block down that is open late."

She turned to her escort, the men sweating, hoisting her trunk in the air. "Lead the way, gentlemen."

The pub glowed with the merry light of a fire flickering within the stone walls. Hers was not the only stomach that was grumbling.

She had enough borrowed silver on her person to treat herself to a small meal, even a glass of ale for her wayward chaperones if she tread lightly with her coin. She waited for the men to reach her, her trunk settling with a solid thump on the ground outside the tavern.

"I appreciate the aid, gentlemen. As I've not much coin yet, I can't offer you more than a pint, but I'd like to treat you to that if you're able."

The one who she initially corralled into carrying her things flashed a quick, easy smile, young to be in the guard.

She smiled back, noting the way he stood so openly faced to her, offering no protection to himself against approaching attack. She could fix that, if she proved capable of training these soldiers.

"We're allowed one a day, miss, unless we're off duty."

"And watching me is considered a duty then?"

"Yes, Miss. I mean—"

Her laugh took the man aback. To be fair, she was rather uncertain about its exuberance herself. She sounded giddy, and the knot in her stomach was anything but happiness. Best not to think too long on the sick feeling, lest it manifest into true form. Better to push it aside, and let things unfold as they ought, the dread would pass once she settled into this new life of hers. "Well then, I shall do my best not to make your time any more onerous than it already is. A pint, good sirs?"

The man who was bringing up the rear of their party nodded, eyes scanning the crowd around them, a true soldier, then. He would likely not partake of any refreshment but water. She might join him in that endeavor.

She acknowledged his austerity with a flickering glance of her own, allowing the guard to see that her flippancy was more act than not. A quick bite, and then they would leave. Already the night was nearly past, and morning came early outside the woods.

SHE ORDERED A bowl of stew for herself, and a round for the men. The young one ordered his own meal, and the silent one gnawed on a hank of bread left for the table. The third one gave a yawn and had to fight sleep to drain his tankard. He should have eaten something, but he didn't, and soon was snoring while she and her new companions finished their meal. He woke with a start when the youngster kicked out the man's chair legs. His hand went to his knife first, drawing it partially from its scabbard at his side before realizing the jest against him. She watched. Fast and precise. The prince's soldiers were not soft in their duties. This was good and hinted that they had a chance of growing more proficient if set the right tasks. Mental notes, all of them, jotted down and forming into a plan for the morrow. She occupied herself with a list of jobs, her mind settled on the immediacy of her new job, rather than the uncertainty of what it would entail.

At the end of her meal, she nodded to the men to precede her from the pub while she waited for the owner to take payment for their meal. The elder man waved her off, and she blushed when she realized her new guards had taken care of her fare for her. She would repay the debt at some point.

They wound their way more easily now through the city, anxious to return to their rooms for whatever sleep remained in the night. She bid them fair dreams at the door to her quarters, taking her trunk to her room without further assistance. She had no bed to sleep on, no chair to rest her feet. Her hands ached from the slices across her palms but those were a passing concern.

She spent the night staring out the window, sharpening the sword hidden deep in her belongings until the edge gleamed and cut the air around her.

At the first whistle of bird song, she summoned her courage and stood to face the new dawn, so much brighter than what she knew and understood.

IV

SHE STOOD IN the vestibule, watching as men in uniforms lined up in rows and squared off against their opponents. It was their version of entertainment, thin foils lending skill in developing speed for the attack. Speed and accuracy, as she watched men find marks on their opponents, some even mimicking the movement of pulling a sword free before taking the offensive once more. Still, if real battle were to come, the thin blades would do nothing against an armored opponent, and she'd not heard that the steel had any ability to stop a spell or dragon fire spit at a man.

She could not deny that it was fun to watch, something she'd not considered of her own training within the woods.

The prince paired off with the commander, both men saluting each other before beginning their dance of thrust and parry, riposte and remise.

The movements were easy enough to emulate; the forms similar to what she knew of knife fighting, requiring the same skill.

She stepped from her post at the wall, having decided she'd had enough of this pointless back and forth.

"Is that a girl?"

Her eyebrows rose at the shrill call of one of the men now pushing away the foil of a fellow's blade touching his chest. Truly, there was nothing all that different between his physique and her own. A bulge at the groin, but they both had two legs and arms. So, his breasts were less defined against the cambric of his fencing jerkin. She'd bound hers down so not to get in her way while fighting.

Surely some of these men had lain with a woman before? Just because tradition dictated abstinence amongst the nobility, the lower classes found what amusements they could and a guard was very unlikely to be true nobility.

The prince spun out of an attack by the general, stopping their back and forth to look at her where she stood in the doorway to the practice area.

"What are you doing here, El-li?" He stumbled over naming her, shortening what was once her title into a strange amalgamation of the name he'd known her as at the ball and who she no longer was. She was no longer either person.

She would be "Eli." Yes, the name settled on her tongue and she found it palatable.

"Training, Sir." Eli let her gaze wander over the men ranged before her, some with skill, many lacking.

"Kit, she's a woman. She's wearing breeches."

"For the Darkness' sake." She traversed the parquet floors, ignoring the way the sun glinted off the multitude of colors in the wood and cast the room in a rosy glow. She stopped before the prince and the general and crossed her arms over her chest, knowing that their gazes glanced there with her motion. "If you cannot get over the presence of a distraction on a battlefield, how do you expect to survive a war?"

"We're not on a battlefield, Captain." The general's deep baritone settled deep in her gut, grounding her in the moment. A talent, almost like magic, if he could calm his men with just a word or two. She'd have to remember the phenomenon for the future. "This is simple sport."

No, he didn't believe that, despite the levity of his words. He didn't want her here. He didn't trust her. She wasn't sure she would act differently in his situation. Very well. "Then where am I to train?"

"In the training courtyard, beyond the barracks. We only meet there thrice a week during peace times."

She turned her gaze to the prince, the twitching of his lips into something more than just the congenial mask she remembered him gracing other maidens with during the ball. He liked her sparring with his commander, the irreverence with which she spoke. "Then why fence, if there is no point to the endeavor?"

"Stamina, Captain." The general rested his foil against his shoulder.

"Have you ever tried before?" The prince looked quickly away from her gaze, refusing to hold her stare.

She'd fenced, but not, precisely, in the same way he was asking her. The divot where the blade had pierced her shoulder pained her on exceedingly hot days. And she didn't think he'd enjoy the knowledge of her second time with foil in hand. "I'm proficient with this weapon, if that's what you're asking."

"It's wasn't, no." He turned from her, gripped his gloved hand along the length of the blade and cleaned it of what dust had gathered there in the moment they'd been forced to converse.

Had she angered him?

She hadn't meant to.

Did he truly not want her there?

She wasn't leaving.

The Commander responded. She watched the prince's shoulders tense at the decree. "Geoff, pair with Captain Eli. You're a novice. Go through the motions together and we'll see how you've done at the end of the bouts today."

Bouts?

And he was pairing her with a novice?

"But sir, she's a woman. I can't fight a woman."

Blunt, and amusing, she found the combination worked best when dealing with prissy little boys. "For the Night's sake. Do you think that my lack of cock will really impact whether I can use a sword or not?"

The commander blurted out a guffaw, quickly silenced to not undermine her new authority.

She found another male ogling her, most of them were. "You," she pointed to the unnamed noble, uncaring that he likely outranked her, though his age looked far younger than her one hundred and ninety-seven. "Fetch me a pair of socks and hurry up with that."

"Socks?" The whispered question quickly made its way around the room.

The boy didn't hesitate to obey her order.

This time it was the prince's eyebrow that reached skyward.

She bundled her hair into a knot at the back of her head to keep her tresses from getting in her way, from being too obviously feminine in appearance.

Brazen balls. No woman had held the position of Elichi before she ascended to the title. For forty-seven years, she'd been the best killer in her clan, in all the clans of the woodland folk. She would have lasted longer, if she'd not…abdicated…to follow Kit to the palace.

Yes, she liked that. Abdicated. It felt better than the truth. A lie to balm her wounded, lonely soul.

The boy skidded to a halt, his boots lacking traction on the wooden flooring enough to stop him without sliding forward. One pair of stockings, not socks as she'd requested. The sturdier material would have done better, but she could wind the stockings into the right shape all the same.

She took the silk and braided it into a thick rope, barely six inches long when she was finished. It didn't really matter, as it was a demonstration more than anything else. "If it's a cock you want," she pushed the bundled fabric into the tight fit of her breeches, adjusting the disguise until it looked like the appropriate appendage it was emulating.

The prince choked, bowing forward to fight for a breath free of laughter.

His movement loosened his hold on the foil in his grasp. She snatched it easily from his fingers, slowing her movements enough that the boy in front of her realized she was going to attack before she swung her arm in an overhand slash, knowing that the blade she wielded would easily be blocked and was not used for such a move. Per the rules of fencing, she should be disqualified. But that wasn't the point now, and she shifted forward when he moved to block her, spinning inside his guard and knocking her opponent back a step, snagging his dropped sword before it fell to the floor and ending with the point of the prince's blade at the young man's throat, the second sword's tip just barely touching her sock bearer's *equipment*.

"That is not fencing."

"No, but I wasn't trying to fence. Just prove a point." She pressed a nudge forward, enough to ensure that her opponents felt the press of her blades against their more vulnerable areas.

"Are you quite through?" Prince Christophe stood at her back, his bent arm just brushing against the flowing linen of her shirt.

"Will they disregard my lack of a penis to fight me?" She did not take her gaze off the two men cowering before her.

"I think we will all be quite willing to disregard that rather unique trait of yours."

She nodded. "Then let us fence." With a flip of the foils in her hands, catching onto the blunted blades and extending the pommels back to their original owners, she moved into position to train.

The prince waited to retrieve his weapon, stepping into her guard to do so. "After practice, you'll show me how you did that."

She inclined her head in agreement.

"Fetch her a blade." Voice lowered, he said to her, "And take those damn socks away."

She caught his eye, unable to resist the quick retort. "Jealous?"

His face flushed red, eyes glancing down at her displayed groin before squeezing tightly closed. "I'm not sure that's something I can—" He gulped.

She laughed. "And yet men parade about the same every day. How disappointing."

Kit didn't respond, though his cheeks grew a brighter shade of red beneath her gaze.

A man tossed her a foil and she caught the hilt, swung twice, before resting the blade on her shoulder and waiting for her prescribed partner to regain his feet from where she'd knocked him to the floor.

The prince turned back to his bout, and she parried her partner's thrust.

The boy managed a good defense, but was too timid to attack, whether because of her sex or his lack of command with his blade she didn't know. After the third such advance, she pulled the boy to a corner of the room left free of fencing men and adjusted his grip on the hilt.

"It's a light blade, that's true, but you can't hold it like it will sting you same as your opponent's weapon."

They parried and thrust in tandem, her pupil mimicking her movements until he moved smoothly, or nearly fluidly, through the sequence. She worked with the lad well past the time the other partners stopped for a rest, her student more than willing to listen to her advice now that her skill was proven with more than just cheap thrills and tricks. They both panted with exertion by the ringing of the midday bell.

"Last bout, gents, and lady." The general called the match.

She made to salute Geoff but was stopped before her blade rose in the motion.

"His highness would see your skill for himself, Captain."

Her gaze traveled over the general's face, noting the slight grimace with his command. If she were him, she would not want someone like her partnering the royal personage without proper vetting. She couldn't fault the soldier for his caution.

That didn't mean she would back down from the bout though.

Eli, the name settled on her though she'd only had it for an afternoon, squared off against the prince, watching Kit adjust the gauntlets on his wrists.

She'd refused to call him by name during the ball, not wanting the intimacy of it to further compel her heart to his. Did it matter now, how far she fell? She was stuck with him for the next four hundred years at least, would it not be easier to regain a part of the companionship that had existed between them a night ago rather than this stalemate between their persons?

Yes, if she managed to force the feelings simmering in her gut to friendship, then love would flee.

"*En garde*."

He thrust, and she parried.

They moved back and forth along the lines of the floor, neither forcing an attack while they tested the other's mettle. She found him to be competent, willing to hold back rather than show her his skill at the forefront of their engagement. A wise tactician, so it would appear. She followed a similar mindset, though it took her only a few moments to know that her skill outstripped his. Of course, her skill was based on ignoring the rules of engagement and creating her own, better suited to a true battlefield rather than a test in a controlled room.

She refused to lose regardless.

He scored the first hit, and she quickly followed with her own, a second and third and the match was hers. She could have taken his sword at the end; he'd left himself open to the maneuver, but she was congenial, and did not divest him of his weapon before his men. His eyes narrowed at her like he knew what she'd done. She shrugged, her only acknowledgement of his belief.

"A wonderful display, your highness. And Captain, a true swordsman has entered our midst. I look forward to watching you upon the practice field with real weapons in your hand." The lie made her smile. The commander was dreading her appearance in the lists, for, with a real weapon, she was all the more likely to move to kill his prince than with a foil. Accidents tended to happen on the practice field.

Eventually, Marius would realize she was dedicated to ensuring no accidents befell the prince. She would prove it to herself as well.

The men dispersed, only the prince and his personal guardian remaining behind with her.

"You had me. You had my sword, but you didn't take it."

He did not pose the remark as a question, so she did not feel the need to respond with an answer.

Before he could ask her why, she moved to his side, tossing the general her blade to mirror Kit and his stance beside her.

"General, do you remember Kit's" the prince stiffened at his nickname, "stance for the last exchange?"

The man nodded, raising her blade to mimic his lord's position.

"Good. Now, do you see…"

THEY SPENT ANOTHER hour discussing technique, practicing the movements that she'd honed beyond an art form into a deadly dance if the blades were tipped and she were aiming to kill. She squared off against Kit, practicing with him once more. This time, when he opened himself to her attack, she took his blade and knocked him to the floor.

He went to stand only to notice that her blade was at his throat.

"That's enough for today. You're exhausted. And I'm exhausted. The longer we drill, the less you'll learn and the more likely you're to be injured."

"Or you."

She smiled at his sullen response. They both knew that if one of them was to be injured, it would not be her.

Marius returned to the room, she'd not noticed him leave, with a platter of sandwiches in his hand, a pitcher of water on the tray. "It's nearly supper already. You've been at this since midday. I thought I'd have to physically separate you if you weren't done by the time I returned." He paused to truly look at the scene before him.

She'd knocked Kit to the ground before.

This was the first time she'd pinned him with a sword too.

His voice tried for nonchalance, though his eyes hardened at the sword she had pointed at their prince. "Perhaps I'm too late."

She pulled away quickly, a final salute, before she extended a hand and helped Kit to his feet. His fingers lingered in hers a moment longer than necessary. He did not meet her gaze though, and she felt a flash of something at his denial.

"Thank you, Marius."

The general placed the tray of food on a side table and handed Kit a towel from his shoulder.

She stood there, an awkward third to their easy comradery.

She was not jealous of the exchange between them.

She wasn't.

But she missed having Kit to herself. Even in a crowded ballroom, they'd been alone together.

Stop it.

Stop thinking of that. It's over and done. No more. It will never happen again. She would damn sure not cry.

Killer. Assassin. Guard.

Lover was not a name that she claimed.

She'd given any hope of a lover up the moment she'd attained the position of Elichi. Tomal had refused her bed after she'd proven the Darkness in her heart. She'd refused Kit who was her second-best bet. A lie, about being second.

Her gaze skittered to his when he sat at the small table and read the papers that had come along on the tray from his commander.

They'd not dismissed her. And yet they ignored her presence like they had.

She was not used to being unseen, at least when she was not trying.

Eli didn't like it.

Her fingers tightened on the hilts of the swords she carried. She wanted to go back to sparring. Wanted his focus on her once more. But he laughed at something the commander said, and her thoughts were too angry in her head for her to hear the man's response.

It took all of her concentration to exit the room unnoticed, to leave the two men behind without looking back and hoping they would call her to stay. She deposited the foils in a large stand with the other noble's blades piercing the wood.

She didn't care. Truly. She didn't care.

She didn't sit on the bench outside the practice room waiting for him to emerge because she cared but rather because someone had best guard him for a few days unless an assassin attack or some other such fool made to hurt him.

When he emerged, walked past her without noticing her in the shadows, it was harder to hide the hurt his lack of recognition caused her.

She followed him regardless, gritting her teeth to keep from calling out to him to turn.

V

SHE WATCHED HIM as he shrugged the fencing jacket off his shoulders, the thick material bunching around his wrists until he freed the cuffs and caught the coat before it fell to the floor. His undershirt was wet through, a testament to the state of his training. He was not weak willed or prissy, this prince of the thousand balls. She was desperately hoping he was weak willed, had some other tendency that she could look upon with scorn and derision. Every time she saw him, her heart fluttered and those damn feelings she shouldn't have felt but gave into on the forest road tried to consume her.

She smiled at the thought.

But he didn't smile.

Eli was finding that rather irksome.

His back was to her, so he didn't notice her intense scrutiny, was unselfconscious in fiddling with the closures of his breeches and—

"You might want to keep those on for a moment."

So bashful, her prince.

He turned towards her intrusion, clasping the front placard of his trousers tightly closed. "How long have you been standing there?"

"Long enough to see you strip off your jerkin but no longer. I stopped you before you grew too interesting."

It was a definite difference between her people and his. Where she was used to the male form, having trained since birth to fight against them, sharing in the same summer ponds and bath houses with everyone else, his people were most strict on separation of the sexes. They built walls around walls around walls, city, home, and heart. Poor fools, and yet he didn't seem as perturbed by her appearance as she would have expected. Not that the light blush across his cheeks wasn't noticeable. He was very pretty when flushed.

"Was there something you needed, or you just happened upon these quarters while investigating your new barracks?"

"The second, if you must know. I was looking for the baths." He didn't need to know she had her own in her chambers.

It was a likely excuse.

"They're underground. This is the royal wing."

"Which no one told me."

"And you asked who, precisely?"

She would have asked him, but the moment the general brought Kit's food, she was forgotten. "I know no one but you."

"Which precludes you from speaking to any others?"

"No."

He did not seem pleased by the admittance, or the disavowal, or whatever it was she was answering to. Damn, but she had no footing with him. Yes, with a sword in her hand, a knife in the other, she might be able to knock him back a peg, and he was quick enough to make it a match, at least until she grew bored and wanted the win. But this wasn't the man she'd spoken with the past three nights. The man who'd danced her around a ballroom filled with the most opulent of dresses in a rainbow of colors and her in black, darkest night, looking so out of place among the glittering throng.

"I'm sure they'd be accommodating if you voiced a question. As it is, I'm rather indisposed at the moment and would prefer my privacy to continue."

"I rather like this room and think I shall take a rest. Hard day's work and all that. Please, don't let me distract you."

She ensured her gaze held his while she moved into the room proper and took a seat on the bench where his change of clothes was laid out. Sitting put her eyes level with his naval, his height far greater than hers, though he was unsure of its advantage. Perhaps tomorrow she would show him that a smaller, lighter person could easily unbalance him and land him in a bind. It would prove a good lesson for the military corps in general. Well, she would not lie to herself and ignore that half the appeal of the lesson was watching her young prince beaten back.

"Really?" The incredulity in his tone brought her gaze to his.

She really must stop her mind from wandering. Not that wandering did much good, eventually she always came back to the present and the mess she'd made of her life. Funny, that said mess didn't feel so messy at all right now.

"This seat is quite comfortable. Go on, I promise, it's nothing I've not seen before."

She may have been mistaken, but she thought she caught a hint of anger in his gaze, along with the blush on his cheeks, at her mention of having seen other men undressed.

Rules of propriety: A woman and man mustn't meet before their mating.

Stupid city rules, all their walls they put up trying to keep themselves separate from the world and each other.

He'd barely worked up the nerve to kiss her and then that had been ruined by her brethren's interruption.

No. Not brethren. No more.

Her enjoyment in tormenting him dimmed with the thought.

There was something about him that called to her, begged to be tempted and pushed until all that he was overflowed and consumed her in the flood. The Darkness in her soul yearned for his light, and it was a strange yearning, almost peaceful in its craving.

"Fine then."

He met her gaze and did his best to hold it, mouth set in a grim line, eyes cold and stormy staring down at her. She let him think her caught, watching his fingers fumble at the ties of his breeches before he managed to push the cloth past his hips, small cloths remaining behind for a hint of modesty. Her eyes dropped to his waist, the trim hips, defined muscles his clothing covered so elegantly, even clothing meant for work fit him perfectly. If she'd said yes to him, if she'd given in to desire and left with him, all this flesh would be hers to touch and more.

When she stood, he stepped back, trying to keep space between them. It didn't occur to her not to follow, a predator stalking her prey. He continued to back away and she advanced until his knees struck against a second bench and it was her hand grabbing his arm that helped him steady. "You're more graceful on a dance floor."

"More room to spin in."

"Or flee."

"I don't flee."

"Liar."

He hadn't noticed that she'd taken his clothing in one hand, so focused on her approach he hadn't been watching her fingers. Another lesson for another day in the lists. Good, she was beginning to develop quite a curriculum to aid in protecting her new liege.

Eli wanted him to survive.

Who better than an assassin to train him so?

"Stand still, Prince. Best to get you changed before someone else barges in on us."

"There is no us."

"Precisely."

She sank slowly to her knees, ignoring the body before her in favor of focusing on the task at hand. With quick, efficient movements, she stripped him of his soiled garments, piling pants and undergarments together in one hand while she passed him his cleaned clothing with the other. A hamper lingered along one wall. She took advantage of the basket to deposit his practice clothes into while he pulled fresh breeches on. He sucked in his breath, stomach contracting into rippling muscle when she returned to him and laced him into his leathers.

She held his shirt out for him, and he snatched it from her hands too quickly.

"You don't smile like you did at the ball."

He stopped with his head stuck within the mess of cotton over his hair.

She couldn't help herself as she reached up and untangled his shirt, her hands running down his sides in the pretense of helping him dress. His arms remained in the air over his head while she touched him. For this moment, she did not meet his gaze, instead focusing on her fingers smoothing out the wrinkles in his tunic, tying the laces at his throat. He'd cover his shoulders with the blue jacket she'd left on the bench, hide this physique behind layers of cloth. She didn't understand this need to be covered, but, then again, walls were not only made of brick and mortar.

He swallowed, the bob of his Adam's apple drawing her gaze. Almost, she could imagine his head thrown back in passion, the way he would struggle for air, tortured by pleasure.

She shook her head, trying to clear it of the image.

"I smile."

His gaze found hers. She recognized the ploy for what it was. If her focus was on his face, then other things could be ignored. She let him distract her, though she could see the lowering of his arms from the corner of her eye, the way he leaned into the scant space between them even while the whispered words and the grim set of his lips hinted at the desire to escape.

"Not like you did at the ball."

"We are no longer at the ball, Captain. This is the real world again. There is no time for fancy twirls and grand costumes. You will have to grow used to the change same as anyone else."

That wasn't what she meant.

The change, as he so roughly put it, had nothing to do with the ball and gowns and aristocrats swelling the palace walls. The change had to do with him, the way his lips would tilt upwards at the corners, his teeth would sparkle in a beam of sunlight, and his eyes would remain dark and bruised to the flirting and the posturing and the politics around him. There was a hint of a smile in the fencing room this morning when he took his blade to the general and beat the man back rather soundly. Maybe even a hint when she disarmed him and then showed him how she'd managed the feat. But now his smile was the one he wore for the court, and it was not the smile he'd given her.

She missed that smile.

"Of course, Kit."

"Prince Christophe. Highness. Or My Lord, Captain. Never Kit. I will not tell you again."

The correction took her aback. They were in private. Surely, he would not insist on such formality between them—but they were no longer at the ball, and she was no longer a woman whom he was asking to dance.

She killed her people to spare his life.

It was the killing of his heart that was the true wound.

"My apologies, my Prince."

He did not correct her claiming.

They stood facing each other, his garments in order, her slighter frame blocking him from his jacket and an exit from the room. If he wished her to move, then he would have to ask or push her from his way. She was used to silence and doubted he had suffered the same treatments in his life.

"Excuse me." His words were curt though proper in every way.

"Of course, my Prince."

She stepped easily aside.

He walked past her, picking up his coat and slinging it over his shoulders.

She held the door for him when he exited, followed in his wake the way a guard should.

"Are you planning on being my shadow the entire day?"

"Yes, Sir, it was my assigned task." Not precisely true. All right, it was almost entirely a lie. But he didn't need to know that.

And besides, she was sure she could make a good excuse as to her presence. The prince's death had been prophesized for a long while, who was to say there was not an assassin waiting just around the corner to steal his life?

"You plan on entering the city in that?" He looked over his shoulder at her, eyes moving down her flowing shirt and the black breeches covering his legs.

If she wanted, she could be a shadow in the streets. Easier to be a shadow dressed in black than in skirts. "Yes."

He sputtered, unsure of how to respond.

"Is there something wrong with my attire? You didn't seem to have a problem with it during drills this morning?"

"That was drills—"

"Yes, and this is guard duty, not a grand ball or a picnic outing."

"Is that what you think I'm doing? Going on a picnic?"

"Dressed like that? I don't know what you're doing, my lord." She did not try to keep the sarcasm from her voice. Honestly, she rather liked the way he was dressed. He wore his fashions fitted enough that should he be in a fight; his clothing wouldn't hamper his movements. That they had the added benefit of endearing him to the feminine eye at the same time was not something she would share with him. He looked like he could go to a picnic or summit meeting or whatnot dressed the way he was.

He searched her face. It was disconcerting to be so studied, yet she stood her ground. This was not the study of the changing room, laced with a heat she didn't think he even recognized. This was something different, a soldier recognizing his opponent's skill. Why this perusal threatened to bring a blush to her cheeks and the other did not, she couldn't say, but she liked it.

"Fine. Tomorrow you're off guard duty."

"That is not your call to make, my lord." The pink in his cheeks was not from embarrassment this time. "I was assigned this duty by the general as I am the best at presenting an unassuming tail. I will be a ghost. I swear it. You will not even notice me there."

His teeth grit, jaw clenching, fighting back his instinctual denial of her demands. The play of emotion over his face was eloquent, and quick, too quick given that she would have enjoyed watching anger chase away embarrassment, fade to joy if she could manage to make him grin.

The blasted court smile turned his lips, eyes shadowed with anger. "Very well."

She liked his ire. It was refreshing from the solemn disinterest he'd shown her since their return to the palace. She liked it but would not be swayed by it.

She'd keep her word and be his shadow.

He did not look behind him to see if she followed or not.

He would not have spotted her regardless.

CHAPTER TWO

I

KIT COULDN'T FORGET her presence behind him.

She kept her word, and was like a shadow, blending so easily into the city around him that if he hadn't been tuned to her every movement, her every breath, he would have lost her entirely. He had to constantly remind himself not to stop and look for her, not to turn around and invite her into a conversation with him.

She wasn't the woman at the ball anymore.

How could he have been so stupid as to think three nights of dancing would have endeared him to her, or to any woman for that matter?

And she was an assassin.

Sweet gods, she could have killed him at any time if she so desired.

And when she trained with him that on his birthday—

He turned around, spun really, in the middle of the crowded street, left then right trying to find her.

She burst from her position against a wall, moving to his side with a speed he envied and a grace he could never hope to emulate. He grabbed her arms when she reached for a knife at her belt, a knife he didn't even know she had or how she'd come about its possession. "You were my opponent on Samseiet!"

Her lips parted but she spoke no words to him. He waited but she seemed unable to find her voice, not to affirm or deny his remark. She came to the fencing room before today. She'd come in trousers with her mock cock and her hair tucked beneath a cap that he'd found odd but hadn't questioned his young opponent. She'd come as a boy learning the art, not as one of his men well trained to the sword. And he'd stood opposite her, him, whatever, and parried gently so as to aid the boy's approach to the bout.

"Why?"

Her eyes rolled to his, chin tilting just far enough that he thought she might be clenching her teeth, unsure if it was displeasure at his manhandling, or a vein of temper at being so questioned by him. Did she think he was unaware of her skill? Was that what her look was about? She held his stare and shrugged.

His lips drew back in an unhappy snarl and it took all his will not to shake her. "Why, Eli? To kill me before my men? Show how woefully unprepared we are for you and your kind?"

"My kind no more."

He didn't understand, didn't know why the tone of her voice caused a wave of pain to pierce his heart. "Why then?"

"To know you," her hands touched his elbows, completing the circle of their arms though he could not decide if it was intentional or some form of guardianship he was unfamiliar with. His soldiers rarely touched him except to pull him from whatever harm they suspected.

"And yet you were so against the knowledge yestereve."

The blush that came to her cheeks was nearly hidden, nearly undetectable if he wasn't so attuned to watching every subtle nuance of her face, so captivated by it. "It was two days ago, now."

"Damnit." He shook her, a gentle shake, his fingers lightening their hold on her arms, so he didn't hurt her. "Do you truly think this has anything to do with when the conversation occurred? You lied to me, thrice over!"

"I never lied."

"You didn't tell the whole truth."

"You're a politician, Prince. You always tell the whole truth?"

He had no response to that, and damn her, he knew she saw that too.

"Push me away; throw me out, exile me from your kingdom, or allow me the job you offered and take your hands from my arms."

How sick of him to admire this anger of hers, this strength.

She was in the wrong. She had to know she was in the wrong and yet she acted like she had more right to her anger than he did his. She was the one who lied about who she was, invaded his palace, her woodsy ways so at odds with his culture. And she'd refused him when he offered her a chance at his hand.

That's what irked him most.

That she was the better swordsman was unquestioned. He had her in the ballroom. They both lied easily enough, convincingly enough to one another.

No, he had never lied.

Had he lied?

"Are you going to let go?"

Kit dropped his hands from her arms, stepping back quickly. The moment she came close, all reason deserted him. He was a prince, a politician, a soldier, a general. He knew better than to allow himself to be distracted, knew to listen first and speak second. Yet she interrupted him without regard, her words as pure as though there was no filter between her thoughts and her speech. Guileless, though secret filled.

And his heart still beat for her.

Of everything that had happened, that he could not remove her from his desires, that her betrayal, her lies and secrets and, for the gods' sakes, her victories in the practice field, meant nothing to him when she was near, were the things he should not forgive, and yet could not hold against her.

He held her gaze, standing in the middle of the street as washer women and craftsmen and soldiers on patrol passed them by, said soldiers walking slowly to ensure he was not in need of assistance.

He shooed them, and they quickened their pace.

"And if I exiled you, where would you go? Would you then pit your skills against mine? Return as my assassin in the dead of the night?"

"No." He didn't miss the way her voice grew hoarse at the suggestion, the flash of horror in her eyes that she might attempt to kill him. "I wouldn't return as your assassin."

A moment longer. He wanted a moment longer to look in her eyes, pretend that they weren't in some unknowable battle of wills, that he wasn't supposed to hate her, and she wasn't supposed to hate him and that that flare in his chest meant nothing.

"Fine then."

He turned and walked away heading towards the center square and the vendors setting their wares out for the day. Already the fresh scent of baked bread and apple tarts layered the air. If nothing else, the smell calmed his raw nerves, recalled his childhood where he would sneak out of the palace and race to the marketplace and Cinta would pass Kit a sweet bun before going back to his oven.

He hadn't been to the baker in years.

Every time he thought to leave the palace for a moment, something else would come up: another meeting, a request by a steward for something or other, a noble wanting a quick word.

The only reason he managed a respite this afternoon was that he'd left before anyone could stop him. He never left straight from fencing, but she'd distracted him, turned his head, and now here he was in the city. Yes, he knew the palace was like a city unto itself, but he enjoyed walking the streets of Tornald, seeing the people, speaking to them. He wasn't going to live his life afraid to leave his rooms because there was a bounty on his head. His people protected him. He would honor that by proving he trusted them enough to be part of their lives and not remain secluded from them.

Pigeons swooped around the baker's stall, the breads and rolls lining the table did not rise to their usual appeal. The red of the awning hung partway open, like it had been done in a hurry and not done well. The baker himself was nowhere in sight.

Cinta had never been so lazy or so lax in his shop's appeal.

Kit stepped towards the stall and frowned when her hand closed around his upper arm, drawing him to a stop. He looked back at her, and she nodded to the ground and the dead pigeon and two dead rats, half hidden beneath the wrinkled tablecloth covering the stand.

His hand went to the sword at his hip, and again she stopped him, stepping up to his side rather than the foot behind she'd been following.

She turned so that she faced him, keeping her lips averted from the store's front window. "I need you to slap me and walk away in a huff, find the patrol that passed us and get back to the palace."

"That's not happening, Captain."

"Something's not right here, you know it as well as I."

"Yes, and Cinta and his family have been friends of mine for years. I'm not leaving until I know what's wrong. They wouldn't betray me."

"They might not have had a choice."

"All the more reason to stay." But he understood the need to playact a scene, not to rouse more suspicion around them than his being prince already did. He pushed her hand from his arm, turned to walk towards the stall as was his original intent. He wouldn't actually get close to the thing, just close enough that it appeared he was oblivious to the threat.

"Sweet Darkness."

He heard the whispered curse behind him before her arm came from his back to wrap around his throat, her knife pressed against his pulse. A quick jab to his side had him bending at his middle to protect the injury, not having expected the attack, not prepared for it. He doubled over, seeing spots, wondering if this was all an act or if he'd put his faith in the wrong person.

"The bounty's mine, you bastards."

He struggled at that, fighting to pull away, lash out. She was quick enough to avoid his attempt, pin an arm at the small of his back, press up on his captured wrist until he rose on his toes, trying to relieve the strain on his shoulder while she forced the appendage at its unnatural angle. Kit fought to control his breathing, unable to look up as she held him bent over, the knife at his throat precluding him from turning his head to try and read the situation.

"You should have killed me in the forest."

"Shut up, your highness."

She held him prisoner to her, slowly relaxing her grip until the hand captured at his back slipped to her waist, the knife holstered there, her fingers helping his to curl around the hilt, hidden between their bodies. The weapon did nothing to relax him, only tensing his muscles further, undecided if she was friend or foe, praying for friend.

She bent towards him, a quick look beneath his bowed spine, to his sides, her face hidden by his body. "Play along, Kit, or we're both dead."

The withheld breath eased from his chest, letting the simple command calm him, knowing he shouldn't trust this woman and unable to stop himself at the same time.

He didn't know what had spooked her, didn't know how to ask.

But the door to the bakers crashed open. Three huffed breaths, three rancid scents, filled the small street, stormed from the room and shifted over the cobblestones, drawing neither closer nor backing away. She pressed up on his bound arm, forcing his bend more severely, minimizing the target he presented, no clear sight line to his heart from behind, her body a shield from the side and front. She'd relaxed her knife enough for him to see the situation but maintain her capture, his gaze just able to pick out the unshaved faces looking at him, the hint of more boots out of his peripheral vision.

He heard the table clatter to the ground, a poisoned roll rolling towards his feet, splintered wood having crossed the cobblestones to land near his boots, evidence of the violence of the men's approach.

Three men.

She'd taken four without problem.

He could hold his own in a fight, despite what she might think.

But this wasn't about killing the enemy.

Kit knew the faces of his townsfolk, knew the men and women who worked outside the palace walls and within the city limits, those who'd come before the king begging sanctuary, who'd pledged their allegiance to Kit when they were given shelter.

These men did not belong here.

That there was no alarm suggested that their arrival had gone unnoticed. And if their arrival was unnoticed, perhaps the baker and his wife and son were alive within the small house.

How long would these bastards have spent hoping to catch Kit out about the city? He never kept to a schedule. There was no one who knew he'd left that afternoon but his guards, and they were discreet. None had left before him except the group they'd passed, and they were gone before he even escaped the palace that day.

Her body stiffened next to his, tension or hesitation, he couldn't decide until the pressure of the knife changed, and she forced him to straighten, allowed him a view of the street around them, the men circling their position.

"Tell the rest of your men to come out. You five aren't worth my time."

Shit.

The tailor from across the street, the bookseller's and the printing press, disgorged their cohort of mercenaries, enough that even with the guards walking the city, Kit and Eli would likely die.

Twenty men against two. If his guards came, that added five to their side. That she had a knife to his throat was buying them time, but not nearly enough.

"Looks to me like we've got the better claim to the lad, elf."

"Looks to me like you have more men and think that makes your claim better." He heard the cruelty in her words, the edge he didn't know how to respond to. "In truth, it makes the split of the bounty smaller, which is why I always work alone."

She took a step back and Kit followed with her, allowing her to move him where she would, his strings pulled taut. The men at their backs shifted, stepping forward to threaten her retreat. Her lips pressed to his throat, teeth pressing into her skin in threat; her knife drew a small line beneath his jaw. She tsked at the mercenaries, smiling against Kit's skin. "Do you know who I am, hunter?"

The man paused, looked her over, shrugged. "Another elf looking to make a name for himself." He waved a hand in the air, dismissing her. "Passed your kind on our way in. They were smart enough to wish us luck on the kill, Precious. You should run back to them."

Kit felt her stiffen against him, her people responsible for their present circumstances, or at least instigating it to move along faster. They didn't attack themselves, but free reign to others apparently.

She made no verbal response. He couldn't decide if her playing assassin or keeping her name hidden would spare them. Not that it mattered when she drew a second line of fire over his skin, thin, not much blood, barely a scratch but enough of a threat for the men around them and his focus returned to the moment rather than debating the merits of irrelevant thoughts.

"You kill him, we kill you, the bounty is ours and there's plenty of time on the road between here and Kirbi for men to die."

That the merc made the threat before said men acknowledged how fragile the confederacy between them.

Kit wondered if their destination of Kirbi was a lie.

The island continent was across the sea. No one came from there but hired swords. Their bounty would not come from the other country; their master hidden somewhere closer to Kit's home.

He hissed when she pressed his arm further up his back. "I'm willing to split the bounty five ways, boys. Maybe throw in something special for the lads that help a poor lass out." His body reacted without thought to the implication, struggling in her grip which she ensured the gathered men noticed her hold on him, how easy killing him would be. "Best make that decision fast gentlemen, before I lose patience." He couldn't decide what angered him more, that she would offer sex as a reward to his potential killers, or that she refused him in the same.

He didn't want that with her though. He wanted more. He—

She'd kept them moving, her steps even, steady, unhurried and ignored by their hunters. The tanner's shop was at their backs. A heavy kick to the door, a fast retreat, and mayhap they'd find some safety in the small house until reinforcements found them.

If she was with him, and this wasn't a ploy.

Stop thinking!

The leader drew a crossbow from his accomplice, aimed the weapon at Kit's chest. "Twenty against one, little miss. It's been a lark carryin' on like we 'ave, but we've wasted enough time now."

With a smile, the mercenary fired at the same moment Eli pushed Kit aside. The crossbow bolt thudded into the heavy wood behind them.

Kit didn't stumble away, using her push to spin around, her dagger in his hand, let fly against the leader while she kicked the door in. He followed her into the room, overturning the cabinet inside the threshold to act the barricade to the broken latch. The wood would hold for a time, enough deterrent that the best avenue of advance into the space was through the windows, bottlenecking the men attacking, their advantage of numbers minimized.

Her knives flashed in the dim sunset of the room, slicing through the shattering of glass to strike the first man through. Kit pulled the sword from his hip, barely enough room for him to raise the weapon against the male sent tumbling towards him when she passed the mercenary back for Kit to finish. A quick slice, empty hands raised to the red smile cut along the male's throat, and Kit turned his head to his next opponent.

The table at Kit's back threatened to trip him, acted to the killer's benefit when Kit was forced against the wooden surface, rendering his sword useless. His fingers scrabbled against the table, searching for anything to use against the man atop him. A handle slipped into Kit's fist, and he didn't care what it was, swinging wildly against the man, ignoring the momentary shock of blood spraying over him when the knife slashed the carotid and the man died above him.

Kit's fingers tightened against the weapon, both hands full of metal to meet the next attack, unable to spare a moment to see how Eli fared at the front.

HORNS SOUNDED IN the street.

The ground shook beneath the clomp of hooves. Soldiers sent to join the fray.

The mercenaries stuck within the tanners with him and Eli tried to flee, but there was no other exit from the small room. Kit swung high, took the head of one man, watched her sink two knives into her opponent's sides, draw the weapons up, slice the belly open. The man dropped.

Kit leaned against the table, trying to catch his breath amidst the dying men at his feet. His gaze scanned the decimated bodies, counting the dead they'd slain.

His eyes closed at Marius' shout. "We're clear out here, my prince."

But "clear" was not enough. "How many mercenaries out there?" Her words echoed around the room, spinning through his brain.

He tried to lift his head, stare at anything but the blood-soaked ground at their feet, but it was difficult, so difficult, each breath a challenge in itself. Her hands cupped his cheeks, raised his gaze to hers. He hadn't seen her move towards him. "Are you hurt?" The soft whisper of her words broke the spell in his head, the catch of her eyes with his.

"Nothing serious."

One hand slid from his cheek to the red staining his left arm, drifted to the blooming gash on his side beneath the linen shirt he wore.

"We've seven here, Captain."

"There are nine in here with us."

She nodded at Kit's words but didn't relay the message outside, her gaze held on his slight wound, fingers pinching at the skin, making him hiss.

He turned his head to the chamber, searching corners, counting bodies again, anything but looking at her. "I counted twenty men out there."

"Twenty-one, there was a rat on the roof above us, too young to be part of their brotherhood, but a member all the same."

"A lookout?"

"A spy."

"That's five men unaccounted for." He said.

Her cheeks twitched in what might have been a grin but never fulfilled the promise of false gaiety it strove for. "What are the odds we've made them rethink the bounty on your head?"

He gave her a grim smile in return. "You did a good job of ensuring they wouldn't, Captain." Her brow furrowed at his response. "Less to split the bounty between now."

"Shit."

Marius entered the small room, hands held wide, intending no harm. Kit's arm rose, sword ready for another attack despite the approach of his friend. The arm she'd been examining tightened around her, pulling her close lest the known general prove less than trustworthy.

The commander dropped to his knees before Kit, ignoring the woman standing as shield in front of the prince's body. "I've failed you, your highness."

Kit met the dismal gaze leveled on him, his grip relaxing across Eli's shoulders. "I'm alive."

"I should have sent guards with you."

"You didn't know I was leaving." Kit stared down at his general, tsked when the man failed to look up. "You got here in time to save our lives. Find the rest of the bastards and consider the debt paid."

Marius rose, eyes scanning the room now that he was forgiven by his prince. "More?"

She spoke. "At least five within the city. Not counting if they had others waiting beyond the walls."

Marius turned his gaze to Eli, the elf unflinching beneath the glare. "I heard you had a knife to Kit's throat."

"I heard I saved his life from those who would have taken it without my knife there."

No trust between them then, and perhaps Kit shouldn't be as trusting of her as he was.

"She's my captain, General, named and witnessed by you and our men. She saved my life."

Blue eyes landed on the red stain at Kit's throat, though how Marius could see the small gash beneath the flow of blood from their adversaries was beyond Kit. Too much blood.

The slice at his side burned; the one along his sword arm was numb so long as he didn't move but flared hot with agony any time he adjusted his grip on his weapon. Eli'd already surveyed the nick to his left bicep.

Would mercenaries resort to poison? Or would that be too hard to prove who made the kill?

A lifetime spent with the threat of death over his head, and this was the first time he'd ever taken a life in defense of his own.

"Kit."

Marius stepped forward, and Kit took a moment to close his eyes, gain control of his breathing, ignore the stench of the dead and dying, of blood and spilled guts around him. It bothered him, to have had to take a life, but worse would have been dying and fulfilling the demise of his city through prophecy.

She stepped to his side, her fingers wrapping around his forearm, the trembling in his limb from over exertion. She clenched her hand, and he flinched at the bite of her nails in his skin. Marius ripped a hank of the hem of his shirt off, bound the cloth around Kit's right arm, a makeshift bandage until they reached the palace.

The two worked smoothly together when he was the focus of their energy.

"Are you all right? Do you think the blades were poisoned?"

He shook the arms off him, pushed against the table so that he could stand on his own, force his soldiers away to give him room.

Marius edged Eli aside.

The snarl she leveled at the commander had Kit's head snapping to the woman.

"Enough. Whatever it is between you, put it aside." He made sure to meet both of their eyes, hold them in his glare. "I trust her same as I trust you—"

"She held a knife to your throat!"

"Yes, and she had me alone against four of her brethren and saved my life at the cost of theirs." He didn't intend to raise his voice, so very rarely lost his temper that it was a shock to his system as much as his soldiers.

Kit closed his eyes, breathed in, waited for the world to calm a moment before he continued. Marius wasn't the only one at fault; at least, Kit didn't think Marius was the only one at fault. He'd address the issue regardless. "She's ours now, sworn to me. You don't have to like her, but you will accept her as it is my order for you to do so, Marius. She's proven herself more than an ally. She didn't have to fight to save my life the first time, but she did." He turned his gaze to Eli. "And you: Marius earned the title of General of my guard and my army. He has dedicated his life to its service, to me, and deserves the respect owed him for earning his position. He might fight differently than you, he might have lived differently than you, but you are both warriors and will respect each other as such. Am I clear?"

"I know how to protect against assassins better than he does."

"Only because you were one—"

"Yes, because I *was* one." She met Marius furious gaze, met the incredulous tone with the vehement truth of her own.

Kit watched the mask come down over her emotions, veiling her anger or whatever else she felt behind it. Whether she was trying to obey his decree to play fair with the general, or if it was her natural way to hide how she felt, she was giving Marius a direct stare, unchallenging even as it was dominant.

"If I hadn't put my knife to his throat, they would have had a clean shot at his back. Keeping my body between them and his saved his life. If I hadn't put a knife to his throat, they wouldn't have hesitated to kill us both; but another mercenary against them left room for doubt because, despite it all, General, mercenaries and assassins follow a code of honor. It might not be the honor you appreciate, but it is there. I had first claim to him then. They had the numbers over me. Putting my knife to his throat was the only way to buy us time to get into a position where we wouldn't be at such a disadvantage, where we had a chance of lasting until you got here."

Kit watched his commander clench his jaw, a tick working at the man's right eye.

"What would you suggest we do now, Assassin?"

"Captain, Marius. She gave you your title," Kit snapped

"Assassin is appropriate, my prince."

Kit closed his eyes, his head throbbing from more than just the fighting.

"Their leader should be wounded, upper body, maybe head. I don't think it was fatal but left untreated it might be. Whoever is left will flock to him, so we find him, we find them. The problem will be whether they decide to risk attacking right off or wait a night or two hoping our guard lowers." She looked away from Marius' stare, pulling her bloodied knives from their sheaths at her hips to clean the blades of some of their blood along the linen of her trousers. The action drew Marius' attention to the red she'd spilled in Kit's defense, another reminder that she'd been the key to Kit's life. The motion was neither subtle, nor unintentional.

Kit watched Marius swallow back his pride.

"If it were you, Captain?"

She replaced the weapons in the sheaths at her sides. "If it were me, I wouldn't have brought twenty men to do a job a slim knife in a passerby's hand could accomplish. Barring that, I'd strike again, fast. I'd move with the light, hiding in plain sight, unexpected, but they're scared, they'll wait till full dark."

"So, in Kit's chambers."

"Likely so."

"We'll put guards on the doors and below the balcony."

"On the balcony. They had a man on the roof. It's possible they'll try that way again." Both soldiers turned to look at Kit, apparently realizing he was privy to their conversation. That it was Marius' stare that held disbelief at Kit's words, and Eli's that held approval, did not endear the man to Kit.

"I know you don't like anyone in your rooms, Kit—"

That it was for Kit's comfort Marius hesitated with the guards eased some of the ice in Kit's gut. "There will be a threat until I'm five hundred and eighteen years old, Marius. I'm not going to be coddled my whole life. Until these men are captured, you'll have the rule of me, but once it's done, we go back to how we were."

"That wasn't particularly safe, my—"

"Though I named you captain, Captain, in this I do not require your opinion to guide me. I will not be a prisoner in my own country. I won't cower."

"Then you'll learn to fight."

He frowned at the woman who looked so calm and serene covered in blood fiddling with the hilt of a dagger stuck in her belt. "I know how to fight."

"Like your people, yes." She focused her gaze on his face and it was Kit who turned aside. "You'll learn to fight like mine. Like the Dienobolos. Like the Quifolno and their desert-men brothers from Kirbi. I'll teach you the way of the island people of Wen, the Kirannas and the Tuabs, the warriors of Zahni."

Kit snorted at her list, the fantasy of it. "Why not add the lost people of Miest to the list then? Or, perhaps you've seen fairies fluttering about your woods you'd like me to train with?" He could not help the sarcasm in his voice.

Yes, his father had opened trade routes with the Islands of Wen and the desert land of Kirbi. Hells, those same trade routes likely brought his current attackers to Spinick's shores.

Prutwl even sent delegations upon a time, but the crossing to the northern continent was more hazardous and Leon hadn't approved those shipping lanes yet.

But the "warriors of Zahni," the desert dancers of Quiofol, no one knew their fighting styles. They were closed territories, they'd never waged war against Spinick or his father or his father's father. No one knew their ways of battle, not even the once Elichisolos of the Dienobolos.

Or was that just a hope in his heart? If she knew all that she suggested, then how in the gods' names would he stop her?

"The people of Miest left the dragon lands long ago. What's left of their culture is not something to mock, Prince. They're deadly. They had to be. They killed enough great serpents on Zephra to make the land slick with black blood and they survived to tell the tale of it."

She spoke like she knew such men and women.

Zephra was a dead land.

Its people were dead.

But the Dienobolos worshipped the Darkness, so mayhap they walked the shores of the afterlife like it was simply the twilight of this world.

Her anger had the ring of righteousness to it.

"My apologies, my lady. I meant no offense."

She nodded, releasing him from the razor of her glare. "I wouldn't teach you the ways of the Miestians, Prince. You're too faint of heart."

That raised his hackles, and he wanted to retort, but the look in her gaze suggested that, though she might have learned the mythical art of war of the dragon people, even she was not comfortable in its use. He bowed his head, acquiescing to her knowledge on the subject.

He looked to Marius, the shrewd look in the man's eyes, the distrust and raging hunger for the things she suggested, and Kit had little faith in. Kit would suffer for that hunger, forced to train unnaturally to fulfill the general's desire for military acumen. Kit would suffer the training fields and the healer's touch because she was staring at him too, and her eyes held a similar hunger, one far more personal or so it seemed.

"We should get back to the palace."

"Yes."

Eli agreed, led them from the confines of the death filled room.

Kit mounted the horse presented to him, rode through the streets at a gallop, no one willing to let him linger longer in the unprotected and unknown alleys of his home city.

At least no one would be training in new doctrines today.

For once, he almost looked forward to the solitude of being locked in his own chambers.

II

HE SLIPPED THE knife under his pillow, stretched his arms over his head, and flinched when the right protested the movement. His side ached beneath the bandage wrapped tight round his middle, his muscles opposing the strain, wanting simply to relax from the tension of the day. His mind wouldn't relax. Kit doubted his body would.

He'd foregone any bedclothes for the evening, preferring to sleep beneath the sheets comfortably despite the chill outside his windows. He'd kept his breeches on; a lingering worry that Eli might be correct, that his would-be assassins would strike again during the night and he didn't want to be without some decency covering his skin.

Guards stood outside his balcony. He'd offered them blankets for warmth since they were not allowed fire. They'd politely refused, something about the cold being bracing, and shut his balcony doors, closing him inside his chambers. Guards were at the doors to his sitting rooms, at the doors that connected his room to the second set of family quarters, at the main doors of his suite and his bedroom, all doors closed, and all guards sworn to keep careful watch throughout the night. No doors locked in case they had to invade quickly. Easy access for any who made it past the men though

If any of the men died, it would be in his defense.

Marius would say they died doing their duty or they died because they hadn't trained hard enough.

Kit suspected that Eli would hold a similar mindset.

He settled on his back beneath the blankets. The pillows mounded enough behind his head that he had a clear view of his room. The bed curtains wound tight to their banisters, leaving ample space to escape the large four posters and anyone coming to attack.

A guard had even checked beneath the bed and beneath the sheets in case someone had slipped something into his room without his notice.

He'd been confined to the damn space for the entirety of the evening upon returning to the palace. The only one who could have slipped something into the room was Kit, and he hadn't done that. He had no desire to die.

His eyes drifted closed; he turned on the mattress so that he was practically buried between the soft blankets, head cradled within the mound of pillows.

His hand curled on the hilt of the dagger.

HE KEPT HIS breathing deep and steady, no hint that he was awake or aware of his surroundings.

The first thump had been nearly silent, but to heightened nerves had sounded obscenely loud in the confines of his room.

There hadn't been a struggle, and now there was silence once more from the balcony.

His eyelids cracked open enough to allow him a glance towards the glass doors, the shades drawn to keep out the torchlight and the sight of the men beyond the windows. He should have kept the damn things open.

His sword was against the nightstand, close enough that a quick flip would find the blade in his hand, but enough time for a quarrel to find its way to his heart from a crossbow.

The handle of the door turned, visible only in the flickering light of the few candles Kit had left burning on his desk.

There was no bow in the hands that entered the room first, only black gloves followed by an equally black uniform, even the face shadowed by cloth. The mercenary clung to the shadows, moving along the wall towards Kit's bed without stepping out into the open of the room. It kept the man in Kit's sight, poor fool.

Kit's fingers clenched around his knife and the man pressed a knee to the bed. Kit's wrist jerked up and out, slipping through the cloth at the man's throat, into the flesh beneath. Warm liquid splashed over Kit's face and he closed his eyes, trying not to think about the assassin dying in his bed, the men slain earlier that day by his hand.

The mercenary's blade thudded against the quilt, fingers gone nerveless in his last minutes of life.

Kit squirmed from beneath the male's weight, slipped over the side of the bed without rising, presenting as small a target as possible.

His eyes went back to the balcony door, left open now with no one to close it.

Had someone else come into his room in the moment before his attacker died? Was he even now being stalked unaware while the first assassin cooled?

A shadow slipped from the porch, thin and willowy, moving quickly to the bed, not trying to hide its approach.

There would be no surprise this time. The attacker would know Kit was alive the moment he pulled his sword from the sheath.

He stood with the blade drawn, drew the mercenary's gaze though Kit did not attack directly.

Shadows cleared, and Eli crouched at the side of the bed. A quick glance to him, noting he lived, was unharmed, and her eyes turned to the corpse. "You survived."

"I'm not incompetent."

"No, you're not." She pulled the assassin's hood off his head, adjusted the corpse so that he looked like he was simply sleeping rather than sprawled where he lay.

Kit watched her pull the sheets over the body before stepping away.

"The guards on the balcony are dead. I managed to kill the one climbing the wall, but another came from over the roof before I could make the ascent."

"I'm assuming that's the one I killed then."

"Likely."

He didn't like the uncertainly in her response but didn't question it either.

His gaze moved to the other doors to the room. "How many of them could be left? Three?"

"There were more in the outlying parts of the city in case you went to somewhere other than the baker's. There are at least thirty men looking to kill you."

"Why are they so determined? Long as I die before my five hundredth birthday, the city falls. They have time."

"Maybe their lord decided he couldn't wait another four hundred years. Or perhaps he rewards failure harsher than we would reward the attempt."

"In other words—?"

"We might kill them fast, where the master will kill them slowly."

A harsh reality, and one he couldn't refute. She spoke the truth, though if he survived, if any of the men survived the attempt of taking his life, Kit doubted his father would sanction a quick death for any of them.

He slipped away from the bed and into the deeper shadows near the hallway door, back against the wall to watch the room, conceal his presence. She had made a decoy of him in the bed. He'd best use the distraction.

His voice was barely a whisper, but the silence in the room offered no challenge to the hearing of the words. "You're sure it's a male?"

"The lord?" She smiled in the dim light of the room, moving from the bed to follow him into the corner, standing with her shoulder pressed to his against the wall. "A woman wouldn't fail. We're more vicious than men, crueler. You'd die, and yes, we'd obey, and it would be timely, but it would be painful, that quick death, if called for by a woman." A chill slid down his spine at the ambivalence in her voice. "It's a male."

His throat was dry when he responded, doing his best for levity, to ignore the knowledge with which she spoke, the death stalking him. "Sexist."

"Realist."

"I yield to the greater experience."

Another flash of a smile and she turned towards the doors to the second set of apartments, staring hard at the wood separating them.

"How many guards were supposed to be out there?"

His breathing stilled at the question, his chest aching at the implication. "Two at each door."

"There is only one that way."

He almost asked how she could tell, but managed to refrain, unsure he wanted to know if she was using magic.

Oh, he knew about magic. The mages in the city cast spells over the palace once a year that protected it from weather damage. Supposedly the city itself was protected from direct attack, the enchantment built into the walls themselves. Kit knew some mages worked on close magic, magic that worked physically on the people it impacted, and then there were those who worked on inanimate objects, and those who could heal, and there were no dark mages in Spinick, but that didn't account for the other nations of Lornai.

She worshipped the Darkness Itself.

She was an assassin.

What magic would a dark mage wield if they were to call upon it?

"There is one shadow moving beyond that door, and three in the halls outside your room. That accounts for only six men including the two already dead."

"Where are the others?"

Her eyes met his.

"Can you find them, Captain?"

Her head tilted to the side, staring beyond him.

He watched the green of her iris bleed into the white of her eyes, fade beneath the black of her pupil until the whole of her eye was the same vitreous shade of shadow. If she scanned the room, he couldn't tell. If it was her eyes that were seeing, he didn't know. Her head turned, sharp, fast movements, a bird hunting its prey, left, right, up, down. Had she turned her head all the way around, Kit didn't know that he'd be able to abide that. The blackness of her gaze was disconcerting enough.

Slowly, minutely, her pupils began to recede, or perhaps it truly was shadows that were clearing from her vision as the whites and then the green reformed in her eyes.

"They're fighting in the main galley. A distraction for the six sent for you."

"And the guards around my room?"

"I do not think any are left this side of the living."

He cursed. He prayed. "Atha take them."

She said nothing to his fervent whisper, though her gaze turned away as though she couldn't abide his worship where he said nothing of hers. "I do not know your Atha."

"She was the Goddess of War."

"Was?"

He did not respond to her question, not knowing how to, even if he could. Atha was the goddess of war. But his faith was shaken with his mother's death. He resented her patron goddess, even as he offered the prayer to the Woman.

He raised his hand, brushing against the ash on her cheeks, smeared across her forehead, looking for a safer distraction than the gods he worshipped, the Darkness she prayed to. "Did you roll in a fireplace?"

"The cinders help to hide my face in the darkness."

"And you know this how?"

"Do you really want that answer?"

No, he didn't think he did. "Gods," he cursed, not knowing who else to call upon, how else to relieve his pent-up fear and anger.

"Only one, and the Darkness is begging to claim a prize." She touched the blade of her knife to her lips, kissing the bloodied metal before flipping the hilt in her hand so the tip rested along her forearm, a deadly vambrace. "Do not engage unless they get past me."

There was no time to respond, or perhaps her timing was simply that impeccable. The door rattled and bowed inward, three men from the hall rushing through the mess in tandem with the single mercenary from the servant's entrance.

Kit's hand gripped harder around the hilt of his sword, the blade pointed towards the ground, unable to raise it with her so close. He watched the swing and parry and lunge of her knives, the mercenaries' grunts when she struck them, two downed without chance of rising, the last two advancing together against her.

The moment the one engaged, the other dropped away, slipping beneath her guard, trusting his fellow to distract the lady while he went for Kit.

But Kit had killed men that day.

His men had died for him this night.

The man lunged, and Kit stepped to the side, the blade passing safely beneath his arm, never slicing him as he turned, the swordsman's grasp weak enough that the hilt slipped from the man's grip, and Kit's blade buried in the mercenary's gut.

The would-be assassin clenched at the sword in his stomach, unaware of the further injury inflicted as Kit withdrew his weapon and turned to meet his captain's stare over the body.

"I showed you that move once and already you're putting it to use. That's unwise to the extreme, Prince. You need to practice. Instinct is one thing, but skill another."

"Maybe I have both."

"You do, but those skills are untested, and instinct isn't honed. I'll add that to the list of what we'll be working on come morning."

"And will I be wearing cinders while we go about blooding each other, Ella?"

She caught her breath and it took him a moment to realize the name he'd called her.

She responded before he could apologize. "No."

The pounding of his heart eased, the noise of it calming so that the sounds of battle from outside reached them, the fighting having progressed inside the walls of the palace if he had to guess.

Their position was compromised, the doors unable to hold back the wind let alone a soldier intent on the kill. She didn't even bother trying to salvage the wreck, leading him from his rooms, creeping silently down the halls. He didn't dare try to meet her gaze again, afraid it would be dark black pools that stared back at him.

They came to a crossway, silent like the dead behind them, yet she didn't lead him further. Her knives rose, one coming to cross his chest, press him to the stone behind her, far from the little light the dying torches cast into the small space. He sank to a crouch without her command, eyes trained above him where a soldier's gut might be, a raised sword prepared to attack.

She came up under the man's guard, barely stopping the advance of her knife into vulnerable throat as Marius aimed his crossbow at her. She pushed the bow aside and the general's eyes scanned the hall.

"Kit?"

"Here. Is there anywhere safe?"

"The last of the fighting is in the courtyard. All those who marched into the palace are dead. We ensured that."

"Did you keep one alive?" His general looked down at him, and Kit rose slowly, careful to keep his shadow from elongating with the torch.

The commander and captain's head were on a constant swivel, looking over each other's shoulders for attackers at their backs. They might not be fond of each other, but over a common foe, they worked in tandem. Kit filed the thought away for later reflection.

"Whoever survives the square will meet with question-ing."

"Did you tell your men to leave one alive?"

"It didn't need to be said, Kit. We know whose life is at stake. We won't fail you."

Kit scowled. "It's not about failing me. Mine is not the only life at risk. How many of my men have died tonight? Men whose only crime was being sent to guard me while I slept? How many souls are on my head for them?"

"They didn't die protecting you."

His eyes narrowed on the woman before him. Marius' glare equally cold at her words.

"They died protecting this kingdom. Your fate is not your own, Prince. To disdain their sacrifice, to think it so miniscule, is disrespectful. They died to save this country. You lived to do the same. Honor that spirit, instead of acting the whiny brat."

The reprimand was on his tongue. A servant, a soldier, daren't speak to his, or her, prince that way. But he could not deny that she was right, and if nothing else, Marius' silence confirmed her avowal. "My apologies, Captain."

She hadn't looked at him, not even to rebuff him.

She didn't meet his gaze now, striding past Marius and into the hall beyond.

Soldiers formed along the walls, bloodied and tired, but alive and triumphant. Some were kept standing by the brace of a brother at their sides; others slumped against the stone, knees trembling, eyes haunted. There had been no wars to fight since Kit was born. Small attacks on the country, on the capital, but nothing that required the troops train in the field, learn the lesson and the pain of taking a life.

Kit met the gazes of many of the men, wondering if he bore the same haunted look in his eyes reflected at him.

III

THE KING STOOD on the steps of the palace, crown in place though he wore a simple night robe rather than his coat and sashes of the court. He nodded to Kit, eyes widening at the blood on Kit's chest, the bareness of the flesh revealed. Kit almost shrugged but decided the gesture would be irreverent considering the scent of blood in the air and the cries of pain from the men lingering on this side of the veil in the courtyard below.

"We have sought no quarrel with you. We are a peaceful people and yet you brought this terror to our doors in the middle of the night. Our brothers are dead, their lives stolen by the recklessness of a few." King Leon looked to Kit, accepted Kit's bow of deference. "Tonight, we show no mercy. Let those who would make us enemies know we will not yield to their evil or their greed."

The guards took up a chant, hailing their king's wisdom, his anger on their behalf.

Kit focused on the men wrapped in irons, in ropes, some unable to rise, some whose eyes blazed with icy fury, wanting to kill, uncaring of the fate they faced.

"Death to the Prince!"

The lone voice was familiar, drew Kit's gaze to the wall surrounding the outer courtyard of the keep, the man standing alone atop the stone, crossbow in hand, the sun rising behind his back until he was just a shadow come to kill.

The whistle of the bolt reached him over the stricken crowd.

He couldn't see the quarrel though the sound of its passage seemed inordinately loud in the wide space.

Kit raised his hand, whether to bat the bolt away or block the sun so that he could see Death's coming, he didn't know.

He needn't have bothered.

Guards swarmed the tower where the leader stood, a bandage over the left side of his face, likely Kit's doing from the afternoon. The man didn't wait to be overtaken, flinging himself from the wall and laughing the short drop to his death. He struck the ground and was silent though soldiers surrounded him just the same.

Kit looked at the hand hovering before his chest, the quarrel that pierced the center of her fist, caught without a nick to her own flesh, held at bay from piercing his.

Leon stared at Kit, eyes roving between him and the woman who was his guard. "Seize the witch!"

"Not on your lives!"

Kit put himself between Eli and his father. Marius moved to guard the lady's back.

"She is the captain of my guard, Father."

Irrational hate filled the king's gaze. "She's an elf!"

"She saved my life thrice over. Would you reward her with a noose?"

Leon took the step up, Kit's height allowing him to stare over his father's head, though the man had a large enough presence that Kit barely managed the feat. "She will kill you."

"She has killed for me."

The older man's stare ranged from Kit's face to Eli's to Marius, silently asking the commander to what, Kit couldn't guess. "You trust this woman?"

Marius looked down at Eli, and Kit glanced over his shoulder, begging the man to side with him for he spoke the truth. "She's saved him when I would have been too late to do the deed myself. Do I trust her?" Marius shrugged. "No, but she's done nothing to earn my distrust either."

"An elf can never be trusted. Her people were the most violent against you as a babe, Christophe."

Kit and Marius looked to the king's brother slowly descending the steps. Kravn's face held no expression, though there seemed a madness in his eye as he looked between elf and prince and back again.

"You are unharmed, Uncle?"

"No mercenary would dare attack the Wolf of Spinick."

Yes, the Wolf of Spinick, but Kit had never heard of mercenaries fearing anything before, especially not a man so far from his prime as the king's brother.

If Kravn was not attacked, likely it was because the older man had hidden far from the battle, though Kit would not say such to disrespect his kin.

"Of course, Uncle." Kit nodded appropriately, no sarcasm or pity in his voice.

Marius drew Leon's gaze from the family reunion, back to the woman whose fate they were deciding. "I vouch for her, my King."

"As I vouch for her, Father."

Leon's gaze moved to her. Eli held her arm upraised, the quarrel in her grasp unnoticed while her eyes roamed over the crowd, guarding Kit even as she was discussed.

"The Children of the Wood will not part with one of their own lightly."

"I am foresworn, King Leon."

She'd made the choice herself, to part with her brethren. Kit held his breath at her remark.

The monarch's eyebrows rose at so direct an address.

Kit said nothing to this new battle of wills.

"That does not endear you to me, girl."

Kit could not see her face, though he thought he heard the smile in her voice. "I am foresworn, King Leon, for saving your son from my kinsmen. Your general was witness to the aftermath."

"I saw her sword pierce one of the villains' hearts while the prince was vulnerable, my King."

"I trust her, Father."

Finally, the King's gaze broke from the woman in question. "On your heads, be it. But I will not have a girl guarding my son; put her on rounds, city watch, away from him even if he wishes her in his service."

"I am the most qualified of your men. You may ask your general if you do not trust my words."

"And you should learn to hold your tongue in my presence."

Kit had the feeling that his father held little glory over those she'd grown up with.

She was, had been, head of the judiciary of her people. Elichi. Elichisolos. He knew the name, the title he'd kept from Marius. He knew before she told him on the ride to his home. She outranked all of her people but one, the High Priestess of the Dienobolos.

Gods save him.

She was a queen in her own right, and she'd bowed before Kit.

His father likely posed little threat to her, and yet could not see beyond her sex to the threat she posed him, the safety her presence ensured.

"Of course, your majesty." She inclined her head, turning finally to look upon the king while guards hefted the dead and the injured from the field of battle.

Kit's gaze caught hers for a moment, noted the calm glint of her eye, the widened pupil as though she were hiding emotion behind the blank face. These were not her people. A part of him was comforted thinking that perhaps she did not revel in the spilling of unnecessary blood despite her occupation, her past.

"Most qualified or not—"

"Captain." The king turned to stare at Kit's interjection. "She is the captain of my guard, Father. Qualified, trusted, or not, she deserves the respect the position demands."

"She has not earned it in my estimation."

"She has in mine, and as I am your heir. I would hope my word carries some weight with you."

"Kit," the king sighed, shaking his head before looking back at Eli standing patiently before him, quarrel in her hand held unthreateningly at her side now. Leon turned his gaze to Marius. "Ensure that she is relieved from duty before I need see her in my son's presence. And pray your trust is not misled, for it is all our lives if Kit should die."

Stated so bluntly, Kit blanched.

That his father would state such a truth in the aftermath of so much death was unseemly, threatened to consume Kit with anger, with despair.

"He will not die so long as I am with him, your majesty. I swear it to you, by the Darkness that Rules the Night."

The old man flinched. Kit's uncle and the commander flinched.

It was one thing to know she was from the wood, to discuss belief and magic when fighting for one's life. But that her beliefs were so different, so alien to him and his people, thrown so bluntly into their faces, made Kit flinch, fear what his father's response would be.

"By the will of the Gods, your oath is witnessed."

"And binding."

Kit's gaze went to Marius, the general's solemn face staring at the woman who offered herself to Kit's protection.

By her faith, and his.

IV
One Month Later

"I WAS AN assassin, my prince. I killed those who deserved to die, no more. War is a different battleground, but even then, if a life can be spared, the Darkness does not seek to claim it."

She extended her hand, offering aid in rising while he rubbed at his ribs where her sword had struck beneath the shield of his light armor. Trying to kill him or not, she'd found her way around his defenses over and over. That it was part of the exercise did not endear him to the instruction.

Try this. Lift that. Lunge now.

No matter what he attempted, her blades whirled faster, kept him at bay while she struck true.

When he asked what form a particular attack came from, she gave three names, none of which he knew, a hybridization of what she'd learned over her life and adapted to her own style. Of course, she said she was born knowing the ways of death, which he was particularly willing to believe considering how easily she managed to keep him from striking her down.

They'd been at the same exercises for weeks now.

He had bruises on bruises, no time to heal from one bout to another, forced by his father, by her, to practice daily without fail, more if court sessions were short and his schedule allowed.

He didn't dare point out that there had been no subsequent attacks on his person, or that there were no current rumors of attack or threat to the same. Rumors were often silent, and Kit so rarely left the safety of the city walls, he wouldn't know of any planned attacks or not.

The king commanded, and Kit's elfin assassin was surprisingly willing to obey the orders she received to keep him in the lists longer and longer.

"You hesitate on the attack, your highness. Rather than raising your blade to kill, you raise it to practice." She shifted position until she was at his back, her arms wrapping round his waist, cupping his forearms for her lesser height did not allow her to reach his wrists. "Your arms are too tense, too focused on maintaining your form rather than anticipating the strike, defending against it, lunging in turn. You move like one of your knights, strict, straight, unbending; but the monks of Rao Shar could slip between your arms like a lover moving to embrace and you'd find a knife between your ribs before you recognized the danger. They flow like dancers around your rock formations."

"Which means nothing since I am not facing the monks of Rao Shar or the demons of Quiofol or the Forgotten Peoples of Miest or any other person out there beyond the borders of my country!" He tried to pull out of her arms, but her hands only tightened further while he fumed.

Her hands lifted his arms in a parody of the water form she'd shown him the day before, long slashes that rolled like waves against a sea shore, an advance and retreat in one. Yes, the patterns were distinguishable, could be anticipated when made the same each time, but no wave struck the shore twice identically. Her response hadn't stopped him from trying to prove her wrong, flowing through the motions with his broad sword while she danced on the crests out of reach. "It means that your fighting style is too narrow, my prince. And you are not facing them *yet*. They will come if they are hired. Assassins have no creed but that of the orders they accept."

"You said not every attack must be to kill."

"But every attack must be ready to kill." She released his arms, letting him maintain his strict pose or drop his guard at will.

The sword was not meant for the fluid motions of the Rao Shar.

He let his blade point towards the ground and turned to face her.

"We'll start with my people. The Dienobolos fight with short knives, personal, close. It leaves your longer swords at a disadvantage when your opponent is skin to skin and your blade too long to turn on them."

"My sword allows greater reach to keep you from drawing that close in the first place."

"Not if I am fast enough to duck beneath your arm and close upon you before you can respond in kind."

And she was fast enough. How many times had she proved that point over the past month?

He refused to admit she was correct. She was, but he didn't want to feed the lack of ego she already employed. The woman knew her strengths, didn't flinch from them or preen over them. She simply was and while Kit admired it from a military and scholarly standpoint, the swordsman in him resented being constantly beaten back. "Then what do you suggest?"

"If you refuse to learn other weapons than that long sword you wield, then you had better be faster than all your opponents. If you're not fast, then learn blades that can protect you against those who are, the stratagems and movements ingrained in your being so that it is instinct to defend and attack, not thought."

"You said instinct wasn't enough."

"Practice leads to instinct. Once muscle memory takes control of your actions, then instinct is what you can rely on. That allows for a thorough defense." She weaved, her daggers close to her body, nearly pressing them to her chest as she spun around him, her knives arcing so quickly that he missed the lift and draw of them but knew what the motion should be from having practiced it so many times now. The sword was unwieldy when compared to her movements.

Her forms added protection to her person while being deadly against her foes. "I'll show you patterns for knives, long staves, hands. Subtle ways to kill and brutal ways to defend. I've watched enough. I know what you can do and what I can teach you to do if you'll let me."

"I thought you were already teaching me?"

"This was testing. Now the training begins."

He watched her clean the steel of her blade against her slacks.

The silver glinted in the afternoon light, shining along the edge of the weapon. He reached towards that glare, pressed the tip of his finger to the blade, felt the razor sharpness of it against his flesh. A hiss slipped past his lips and he sucked his bloodied digit into his mouth, glaring at his new trainer who was using edged blades against him in practice.

He should be dead one hundred times over.

That she hadn't killed him with her knives was impressive of her skill and depressing that her skill was what had kept him this side of the void.

Her lips quirked when she noticed him glaring at her. "A spell, Prince, to blunt the edges for practice but that obeys my will when the blade needs to be used in defense."

"It saves you from having to sharpen the metal daily."

"It saves me from ever being unarmed, even when the weapon is perceived harmless."

She spun the hilts of her knives in her palms, catching the weapon by the handle when the blade pointed away from her body, an impressive display of timing and skill.

Kit found the motions hypnotizing, unable to look away from the twirl and catch before him. Other soldiers were in the practice square. Distantly he was aware of the clang of steel against steel, had known that he was not alone though likely the only one getting his ass handed to him routinely. But the knowledge did nothing to distract him from the woman before him, or more precisely, from letting the motions of her knives lull him into a near daze, his exhaustion making its untimely appearance. The thought of returning to the lists for another round made his chest ache like a boy about to lift a sword for the first time, remembered terror and pained future exertion.

"Not tonight, Highness. A few days perhaps, to recover, before we begin again?"

He shook his head, blinked away the dust and sweat in his eyes. What had she said?

Her eyebrows rose, the half-smile lightening into a grin at his lack of comprehension. "Have I worked you that hard, Prince?"

He couldn't help himself. The smile came to his lips without thought at her words, easy to grin at the playfulness in her tone, the lack of biting critique or harsh command. "Gods yes."

She laughed, though he felt her gaze on him, lingering where she had struck him throughout the day, and the days prior.

He met her green stare, watched her lips turn down, felt his face morph to match. "Is everything all right?"

Her head tilted at his question.

He waited for her response, worried that she was going to renege on her offer of a few days of rest.

"You haven't smiled like that since the woods. I thought I'd never see it again."

Heat flamed in his cheeks, likely unnoticed beneath the layer of crime covering him. No one ever seemed to call him on his smile, only her. "You're the only one to comment on my expressions."

"No one else realizes that the upturn of your lips is anything but what it's meant to emulate." She took both knives in one hand, extending the other to take his sword from him.

He took her weapons instead, chivalry demanding he at least pretend to treat a lady as a lady even if said lady was deadlier than he.

She followed him over the hard-packed sand of the arena towards the barracks, the weapons master who claimed each practice blade, ensured that wet stones and swordsmiths were at the ready if someone needed an edge.

Five men ringed a pair of combatants, soldiers having reverted to wrestling when the sun waned beyond the outer wall of the courtyard. Groups of the same stood along the sentry points, staring out over the city shielded from view by the sandstone built around the palace.

Kit knew the view from atop those walls. The spires of temples reaching into the sky, thatched and shingled roofs, some flat with small awnings atop their backs for residents to escape the crowded streets for a night beneath the stars. How many times had Kit wanted to spend the night atop one of those small homes, staring at the sky rather than stone vaulted ceilings blocking out the night around him. Or looking beyond the city, to the green pastures, yellow corn fields, a patchwork of nature far beyond what he could see, supporting the lives of the men and women who called his country home. The woods too, great trees standing unbent in the distance, their secrets hidden beneath a canopy of leaves.

The days were finally growing warmer, though winter's bite had yet to truly lift in the air. Soon enough warm would turn to heat and then to snow once more.

Her touch on his hand drew him back to the moment, had his fingers tightening on the blades though she held his wrist to stop whatever attack he would have perpetrated.

"Instinct."

He managed a small grin, not forgetting her words from before, not willing to smile in truth, needing to keep the expression to himself lest he forget not to fall under her spell once more.

She handed her knives and his sword to the blacksmith. "I'll need another set, two inches longer, an ounce or two heavier but no more. You'll have to keep the blades proportioned but light."

“Like the steel used for these beauties?” Grizzled hands touched the tang of each blade with care, honoring the weapons, their intent and craftsmanship.

Kit would have found the gesture odd, but the man was an artist even if his craft was warfare. Not that his brain had enough energy to care.

“Exactly, just like I showed you.”

Showed him what? Him? Kit? Or the sword master? What were they talking about?

“And who are the blades for, my lady?”

“The prince.”

“Now wait a moment—”

She turned to meet Kit’s gaze, brows raised at his stuttered complaint, and he tried to recall the train of the conversation he’d heard but not been listening too.

Her arms crossed over her chest in silent reprimand to his inattention.

How did she do that?

She was, technically speaking, his servant, in a way, and yet with a single look, he held his tongue, bowing to her will. He should be furious with her that she had so much power over him. Fine, yes, alright, he could recognize the authority of another leader. But just because he recognized it didn’t mean he should obey. And yes, he’d admit to a small amount of jealousy that she wielded such authority so easily where it sat without much weight on his shoulders.

Kit blamed the last part on the fact that everyone was always tiptoeing around him.

Must protect the prince. The prince cannot be hurt.

Well princes needed to rule, and the constant subversion of his rule was weakening him in the eyes of his people since he was surrounded by a contingent of guards or spoke through his father’s words, his own never acknowledged.

Anger swelled in his breast. He deserved her respect, the swordsmith’s, his soldiers. He was good with a damn blade. He wasn't incompetent despite how she made him appear. He'd survive any battle posed against him. He would, despite what she might think. He was sure that there was someone out their better with a weapon than his elf. There had to be someone out there better than his elf, someone meant for him, who wouldn't run from him after a damn ball because he said he was in love…

The humor in her gaze changed to concern. He forced his fists to relax at his sides, tried to coral his expression into something benign.

He wasn't this type of person. He was calm, even tempered. Nothing riled him and yet around her, nothing was normal or sane. He was letting the damn pit in his stomach disrupt his life, those strange flutters near his chest anytime she came near distract him, tie him up in knots. It was so easy to say he wasn't going to give in to her, wasn't going to feel anything for her, and something very different to live with the results. Easier to change a river's path than the way she made him feel, look in her eyes and see a complete lack of reciprocation in them.

That was it, wasn't it? That she didn't feel for him the way he felt for her.

He blinked, met that upraised stare. "What do I need daggers for?"

"To learn to fight with."

"And the practice daggers we already have?"

"The way your weapons are formed are different than my peoples. To fight like my brethren, you will need weapons like them. If you find that your style adapts to using your knives with more efficacy than mine, then you're welcome to use your own blades. But as I am your instructor, you will learn my way, and only when I deem you proficient will your considerations be taken into account."

"And that I am prince?"

"Means nothing when it is your defense we are discussing."

She was uncompromising.

Why that helped steady him, he didn't know.

It wasn't just her expertise with a blade he could learn from her, this woman who pushed emotion aside to focus on the need at hand. She made a good instructor, had been renowned as the best of assassins, the head of her guild, if elves formed into guilds. She'd make a wise tactician and general someday, if those skills were required. He could allow himself to admire those qualities in her. A safe way to deny his emotions, accepting a few to bury the others beneath.

He looked at the blacksmith. "How long until the blades can be forged?"

"A week, Prince."

"You're not to deny your other duties to make those weapons. We'll make do with what we have until they're ready. Is that understood?"

"Of course, your highness."

He nodded at the man. "Is that sufficient for your requirements, Captain?"

"Quite, my prince."

"Then are we finished for today?"

She nodded, and he returned the gesture before walking away, needing to walk away.

As expected, he felt her presence at his back, her shadow stretching towards his in the late waning sunlight.

He paused at the door of her rooms.

She did not enter.

"I am going to my rooms, Captain. There are guards on my door, likely one on my balcony. There are no state dinners for tonight, nothing to fear or worry over. A meal with the king, and then bed. I don't need a shadow in my own palace."

"If you think that, then you need one all the more."

"Not tonight." He didn't mean for the edge in his voice to cut her, the small flinch he wouldn't have seen if he hadn't been watching her so closely. She'd made a vow to the king. That was why she was so adamant about keeping him in her care. There was nothing else in her gaze but duty, and he would do well to remember that. "You're relived for the evening, Captain. If you're resolute on having me watched, set someone else to the task, but I'd not have your shadow after mine tonight."

He wanted solitude, for just a moment, he wanted solitude. He wanted to be far from her and whatever it was she made him feel.

"As you will, my prince."

His eyes closed in silent gratitude, and she turned towards her rooms, the sound of her boots loud on the crunching sands of the training grounds, the thunk of her door closing when she left him alone.

He retreated to the palace and to his chambers, a bath drawn and ready for him, his steward urging him out of his soiled clothing and into the heated water the moment Kit opened the door.

Not right away though. He let the servant undress him, take his clothing, ask if there was anything else Kit required before leaving the prince to his bath.

Kit leaned against the sink, eyes closed, preparing himself for a lonely meal with his father, the less awkward drinks in the library that would follow, the formalities over with for the evening. He loved the old man, but his father was king, and his mother had been the love of his father's life. Kit looked too much like his dam to ease the man's heartache, and it was only with alcohol in the king's system that Kit felt truly accepted by the man who'd sired him.

With a groan, he lowered himself into the steaming water, letting the heat soak into his abused muscles, the bruises decorating his chest and back, his arms and legs. Just a few moments rest before the emotionally grueling dinner.

At least he had the day off the practice field tomorrow.

He wondered how long it would take before Marius heard that the captain had planned a brief stay of degradation on the arena floor and came to train Kit himself.

Ah to sink beneath the bath water and hold his breath.

He stood and resigned himself to duty, hardened his heart with the word.

Chapter Three

I

He was sitting in the library, alone now that the bells had chimed fourth hour of the new day, the king finally retreating to his own rooms and leaving his son in peace.

She watched him from the corner. The way his hand cradled his chin, his eyes fluttering closed before he jerked awake.

One month.

Sweet Darkness, she'd been here for a month already, one month of sparring, of training, of doing her best not to see the man beyond the soldier's blade she tutored, the solemn face that rarely smiled in her presence.

No, that wasn't really what was worrying her. What worried her was that she'd been here for only a month, and she no longer thought of the woods of her birth as her home. Not that she thought of the walls as her home either, just that, staring at the prince, she found a peace she'd not felt surrounded by her own people, worshipping her own faith, performing her ascribed duties. With him, with him she found herself.

She'd never shied from killing.

She was what the Darkness had made her, and she wasn't ashamed of the part of her soul that was violent, that was sure, that was a killer, a justice dealer, mercy for the suffering and death for the wicked. There had been no times where she took a life undeserved, where she slayed without reason or cause.

She was, and that had been enough for her until they danced the waltz and she found that she rather enjoyed the way someone else looked at her, liked knowing that he saw something beyond the First of Assassins, beyond the bleakness of her path in life. He'd seen a woman, and she wished desperately that she was still that person to him.

She blinked, met his stare, his body no longer relaxing to sleep where he sat in his chair, one hand at his hip and the dagger she knew he kept there at her insistence.

He didn't drop his gaze, waiting for her to do or say or make excuses as to why she'd disobeyed his order for peace and intruded upon it.

She willed her fingers to relax at her side. Concerns she hadn't felt since before she accepted the Darkness made her stomach turn when she looked at him, that strange tingling in her nerves that failed to flee whenever she was in his presence. "I would like to request to be relieved of guard duty for the next three evenings."

Surely, he'd grant the request. She'd relieved him of training for the same allotment of time. Quid pro quo and the like.

His eyes narrowed, focusing on her in the darkness, searching her face for what she didn't know.

She was grateful to be standing in the shadows to hide her blush from his piercing gaze.

"Why?"

Why indeed.

How much to tell him? What amount would see him grant the request without him asking for more than her faith allowed her to give? The Dark of the Moon were sacred days to her people. There were rituals to perform, offerings to make, sacrifices to endure, rest to take. "It's a religious obligation."

"And you'll return to the woods? To the people who you killed for my life?"

"No."

He must have heard the edge to her words, wondered at it. He must have, yet he did not question her further. That he didn't made her anger rise, but that rising emotion implied a longing for more than she was willing to give him. She should appreciate his circumspection. But that he didn't ask inferred a lack of caring and Darkness take it, she wanted him to care, to maintain that damnable need for her he'd had when he asked her to stay, before he knew who she truly was, when she was simply Ella and he was Kit and prince and assassin didn't matter.

"Will this ritual entail the harming of any of my countrymen?" He asked the question neutrally, eyes holding hers though she saw no emotion in their depths.

"No."

"Will the obligation damage my land or my people's homes?"

"No."

"Will the evenings be enough for you to complete whatever it is you're doing, or do you require the whole day?"

"It's—" She would have laughed at his ability to ask without asking what she was doing, but she held her tongue. The first two questions cared for his county. The last cared for her. "It must be performed at the darkest hour."

He stood from his chair, hands at the small of his back. He crossed to the fire burning merrily behind the grate in the library wall. She watched his profile, the expressionless mask over his face, the flickering flames that hid the emotion in his eyes.

"We have holy days too, you know. Days of commitment that we hold sacred." His head turned, and she crossed the room to stand at his side, letting him look at her now as she stared into the fire, into the light. "Did you think you needed to bribe me with a few days free of training to grant your request?"

"No," she paused, "but I did not think it would hurt any."

"Would you tell me about it, if I asked?"

That he didn't command soothed her even while her heartbeat sped at the interest the question implied. "None of your people have ever witnessed our rituals."

"I did not ask to witness, Captain."

She shifted, turning to face him, waiting until he did the same for her. She couldn't help herself from reaching up and pressing his strands of midnight hair behind his ear. His eyes widened at the gesture, the pupils expanding at the highly inappropriate touch given who they were and where they were, but he didn't stop her, and she let her fingers linger in his tangled curls, glance over the cords of his neck, his shoulders before slipping back to her side. Her pulse raced. His gaze dipped to the beat in her throat, quickly back to her eyes. "I cannot explain it other than for you to see."

"And is it the type of ritual outsiders are allowed to share in?"

You're not an outsider.

The words were there on her lips, ready to leap into the air between them. She had to bite her tongue to hold the avowal back. "I don't know. Not many visitors entered the Woods, and none who did asked to witness what it was to be a Child of the Night. But the Darkness touches all, even those believing in younger gods. The Night will not rebuke any who choose to reside in Its glory."

"Yet you live in the day."

"Yes."

Whether he shifted, or she did, she couldn't say, only that it was no longer the fire that seared heat into her flesh, and if not for the clench of her hands at her sides, fingers buried in the folds of her slacks, for the grasp of his hands behind his back, she would have wrapped herself around him, uncaring that she refused his emotions and he played cool towards her.

"It would be an honor then, to be welcomed to witness your faith."

"So that you can learn yet more of my people?"

He blinked, and she watched him accept her offered respite from the intimacy of the moment. “Yes, a chance to learn more of your people.”

She heard: more of you. “I would use the glade, at the far edges of the gardens then.”

“A wise choice, beyond the normal prying eyes of the court.”

“Yes.”

He nodded, and the gesture brought his lips a breath away from hers, only a small rise on her toes, and the choice between them would be gone. She knew he waited for her choice, knew that if she reached those final inches between them, he would not let her go back to being his captain, and she would not want to, and it was too soon. Much too soon to be playing games with the rest of their lives. He was not safe. His life was not his own, not until his five hundredth and something birthday.

He needed a captain, someone who could be reason and violence, who would protect him even from himself, and if she kissed him now, despite the odd flutter in her heart at the thought, he would put her life before his, and damn the Night because she wanted that and had too great a sense of duty to allow him to make such a sacrifice.

She stepped away and his head snapped back, the brief play of emotion in his eyes dimmed to its familiar indifference.

“I will leave at sunset tomorrow.”

“I will inform Marius of your absence.”

She hesitated, hearing the dismissal in his voice and debating the sanity of pushing, staying, any longer. “It is a monthly observance,” she nearly said his name, nickname. She offered his title instead, “My Prince.”

“I will inform the General to make considerations as such.”

“Thank you, my lord.”

He continued to stare at her, and she fought the urge to twitch. Her, the greatest assassin of the Dienobolos, fidgeting before a prince of the city.

"Captain."

She nodded, gave him her back, and left him to his silence in the library.

The door closed behind her, and she forced herself not to turn around, walk back into the room she'd left, beg for forgiveness for the distance needed between them.

Instead, she fled through the palace walls, to the courtyard beyond and her rooms, hiding in her small sanctuary, away from her prince and the burning desire for him that wouldn't abate.

II

SHE WAITED FOR the sun to set in her bedroom, watching the last lingering rays of daylight fade into the western sky. Twilight bloomed over the horizon in a bevy of reds and oranges, faded to blue and azure, stars twinkling at the edges of the darkness.

The red bag she found in the pantry sat beside her door.

A stick of incense scented with lilies to honor Pirie, the aspect of the Dark to whom prayers were offered. Seven seeds, two from a peach, one from a rose, four from the grain grown in rows beyond the edges of the walled city, to honor Rouchim, Lady of the Earth, the Giver. She bought a toy boat in the shops near the port one afternoon, a gift to Ashet, the Builder, for the home Eli lived in, be it wood or stone. Her blood she carried within her, a gift to Liaea, to nourish the earth where the body lived upon its death, where all things came from before their birth. There was a knife in her bag, ceremonial and sharp, to honor the flesh and the darkness that filled it.

For Echi there was pain.

She was a servant of Justice, even stripped of the title. Her soul was bound to the Judge of the Night.

She had taken four lives unsanctioned by her people to save one not of her own. She could argue that since she was the highest of her order, her taking of the lives was sanctioned and deserved no recompense, but she was not afraid of paying the debt.

Her eyes scanned the bulge of the martinet in her bag, the flogger handed down through generations, held by the hands of the Elichisolos before her, should be held by those who followed in her stead. She'd spilled her blood by the weapon in the past, once for every time her soul needed purging. Never before had shame filled her at the need to touch the weapon.

It was sacrifice.

The Darkness demanded it.

In her soul, the deepest, blackest parts of it, where her connection to the Night pulsed strong and true, she held no regret, held no sorrow at her actions in saving the prince.

But justice was demanded.

She would abide by tradition, especially here, where her traditions were unknown, subverted, ignored.

She was not ashamed of the demands of her faith.

She donned her cloak, pulling the hood over her head, hiding her auburn hair beneath the deep blue velvet. The bag she slung over her shoulder, settling it against her side.

A patrol marched past her door, and she slipped out at the passing. Her feet found the path around the castle and to the gardens beyond.

She padded over the stone paths, walked into the darkness without a torch to guide her way.

She had not sought him out during the day, neither rescinding nor reminding him of her offer the night before. A part of her hoped that he would not be there, in the glade, when she reached the area. Another part hoped he would, for she had never been alone for the Offering, and she was so alone here in the city, separated from the ones who knew her, and the ones who would have worshipped as she did, even if they were not familiar with her person.

He wouldn't understand the rituals involved in the service. He had too much honor to understand beating anyone, let alone self-inflicted penance.

It wasn't something she had to worry about yet though.

It wasn't something she was likely to have to worry about regardless.

She stepped onto the cool spring grass, the earth cold, only the barest hint of summer in the air. The first spring blossoms were beginning to bloom. Shoots of green rising after a winter buried beneath the snow. A mild winter, considering. They'd not had more than a few feet of white, not in the woods and not without them.

The earth was dry.

Rain would be a blessing so long as it did not turn to sleet.

Perhaps she would add that to her list of prayers.

She entered the grove, the trees surrounding the small fountain built for lover's trysts within the woods. Not that the denizens of Tornald would engage in such physical exertions, not with their taboo on a simple kiss.

Eli slipped the bag from her shoulder, knelt to lay out the contents on the ground. She stripped the cloak from her shoulder, layering the earth with the velvet for her offerings to rest on.

Naked as the day she came into the world, she genuflected with her hands folded in her lap, head tilted back to the sky, the cold of the late night raising goose pimples on her skin. She waited for the witching hour to come, whispering the silent prayers of her people to the wood.

SHE OPENED HER eyes to the darkness, her magic mingling with the night around her, wrapping her in shadows, cradling her in its embrace.

With a flick of her fingers, she lit a flame at the end of the stick of incense, letting the sweet scent of flowers fill the small grove, cast a hazy fog within the Shadow.

Her fingers found the offerings easily enough. There was no fumbling when she lifted the seeds in her hands, cupped them to her lips and blew. Black tendrils of shadow rose to enfold the little stones in their embrace, sinking into the hard shells of the pips, seeking out the essence of life held within each tiny bulb.

The seeds turned to hard gems, the offering accepted and remembered by the Darkness.

It took only a thought to pass the gems through the cloth covering the ground, burying the offering within the winter firm earth, something to wait on the warmth of summer to grow.

The small boat sailed along on a wave of Night, flowed over the air around her, towards the fountain in the center of the clearing, set to float along the gently rippling water, buoyed there despite the chunks of ice dotting the basin.

Eli watched the boat disappear around the edge of the mermaid rising in the center of the pool. Her people were not seafarers. She'd never set foot on a boat and doubted she ever would. If they fished, it was at the edges of the lakes and ponds throughout the forest. But there was something beautiful about the waves. She'd listened to them beating the shore late at night at the edge of the city. The rhythmic rush and fall of sand roiling soothed her like the sound of wind through leaves.

She lifted the knife, pressed her lips to the blade beneath the hilt, offering a silent prayer to the glinting blade in the darkness, shining despite the lack of light around it. Her free hand opened, palm flat in the air before her. Economical, she pierced the center of her hand with the knife, opening her skin until a pool of blood formed. She cut over the length of scar from the sword stained with Beracsh's blood.

She replaced the dagger on her cloak.

Her predecessor, the Elichisolos who ruled before Eli offered herself to the Darkness, had chosen the cougar for his sigil, the cat an elegant creature, strong and sure in its presence. Before him came the wolf, a man who believed in pack, who held the woods against the city dwellers, the trolls and the dwarves, the demons from Quiofol and the dragons of the sleeping lands.

When offered the position, she took the emblem of the fox. Quick and agile as the cougar, proud and strong as the wolf, all with the cunning of the hunter and the terror of the prey. The fox knew both sides of the stalking ground, something humans too often forgot in their own arrogance.

She dipped her fingers in the pool of blood in her hand, traced the outline of the fox branded into the skin on the right side of her pelvis, shivering in the chill when the cold air dried the blood on her flesh.

The marking complete, she clenched her bloodied hand into a fist, leaned over her cloak to ensure that five drops of red fell on hard packed earth.

With the last drop, the wound on her palm healed, a black swath of night wrapping her hand for a moment before disappearing, taking the last of her sacrifice with it, carried on the wind to join with the offerings of the rest of her brethren.

The Priestosolos would gather the offerings of the elves within the great Mother Tree this night. She would commit the gifts of blood and grain and wood to the temple altar, allowing the Darkness to claim the devotions of the children of the wood.

Eli had never seen the ceremony. She was not a priest and her only experience within Eao, the Great Temple, had been when she offered herself to Echi and been accepted as the Blade of the Darkness.

If she'd been invited to see the inner sanctum as a child at her mother's heels, she didn't remember it. The Priestosolos had never been comfortable with Eli after the offering ceremony. She and her mother, one executioner, one healer, could not see eye to eye, though the High Priestess had taught Eli much over the years. They'd never been close as family. Eli had no connection beyond blood between her birth mother and birth father, each honored for their place in the tribe, as Eli was, had been, honored, their teachings respected as elder law.

She opened her eyes, watched the last of the darkness clear around her until she knelt in the dim light of the stars, bare to the Night.

She was a servant of Echi, not her mother, no longer the woods.

Echi demanded that penance be given in the open, exposed to the world as it was meant to be naked to the soul in judgment and salvation.

Her tongue formed the words of her people, head bowed in supplication, in atonement. “I do not know my purpose. I have failed You as I was meant to be and flounder as I now am. I beg guidance. I beg forgiveness. I offer my suffering, so You would know my sincerity and grant Your wisdom on Your child.”

“The Darkness does not listen to outcasts.”

She considered the shadows between the trees, watched five of her once brethren emerge, dressed in black cloths, swathed from head to toe so that only their eyes were visible to the Night. “You would kill me on our sacred day?”

“Kill you?” The woman was smaller than her companions though the men with her yielded to her words. “No, we would not kill you. We seek only the justice of Echi against one of the Dark’s own.”

“I have committed no crime against Echi. I am the Judgment of our people.”

“The prince’s life was forfeit long before you took the position.”

“I am the Judgment. I decide whose life is forfeit and whose life is sacrosanct.”

“At the cost of your brethren’s lives?”

“They knew the cost of attacking their Elichisolos.”

“Yet you did not return. You did not announce their sin but ran away. Your actions find fault in yourself, not the dead.”

Eli blinked, stood. She did not take her gaze from the woman, even as the men flooded the grove to surround her. “I accept my exile. I have not stepped foot within the woods. I honor our traditions.”

“You defame them with this farce we have witnessed this day.”

She did not argue that her offerings had been accepted by the Darkness. The truth would bring no peace to these elves surrounding her. "What would you have of me then?"

"Penance."

Eli didn't expect the strike of the whip, nor the skill with which it was wielded.

The cord wrapped around her wrist, pulling her off balance while a second struck her opposite side, laying open a line of fire along her flesh.

Echi demanded three times repayment the suffering caused.

Four lives were at her feet. Twelve strikes to balance the scales.

She didn't fight the lashes landing against her skin, from the accidental strikes that lacked strength, to the ones that broke flesh and drew blood to the surface.

"Nine."

The female unleashed the whips at her hips, taking the handles of each in hand, uncoiling the twin tails on the ground before her.

"Ten."

Eli ducked her head, squeezing her eyes closed when the lashes cut across her cheeks and chest, drew blood from the barb tipped tails. Her knees buckled. She barely caught herself on her hands, fighting nausea now that she counted the offering complete.

The woman drew back her metal tipped whip, letting the left fly once more towards Eli's face.

With her hands pressing into the dirt, her knees on the bloodied remains of her cloak, Eli called the Darkness around her, a final offering to be accepted or denied. The whip came closer. Eli watched the barbs' approach.

A wave of midnight surged around her, enclosing her in a shield of ebony, accepted and protected by the faith she worshipped. She touched her hands to the miasma, laughed at the gentle thrum of power seeping beneath her skin. The Darkness surged through her veins healing welt and reel, clothing her in its armor against her once brethren, betraying the condemnation of their beliefs.

Starlight flickered into the glade, pierced the shell around her.

The Darkness faded, left her protected in its warmth to face the men and woman.

"The penance was twelve strikes. The Darkness accepted my offering. I am still Its child. You have betrayed Its teachings for vengeance sake."

The woman snarled, drew back her whip for another strike, no pretense of penance in her attack.

Eli growled.

She was faster than the strike of a whip. Had she chosen, she could have dodged each blow landed against her. But she had owed the suffering to the Darkness, had paid the debt willingly, letting the lives of her people be the penance for leaving the fold of the faith and home to be with her prince, so far beyond the Darkness' reach. This was not the same. This was battle. She was not of the forest any longer. She'd made her offering and it was accepted. The holiness of the day acknowledged and the ceremony complete. She broke no laws in fighting those who would attack her now.

The whip with its barbed tail curled around her wrist, dug into her flesh.

She twisted her arm, yanking the handle from the woman, pulling the whip to her own use, her speed making the others step away from her attack.

"I am not of the Dienobolos any longer. I am foresworn, outcast. I am allowed to defend myself even against my once kin." She smiled at the men around her, baring her teeth in a sneer, ignoring the woman struggling back to her feet. "If I kill you all, I suffer no greater penalty than that which my soul feels at killing those who would kill me."

"You are exiled for four hundred years—"

"Yes." She stared at the men. "But I can kill you with impunity because of it." The snarl faded from her lips, sadness at the unnecessary loss of life replaced the cold emotion in her eyes. "Do not make me."

It was not a plea, and yet it was.

The choice was on their heads.

One of the men nodded, wound his whip around his arm, the others following his example.

Her blood dripped at her side, the barbed tail embedded in the flesh of her wrist, ignored until the threat faded.

The elves stepped back into the woods, back into the garden to make the climb over the wall that surrounded it, return to the wild forests of their homeland.

Eli pulled the barbs from her wrist, coiling the whip, her concession from the woman who would have broken the laws of their people. She watched the female stand. The elf's arm drew back, and Eli heard the broken step of a booted foot sliding to a halt to her left.

She was quicker on the throw, more accurate, her commandeered whip wrapped in jagged lines around the woman's throat, tearing gouges into the flesh.

Kit hissed, but it was the stranger who died, the wicked metal barbs having pierced the thin covering of cloth and skin and nicking an artery in the woman's throat.

The fresh scent of iron tinged the air.

Eli watched the black cloth darken with spilled blood.

His sword rang from his scabbard. He moved to flank her at her right, giving her the dominant position though she doubted he realized that's what he did.

He did not ask if this was part of the ritual.

She did not offer an explanation as the woman gasped her last, clutching at her throat, spasms racking the dying body before going motionless on the ground.

He tensed when shadows filled the trees, spilled out on the ground, hiding the glade in its dark embrace. She caught the tightening of his shoulders from the corner of her eye, the way he shifted onto the balls of his feet, preparing to meet whatever attack was coming. His sword disappeared within the shade, nothing to defend against, held steady though he did not swing.

Her gaze strayed to the darkened tree line, the black clad eyes staring out at her from within the first blossoming of leaves.

She blinked, and the darkness cleared, the body gone from the ground between elf and wood.

"Will they return?" His voice was steady, his arms unshaking at her side, eyes roving the tree line, not trusting her brethren's retreat.

"No." Her lids closed, heart steadying now that the threat was passed, both to her and to her prince. "The attack was unprovoked. They'll return the woman to the forest, but she betrayed her faith by intending to kill on this night."

"You killed."

"To defend my own life. To defend yours. My actions were just, Kit. Hers were not."

He sheathed his blade.

His eyes went to her body, trailed down the shadow silk armor covering her, the metal plates a harder substance than any steel he could touch, lighter than air.

She had not expected him to take her arm, flinched when his hand rose to hers. He didn't pull away, keeping his grip on her bicep while turning her hand towards him, looking at the blood seeping down her wrist from the slice of the whip she'd stolen.

He was bloodied too, a rent in his shirt showing a growing stain of red from where the woman's whip had struck.

Eli'd not been quick enough to spare him any injury.

"But you spared my life."

She pressed her free hand to his chest, staring into his steel gray eyes, knowing that hers were eerie, at best, when she called the darkness to her. He didn't flinch away, not when she felt the flickering of her pupils, or when strands of shadow magic uncurled from her fingers and eased into his wound, mending torn flesh, leaving only a scar in its stead.

He cupped her cheek, his thumb brushing the ridge below her eye, brushing until the magic faded. "You didn't heal yourself."

She looked at her seeping wrist. "Penance, for the life I took to save ours."

"You said it was just."

"Just" didn't mean guiltless.

He didn't press further.

Her cloak, the incense, the seeds and boat, all of it was consumed by the Darkness. All of it gone but for the ceremonial dagger glinting in the pale star light. She caught her breath when he bent to retrieve it, lifting it carefully from its cradle of grass, handing it to her with the reverence ritual required.

"Thank you."

He nodded.

She slipped the knife into a pocket of the flowing shadows clothing her. He extended his arm and she wrapped hers within his embrace, letting him lead her from the grove. Her bare feet made no sound on the cold stone, too used to moving quietly on any surface regardless of shoes or not. He matched her, silencing his steps best he could. She said nothing for his efforts, though she smiled at his attempt. He'd grow silent under her tutelage soon enough, but he was not training to be an assassin, and sometimes a stampede succeeded in instilling fear where silence did not.

III

HE LED HER to the palace, ignoring the turn to the barracks and taking her into the lower level of the great castle, to the rooms she'd not yet explored.

His hold on her arm tightened as he helped her down the stairs to the servant's quarters and military council area. She'd heard of the rooms, if not been there. He was solicitous, though she didn't need the aid in walking, enjoying his touch all the same. "The baths," he nodded to his right at a wide door from which heat seeped. There was no sign to the room, but it would have been easy enough to deduce what loomed behind the doors based on the sound of running water coming from within.

She used her private bath.

But it was good to know the location, even if he'd told her, obliquely, that first day where the public washrooms were.

He pointed with his free hand, directing her gaze to the far end of the hall bathed in darkness, rare torches lighting the way at this hour of the night. "The healer is at the end there, his rooms taking up the southern wing of the palace with the healing ward. He's some skill with magic, not like you, but something similar when it comes to the healing of the flesh, though he prefers not to use it, I think." He didn't elaborate, and she nodded like she understood.

Of course, she probably did understand better than he. For some people, their magic was finite in its strength and power. There were other means of healing someone if the wound wasn't severe enough to merit calling on enchantments deep within.

Her eyes turned up to his, meeting the gaze he leveled at her, his steps slow and steady while they walked down the hall. "Is allowing him to look at your wrist against your customs?"

The question was unexpected, and she stopped, pulling him to a halt beside her.

She liked the caring it implied, for her, for her faith.

"No, I do not need to see him; and no, it is not against my beliefs to have the wound attended to by another healer. But I am a Daughter of Echi."

"Your god of justice."

"The Aspect of the Darkness that deals in Justice." She watched his brows knit over his forehead, lips open to argue semantics with her, close.

The Darkness was. It was not a being like his gods. She'd tried to explain it before but failed. It was why she was a servant of the Night, and not a priest in the temple.

"I tend my own wounds when I can."

He took the out she offered, not arguing theology with her, though she knew it was not an argument he sought, just knowledge. "Very well."

He drew her forward, continuing, leading her the Darkness knew where.

The door he opened had a frosted glass window, the wood warped so that it bulged towards the hall even though it swung forward into the space it guarded. Coals burned merrily in a grate in one corner of the wood paneled room. Despite the obvious upkeep, she had the impression the chamber was seldom used.

He ushered her into the space, closing the door behind them.

Two tables sat in the center of the area, cushioned to lie upon though the reason why someone would choose to sleep here rather than their own beds was beyond her. But she was not a prince, not hunted by assassins and guards every minute of the day. This well could be a place of peace for him.

"Do you even realize that you are shaking?"

His arm no longer linked through hers, instead curving about her waist, holding her to his side while she took in the small area. And it was small, yet she felt like she'd yet to see the whole of it.

Her gaze snapped to his, but the motion took an eternity to complete. She'd felt the shaking, yes, but had thought it was from him, ignored the odd lethargy suffusing her limbs.

It wasn't poison. Her body would have fought against poison, warned her if that was what was attacking her system.

Her hand shook when she raised it to her forehead to wipe the sweat from her brow.

He sat her on a table, and it was the most natural thing to allow him to step between her legs so that his arms could remain wrapped around her, supporting her. "Was your wrist the only injury tonight?"

Her head tipped to the side, eyes blinking rapidly up at him.

He would not like to know that she had been whipped, or that she'd been planning on whipping herself.

She raised her hand, brushing back the stubborn lock of hair that was always falling over his eye. So black, his hair, like the Darkness in her eyes when she called magic to her. The smears of red on his skin looked wrong. She tried to brush the blood away, but it smeared further. A small yelp escaped her lips when he pulled away and swung her legs onto the table, laid her down before standing at her side, looking down at her wrist in his hand.

The shadow silk was slick through with her blood. It stung when he peeled the fabric away from her flesh, revealed the marks where the barbs broke her skin.

"Damnit, Ella." His fingers clamped on her arm, squeezing her hand to his chest.

She should pull away.

She meant to, but his grip was too strong, and she liked the way he held her to keep her close, keep her present.

Her eyes blinked open, his lips moving but the words were distant. "Come on sweetheart. Heal the wound, Ella. Call the darkness and heal yourself."

It was the Darkness, not darkness. She wanted to tell him that, but he looked so worried that she decided that discussion could wait for later.

She closed her eyes, his free hand shaking her shoulder, jostling her awake once more.

"Don't fall asleep. Stay with me."

"I'm calling my magic. It hurts to concentrate."

His mere presence was distraction, but she managed to pierce the veil, call the otherworldly Obsidian to her will, force her flesh to heal, seal the arteries and veins beneath, encourage her blood to replenish and flow throughout her body once more. The last calmed the rasping of her breath, eased the tension in her chest. Her eyes focused on the scars, the faint lines visible between the grip of his fingers.

The woman had nicked an artery, multiple times, it appeared.

Eli hadn't realized the severity of the wound.

She might have survived it, even without treating the injury, if the Darkness was merciful. Likely she would have remained at her vigil in the glade and passed into the night without anyone the wiser.

Her gaze focused back on him, noting the intensity of his return stare, the way his fingers brushed against her skin in a gentler caress now that the wound was healed.

"Thank you."

"For what?" The gruffness of his voice had her fighting a smile, a blush at the way his gaze pierced her.

"For saving my life."

"I didn't do anything, Captain."

"You recognized that something needed to be done. I wouldn't have realized until too late."

He smiled down at her before flinching and backing away, letting her hand drop to the mattress, separating them now that the immediate threat was annulled. "Only thrice more and we're even then."

"Are you keeping score?"

He didn't respond.

Her body was weak, but she forced herself to sit all the same, hands braced on the sides of the bed as she stared around herself at the room she was in, better able to examine it now that her mind wasn't muddled with imminent demise. Her lips quirked with the thought, quickly stilled and willed away. "What is this place?"

He looked away when her gaze landed on him though his eyes flicked back towards her though he tried not to stare. "A sauna. My great something or other grandfather had it installed for his wife. Apparently, the lady was from Wen and enjoyed the balmy island climate there, ours too cold for her."

"The lady? Don't you know her name?" Eli grinned at the question, hoping it would put him at ease, annul the tension between them.

"She left soon after her arrival here. She's not even in our history books."

"A harsh fate."

He looked back at her, one hand resting behind him to lean against the table opposite hers. "Yes. But she was unhappy, and Grandfather kept her name from our histories so that she might have a chance at a life outside of our realm. Perhaps she found something more to her liking somewhere else."

"That's a compassionate way of looking at a cuckold."

A bark of laughter escaped him, and she smiled at his response. "He wasn't happy with her either. Between the two of them, the only time they spent together was in this room, someplace where silence and rest was appreciated, and they didn't need to speak to one another."

There was a wistfulness to his words that she wondered if he heard. "And why do you come to this room, Kit?"

"Because I can be alone here, Captain, and I find it restful."

Yes, she could understand that response, even commiserate with it.

Of course, she found being with the man himself restful.

"I'm sorry I was late to your ceremony. I might have been able to aid you against the elves who attacked had I been on time."

"From my perspective, my prince, your timing was perfect."

He moved from his position on the bed, walked to the coals and ladled a cup of water over the gentle heat from a bucket built into the wall itself. Coils of tubing pierced the grate, allowing for a slow trickle to constantly feed against the heat of the stones, keep steam circulating within the chamber. But the ladle added more fuel to the flame, increased the heat of the temperate room to the inhabitants liking. He seemed to enjoy the added moisture, eyes closing as the steam drifted towards his face.

Her clothing began to stick to her skin, and she was not as thrilled with the result, though said nothing to disrupt him, to ruin this moment between them.

"You will worship again tomorrow and Vernoui?"

"No." He glanced at her from over his shoulder, continuing to move about the small space, never letting his attention linger on her form. "They are days of rest for my people. We live in the woods. We hunt; we forage. We are constantly working with and against nature, so we built in time to rest."

"That's what Timresiet and Samseiet and Parlquoet are for."

"In your culture, yes. Not in mine."

"You do not have weekly days of rest."

"It is not so much to work thirty days of each month when three are meant for our ease."

"You make me feel lazy."

She smiled when he turned to face her, shadows keeping his face in darkness, his expression from her eyes. "I've seen you on Samseiet, my Prince. You don't take days off either."

"I'm a prince."

There was no joy in accepting the title.

"Even princes need to rest."

His arms spread wide, fingers grazing the smooth wood of the paneling. The gray of his eyes shadowed for a moment as he leaned against the wall, breathed in the moist air. "That's why I come here, fair Captain. No one ever seeks me here."

She stood carefully, testing her balance before she stepped away from the bed, rounded the wooden table to stand before him where he leaned in the corner. The slice in his shirt was shallow, the barbs of the whip having cut his skin, true enough, ripped the shirt, yes, but not done much damage beyond the surface. He would have a scar, but that was because of her magic. Had the wound been treated with tinctures and a wrap, likely nothing would have remained to tell the tale of tonight's adventure.

He didn't stop her from pressing the pads of her fingers to the mark, tracing the line from collar bone to the ridge of his sternum. "This is your sanctuary." She flattened her palm to his chest. "I did not mean to disturb it."

"You haven't."

Too far, always just an inch beyond a simple tilt of the head to press her lips to his, taste this prince who was far too pure and too honorable to be of the city she hated and yet was growing to care for because he lived within its walls.

"You're welcome here, Captain, if you need the space to retreat to."

Her rooms were her sanctuary, but that's not what he was offering her. If no one else could find him, she would know where to look. He gave her the key to his small place of peace, a place where he was alone, and she could be alone with him.

Poor man likely hadn't thought of all the implications of his offer.

Her smile dimmed with the realization, the want. "I would have us be friends, Kit."

He looked down at her, covered her hand on his chest, squeezed her fingers in a gentle caress. His pulse was steady beneath her touch, wonderfully alive against her, even as she knew his answer would be other than what she wished for. "I don't know that I have the strength to offer that, Eli."

Especially since friendship was not what she longed for, not what he longed for.

He'd offered more once, and she'd denied him.

"Please."

A final squeeze before he gently pushed her away, creating space between their bodies so he could brush around her, walk free.

She remained in her corner, eyes focused on the wall before her, unwilling to see whatever expression was on his face, if he would acquiesce or deny her request.

His footsteps paused at the door. "Ella."

She turned to him, her gaze carefully neutral so he would not see her hope or despair.

"I'll try."

He was gone before she could respond, the door closing at his back.

Her prince fled, and she wondered if she should give chase.

She looked at the glass window, knowing his rooms were only a story above her, easy enough to catch him if she chose.

But perhaps it was better to let him find her, be the one pursued rather than do the hunting.

After all, he'd never returned the shoe she'd lost that third night of the ball.

BOOK TWO

Chapter One

I

The One Hundredth and Thirty-First Ball

HE DID HIS best not to whimper as he shifted on the padded table until his arms were pillowing his head and the spasm in his back had eased at least a little. Pride was the only reason he was lying alone, in agony, in the palace sauna rather than on the medic's bed guzzling something to dull the pain.

It was his own fault.

He'd known there was something not right with the horse before he even tried to mount the beast, but his uncle had been there, daring him to the feat, and Kit hated to look weak before the man who constantly reminded Kit that Kravn should be heir to the throne.

"Apologies. I had not thought to find you here."

The jerk of his head towards the door made his muscles tense, agony spearing through his shoulders, down his spine, stealing the air from lungs surrounded by bruised ribs. Kit managed to turn his moan into a hiss.

Her eyebrows rose, lips fighting the turn at their corners, and he knew he'd failed to hide his current state of misery from her.

He closed his eyes, not wanting to see pity in his Captain's gaze as she looked at him, the black and blue mess of bruises covering his back and chest. Her footsteps sounded over the wooden floor, the door closing behind her. Kit grimaced when her gloved fingertips traced the swelling along his left side, even the light touch unbearable.

"I heard you were thrown from your horse."

This flinch had nothing to do with his physical pain.

How quickly would the rumor spread?

Prince Christophe de L'Avigne fell from his horse. The prince was injured trying to ride a foal. Poor Kit. Fool boy.

Gods, every woman at the ball tomorrow night would be petting and cooing over him. If he couldn't stand, if the healers said he needed to remain seated for the evening, he would have no way to escape all the inane conversations, no excuse to find a different dance partner since he wouldn't be dancing.

When he groaned this time, her throaty chuckle greeted the sound. "I heard it from the Commander, my prince. Most of the guards haven't been informed though the fact that the stallion in the western pasture is being kept apart from all the rest of the steeds has led to some debate."

"The debate being what? When to put the bastard down?"

"Most I've heard is whether the stallion's in rut and if a mare will be brought to it."

"Lucky horse." There was an edge of bitterness to Kit's voice that he didn't try to hide, wishing, for a moment, that he was that horse waiting his mare, hoping she didn't hear his longing, hoping she mistook it for sarcasm or whatever else.

He didn't want the horse dead. The creature had suffered enough, Kit could see that. But that didn't mean he was noble enough not to want a bit of revenge.

He turned his head to look at the woman standing at his side, meet her gaze as she stared down at him.

A ball to find a bride when the one he wanted was standing next to him unavailable.

Another wave of bitterness assaulted him.

No. He didn't want her. He'd spent a year convincing himself of the fact and he'd damn well near succeeded. She was his shadow, walking where he went, in court or beyond the walls of the palace. She was his spy and his eyes when he was relegated to ceremony without means to escape. She was his sword and his shield and his instructor.

She was not his lover or his fiancée or anything that might have an emotional attachment to it.

The lie only tasted slightly unpleasant on his tongue.

He would have smiled at the thought, but he was in too much physical agony. Better to focus on that than the woman he didn't want to take his eyes from.

Besides, she was too observant not to question what a turn of his lips meant, especially while he was lying too hurt to move.

"How bad is it?"

"How bad does it look?"

He watched her smirk, felt the air pass along his skin when she ran her hand just above his flesh, no longer touching him.

"Did you see the healer?"

Kit closed his eyes, letting out the breath he hadn't realized he'd been holding. Easier not to breathe than force the expand and contract of his damaged ribs.

Her footsteps moved away from him.

His head snapped up once more, his quick motion, unintended moan, drawing her attention back to him, her hand on the door to the small anteroom and its lockers and benches within. "Please."

It would be beyond improper to ask her to stay, and yet he didn't want her to leave.

His mouth opened but no words emerged, not that he knew what he would have uttered regardless.

"Do you mind me joining you?"

"No."

"I assumed you would prefer me to fetch a towel rather than join you as I am."

He knew enough of her culture that "as I am" meant without the human trappings of clothes to guard her, or, more likely, his modesty.

Heat flamed in his cheeks. He put it down to the rise of fresh steam in the room.

A nod, which was a poor choice of response, and then she was gone, the squeak of the hinges heralding her departure, heralding her return too.

Kit let his eyes close though the rest of his body tensed, waiting for the unoiled swing and the softened tread of bare feet on damp wood.

SHE DID NOT move directly to the opposite bed in the room. She had to walk around it to reach him, and that was what she did. One eye opened to watch her settle the jar on the side of his bed, the evil scent of Witch Hazel wafting from the uncapped container. He groaned at the implication, not wanting the foul lotion anywhere near his skin, knowing it would help in the end.

The last time he'd been forced to use the salve was after their first training day. She'd brought the jar to him as he hobbled to his room, barely able to stay on his feet.

A home remedy, she'd said.

He'd nearly dropped the jar when she opened the lid for him.

"If you use it, the swelling will go down and your muscles will relax. You'll be able to fight in the morning rather than moan around in pain, not that the moaning will get you out of anything."

Princes didn't moan, he'd told her, handing the jar back without using it.

He moaned the next day as she said he would.

He took the foul jar that night and rubbed the lotion into his tired muscles.

Damn if he didn't feel its effect the next morning.

Now, she lifted the jar closer, and he closed his eye again, not arguing over the necessity of the liniment for his aching body. The slurp and suck of her fingers dragging a dollop of the ointment into her hand reached his ears, muscles tightening further in preparation for the salve, knowing tension was the cause of many of his aches and relaxing would be the best solution. Her nails scratched at the back of his neck. How she found the ticklish spot, he didn't know, but she took delight in tormenting him when she could. The brief touch eased him now, focusing on her presence rather than her ministrations, a different, no less painful tension centering him even as he relaxed into her touch.

The lotion soothed over his skin in a light coating, heating slightly at the application, cooling slowly despite the warmth of the room.

Deep breaths came easier. His arms still felt brittle and breakable curled beneath his head, but the rigid line of his spine grew more malleable. At least, it was less stiff until her fingers traced the line of the towel at his hips, slipped beneath the edge to unwind the cloth from his lower body, treat the bruising that covered his thighs and calves.

"No."

"Stop being a prude, Kit."

The use of his nickname, the informality of it, the friendship, made him hesitate to rebuke her. In quiet moments like this, when they were alone, and he didn't have to be a prince and she was not just his guard, she would call him by name, and he allowed it. He enjoyed the softly spoken moniker, the way his heartrate sped at the implied relationship between them.

Yes, he knew it was insane to allow her the familiarity the name implied. But when she used it, he remembered those first three nights of dancing when she stared into his eyes and there wasn't a brittle wariness in her gaze as there was now. She had to have known he was the prince. But he hadn't known she was an assassin. There had been no dissent betwixt them then, not until he followed her into the woods and would have asked her to marry him if she hadn't told him "no" before he'd voiced the request.

But that was long ago, and she was nothing but a friend now, completely platonic; an instructor in the art of war, nothing more.

"No, Captain."

"The bruising continues down, Kit. You'll not get any relief if I leave half of you untreated."

"I can do the rest myself."

He felt more than heard her bite her tongue, her fingers lingering at his waist pressing more firmly against his skin before she acquiesced to his request and released him from her touch.

"Suit yourself, Prince."

Not "my prince."

He'd managed to sting her pride. She only refused to claim him when he'd done something mulish that she disagreed with. Amusingly, it tended to happen most often in moments when there was an unaccounted intimacy between them that she'd shunned first.

"You'll not dance well for your ball tomorrow."

She knew he didn't care.

Her teeth clacked together. He didn't think she realized she did that any time she was frustrated, a sound most would ignore, wouldn't recognize her making if confronted with it since usually it was accompanied with a sugary sweet smile hiding the anger within. She slurped more of the lotion from the jar and slopped a fresh layer of the goop over his back.

He laid there quietly, soaking in her attention. Her fingers slowly began to knead his back, the liniment working enough that the pain of the fresh bruising abated, only tightened muscles remaining. She worked the kinks from his body, the tension slowly slithering away beneath her touch. When she pressed his more tender areas he fought back a growl and she eased the pressure slightly.

"It will hurt worse if I don't."

This growl was not stifled against his forearm. She laughed at him, though there was an undercurrent of emotion to the sound that he did not expect, something that bordered on concern.

Her hands left him, and he opened his eyes, trying to sort her out in the dim light of the room.

She stood beside him still, adjusting the towel wrapped around her chest back into place.

He meant to close his eyes, look away, managed only when she knotted the cloth once more, sufficiently covering herself before glancing back to him.

He heard the smile in her voice.

"You are terribly boring to temp, Kit."

A man should meet his wife as pure as she on their wedding night. Pure in sight, in touch, in taste.

The damn protocol was from the birth of his civilization. The first kings swore to obey the law and passed the tradition on to their kin. Not all of Kit's ancestors followed the doctrine. There were bastards roaming the city, beyond, if Kit looked hard enough to find them. Not many, to be sure, and those that were likely didn't know they were descended from the kings of Spinick, the bloodlines diluted over generations.

But King Leon expected Kit to obey the law.

And Kit hated the rules.

Hated looking over the nobles who gathered during court sessions, at the balls, sat on the long tables aligned for meals in the great hall, and knew more about relationships than Kit ever would. Hells, he couldn't even call what he and Eli had a relationship. Well, he could, but he shouldn't, hence the rub of it all. He knew more than he should, was tempted more than was allowed, enjoyed the temptation she presented, and was grateful all she did was tempt for it would take precious littler persuasion on her part to have him breaking all his vows.

It was a bitter pill upon his tongue, knowing that she could move about his soldiers and guards and courtiers without distress, while he watched from the corner, silently denying his lust even as his gaze strayed over and over to her.

Even Marius called him a fool.

And in the end, did it matter if he looked when she stood before him? He wouldn't act on his desires. That was what mattered most to his father.

He fisted his hands beneath his head, and squeezed his eyes further closed, desperately denying himself any further lure.

Besides, if he'd been going to break his vow, he would have done it that night on the forest road.

He shifted, and her hands were there, helping him move so that his numb arms could relearn the flow of blood through them. She massaged the liniment into his skin, settled one arm back beneath his head to repeat the process on the other.

"I'm a soldier, my lord. Just another one of your guard."

He glanced up at her, holding her gaze while she ran her fingers through his, linking their grips for a moment in her gentle caress.

"Soldiers see each other in stages of undress all the time."

He snorted out a laugh, even as he was grateful for the excuse she offered him. Gods save him.

She released his hand, letting it dangle over the edge of his table, the small space between the two beds in the room. "Let that sit for a while. I'll apply more before we leave for the night."

Would he still look a discolored corpse in his mirror when he left? Would the bruising change from blue to yellowed green? He was almost afraid to ask, even while he couldn't care less.

No doubt his father would find fault with the state of his skin.

A small, quiet dinner for final announcements before the ball the next eve. A dinner with just himself and the king seated at opposing ends of the great table, a dossier set before each to review together all those who Kit had to dance with and those who Kit could beg off as not quite important enough to receive special attention from him. Drinks to follow before the fireplace in the king's study, a less formal affair, where his father would discuss past ballroom debacles and triumphs, both of his and Kit's doing. A pat on the shoulder when Leon was well and truly sloshed, and Kit could finally be excused at the crack of dawn, only a few hours of sleep required to endure the torture of the next three days of sit down, stand up, dance around, do it again.

Ritual meant everything to Leon.

Kit despised the entire affair.

"Surely it can't be that bad."

That she knew his mind had turned to the ball spoke volumes to how well she knew him despite their supposed indifference. "It's horrible."

"You seemed to enjoy yourself last year."

He didn't say that last year had been different or that it had been a first for him, that her presence alone changed things, and would darken them this time yet further.

That he'd taken a verbal lashing the day after for chasing off after a woman only to bring her back as a captain rather than a wife remained firmly locked behind his closed lips as well.

His eyes opened to watch her add a ladle of scented water to the coals in the corner of the room, fresh steam filling the air. He didn't look away as she settled onto the second bed and adjusted her towel to remain properly covered for which he gave her a smirk and she stuck her tongue out at him before laying down on her back, her head turned towards him as she relaxed.

"Thank you for the aid."

Her lips turned up in a small smile while they stared at each other.

"So, tell me about the horse?"

"Which one?"

Her forehead furrowed at his retort, unsure of what he meant as there was only the one horse who had thrown him.

He grinned, shifting his arm to take the hand she dropped between their beds.

It was such a simple motion, not meant to mean anything.

Her fingers laced with his and he squeezed gently, enjoying the clasp of their hands together. He wasn't going to question whether this was an intimacy he would be better off foregoing. The simple, small touch eased something in him, and as he watched her eyes, he thought that same something softened in her too. That same something hurt near his chest where the wall of ice he'd carefully constructed to surround his heart twanged as though hit by a blacksmith's hammer intent upon a crack. He didn't let go of her hand though, determined to take the beating of his wall and stand strong.

"Well, I suppose my father's closer to an ass than a horse, though he'd argued there is merit to his particular version of charm—"

"That's rude, Kit." But she smiled as she reprimanded him.

"Also true, Captain."

She didn't deny his words this time. Her chin tilted into her neck, considering. "Am I an ass?"

He shouldn't tell her that she could be particularly stubborn on many occasions, but no, she wasn't what he would consider an ass. Then again, his opinion was biased.

Kit scanned her face, lingering over the sharp cheekbones, rounded eyes shadowed by the most brilliant set of lashes he'd ever seen. There was a bump in her nose, likely broken at some point in her life. He'd never met a lass with a similar injury, but then, no woman had ever fought for his guard before either. He didn't dare look at her lips. He wouldn't be able to look away.

He coughed before responding, trying to force back the rough note he was sure would color his voice when he spoke. "Nay," he whinnied, and he was rewarded with her husky chuckle.

"Very amusing, my prince."

"Thank you, kind lady."

This time it was her hand that squeezed his. "What happened with the horse, Kit? I've never seen you fail to control even the most troublesome of animals. You've a way with them."

All but her, his most skittish and unruly animal and she didn't even recognize the comparison.

Kit thought about the horse that had thrown him. The poor beast had panicked, and in its panic, Kit had failed to sooth the creature.

He could ride a bucking stallion into the ground on the best of days, tame the most stubborn of mares into carrying an infant safely on her back, but the moment he launched himself into the horse's saddle, he'd known this wasn't the type of stallion that could be tamed. There was something wrong with the beast, something hurt. And he'd stayed on the stupid animal out of some misplaced sense of arrogance.

Surely, he, who could calm any creature, could likewise do the same for this one?

He probably would have succeeded in the end, but the girth strap slipped a notch, and the saddle went out from beneath him just as the horse bucked. It sent Kit into the stalls. He was lucky the grooms were there to keep the beast from trampling him. The look in the poor creature's eyes said he wouldn't stop at throwing Kit; would only stop with blood and broken bones and Kit had been too stunned to get out of the way if the animal attacked.

"He was hurt, Ella." It was unconscious; using the name she'd given him, forgetting it wasn't the name she bore. "Apologies, I didn't—"

Her gaze sharpened on him, eyes searching his face while he wished the heat would fade from his cheeks. "Does it give you comfort, to call me that?"

He tried to drop his hand from hers, pull away so he wouldn't have to feel her revulsion at the reminder of one year ago.

She didn't release him.

"It was unintentional."

"How many names do you have for me in that royal head of yours, Prince Christophe?"

He heard the smile in her voice, eyes closed so he wouldn't have to look at her face and the disgust he expected there.

He blinked, met her stare, too much pride to shy away that much.

She was grinning at him, though there was something else he read in her face that he couldn't name.

"I haven't counted them, Captain."

"Too true, Prince. I haven't counted all those nicknames I have for you either."

"Should I guess at some?"

"I'd rather not be sent to the whipping posts for those thoughts of mine, my lord."

He laughed, and when he pulled his hand away this time, she let him go. Arms curled once more beneath his head, content to relax in her presence, comfortable where he was so often tense with everyone else. "I should have seen it in his eyes when I mounted, but a groom was holding the halter, and I'm an arrogant bastard on my best of days. Soren didn't deserve me for a rider."

"Can he be saved?"

Kit thought about his answer. His first response was yes, but was that pride claiming to be able to tame the animal or actual insight into the beast's salvation? He didn't want to see the poor horse put down, unbiddable. His uncle would do it, would kill the creature without a second thought. Likely it was Uncle Kravn's fault that the beast had been ill-treated in the first place.

Kit and Kravn had different mindsets when it came to training their steeds, but Kit couldn't turn down a gift from his father's brother any more than his uncle could sneer at Kit being heir by his birth. There was no love lost between nephew and uncle; they played a cruel game with each other, barbed comments and equally barbed gifts, so it would seem. But at the end of the day, they were family, and Kit respected that and expected his uncle to hold himself to the same standard.

He didn't tell her about the saddle fraying beneath his seat.

Could the beast be saved?

"Yes."

"And you'll take on the task yourself?"

"Are you willing to rub out the bruising for me if I do?"

She laughed again, and he smiled against his arm.

The horse was the least of his worries now. He only prayed the ball left him with no more bruises than he already bore.

II
The Two Hundredth and Twelfth Ball

"YES, FATHER. I understand. The very best one yet. I will find a bride this time 'round without fail. My word to you."

Kit placed his folded hands against his heart, bowed his head to imply his sincerity. What number ball was this now? Two hundred and twelve? Both he and the king played the same game year after year: Kit promising to find a princess to wed, the king threatening to make the choice for his son.

King Leon would never take the decision from Kit. He had married for love, once upon a time, and though "suffering through a similar fate" was not what he wished for Kit, the king would let the prince make his own choices.

And Kit, for all the smiles he'd received, and hearts thrown at his feet, knew there was no one among the glimmering throngs of women who danced at the balls that would capture his heart as it was already held and trampled upon by another.

"Dismissed. Perform your rituals, boy. Leave me to my melancholy and I will leave you to yours."

"Gratitude, Father."

Kit backed from the room, bowed appropriately for a meeting with his king.

The moment the doors closed his father away, Kit straightened, rolling his shoulders to ease the ache in them.

He'd only returned this morning from LarkTown, overseeing the expansion of the kingdom's walls to include the small village that reported being hammered by a phalanx of trolls over the past few months.

Trolls.

Trolls hadn't been seen in years, and yet Kit couldn't dispute the evidence of the attack, especially when said trolls heard he was in residence within the town and decided to batter the poor defenses in an attempt to get to him. His men, the legion who'd come with him, had held the line against the mammoth sized males, the clubs and hammers of the mountainfolk as deadly as the swords and bows his people wielded. He'd seen good men smashed beneath the sledges the trolls swung. Smashed, truly smashed into piles of gore on a killing field that should have remained just a field at the far edges of his father's country.

And as they fought to secure the town, the engineers fought to erect the high stone walls that would withstand the brutal battering of the trolls coming against it. The wall wrapped the small city, was woven into the existing walls that protected the main land of Kit's kingdom. Soon there would be no more farm land to pass through that was not divided up by great grey blocks held together by mortar.

A part of him wondered if the walls coming down would be such a bad thing, but that was wondered as he sat at the bedside of a young officer whose leg was so badly destroyed the best healers said the only thing to do was to remove the appendage.

He held the man's hand through the sickening wet crunch of saw on flesh and bone, promising laurels and odes to the man's bravery upon returning home to the city. Infection set in, and the healer had no magic to aid his efforts, potions not enough to stymy the poisoned blood. Elderberries and feverfew held the soldier's soul to his flesh for a week, and when Kit checked on the poor man the next day, the body was already cool to the touch.

The trolls attacked, and his soldiers fought hard, and soon the few trolls who had caused the most damage were too wounded to keep up the fight and bowed before Kit in defeat.

It was not soon enough for the men Kit lost on the field, nor the townsfolk who cowered from all the blood and gore surrounding them. Kit survived because he had trained with Eli every day since she came to his people. He survived because he knew how the Faousteners fought, the trolls with their strength who forgot speed worked against them.

They won the skirmish, saved the town. They orchestrated a truce between them, the trolls and the humans. A truce paid in blood and gold and the lives already lost upon the field because the lord who bid the Faousteners to attack cared little if the mercenaries all died in the attempt. Cheaper, to renege on the accord with a nameless patron than lose the lives of their best soldiers to Kit and his people. Let the Other send men to die, the Faousteners wanted no more.

The final wall went up.

The trolls faded into their lands, behind hillock and dale and mountain face.

The people cheered.

Kit waved goodbye and managed to make the palace gate by midmorning the day after it all finished. Three months of fighting. Two months of labor. It wasn't that much in offering to his people, but it was enough for now. Five months he'd been away from home, and yet he didn't miss the palace walls that were his prison. That his father had let him leave at all was a miracle. That his guards rode with him had saved the people of LarkTown, had saved him.

His back ached from having worked side by side with the masons to make sure the walls were sturdy. His hands were swollen from chiseling and hammering, and it had taken too long for him to realize that he had an allergy to the composition of the cement between the stones, but the swelling would diminish with distance, the medic said. Kit forced himself to smile when he road through the streets of Tornald and his father welcomed him home.

It was done, and he had a godsdamned ball to look forward to and all he wanted was to sleep for a year and forget about everything.

And Eli hadn't been at the gate to greet his return.

He hadn't had a chance to ask where she was, afraid to hear she was away on some adventure he was unable to attend, afraid it was a fight which he'd seen too much of lately.

Kit retreated to the only place no one would follow, no one but his elf.

It had become a ritual between Eli and himself. The most stressful days of his year granted a few hours reprieve in her company away from the lists and duties of being a prince.

Funny that he hesitated over his traditions, not wanting to relax in the sauna if his captain wasn't there to keep him company.

He looked forward to their yearly chats. The small steam filled room had become a balm to him, the one place he was able to speak freely, feel like a person rather than a court monkey sent from one errand to another without relent. She smiled as rarely as he did in public. Yet there, with a little bit of time for themselves, it was like that first ball, and he was speaking to her as just a woman, and he was just a man.

His jacket fell to a heap on the floor, shirt and breeches, small clothes all following. The towel he wrapped around his hips was immodest, but no one would see, and no one would care. Servants would be in to clean up the mess of his garments on the ground while he let the heat soak into his muscles. And still he hesitated at the sauna's door, dreading walking in to an empty room even as he craved the silence of solitude.

She looked over her shoulder at him as he pushed the door open, a small upturn of her lips all that she managed before he was across the room with one arm around her waist to support her. The bandage around her middle was stained with a spreading line of blood across her side. She trembled in his arms, her legs weak as he held her.

"What happened?"

"Gouldaria. They hired the mercenaries." Her eyes opened to look at him. He caught the hand she raised to his cheek, her arm heavy in his hold, limp. "I found the camp and took care of them."

"But *I* beat back the trolls near LarkTown." Had she been his shadow at the wall? Why not announce herself if she was? "You did not find me there?"

She blinked, eyes unfocused on his face. His hand cupped her cheek, wet with her blood he hadn't realized now stained his flesh. Her lashes fluttered, gaze finding his once more. "The Dwarves. From the West. They attacked Sneed before you left for LarkTown. You were supposed to be safe in the north, away from the fighting. Marius sent me so you would be safe in the north."

"He sent me north to another battlefield."

"It was not supposed to be a battlefield. Trolls are hermits. The reports were not supposed to be true." Her knees buckled, and her full weight fell into his arms, her pulse fluttery at her throat, eyes rolling white in their sockets.

"Sweet Atha. Eli. Eli!" He shifted his grip on her, raising her arm to wrap around his neck as he bent to lift her at the knees, ignoring the feel of her bare breasts against his chest as he laid her down on one of the cushioned tables. There was blood on his chest when he pulled away, so bright a red that it hurt his eyes in the dim light of the room.

Her head rolled on the cushion. Keep the wounded awake, she'd told him, the healer in LarkTown told him.

He cupped her cheeks, brushed his thumbs over her forehead, across her eyelashes, uncaring that her blood wet his way. "Captain, come on Eli. Look at me now. Talk to me. How many Dwarves were there? How deep is the wound? Captain!" He used her title, a snap in his voice calling to the soldier in her, cracking her pain filled eyes open and up towards him though their focus frayed, and he tapped her temples, the small pain to keep her with him. "How deep is the wound?"

"Not too—" Her eyes fluttered and no number of fingers beating against her forehead could rouse her to him.

"Ella." He shook her, trying to wake her from her sleep. "Damnit, woman, wake up!" She did not stir.

His gaze travelled down her face, her throat, spying the pulse rabbiting in her neck, the stuttered rise and fall of her chest.

The wound still bled, dripping down her side, her bandage, to the cushion beneath her.

"Damnit."

He gathered her fallen towel from the floor where she'd dropped it, bundled it together and pressed it to her side, turning her onto her wound so that her weight acted as pressure to staunch the flow while he rushed for the healer down the hall.

The elderly man nearly fainted at Kit's appearance, bare footed and bare chested, naught but a towel around his hips. Silas recovered himself quickly enough, followed Kit to the sauna and examined the patient on the bench. The healer made Kit turn aside, avert his gaze from the naked woman on the bed like he had not found said woman in her current state of undress to begin with. But whatever the healer wanted, Kit gave, did, didn't matter so long as Silas saved the captain's life.

"Not quite that grave, boy."

Grave enough, though Kit did not argue the point.

Guards came quickly after that, rumors of their captain's injury spreading throughout the palace and grounds fast as fire set on dried tinder. They were summarily dismissed upon their arrival, the healer calling for his aids rather than a posse of soldiers wanting to protect their injured comrade.

When the medic's minions arrived, Kit was ushered from the room. Servants bundled him into a robe sashed at his waist.

He paced the length of the changing area, waiting for news.

Marius joined him at one point, both men caged within the small space, dodging benches and each other while their bare feet and boots slapped against the flagstone flooring respectively.

"You may enter now."

Both Kit and Marius crowded the door, Kit's entrance allowed first only due to his station as prince and Marius' as guardian.

Eli was covered now with a sheet. Her breathing easier, though her skin was pale against the mahogany wood and cream cushions of the room.

"How is she?"

"I've patched her up. She lost quite a bit of blood but she's a strong lass. I expect a full recovery. From her scars, many of her other wounds have pained her more than this wee little scratch. Right as rain in a week or two, I'd say."

"She was supposed to take guard duty for the ball tonight." Marius' words were jokingly said but did little to hide the man's concern.

Kit tried to respond in the same sarcastic vein. "Perhaps father will be persuaded to cancel so we don't inconvenience you." There was irony, to be sure, but the biting anger at her injury shadowed his words more.

Marius's eyes narrowed but he said nothing to Kit in front of the healer.

"Yes, well, she won't be guarding anything for a few days at the least. I'll leave you with her for a moment while I arrange transport to her chambers. Call if she wakes and needs anything."

Kit nodded first, and Marius followed suit, both men remaining on their sides of her sick table until the healer was beyond the door and the heavy wood enclosed them once more.

"I don't consider it an inconvenience, Kit."

"More fool you then."

The General stiffened, spine straightening at the unintended insult, nerves tweaked too far for this night. "You're worried, so I'll forgive the affront this once." Forgive, but not forget. Kit nodded, accepting at the recompense that his friend would mete out upon a day.

"I know you hate the balls, my prince." Marius walked slowly around the table, moved to Kit's side though the hand he would so casually drape around Kit's shoulders remained rooted on the hilt of a knife at the General's waist.

Kit noted the motion, the tension it implied. He let the ball distract him, for a moment, from the woman lying so still before him. His fingers brushed softly over her hand he clasped in both of his, hoping to feel her fingers clench his in response. "Hate seems too mild an emotion for my feelings on the damn dances."

Marius' smile did not quite reach the man's eyes. "There is an easy solution, if you would permit me to say so."

Kit shook his head, unable to help the quick grin at the common parlay between them. *Marry a bitch and be done with it*. Poor Marius had lost his tact somewhere around the hundred and seventieth ball. He held out far longer than Kit did.

Eyes closed to disguise his uninterrupted stare at Eli's face, Kit slowly shifted his shoulders, hoping to release some of the tension that would not fade until she met his gaze without a fog clouding hers. Easier to consider Marius' suggestion, a marriage Kit never wanted and yet could imagine easily enough. Bright green eyes meeting his from down a long aisle framed with multicolored gowns, their wearers crying as she walked towards him and they remained on the sidelines, only witnesses. She'd hesitate when asked if she would marry him but finally acquiesce to the priest's question. His lips would finally find hers, claim hers despite the crowd that watched on.

He forced the thoughts away, blushing at the womanly imaginings, hated that he was the one to consider such a thing, knowing his captain never would. Kit cleared his throat, forced his gaze to Marius'. "Unless your suggestion is abdication and summary eviction from the palace, I do not want to hear it."

"You'd rather lose your chance at the throne than marry?"

"I'd rather kiss a toad than partner with any of the rats paraded before me for a single dance in the hopes of snagging my interest.

I'd find more entertainment with a fishmonger's get than being groped by the gloved hands of the nobility who I dance with."

"You are the only man I know who complains about that particular problem, my prince."

"They're allowed to act on their desires."

"So you desire some of your accosters?"

He had no safe response for Marius' question.

Eli drew in a stuttered breath, saving Kit from replying, drawing his attention back to her, back to the moment. He saw no more seeping blood from her side. Her chest rose, steady and even beneath the thin covering of the sheet. He squeezed her hand. She responded in kind, cool fingers gripping him back, no strength to the motion.

Her eyes blinked open.

His hand shifted to her cheek, brushed the paleness of her usually sun kissed skin. "How do you feel?"

"Like a fool," she rasped, her voice hoarse to his ears. Her muscles tensed, chest expanding as she drew in a great breath. He supported her neck when she turned to her side to cough, the clearing of her throat leading to the harsher sound.

Kit helped her settle back on the cushion, another throat clearing his warning to remove his hands from their overly familiar touch on her body. He forced a slight smile to his lips, a laugh to his words. "I see no fool."

Marius shifted closer to the bed, pushing his way to her head, Kit to step further away, a commander addressing his subordinate, the title of prince holding little rank in military matters. "What happened out there, Captain?"

"Gouldaria." She coughed once more. It was Marius' hand that helped her shift so that the pressure of her chest found relief and Kit watched on, helpless. "They're amassing an army on the border with Faoust. Their troops are filtering in, coming from different directions, more every day, likely so that any spies we might send can't make an accurate accounting."

"Spies, not accounting for yourself?"

Her lips turned up in a pained grin. "Easy enough to make simple calculations, General. At least ten thousand already gathered, supplies for three times that many, enough to last many, many months. They've already secured access to provisions further inland where we can't gainsay them unless we take their land which we've not the men to do."

"Buy why? We've been at peace for over a hundred years. Why war now?"

"You."

He did not resist taking her hand when she reached for him. Her fingers were warmer now, no longer chilled against his skin. Perhaps it was his flesh that was cold in response. "Nothing has changed with me. I've always been hunted and cursed. What use declaring war when assassins are more likely to succeed in the dead of night?"

He had not meant her. Did not mean to imply that she—But she simply squeezed his hand, unjudging.

"You've survived the attempts, Ki-Prince. Draw you out of the castle, onto a field where death surrounds you at all time, and mayhap it will finally find you where it has failed so far."

"Death did not find me in LarkTown."

She huffed out a breath, the closest to a laugh in this dire conversation. "They made mention of stupid trolls. That's what you were saying before? You fought trolls?" At Kit's nod, she groaned, eyes closing before she struggled to sit.

Kit's were not the only hands forcing her flat to the bed, holding her down. "The healer said to rest."

"That wound needs time to heal."

"There's no time left! The first attack already failed. They'd thought to use the trolls as a distraction while they finished gathering their men but Kit won. Marius, Kit won, and now our eyes will turn to the west, to the Dwarves on the far side of our border— Darkness," she stopped her mad rant, eyes raking over Kit as if just seeing him, thoughts turning in her head that he wasn't privy too, didn't think he'd enjoy when she shared them. "They weren't preparing for war but to take over our lands once the walls fell. The trolls would be defeated because we would kill the bastards that killed our prince leaving the Dwarves free to invade."

"But the trolls failed."

"It wasn't meant to be war."

"But it will be now."

"Because I lived." His captain and his general turned their stares back to him. He dropped her hand and backed slowly away, needing room, needing to think, needing to escape. "How many men must die so that I might survive?"

"Kit—"

The hand he raised was feeble barrier against the weight of his name on her lips, the desperation and despair in her gaze. All of this, because he was a prince and fated to die. Yes, he knew that he was not the only prince under constant attack, but how many others had the weight of their lands on their shoulders? And yes, he knew that answer too. Knew that any man destined to rule bore the fate not only of himself but of those who bowed under his leadership on his conscious. He had a city who offered its life for his. Guards and friends who already had died trying to protect him, were injured and maimed in his defense. Would trolls and Dwarves and gods knew what else still be so adamant on the attack if Kit were just another noble in line for a throne?

"Men die all the time. Some die for honor; some for loyalty, others for greed. Everyone is walking towards their death for one reason or another. You're probably the only fool having to walk towards life resenting it."

"I don't resent my life, Captain."

"Then start acting like it. Men are going to die. At least they die defending what they believe in." Marius no longer pressed down on Eli's shoulders to keep her flat to the bed. His arm wrapped across her back, letting her lean into his side as she sat, both staring at him with similar looks of hope and disgust. "Grow up, Prince.

War comes to everyone. You're the one person most likely to live through it. Stop acting like a child."

"Caring about my people is childish?"

"When that care leads them to be enslaved under Dwarves or trolls and whatnot? Yes." Her hand was shaking as she held onto Marius arm about her shoulders. "Will you help me to my room, General? The prince has a ball to prepare for, and we a war."

Marius held Kit's stare. "Yes, my lady."

They left him alone in the sauna, its heat oppressive where once it had been relaxing. How quickly feelings changed.

He wasn't being childish.

It was a king's place to look after his people. That meant weighing the cost of war in lives and livelihood and whether the country could withstand the onslaught of the invasion. Dwarves were fighters. They were swordsmiths and weapons masters. They were mortal. They had fodder to throw into the fight that could last multiple of their lifetimes and only one of Kit's. And if the dwarves fought, what would keep the rest of the nations from joining in the battle?

KIT WAS COURTEOUS enough to knock before barging into her rooms, forcing the door open before she had a chance to move out of the way of its swing. His hands caught her slender arms, the strength he was so used to diminished with the weakness from her wound. She nearly stumbled, and definitely trembled in his arms while he forced her to stand rather than lie in her bed and recover.

It was second nature to pull her close and let her use his body as a prop.

He should have taken her to her bed but couldn't help spying out his captain's quarters, the green overflowing from plants and shrubs and he was almost positive there was a tree just beyond the simple doorway from the kitchen area he stood in. His fingers ran along the wooden wall, the white paint chipped away to reveal the brown of nature beneath. There were no white flakes on the floor. Birch trees, like the ones in the King's Gardens. They were not natural to his part of the world. An elf likely would never have seen them before making her home within the palace grounds. A piece of his land, that she'd integrated into a piece of hers. The plants were not forest dwellers, dependent on more light than would ever breech the thick canopy of densely packed trees. She'd replicated what she left behind as best she could, and he'd never noticed how deep her longing for what she'd lost was.

She curled her fingers in his shirt, the cambric not the finest quality he owned but enough to pass muster for the opening of the ball a few hours hence.

"What are you doing up? You should be resting."

"Someone was pounding on my door." Her words were faint. The whisper didn't hide the pain in her voice, the struggle and exhaustion movement entailed.

He made to lift her in his arms, and she swatted at his chest, lips snarling at his attempt at chivalry though she didn't protest his strength around her waist as they walked slowly through her apartments and to the canopied bed in the other room.

She slid carefully beneath the sheets, black sheets that did nothing to offset how pale she was. They swallowed her in their depths but that didn't stop him from pulling them around her, tucking her in. Only her arms remained unburied beneath the linen. Her hand rested empty on the mattress and it was second nature to lace his fingers through hers, relax at the squeeze of her grip in response.

"Did I not make it clear that I was through talking to you for today?" The question was muttered on a low exhale. Her eyes were closed though her head tilted to where he sat on top of her blankets, hip to hip though separated by cloth. The half-smile on her lips took the bite from her words.

He snorted, ignored her comment in favor of lifting her hand from the bed, tracing the faint stains of red that hadn't been wiped fully away yet. So small, her hands compared to his. So deadly. "How were you injured, Eli?"

"I don't know."

He pulled his gaze from their linked fingers and caught her eye.

"I was fighting, Kit. I was fighting, and I didn't feel anything. I mounted my horse and rode away from the killing field; left the corpses behind me and felt nothing until I was within sight of the city walls, in sight of the barracks and saw the people lining up at the gates awaiting the ball, so very early for the festivities, and then the pain struck. It wasn't in our street, that's not what I mean. But I don't know whose knife cut me, or if it was a knife or a sword or a lance. I fell off my horse in the courtyard, managed to bind the wounds before anyone saw, and went to find you."

She struggled to sit, and he pushed her down, forcing her to remain reclined on the bed, one hand all it took to hold her in place. Her fingers remained in his, and he was loath to pull his other hand away lest she tried to sit again. He brushed the matted strands of her hair from her shoulder, wiped the sweat from her brow, no fever that he could detect though he was no medic.

"You should have sought the healer. He would have sent for me or Marius."

Her eyes opened to meet his gaze. He stilled.

"Kit…I—"

The bells tolled outside in the tower. His guards would be coming to fetch him and lead him down to where his father waited to enter the ball. Whatever she would have said, he would have said, would wait, be forgotten in the events of the night.

"I'm not afraid of war, or of fighting, or of men dying. But the numbers of men who will fall on that field, human and dwarf and whoever else becomes embroiled in the fight…" He sat back, pulling his fingers from the tangles he'd made of her hair, from the heat of her hand in his. "I meant only that I wished there was another way than bloodshed."

"With the bounty on your head, and our world seeking your throne, I do not think there is much other choice."

"I know." His smile was brittle, though he tried, for her, which did nothing to help maintain whatever shred of dignity and distance he kept between them. He pat at her leg awkwardly, tempted to press a chaste kiss to her forehead, knew it was against the code his father expected him to uphold. "Rest well, Captain."

Her voice stopped him at the door between her bedroom and kitchen. "Prince."

It took more effort than he would admit not to turn back to her, to just look over his shoulder.

"Try to enjoy the ball. It might be the last one for a while."

"To forego war, I would suffer through a million more."

Kit didn't wait for a response, nodding once before leaving her to her rest and him to slippers and gowns.

III

The Three Hundredth and Thirteenth Ball

HE MANAGED TO get himself back on his horse, pulling hard on the saddle horn, forgetting for a moment to use the stirrups to help him mount. Exhaustion was beating at his shoulders, his head hanging low, too tired to lift and view the battlefield around him. There was more blood on him than anything else. Between the shallow slices from his enemies' swords to the blood spilled from the men he killed, he was soaked through with the red, and the thought nearly sent him to his knees, wanting a moment to disgorge the non-existent contents of his stomach.

The day had started on the western flank, but soon enough he'd been forced to split his attack in two to stop the advancing Westerners from overwhelming his forces. Two fronts, and yet the day was theirs. He credited their victory to Eli's training of his shoulders, her sword work and skill in battle the turning force. He'd lost her at some point during the day, her black banner travelling away from him during the fight. He wouldn't acknowledge the subsequent queasiness to his stomach that she might not be at the camp upon his return.

His horse made the weary journey back to the tents. Even the animal was exhausted.

Kit slid from his mount's back, using his sword as a crutch, the wound in his thigh aching fiercely as he hobbled into the war tent.

"Uncle." He nodded to the older man as he moved to the pitcher of water and the glasses on the map table. Armor as stained as his own, back bent and weary, were all he saw of the man speaking lowly with the gathered soldiers and commanders of the Spinician army.

"Highness."

Kit barely glanced up from his long-needed drink, listening with half an ear to talk of the new weapons invading the field of battle.

Ballista launched with the aid of fire.

Casks of ground charcoal powder that exploded when lit. Unsophisticated. Unpredictable. Deadly.

Words were bandied around with varying amounts of awe and horror. The dwarves, master craftsmen that they were, tinkered with every element at their disposal. They were as likely to destroy themselves as make weapons that would destroy others. That these new weapons were unpredictable now did not mean they would always be so. And the longer the war persisted, the more likely it was that their enemy's weapons would lead to Kit's downfall.

"Have we any of the substance to examine for ourselves? Any of their weapons to replicate on our terms?"

"No one would dare steal from a dwarf, Kit."

The mocking tone of his uncle's voice made the scowl on Kit's face turn dark with anger. "War is war, Uncle. We collect weapons at the end of battle every day. I want these new weapons collected, destroyed if we must, examined for certain. I will not send my men to face an arsenal we've no defense against."

"Then you will forfeit this war?"

"Then I will find another way to win it. I want our engineers at the field. Marius," he turned to his most trusted advisor, meeting the equally fierce expression in the other man's gaze. Kravn made no allies denigrating Kit before these men under his command. "See that they're brought to the front. I want a report on the abilities and power of each of these trebuchets."

"Cannon, Your Highness."

Kit looked at the young man who spoke, new to the council having replaced another who fell during battle. "Thank you, Lieutenant Morrisee. You'll assist General D'Corre in the management of this task. Report directly to me with any discoveries made."

The man paled at having been commanded directly by the prince but seemed to steady under the order all the same. "Yes, my lord."

"Good man," Kit turned his gaze back to the rest of the troupe. Marius looked at his recruit with a regarding stare, hesitation at taking on the new man warring with what Kit thought was a bit of admiration. No one else had taken the chance to correct Kit before. Marius nodded but said nothing in response, likely saving whatever speech he would give for the soldier himself.

Satisfied with the proceedings, Kit addressed the crowd. "Was there anything else, gentlemen?"

"We were ready to disperse, your highness." Kravn left unsaid that they all would have done so had Kit not stuck his nose into the conversation.

But it was his war tent, and his army, and Kravn was allowed voice in deference to his former military experience and position as brother to the king. That he had little admiration for Kit meant nothing except to ruffle feathers already on edge from a day fighting.

"I'm glad I forestalled that for such an important command. Best to face new threats head on than wait until we've no hope of surmounting them." He did not look away from his uncle's stare, held steady beneath the older, crueler gaze. "To your rest, gentlemen. Gods keep you."

"Gods keep you." "Thank you, Highness." "And to you, my lord." "Happy birthday, Kit."

It was the last that caused Kit's contest of wills to break from Kravn, head turn to stare at Marius and his damn open mouth.

"I'd forgotten. Happy birthday, my Prince."

"Aye, to the Prince!" A round of cheers; a raucous chorus of men calling for dancers lest the prince miss another ball; the clamoring of hands clapping to ill-sung songs and laughter, finding what gaiety they could amidst the death surrounding them.

They pulled Kit from his tent, all but Kravn following the procession, pushing Kit towards the nearest campfire, its patrons roused from their light dose at their approach. Cheers rang out. Instruments, flutes and violins stashed within trunks carried from battle line to battle line, found their way into minstrel hands. The men clapped and sang and not a few of them brandished flasks passed from one to the other. Kit took a sip, managed not to choke on the astringent liquor that struck his empty belly. He'd had worse to drink over the past years. The men cheered, again, and some clapped. A few took advantage of those soldiers already standing and swung them around in circles mimicking a dance. It was amusing, or would have been, if Kit didn't see the faces of those soldiers who would never rise again. He wondered if the smile on his face looked as worn and weary as it felt. But it was good to see something other than pain and horror and fear of tomorrow on their faces, and if it came at his expense, so be it. Let them have this moment, for gods knew they were far too few of late.

His personal guards nodded as he slipped away from the impromptu festivities, hid once more in the confines of his near-empty tent.

"Damn you, Marius."

"You know as well as I that the men needed a break." Marius shrugged. "Best to put you to use, my prince. Make those highborn sensibilities good for something."

"So long as I'm good for something, though Eli would be disappointed in your assessment of my accomplishments."

"Eli isn't here now, is—"

Kit said nothing, and Marius did not finish the question or reply with something equally mundane and filled with false hope. They didn't know if she was out there somewhere. They didn't know if she was coming back. That she always did was no guarantee for the future. Kit knew that. He did. He just didn't want to consider it at present.

"Goodnight, General."

"Goodnight, my lord."

He clapped Marius on the shoulder, waited until the tent flap closed before moving deeper into his small sanctuary and the bedroom cordoned off by thick curtains.

He barely raised his sword in time to prevent the assassin's blade from piercing his heart, armor not strong enough to deflect such a well-aimed, well-powered strike.

Kit growled at the attack. How dare the Gouldarans resort to such cheap ploys? Even if Kit fell, his army would stand to protect the country. Spinick would never be destroyed, no matter what some prophecy said. At least, that was Kit's hope and prayer.

He attempted to call for aid, his voice echoing inside his head, the silence around him unnatural. Not Gouldarans then. He should have known the moment the man came from out of the shadows to attack him. Almost he laughed at the absurdity of the woodland elves finally making their move against him, joining a side in the war that was not his. It had been two hundred plus years. Surely that was long enough for them to have tried to kill him numerous times, but this was the first direct attempt on his life by one of their own. Was it because Eli wasn't here to guard him? Was their confidence deserved today where it hadn't been before with her at his side?

No. He refused to think like that. Better to think of his anger, his pride. He wouldn't die by an assassin's blade in the back during the dark of night. At least the bastard wasn't toting one of the rumored canon against him. Certainly, the elves would be most like to have the weapons before humans managed the same. Could one dodge canon? Had anyone survived a meeting with the same to tell the tale?

Step. Lunge. Parry. Dodge.

Questions could wait. He didn't have the strength to wonder and defend at the same time, eyes already heavy, fighting the spells the elf attempted to bind him with.

Minutes. He had minutes to kill the man before he fell himself. Minutes only, and he managed to force the assassin back until the man stumbled against Kit's cot and sprawled on the ground. Kit speared him through with his sword, slicing the hardened leather armor covering the man's stomach, piercing to the ground beneath.

The assassin didn't cry out in pain or writhe on his doom. Black cloaked eyes turned towards Kit, and he met the hooded gaze, wary still for so long as one breath remained, the elf was his opponent. "*Sli muelfan duoui.*"

The cloth door of his sleeping chambers pulled open.

He didn't turn his head from the threat before him, catching her form from his peripheral but never relaxing.

Eli didn't stop in the entrance, moving quickly to his side, and pulling a knife from her hip to slit the assassin's throat, a plunge to bury the blade through the male's heart.

Her hands cupped Kit's face, turning him from the corpse bleeding around them. "You are uninjured?"

A quick nod was all he managed until her gaze found the blood on his leg, the wound untended though the bleeding had long since stopped. "Not from him.

She nodded, hands lingering on his skin a moment longer than necessary. He held her black tinged green gaze. He did not shirk from the manifestation of her power in his defense, a reaction cultivated from long practice though he hoped she did not realize her magic still unnerved him.

She pulled away quickly enough. The warmth of her skin left him feeling cold in its absence. Watching as she unwrapped the cloths that covered the assassin's head, the reverence with which she unmasked his would be killer, did nothing to warm the unease in his heart. She never mentioned missing her people. Kit didn't fool himself into thinking it was easy to watch one die. Likely, she'd finished the kill out of mercy. He would have done the same, but he had no knife at hand, his buried in a skull somewhere out on the field.

"He was kin?"

She replaced the mask over the man's face, the features unfamiliar to Kit though that meant little to him. At least the male didn't have Eli's look, and he could pretend he hadn't killed a father or brother in self-defense.

"An elder to me. He taught me for a time when I was younger."

"*Sli muelfan duoui.*" She looked at him askance, and he wondered if he had mispronounced the words. "It's what he said when he fell." The euphemism did nothing to disguise the truth of his actions. He'd run the bastard through, but it seemed kinder to allow the man some dignity, in honor of the role the assassin once played for Eli, than to feel petty anger against one who almost managed to take Kit's life. Besides, better to honor the dead who fought at the behest of another, then scorn their lives lost.

Her fingers lingered on the black cloth over the man's face before she replied. "*She trained you well.*"

And it was true. A second slower, a small amount of hesitation at meeting the attack, attacking in turn, and Kit would be the one lying on the floor of the tent.

She had indeed trained him well.

He bowed his head to honor the dead's final words and the veracity of them.

"We should call for your guards."

"Will another attack tonight?"

"No."

But the guards should be called all the same, despite his need to be unseen, left in peace, alone. That an assassin so easily breached Kit's chambers was worrisome. Time enough to discover the reason why. "How many would he have killed to reach the camp?"

"I don't know, my prince."

Kit raised a hand to rub at the bridge of his nose, stopped with his bloodied fingers hovering in the air before his face. His blood. Elf blood. Dwarf blood. He couldn't tell the difference between the tints of red covering him. Gods, but for the lines drawn on parchment, who would know the difference between human and any other species? Some elves supposedly had pointed ears. Eli's were a tad more elongated than his, perhaps, but in no way pointed at the tip. Dwarves had the bulk of men who worked iron and ore for their living, no soft muscles of a lord's life amongst them. The Giants were bred tall. The Goblins reportedly short. But all similar in shape. All with the same red pumping through their veins, a similar heart buried deep within the flesh that gave life. All so easily killed when a breast was pierced by steel or lance or fire-thrown projectile.

Iron and earth. Salt of tears. Stink of bowels. His tent smelled the same as the battlefield, the same as what already burned the memory of forest and flower from his nostrils. "Will I never be free of it?"

She took the hand he held in the air, cupped his cheek with the other, leaning forward into the space between them over the body lying broken on the ground to press their brows together, a moment where he needn't look at the death around him. Just a moment.

At least she still smelled of forest, a breath of fresh pine and crushed leaves, smells foreign here where all the trees were reduced to firewood and spear, arrow shaft and pike. He'd never appreciated the forest before. Now he longed for the sight of thickly shadowed roads overhung with branches and leaves.

Gods above, a hundred years.

A hundred and twelve years now. Saplings planted at the beginning of the war were now timber for the pyres burning beyond his doorway. So much land devastated because dwarves threw generations at humans and humans fought because they would not yield, could not yield to the other race, must not.

Her thumb stroked the hollows beneath his eyes, dark, he knew though he did his best to avoid his reflection at all costs. The hairline scar running from temple to just behind his ear. A few inches either way and he would have lost his sight or his life. That all that remained was a fading pink line, barely noticeable beneath the grime coating him, was a testament to the healers who treated him first, even when others were more severely wounded. She dropped his hand and he brushed her escaped strands of hair from her forehead, losing himself in the simple action, surrounding himself with it. She touched his hip, the skin broken beneath his ruined armor. He'd need it fixed before morning. He'd need to treat the injury before infection set in. She didn't tell him to see a healer any more than he would tell her to do the same.

"There is a pond, Kit, a little way to the west, guarded by mountains on three sides. I do not think anyone else knows of it yet."

He smiled at the rush of her breath against his cheek, the whispered words that were secret and offering both. "And how do you know of it?"

"Assassin, my prince. Spy."

Which told him nothing of the lake's origins or her knowledge of it, but he did not protest her evasion, unsure he had the strength to do so regardless.

The reminders of her past life no longer unnerved him. He'd relegated himself to a lifetime of looking to her to teach him ways to kill, respecting her skills even as he feared them, used them.

"I don't know how long before it is discovered, but we should be safe enough for tonight."

"Water is more precious to drink than to bathe in."

"Yes."

The decision was left to him then and he desperately wished honor did not demand the sacrifice be made.

"It leads to a stream that runs into dwarfish territory."

But did he dare attempt to pollute their water same as they would his? Was he not better than that?

"The water will wash clean long before it reaches their greedy hands."

His lips quirked, more at the sigh in her voice, the knowledge that her honor and his were different and yet just as strong between them. "We can cordon off a section of the water for troop use?"

Her smile answered his though he did not need to look to see it. "Yes, so long as you take this night for yourself."

This night.

He should have known she would not forget his birthday any more than Marius would.

Did it make him weak, wanting to give in to her gentle command? Wanting to forget the face of the boy whose throat he'd slit that morning? The sickening crunch of his horse's hooves over dead flesh and bone? The screaming that sounded like music, so varied in tone and breath that the dying made a symphony of anguish with which to sleep to? How easy it was to pierce a sword through armor and muscle and bone and pin a man to the ground?

"One night, Kit. Even soldiers have rests during the fighting, regiments changing and rearranging on the line. Take the night."

"Evil temptress."

"Yes."

She stared at him, the green of her irises fading to black as she called upon her magic, the darkness that was as terrifying to him as it was honored.

"No cheating, Eli."

She blinked, and he wondered if she even realized her spells were settling around her.

He sat back on his heels, watched his black armored captain stand before him, her gauntlet glinting red in the faint light of the few candles still burning in the tent. Her fingers extended towards him, and he took her hand, the damsel to her knight, not even blushing at the comparison, too tired for that. She helped him to his feet, and he stood before her, steadied her when she stumbled against him, somehow unhappy that her strength was as depleted as his.

He stepped carefully around the corpse at his feet, pulled her into his arms when he was clear of the desecrated ground. "Why were you not here when I returned?"

"It doesn't matter."

"Why, Ella?"

A sigh, her face buried in the harsh metal of his breastplate. "A dwarf."

Not hurt, no, she didn't heal hurt dwarves. And he'd told her not to be the one to question the soldiers they captured.

He didn't expect her to listen, just as he didn't ask for details, knowing he would have the answers gleaned before him come the morning.

"I'm not the only one needing a break, dear captain."

She smiled tiredly up at him, head tilted up, dark hair coiled in a thick mess against the crown of her head, better to fit her helm. "No, dear prince, you are not."

"Show me your pool then."

She nodded, stepping from his embrace to usher him from his tent. His guards caught the fresh glint of blood on his armor, the even more exaggerated haggardness of his face and shoulders upon his exit. Most of the revelry had quieted down once more to simple sleeping fires but still the final notes of flute drifted off when she motioned inside his tent and the body was discovered within.

"We'll set guards, my lady."

"They should already have been in place."

The soldier nodded, bowed to Kit.

"Have the body removed and burned with the rest."

"And have his tent moved from the fringes of the camp to its center. Harder to go through an entire army than sneak in through the back."

"Eli—"

"You've your orders, soldier."

Kit's protests were ignored, as was his glare as his guard fell in around them as they walked from the camp and to the promised pool at its edges.

THEIR RETINUE BROKE apart at a sharp slash from their Captain's hand. They left him and his elf to travel to the hidden sanctuary unmolested, standing far enough back to afford privacy while still maintain their guard.

Eli walked until the water lapped at her boots before she stopped. The surface was unbroken by ripples, no fish or fly awake so late at night.

The rock face no doubt fed fresh water to the pool after storms, but laid quiet now, rain having withered away during the heat of late fall, the promise of winter not far off. Likely the pool was fed by an underground source as well. He couldn't be bothered with worrying whether he should search for the spring or not, not when she turned to him, fingers spread to cast them in shadows, hide them from their bevy of attendants while she silently began the process of stripping him from his armor, and he turned his thoughts to aiding her in the same.

He pressed his palm to the moonlit white scar of an arrow that had pierced over her left breast, the flesh revealed as her armor fell away. Kit still remembered the force needed to force the arrow through her back, the head serrated so it could not be pulled away.

She traced the line over his left side, the slash over his ribs, a lance having managed to pierce through his armor and slice at him before he turned enough to keep the point from piercing deeper. Her indrawn breath was enough remonstration to the sword slash that blazed from his hip down his thigh, a maiming strike if not for his armor. She tsked at those, but he didn't have the energy to listen to her admonishment, or she the energy to give one.

Her hand moved to his waist, wrapping her arm around his lower back as he wrapped his across her shoulders, turned so that they could take their tandem steps into the frigid depths.

He would have quaked at touching her so naked, having been touched the same, only a few years ago, before it became second nature to act as soldier on the field and nurse during the nights. His mother would not have understood, nor his father, if word reached the king of his son's actions. Only to see him now, his arm wrapped around a woman's naked waist, a woman not his wife or even his betrothed. He shouldn't find amusement in the situation. But it was easier to remember his mother's harsh voice and imagine his father's shocked expression than listen to the cries of the men around him.

Thank the gods his father never learned of Eli's visits to the sauna in naught but a towel and good humor. A birthday gift, though he'd never say the same aloud. Funny, that here, on his anniversary, with her arm wrapped more intimately around him than any other time, he felt less the cad than ever before. Surrounded by blood, it wasn't feminine curves he took comfort in, but the woman who bore them, the soul within the flesh.

The water was cold against his toes, yet it felt good on his sweat and blood slick skin.

It was a penance, for all those who would never bathe again. The morose thought diminishing his pleasure if pleasure was what he felt at the edge of the lake.

She led him forward, and he followed easily, moving in to the depth of his waist, the water covering her to mid chest. He could not imagine the cold was any more pleasant against her flesh than his, evident by the chattering of their teeth, but she said nothing of her discomfort, and he said nothing of his.

She shifted so that her front was flush against his, sharing his warmth. "I can heat it."

Such an innocent thing to do, such a comfort he did not deserve. Still, he leaned forward, his head just able to comfortably rest atop the crown of hers, strands of her hair tickling his chin where he rested. He felt her smile where her lips pressed to his chest. "Save your magic for the battle tomorrow."

"It would take very little magic to heat the water."

"Eli," this time he cupped her cheek, turned her face up to his, "leave it be."

Even in the darkness he could see the narrowing of her eyes, feel the pressure as her fingers dug into his hips in subtle displeasure. "This is not your fault, Kit. You did not instigate this war and you have done what you could to mitigate the casualties."

"I know, my lady. But their deaths will be on my soul regardless."

"They're on the hands of the Gouldarans who brought battle to our land."

"Yes," he could not help the pass of his thumb over the downward curve of her mouth, her teeth nipping at his skin in response. His breath hitched, but it relaxed the expression on her face, so he held his position, enjoying the press of her lips to his flesh. "But I am their prince and would honor their memory in whatever way I might." Her nails dug further into his skin, and then soothed the marks she left, accepting his will in this if in nothing else. The tension slowly faded into the water around them. He replaced his chin on the top of her head, eyes closing slowly in the dark of the night.

The water heated, not much, but enough that his teeth no longer chattered, enough that the numbness of his flesh slowly warmed. He did not gainsay her offering, grateful for it, though he wouldn't tell her such.

"Is the forest like this? Filled with fresh pools waiting to be explored? Hidden oases to retreat to when the outside world intrudes?"

"Not at all." She twined her leg with his, using his body as a prop to help her stand in the nearly too deep water. "Most of those hidden oases aren't so hidden. The young ones find them first, and adults aren't far behind. For all that we grow up quickly, children are seldom alone or unprotected." Her hand brushed over his arm, cupped water to wash the blood away from his skin. "When the children are gone, parents and ancients and those who've finished their assignments for the day use the pools to relax. Only the wind whistles through the trees then. Silence a commodity we are strangely loathe to go without. It is comforting, being a part of the natural world, forgetting for a moment that life will intrude eventually."

"*Eventually* always comes too soon."

"Too true, my Prince."

He settled his fingers at the small of her back, managing to keep his hands still from running over the delicate expanse of skin he couldn't see in the dark. Some of the scars he knew, scars that crossed her shoulders and spine and layered over each other. Apparently, elves were harsher task masters than any human soldier or commander could be. All the same, he knew the marks she bore, having bandaged lesser and greater lesions over the past years for her. He didn't allow his touch to linger.

She used his hold beneath the water line to tilt back, dipping her head beneath the waves created by their movements. Her hair too was second nature to him, the way the braid was pinned to her scalp by one barrette. He only needed the one arm to support her and it was simple to reach and let the heavy mass of now wet darkness unravel from her crown and drop into the water. She unbound the mass, strands floating around her head in a starburst while he stood before her, looking down.

She made quick work of washing what gore she could from her locks. He cupped the back of her head to help her stand when she was done, the curtain of her hair draping over his arm, down her back, the tips lingering in the dark surf. She didn't protest his aid in gathering up the heavy mass and wringing it of what water he could. He twisted the tail into a tight knot and watched her fasten it blindly at the back of her neck with the barrette he'd stolen before. A last lingering trace of darkness smudged her cheek, and he brushed it away, wiping the smudge of despair they fought against from her pale skin.

"The water runs clean from our washings, though we usually use the sand at the bottom of the pools rather than soap. There were times, as a child, when I would rub my skin raw with the harsher rocks, emerge pink and ugly from the depths of the pools."

"Never ugly, Captain."

She smiled, running her fingers through his hair, the clumped mess that it was. His eye was swollen. Kit couldn't recall if that was from the battlefield or the assassin, but it made no difference when her palm pressed to the bruise and her magic pervaded his flesh, a gentle coaxing of the blood to dispel, the muscles to relax. He couldn't explain it, the feel of the darkness stroking beneath his skin, holding him closer than even memories of his mother's hugs could, and yet so separate, so alien.

He obeyed the command of her magic, allowing himself to sink to his knees in the silt, the dark outline of her body sentinel before him.

When they had moved to shallower waters, he didn't know, but his head rested against the flat plane of her stomach now exposed above the line of the water. She cupped the liquid over his head. He closed his eyes to the thick trickles falling down his face. The salt of blood and tears lingered on his lips even after her dousing and he didn't wait for her permission or approval to dip beneath the surface and wash what remained away.

He didn't try to look through the dark murky waters. He didn't need to see seaweed or fish nipping at what floated free of his skin. The feel of slimy vines wrapping his flesh, scales brushing against him, was enough sense without sight added. Already it took more will than he thought it should to remember the hands that grabbed him and held him beneath the surface were made of vegetation and not the souls of those sent to the afterlife.

She hauled him to the surface and he gasped out a breath, refusing to meet her gaze before pushing away from her and deeper into the depths of the pool. He wanted a moment to think, to process, to be alone. It would be so easy to slip back beneath the waves and-what? There was no escaping his reality or the nightmares that plagued his sleeping and waking life.

"Kit," she had to swim to him, unable to walk the bottom as far as he could, her arms displacing the water around her as she trod the surface once more a foot before him.

"We're clean enough now."

"Kit."

"Leave it be, Captain. The sun will rise soon. Best seek what sleep we can."

He did not offer aid in retreating to the lake's edge. He did not wait for her to follow as he stepped from the water and stared down at the pile of his bloodied armor and clothes. Her footsteps shushed over the sand beside him. She reached for her things first and he followed, only the distant sound of soldiers shifting guard duty, some rousing to begin preparations for morning rations, others grumbling as they went back to near quiet forges that made only the most rudimentary of repairs day to day. He slipped into his clothing, slung the armor over his shoulder, and walked back to the fray. She followed, another shadow keeping watch until the fighting began, and they were separated on the field once more.

IV

Months Shy of the Four-Hundredth and Eighteenth Birthday of His Royal Highness Prince Christophe de L'Avigne

KIT WALKED THROUGH the narrow aisle created by his men. Their hands were held to their sword hilts, their eyes cast steadily forward, his honor guard of thousands come to witness the dwarfish defeat. He didn't need to meet the gazes of his people to know the ache of exhaustion that suffused them all, the morose uncertainty that the dwarves hadn't surrendered only to attack when their shields were down. It would be like the dwarves to do such.

The prince made his way slowly up the aisle, no pretense of being unarmed as he stopped before the dais with the Dwarf king upon its back, his army kneeling behind him.

Kit waited until the sled pulled behind him entered the small clearing, delivering the bodies of both grandfather and son to the king upon the throne.

How many sons had the dwarves lost to this war?

So many of their children lost for greed. Had the fighting continued, Kit imagined that soon there would be no dwarfish men left to breed the next army sent to slaughter. Enough of Kit's own people laid dead in the fields that he feared similar repercussions. Humans bred slower, bred fewer, than their mortal counterparts. Neither nation would be the same, not for many lifetimes to come.

The sleigh with its covered bodies moved into the space between Kit and Torean Thunderclap.

When he was a young boy, long before Kit had met Eli or gone to war or anything else, he had heard stories of the Thunderclaps. The greatest of all blacksmiths in all the lands of Lornai. The king's name was Caerllion when Kit was born, and for all intents and purposes, the dwarf had been a fair and just leader. Rumor said he'd offered a sword for Kit's hand as a birth present, though the sword at Kit's hip was not dwarf made now. Once, Kit had learned the entire succession of the Dwarf kingdom, but the names fled him now, and did not matter when faced with the current king and his dead kin.

"As agreed," Kit said, nodding towards the cloth covered bodies between them. He offered no title, waiting to see if the dwarven king would honor the peace tentatively agreed between them or forego it now that he had his son and father back with him.

Dwarfish skill at crafting weapons was unquestioned. Dwarfish honor was not so trusted.

Torean stood. His sword made an eerie screech as he drew the blade from its metal scabbard and held the weapon before him as he descended his wooden platform.

There was a ripple of ringing metal behind Kit, soldiers arming themselves at the king's approach though Kit made no motion to reciprocate the dwarf's greeting, standing unconcerned at the man's advance. Torean stopped with a sword's length between them, a thrust of his arm enough to bury the blade in Kit's breast.

"It would be so easy to kill you and take everything you've taken from me over these terrible years. So easy, Prince."

"Would that you had not started this war then, and not been the cause of all the loss, Majesty." Kit matched the dwarf's incensed tone with calm. He hoped the morning light was too dim for Torean to see the clench of Kit's hand around the hilt of his sword; that the king would mistake the fear in Kit's shoulders for tension at the meeting. It was one thing to stand openly on a battlefield, sword at the ready, waiting to die, and another entirely to affect indifference when an opponent was armed, and he was not.

"You killed my son."

"I fought for my life against your son as he fought for his. I proved the victor."

The dwarf surged forward. His sword tip pressed beneath Kit's Adam's apple. Kit maintained his studied indifference. The new position of the dwarf forced Kit to tip his head back to meet the angry orange gaze, his own near seven-foot height slight when compared to the king before him who was at least a head taller.

Kit raised his hand, stalling the forward movement of his men whose energy surrounded him, begging to be released upon the dwarfs reneging on their talks of peace. "Drop your sword, King Torean. Or see your word broken and your life forfeit." Left unsaid were the words that even should Torean kill Kit, he would not leave the ensuing battle alive.

"So easy, and then I would not have to worry about your army any longer for they would die with you."

"The walls would fall. Not my people."

The blade pressed closer and Kit felt the skin-tight shield Eli had cast over him dent with the force of the sword trying to break through. He did not think the king realized the charm would protect Kit, at least long enough for him to draw his own blade and defend himself against the attack.

Kit met the man's gaze evenly, watched the king's face when he turned to look at the men at Kit's back, each with sword ready to defend, centuries of experience to bring to the field, while Torean's army was young and world-weary and defeated with the death of their prince who was their hope and now laid on a slab set before them.

Torean's sword dropped, the tip digging into the earth at Kit's feet. The king sank to his knees, resting his forehead against his hands which gripped the hilt of the blade.

"Take your people home, Torean. Cross Faoust and your border and take your people home."

A simple demand made from a man whose voice did not hold the weight of a monarch but of a general. Kit commanded they return from where they came, and the dwarf king rose, and motioned his army back.

It took several days before the treaty was finalized. Provisions and clauses and cessations and taxations were discussed and modified and organized between the King of the Dwarves and the Prince of Spinick.

The meetings ran late into the night every evening. Kit's advisors ranged the table on one side, Torean's on the other. They argued till their throats were hoarse, passed notes and plied pens until their fingers bled and still nothing seemed amenable between the two parties. Not until Kit remained in the small tent long after the rest of his men had left with only the dwarf king as company.

There was no reason to take a penalty of land from the dwarves. Faoust stood between the two countries, and even if the land seemed already to belong to Gouldaria or Spinick, it technically was neither mans to haggle over. Gold could be exchanged, but both kingdoms were rich and gold was not the commodity it once was. The dwarf had no daughters, and Kit breathed easier upon the knowledge, not having wanted to marry the woman but willing if it would save his people. They agreed upon a tithe, an exchange of weapon technology, the chance to learn from the other.

And Torean agreed that if he had contact with the shadowed man who had invited his armies to the border of Kit's land, he would inform the prince, and there would be a reckoning by both parties against their common enemy.

"You proved a stronger leader than I had thought to meet, Prince." The bear of a man leaned back in the high seat he used. No more than sixty, barely a child by Kit's standards, the king fought with the strength and knowledge of his forbearers and the wisdom of their stratagems to guide him.

But Kit had fought many long years against this king and his father and his father's father. The dwarves did not accept change well or often. They might vary their battle plans from generation to generation, but always they returned to similar tactics, and Kit reacted accordingly.

"Your guns nearly undid me, Your Majesty."

"Aye, nearly undid myself with them as well. And your men improved readily enough upon the design."

"Yes, not soon enough though." True. The war had turned bloodier, uglier, as the canon turned from unwieldy canisters to slimmer, personal implements of death. "We tried to make the compound on our own, from elements we knew of here on our continent, but found nothing to match the chemicals in our lands."

"Nor we, though with the trade routes to Kirbi, we had no fear of a shortage of supply."

"Not until they began supplying us as well."

"And not until you sent your navy to block our ports." A burly hand reached for a glass of wine lingering on the table between them, the heavy, earthenware jug of sweet red was much lighter than when the evening started. "If I had not fought you, Prince, and you not taken my son's life, I might have found you a true companion for my people."

"If," Kit laughed without humor, reclining in his own chair, hands hanging limply off the edges of the armrests. "There are far too many *ifs* to play that game, my lord. They date far further back before your birth than you likely even realize and will remain long after your death."

A snort, the tired raise and lower of the glass to lips purpled by the drink he gulped; and Kit watched the king opposite him and tried to hate the man and felt only sorrow at all that had occurred between them. Poor bastard hadn't even been alive at the start of the war, didn't even know why it had happened, and never would. Kit never would for this king's father had died, and the king before that one had died, and the first king of the fighting had died with no one the wiser but the hint of a shadow moving at the fire's edges, nudging a warrior race to battle with the promise of a kingdom in return. The warriors were dead, and those alive returned to the same kingdom they thought to leave.

"You still look so young across from me. I see you sitting there and cannot think anything but that you are the age of my son and I should not hate you for you fought for the same life that he was stripped of."

"I'm young, by my people's standard. Barely a third of my life gone before me, far too long according to most. But I am not your son, nor your son's age. Though a better fighter I'm hard pressed to name." A lie, for he could name one without thought, but it was a lie to balm a wounded soul, and he took comfort in the offering of it to the king before him.

"He was young and brash."

"And brave."

"What is bravery? What is bravery if not bringing the body of a man's son to his feet unarmed because his honor dictated it? What is bravery if not treating the enemy with the respect he would not have shown your corpse had the situation been reversed?"

"Bravery is none of those things. Simple stubborn pride, I'm afraid."

"Pride," the king sat forward, replacing the cup on the table, taking the pen with its inkwell and pulling the harshly scrawled treaty before him. "Pride would see this shredded and the fighting resumed." His signature was a quick flourish which left a black slash across the page that Kit couldn't read in reverse and which he doubted he could decipher when looking upon it right side round. "That," he nodded to the document which he pushed across the table and which Kit took humbly in his hands, "is bravery."

"Peace always is."

The pen was surprisingly light in Kit's hand. A thing of such weight, signing a treaty that decided his and his peoples' fates for a hoped for long time, should feel heavy, but the pen was light, and his name in black ink was a surprisingly simple mark to make. He scrawled his name in more legible letters beneath his signature. This document, scratched out and scribbled upon, not meant to be binding as details were discussed and dismissed, was now a thing of great weight between two countries long at war. It promised peace, and aid, and reciprocation of the same. It masked despair with hope though no nation, no man, who fought would be fooled by the flowery words and platitudes within the document. It bound both parties to their own lands, and any trespass an opening for swords to sing once more. But it was a peace, in which neither country gained or lost anything to the other. A nearly two-hundred-year war waged for nothing. Kit lived. And both sides had lost too much.

"I think, Prince, I will always hate you." The man's fingers smoothed over the tattered edge of the table. Two hundred years the wood had withstood the test of Kit's temper and men's shouts and worse. Most of the details carved by generations past were gone, only splintering sides left of what was once a gorgeously decorated piece. Kit's father's war table, and now a table used for peace. Torean pulled back a splinter. Kit stared at the chipped wood held before the monarch's gaze. "No matter what logic says, I think I will always hate you for your part in this war, for your survival."

Kit met the king's stare. "As I you in your place, Your Majesty." He replaced his pen upon the table, noting absently the drop of black that smudged the curling loops of his last name. Just another smear on the page to match all those that came before it. Kit found he didn't care what the parchment looked like, only for what it said. "But I will not hate you enough to throw my people back to the slaughter."

He pushed the treaty to the middle of the table, watched the king's gaze glance towards the black words and letters and the power they held.

The king blinked, and Kit watched the struggle on the man's face, the lips that trembled away from a snarl, the eyes that squinted and blinked more rapidly than natural ease would allow. There was a tick at the dwarf's temple, but Kit didn't reach for a knife, or shift from the table, away from the document sealed between them. Shoulders tensed and pushed deeper into the hard chair at Torean's back to keep himself equidistant from the truce as Kit held himself. "Yes, I will struggle not to hate you enough as well."

The cost of the words was great. Kit recognized the pain of a father speaking to his son's killer. It was a bitter reality to accept. But Kit did not break beneath the harsh king's stare, for he too would do what he must for his people. Men died at war. Gods, but it took the signing of a treaty opposite a man who truly hated him, to learn that most difficult of life lessons Eli was always arguing with him over.

His men had died to save his life. Even now, his men laid in tents waiting to be tended by healers too tired to do more than offer a hand to hold as they passed from this world. Supplies were low, spirits the same.

He had killed men to save their lives.

"No disrespect, my lord, but I hope to never see you again, just as

I hope that our nations might find a more amicable accord in later years."

A nod in response. "You will see my heirs'—" Torean stumbled over the word "—reigns; you will remain long after I am gone. Perhaps one of them will find a way to forgive what I cannot, no matter the peace between us."

"I expect no less, Majesty."

Kit did not offer his hand for the king to take, would not insult the man by forcing him to touch that which had stripped him of so much.

He was raised a prince. He was raised to be a dignitary. He did his job as he had as a soldier on the field of battle. Here he made peace and not war. "We will see your people across the border come the morning sun."

Torean nodded though he did not tell Kit the escort was unnecessary. He took with him a father and a son lost to this world. Kit returned home scarred, but hale.

The king stood.

Kit remained seated, the dominant power in the room.

It was with a heavy exhale that he shut his eyes when the tent flap fell closed, and Torean was gone from his sight.

A sennite to come to terms.

Gods above knew how long the journey home would take.

He tipped his head back against his chair. The thick wood was uncomfortable but served well for a pillow as the first rays of sunlight slipped through the opening of the tent with the black shadow come to find him.

"I did not think he would sign."

"Nor I." Kit's blurred vision found her slim form as she knelt at his side, took his hand in both of hers, soft leather gloves stroking over his skin. "How is he?"

Her lips turned up, knowing he did not speak of the dwarf so recently departed of Kit's company. She turned his hand over, palm to the ceiling. Her fingers traced the deep lines in his skin. Calluses born of training with her so very long ago, honed by years holding a blade in defense and death, soothed beneath her touch. Were she barehanded, her skin would be as harsh as his. But she wore her gloves and he knew it was so that her touch upon those she could aid went unnoticed, could be passed off as those of a healer and not the warrior she was. "He'll live. Annoyed, and bitter, but he'll recover, given time."

He blinked, watched the darkness behind his eyelids. "We are at peace. He shall have all the time he requires."

She did not mention that peace meant little when the attempts on his life would continue regardless of war or not. Now the assassins would just have to be more creative of how they attacked him, rather than finding their paths on the battlefield.

He stretched his legs out before him, ankles crossed beneath the table. Her head lowered until her thick crown of hair tangled between his fingers where she rested against his thigh and he stroked her curls back from her face. She would wake long before anyone entered the tent to spy on them. And the sun was rising. Whatever rest they found would be short in the taking. He doubted any would disturb him until he rose and welcomed the attention himself.

An escort for the dwarves. An escort for his wounded and his soldiers. An escort home, blessed home.

They were finally, blessedly, going home.

V
The Three Hundredth and Eight-Eighth Ball

THE JOURNEY BACK to the capital took a month and a half to make.

Kit ensured that all the injured were attended to, not a man left behind. He walked beside his horse, having harnessed the animal to a cart, ensuring that Marius was cared for and returned to the city the hero he was.

His commander had taken a lance the final day of the conflict.

The tip had been aimed at Kit.

Only luck had saved the man's life, luck, and Eli, dark magic swirling in her eyes, while she pressed her hands to the wound in the commander's side and Kit pulled the blade from the flesh. The bleeding had stopped, and from what they could tell, any internal injury had been subverted, but Marius was weakened, and Eli insisted that though she might have staunched the wound, any strain could see her work subverted.

So, Marius rode in the cart, and Kit walked, willing to suffer the inconvenience in deference to honor those who had fallen in defense of his kingdom and those who needed the aid to rise again as heroes.

Eli travelled between pallets.

Kit didn't watch her; allowing her passage amongst the men without interference from him. When they stopped at night, she would slip into his modest tent, the war tent having been left at the field of battle, Kit not wanting the reminder of it at home, leaving it as a remembrance to all those who had fought and died that he stood with them, would stand with them again, as long as they needed him.

She would come to him at night, chills racking her body as she crawled into the bedroll beside him and he held her to his warmth while she wept. He dared not look in her eyes. He had learned, after the first such night, that the darkness rode her hard after her day spent with the injured, and the darkness was not the merciful master he would have wished it to be, as willing to destroy a spirit as it was to save. She protected him as best she could from her magic, the demands it made of her, and he offered what comfort he was able in turn. In the morning, her eyes would return to the bright green of spring leaves. The mornings that the edges of her iris remained black were the ones that she left him riding a wave of anger and returned to him looking as bloodied and haggard as any day fresh from battle.

He offered himself as her beating post. She railed against him, cursing and yelling until finally she fell silent and he held her. The energy she loosed left her limp in his arms and he cradled her through the night, wiping her brow when the fevers began, wrapping her in blankets at the chills. The strain of channeling her magic the morning after was that much harder for her, but there was a peace to the actions that most days she couldn't find.

The ebb and flow of the darkness of her aura let him glimpse the magic of her people, and the agony of wielding it. He said nothing, not offering platitudes for a duty she believed was her own, even as he knew that without her they would have been lost and the duty was his that she took upon herself. He held her, and offered what comfort he could, and it was enough as she went about her mission to save his men and he marched the injured home.

THEY REACHED THE outskirts of the city on the day of his birth.

People cheered in the streets, riotous cheers, welcoming him home, the army home, their brothers and fathers and cousins and husbands amidst those slogging the long road to the capital.

The soldiers cheered, free to run to their families now in sight, relieved of their duty though unable to forget the horrors they'd seen. Many walked the whole way with their prince and his guard, all the way to the steps of the palace, honoring his courage in leading them, Kit honoring them as he stood on the steps of his home and bowed to their bravery and fealty. It was unprecedented, and yet he knelt for those who had fought for him and those who had died for him, and the nobles who had come to witness his triumphant return were obligated to follow suit, kneeling in their clean breeches and intricate court dresses like their prince. He could hear the grumbling, most of the dandies not understanding what the cost of war was, held home, safe from the fighting, for their families' sakes. Kit felt no kinship with them, even as they vied for position at the ball that night.

Uncle Kravn stood as an ambassador, having been recalled from the field of battle as he was old and better used as an advisor rather than a soldier. He did not bow when Kit led the movement, but it was not expected of him as the second in line for the throne should Kit fall. Kravn wished Kit a welcome return, though the smile did not reach his eyes. Kit did not fault the man his hard heart. They were all hard after the fighting.

King Leon waited at the top of the steps, head bowed in support though as the king, he too remained standing tall. He embraced Kit upon the stairs and opened the palace to the soldiers and the peasants and any who wished for a birthday celebration unlike any other.

The prince was home.

The walls still stood.

The cheering deafened Kit as he stared at his father, and the thought of celebrating anything turned his stomach, threatened to unman him in the streets as his soul begged for quiet and was met with another battlefield, this one filled with fans and court dances, as deadly as the fighting. Not to his person, no, but to his soul.

She did not join him in the sauna as he prepared for that evening.

She did not join him the night after, or the third night of the ball, and he fought to find a smile that did not appear as weary as he felt while he danced with pretty miss after pretty miss and his tired body begged for a respite that was not coming.

Each night he returned to his rooms, the bed too soft after a lifetime of hard camp cots. He stripped off his velvet doublet, the silk shirt and fawn breeches. He stood at the window in his bedchamber, naked to the moonlight streaming through the glass, letting the gods above stare upon the bruises that discolored his skin, the bandages he'd not revealed, knowing others more injured than himself. He washed his flesh with the water in the pitcher left on his dresser, scrubbed with the cold, trying to remove the memory of blood from his skin.

IF HE MADE it through a night without waking in a sweat, he didn't remember it.

The slightest sound of a knife cutting meat or being removed from a sheath made his muscles tense in anticipated horror, waiting for the fight to begin again.

He ached to the deepest parts of his soul and found no relief.

She appeared as tired as he, always running from one meeting to another, a valued advisor now that the war was finished. They broke pleasantries with each other, but little more passed between them.

Their stolen moments were a balm until she fled to another meeting, and he to his, the days passing in similar blurs.

She did not come to him for comfort during the black of night.

He dared not seek her out to relieve his own soul.

The year passed.

A year filled with dinners and praises and accolades that he was obligated to accept and begged leave to distribute to the soldiers for they were the true heroes. His generosity and humility were applauded, yielded yet greater honors and he longed to be left alone, forgotten, just another common guard instead of a prince.

The first night of the three hundred and eighty-ninth ball, he barricaded himself in his room. His barricade was pushed through and he was found on the floor of his bathing chamber, stomach heaving, chills racking him.

He was excused from his duties for the evening and told that the king wished him a speedy recovery so that he might dance with young daughters and sisters on the next night.

He was no better the next day or the one after.

The healer was called and pronounced Kit sick with an intestinal discomfiture. His father left his suite. Kit glanced at the healer, who patted his leg with a small nod, and left Kit to his solitude.

He remained abed.

It was not just soul sickness. Each beat of his heart strained, felt false, left him gasping, waking in the middle of the night feeling choked.

After a week, his father sent for the healer again, but it was Marius who came for him, forcing Kit from his room, from the palace, out of the city towards the edges of the Forest, the forest ruled by elves but used only by the city dwellers. The piece of land had been overrun by Spinicians long before Leon's time upon the throne. And no elf would dare take a life within their own woods if they could help it. The forest was a safe place, safer than palace walls, for a hunted prince to find a measure of solitude.

Kit and the commander disappeared into the woods for a fortnight to hunt. They killed nothing, riding the forest paths during the day, sitting around a fire at night watching the wood burn with cheerful flame enclosed by the silence of the trees. The outing centered Kit, calmed him.

She did not come for him the next year on his birthday. She had not broken more than the passing courtesy to him since his excursion with the commander. It was not that she was jealous. One cannot be jealous of something they don't know about or are not invited to. Kit would have invited her, but Marius disallowed the offering. He did not think her avoidance was disgust or despair but avoidance he couldn't deny.

The ball passed, the third in such disharmony, in such gloom for him.

She did not join him in the quite of the sauna, or in laughter at the dance, or after in the lists where his sword arm shuddered at the lifting of a blade even as he knew the importance of preparedness. So, he looked towards Marius and the hunt to relieve the pain in his soul, and rebuilt ice long since melted, the cold hurting more than it had the first time she had rebuked him.

He would not beg her audience. He was a prince and he had some pride after all.

The ache in his chest healed. After a time, more years than he expected, Kit returned to fencing and training and sparring and even managed a smile at the honing of skills long memorized against men just learning to fight with him.

She hid from him, and he hid from her and the memories of comfort in her arms.

He was cold, grew colder every time she passed him in the hall and all he saw in her gaze was vague recollection and he fought not to beg for his friend back. He'd accepted the offering once. He would have accepted it again.

But she didn't come for him.

Chapter Two

I

The Four Hundredth and Sixty-Ninth Ball

IT WAS NOT as easy as she pretended it to be. The pretending that she didn't watch him any time he walked in a room or stopped in the city streets to speak with a soldier returned home from the war, or a vendor thanking him for some such kindness or other. Nearly a hundred years, and it still wasn't easy pretending that he was a prince and she had no right to interact with him beyond her role as captain of his guard. He made ignoring her look easy, and perhaps that's why it was so difficult for her to accept that he no longer thought of her as his dance partner while she remembered too clearly, no matter her distance.

What had he asked her? Is it the chase?

Who would have thought that she was as likely to be caught up in it as he?

And damn him for giving up so easily against her.

She'd tried, over the past few years, to bridge the gap that had developed between them. A smile when she knew he was looking at her, a joke she told to make him laugh, that he ignored and failed to laugh at, a stumble when he was near enough to catch her…for his benefit, not hers, and he said nothing. Oh, he did all the right things, offered a hand to help her up, the silky court laugh that he doled out by the barrelful during the balls, a nod to acknowledge her smile though nothing more, no words exchanged beyond the pleasantries dictated by court procedure.

He'd not asked to partner her while fencing. He went earlier than her and left the moment she appeared. Her poor partners in the duels dealt with more than they bargained for when she took up her foil.

She stopped going after a while.

At least in the lists people expected the type of brutality she was capable of doling out and didn't flinch from the more aggressive rings of steal when her blade met theirs. The lists were the only reliable place to find her, if he was just bloody look!

The commander's rich baritone sounded from her left. "You'll scare all the good soldiers away at this rate, Captain."

She didn't drop her blade or turn her gaze from her opponent, keeping the young man in her primary sight even as she let the darkness that was part of her blood seep into the air, get a taste for the people around her and the battlefield she was stepping onto. It was one thing to say she was an assassin, another to say that she was a Servant of the Darkness, but to use the power inherent in her being was something different. She'd used it on the battlefield, and he'd seen her use her magic to heal.

Not Marius. She didn't care about the commander the way she did her prince. Kit hadn't shied away from her magic or her touch, had held her all the closer for it and maybe that's why she drew away so fiercely. He couldn't understand her. She couldn't believe he could understand her because if he did she would have no more reasons to put distance between them.

That he was a prince meant little to her. It meant something when she was of the Woods, but not anymore. He was a man and she was a woman and denying the fact that she was attracted to him had done nothing but make the ache in her heart grow the longer she stayed away from him. And damnit it wasn't simple attraction she felt for the blasted man.

Three quick passes and her opponent was on the ground and her sword was pointed at the man who'd started this tangle she now found herself in, her sparring partner ignored in favor of bigger prey waiting for her attention, standing too close for safety's sake when faced with her wrath.

Kit could handle the darkness in her.

His commander could not.

Four words in the back of a cart uttered on a pained breath as she pulled away from healing him: *Stay away from Kit.*

Four words that she'd taken to heart and obeyed because the commander had met her black pitch eyes and flinched at her glory, and she didn't want to see the same reaction some day when her prince found the courage to meet her gaze.

"Did you need something, Sir?" She kept her blade against Marius' throat for a moment longer, a moment of holding his stare, watching him flinch once again.

She dropped her sword and gave a half bow to her commander and there was no way the man could miss the sarcasm the gesture implied.

"I'll be in LarkTown for the ball. Though it is my duty this year, I was hoping you would be kind enough to take over my watch for the next few days."

They'd spent the last century alternating with each other which one of them would attend the ball as Kit's guard. He hated the festivities because Kit hated the festivities. He would never admit that he hated the ball for the same reason she did: that they were forced to watch the prince they cared for dance with anyone but them.

"An honor, sir." The words stuck in her throat. She hadn't planned anything for the three days off that she was supposed to have. She never planned anything, more often than not finding herself in the balconies of the ballroom watching from afar because Kit never looked up and she was safe to stare beyond his gaze. Being with him on the dance floor, so close and yet so far away, was worse.

"Good."

Nothing else, no final commands or orders to keep Kit safe, not to speak to the prince, to maintain proper protocol and etiquette, any of the other inane comments the man had imparted over the past years.

He said "good," and then he turned and walked away.

A soldier had a horse waiting and he insured that his carry bags were strapped tight to the saddle before mounting. "Try to enjoy yourself, Captain. It's not a punishment."

Bullshit.

Of course it was a punishment.

He found the fake smiles and meaningless platitudes as disgusting as she did.

Enjoy yourself.

Not a punishment.

He'd done his best to keep her from her prince for the past century. Was he finally repealing that decree between them?

Marius was already galloping away before she could ask for certain. He was beyond the far gate when she realized mayhap three days was truly not a punishment, but a penance from a man who couldn't allow that much at any other time. And if she was mistaken, there wasn't anything he could do that would hurt her worse than Kit's avoidance did.

She would go to the ball, as Kit's escort, because she'd been ordered to. And she would go to the ball because she was certain Kit would be in attendance.

Her saber swung back at her opponent who hadn't quite recovered from their last session of strike and parry. "I'll see to security, you ensure the prince reaches the ball timely."

Smart boy, to nod at her like he understood and obeyed willingly despite the terror of his gaze.

She lightened her voice, trying to still the ferocity of her command, make it lighter even if it was still serious. "Once you've managed that, I'll ensure the prince remains part of the dance. You're dismissed for the rest of the festivities, Khary."

This time the green tinged skin brightened, and a small smile turned the man's lips.

She considered telling the soldier he should use the time to practice training against a better swordsman or he'd fall on his first battlefield. He might not fall, but harsher truths had a better chance of reaching silly male sensibilities. And yes, she knew her sensibilities were not the most appropriate for a woman to have, but she'd been here quite a long time at this point. The men who served should be used to her by now.

She considered telling him and changed her mind.

Eli tossed the boy her sword. He managed to catch the weapon with only a slight fumble, and she smiled at his triumph before she left the training yard.

She hesitated at the door of her rooms, the small suite she'd taken for herself, made her own. There was a time when Kit used to bring her pots of flowers, small trees to decorate the corners of her chambers, allow her to pretend that she was back in the forests of her childhood rather than the walls of his people's hated city. Inside her rooms, inside her small closet, were her leathers and her uniforms and the few dress shirts and vests she consented to wearing with the skirt he'd bought her for "propriety's" sake. The only dress she had she'd worn before. If he recognized her in the gown, he would ignore her just as he had for the past balls she'd attended and dressed for a part she hated to play.

Not this time though.

She wanted to play the role she hadn't allowed herself since that first night. And for that she needed a dress that would buy her a minute of time to convince Kit to talk to her rather than stalk away leaving the divide to widen between them.

Eli passed her barracks, paused at the gates to the city proper that separated palace from shops, and took that step forward to find a dress to tempt a prince.

II

SHE FELT LIKE a fool.

The dressmaker had been kind enough to Eli after she recovered from her shock at Eli's presence in her shop. The woman had even gone so far as to offer a wary smile as she looked at Eli's sweat stained cambric and the linen pants that were easier to train in rather than full leathers and armor. Eli'd wanted to feel the bruises on her skin when her opponent landed a strike, any strike. Come to think of it, she'd not spent a day without gaining a new bruise for as long as she could remember now. Easier to ignore the heartache when her leg or her arm or her ribs ached from a particularly well struck attack.

But Amarice was courteous in that she hadn't said anything when Eli disrobed at the woman's request and said woman caught sight of the dark blacks and mottled yellows decorating her skin. There had been some whimpering, and then there had been soothing, like the seamstress was coaxing a wounded animal from the shadows.

That the analogy held weight did nothing to ease Eli's trepidation at being in the woman's dressing rooms, naked and waiting to be gowned.

And now here she stood, on the edge of the ballroom, glad that wearing masks was the fashion and that no one could see the panicked hysteria in her gaze hidden by the supple leather covering her face.

Blue.

A blue dress, nearly midnight in its coloring, but just enough color to highlight those odd shadows in her eyes, change the green to something darker, something different. Golden threads were sewn into weaving patterns over the bodice of the gown, ending just at the dropped waist, showing far more of her figure than most other women would be comfortable showing.

"Nonsense," the woman had said when Eli protested that the dress was too, well, that the dress seemed more suited to a harlot than a lady. She'd expected the seamstress to faint at her harsh critique, but the dressmaker only laughed. "A woman who is confident enough to walk around in breeches can wear this dress, and I will make it so that there is nothing indecent about it."

One dress, sewn onto her body, Amarice had said. No time to make it from scratch so Eli would have to bear the needle pricks if she wanted a gown in time for that night.

She nodded and was ushered from the dressing room to a small toilet with a bath, a young handmaiden ready to tackle Eli's red-brown locks and too dark complexion while the dressier made final adjustments to the gown.

If she heard "nonsense" one more time, she was going to murder someone.

But she'd been washed and braided and powdered and, fine, pampered, so that even knowing she was about to commit herself to a potential madwoman with needles, Eli had stood upon the stool and found herself content to be there.

Now she wasn't so sure.

To be fair, the gown turned out well. The fitted bodice, more a corset without an overtunic, had simply expounded upon the curves she usually hid behind loose fitting shirts and wrapped breasts for fighting. The gown allowed for none of that. Beading along the neckline caught the light and glinted like sparkling suns. The fabric covered her bosom enough that she wasn't flashing anything inappropriate to anyone and, as she'd seen since she arrived at the ball, most women had chosen to wear clothing designed to flaunt said same assets.

Hers was the only dark gown though. The first ball had been pastel colors and intricate décolletages. Trends had turned towards jewel tones lately, sapphires and rubies and amethyst silks. So, though her gown might not have been indecent, the color certainly proclaimed her as something unique among the fluttering ladies of the court.

And that was only the top.

Rather than round bell skirts layered with tulle and hoops, the hem of her gown fell in a simple line, as straight to the ground as the bodice was to her top. But when she moved, the fabric flowed in a rippling pool of silk, flowing over the ground so that the shape of her legs were defined for brief glimpses against the fabric while hidden behind the color, left to the imagination beneath the cloth. The small train of the gown threatened to trip the other courtiers who passed her by, but they seemed as wary of ruining her dress as she was of interacting with them.

And where was the bloody prince?

Her hands were starting to sweat.

When she left for the evening, and the festivities were done, she'd have to cut the laces that sewed the dress together. She didn't know how or why Amarice had made the dress the way she had, but Eli'd been told that there was no other way, that a dress like this could only be worn once before losing its awe, so it wouldn't matter in the end.

Eli's response that she needed the dress for the three nights of the ball left the woman in tears.

"I've never had such a woman to design for." "Please, the other nights, you come to me, and I'll make you dresses no one has ever seen and everyone will envy." "Your wearing the gowns will grow my prestige. Pay me what you can, and I'll take the ensuing commissions as the rest of your compensation."

Well if he didn't come to the damn ball like he was supposed to tonight she wasn't going back to the woman to waste another day being tortured with straight pins just, so she could be some sort of fashion pallet for the rest of the court.

"His Majesty, the King, and His Royal Highness, whose Birth We Celebrate, Prince Christophe!"

She turned her head to the stairway and watched with the rest of the nobles as king and prince stepped into the ballroom and smiled at the gathered crowd.

Kit's lips turned up in his court mask, his gaze roaming the crowd before stopping, finally, on her.

She was not some ninny to go dry mouthed at the sight of him.

She was not some girl of two hundred years anymore staring at the most handsome man she'd ever seen. She'd seen him every day, even if just in passing, for nearly the past three hundred years. That he managed to make her as stupid as the boys in the barracks fresh to the court, made her smile turn deadly and his head cock at her feral show of emotion.

Shit.

That would have given her away for certain.

The court smile turning his lips grew a little warmer, and her blush deepened beneath the candelabras. Maybe he wouldn't see.

She listened to the swoosh and sweep of skirts over the parquet floors, boots tapping as people parted around her. Eli kept her head down, not wanting to look at the commotion she could only imagine occurring around her.

The black boots stopped before her gaze.

She sank into a low curtsy, managing not to wobble on the heels the dresser had insisted on and the fact that while the skirt moved with her, there was not enough fabric to allow a full descent to the ground. Not that she need worry, since his hand caught her elbow the moment she started the move forward, keeping her standing rather than allowing her to show obeisance.

"Let's not provide any more of a show, Captain."

The blush flared fast again. She kept her eyes steadfastly trained on the little buckle at the top of his boot.

He stepped closer and she shifted position, shoulders unconsciously pressing back as her spine straightened in the posture for a waltz and the first strains of music reached her ears. She didn't look up as he took her arm to lead.

It was instinctive to simply step into the dance with him, and the steps hadn't changed that much over the years and he led well enough that she didn't stumble over the ones she didn't know yet. Her eyes closed when he dipped her over his arm, closed so she would not be trapped in the grey of his gaze.

"Tell me, Captain," he spun her and her skirt caught around his legs in a gentle caress before she turned back to his arms. She'd heard the catch in his breath at the motion. "Tell me," his voice was deeper, making the leaves in her stomach rustle, "if you refuse to look up, how will you protect me from any threat that should emerge here in the ballroom?"

Her gaze snapped to his, the court smile back in place though his eyes held more warmth than he normally displayed for his partners.

Her lips curved to meet his small grin, relaxing in his arms, allowing him to break the tension between them. She knew better than to expect it to last, but she appreciated it all the same.

He'd made her laugh the first time she danced with him too, told her to relax or her face might break she was concentrating so hard.

"Is it the dress?" His hands moved to her waist, lifting her in time with the dancers around them. "Honestly, you snuck into your first ball, wore trousers to the last interminable number, but you won't meet my gaze tonight. Does wearing a dress discomfit you so much?"

She grit her teeth, turning her head to the side as they promenaded across the floor. "You try being told you'll *be the center of attention* after a lifetime of being the assassin in the shadows. It is not pleasant being brought to the spotlight."

He laughed at her, the sound tinged with the fake gaiety she'd come to expect from their interactions, though his hand squeezed hers where he held her, and that was a bit more that he offered her than any other noble of the court. "Tell me, my lady, what would you offer me if I plead illness so that you might be excused from your duties a mite earlier than the end of the ball? You'd be able to get out of this damn," he seemed to stumble over calling her gown a gown, as stunned as everyone else was at her dress, though the hand at her waist stroked over her side, dangerously close to inappropriate areas considering his people's reservations about what was considered acceptable personal interactions.

"Hmm," she made the sound knowing he would sense the lie in it, the lack of shrewd calculation that it usually implied when any other woman tempted him. His smile lost a little more of its brittle charm, bordering on being giddy if she had to guess. "Your father would have my head if you did that."

"He doesn't know who you are, Captain. His precise words were: *If you don't dance with that princess, I will geld you, boy. See if she likes older men*." He clicked his tongue, a nervous habit the king had that Kit and she had laughed about when they were less inclined to silence.

"I think I should be flattered?" She looked over her shoulder at the king as she made the remark.

"I certainly would be in your shoes." He glanced at her face, and she glanced back. "Speaking of shoes, you don't have boots on underneath this dress, do you?"

She was tempted to step on his foot and show him what type of shoe she wore, the snide tone causing blood once more to rise to her cheeks. She detested blushing.

The last strains of the waltz ended, and he stepped quickly away, leaving her no chance to react to his comment, no further time to speak to the man she tried her best to ignore. She tried to hide the sudden hurt welling inside her at his retreat, until he dipped into a low bow, his hand brushing aside the drape of her skirt to prove she wasn't wearing boots beneath the gown.

Oh was she tempted to stomp on him. It took all she had to simply return the adieu without growling. Her expression was apparently not polite enough, if his laughter was any indication.

He stepped close enough to lean towards her ear, ostensibly to be heard over the resumed music of the orchestra. "Too many teeth, Captain. That's a snarl, not a smile."

She snapped her teeth together, close enough to his ear that he had to have heard the sound. "Better, my prince?"

He laughed, a woofed burst of noise she doubted he intended her to hear.

He backed away, duties to the other women around them, but kept his eyes on her a moment longer and she realized that it was not that he was looking at the woman she was before him, but that he was remembering the woman she was outside these rooms. Remembering the soldier and doing his best to forget the waltz they'd just shared.

The smile faded from his lips. He still smiled, but the warmth was gone, the pleasure, a brittle mask on his face.

She wanted him back. She wanted her prince back, the prince she'd denied and—

"Thank you for the dance, Captain. I shouldn't think there will be any complications for the night. Please, enjoy yourself."

"Kit—"

He paused for a moment, and it took her that moment to realize he did not wish to stay his departure, but that he would not embarrass her further than she already had done for herself.

"I'm sor—"

He met her gaze, a hand raised to stop her apology that was to come. "Lady."

He wouldn't dress her down in this public a forum, just as those around her would know precisely what had caused that tone in the prince's voice.

A woman who overstepped the rigors of protocol.

They might like her dress, but no one would dare speak to her without the permission of the prince now.

She'd called him familiar before all these men and women. She'd taken liberties no one would dare take without his allowance. She'd just wanted him to stay for a moment more.

And she was supposed to protect the bastard, and most would step in her way to keep her from him if he was in need.

She let the smile fall from her lips. The slight slump to her shoulders straightened and she stood the few inches taller than any other woman in the crowd and met the men's eyes around her without flinching.

First, she was a captain of the prince's guard, one of the very few trusted implicitly with the prince's protection. Second, there was glory as a soldier, but she'd lived as an assassin long enough to know the glory in darker works too. These peoples' pity and scorn held no impact for her. She was her own person, and she was stronger than they were.

Funny, how she'd never realized how the bleeding of her heart hurt so much more than a flesh wound.

She wasn't going to leave the damn ball for being snubbed, not until he told her to leave—

—and then she'd come back in breeches and a man's shirt and see if he preferred being guarded by a guest or a soldier.

III

HER FEET HURT from the damn shoes. The dress was so tight that she couldn't slip the edge of her knife into the seam beneath her arm without the worry of nicking herself in the process. Not that she'd tried; she didn't have a chance to try yet.

No, for perhaps the first time in his lifetime, Kit remained on the dance floor and part of the crowd till the very last person left, and they only left because the musicians couldn't play a melody any longer.

She stood in her slippers, at the edge of the king's dais, hands behind her back as the final lady sauntered from the room, waving to Kit as the doors closed behind her exit.

As the night wore on, Eli had drawn shadows to her, dimming the brightness of her dress, hiding her in plain sight as people moved towards the light and she seeped deeper and deeper into the darkness. Not just her body either. The longer she stood watching that fake smile and those elegantly spun turns, the blacker her thoughts became. She wouldn't hurt him, much. Just a small knock the next time she caught him sparring, because it wouldn't be with her, oh no, not with her. Maybe on a short parry, she'd trip and knock him off-balance so that his opponent scored the hit and he lost the bout. That wasn't enough, but it was a start.

"Are you planning to murder me in my sleep, or pummel me into the ground upon the battlefield?"

"We're not on a battlefield, Highness." She clenched her jaw to keep from sneering.

"Ballroom, battlefield, they're close enough."

“I’m not planning on killing you, Prince. And I don’t want to see you on another battlefield.” The second slipped from her lips unconsciously. She hadn’t meant him to know that thoughts of him during the war still haunted her dreams, terror of losing him too close whenever she closed her eyes. “Are you ready to retire for the evening?” Overly solicitous and polite, her smile was as brightly false as his.

“No. If you’ll follow me please.” The softly worded request was more command than anything else.

“My orders were to tend you during the ball and see you safely to your chambers come midnight. We’ve passed midnight, my lord.”

“Then I relieve you of your duties. And since you are now free of any commands concerning my apparent wellbeing, I should like a word with you in private, and as a free soldier at the prince’s command, I’m sure you will be more than willing to oblige my brief request to converse. So follow me, and let’s get this done.” He held out his arm as he would for a noblewoman needing an escort and she didn’t try to hide the scoff of her lips. “Take it,” he said before she had a chance to argue against him.

Her foot touched the floor and she leaned forward into the step, gasping when her legs buckled from standing motionless for so long, when the numbness of her sore feet was replaced by the fire of blood flowing back into the abused appendages. Only her grip on his arm kept her upright, and then only with his shifting to help her lean on him further.

She shook while she used him for balance and removed the first gilded shoe from beneath the hem of her gown. “Damn—”

“FIRE! The doors are on fire!” The alarm sounded throughout the palace, the voices of the guards picking up the warning and yelling it along. Even behind the thick shield of the ballroom, the words resonated.

The smoke billowing into the room was notice enough though. For the ash to thicken so quickly, an accelerant must have been used, no accidental flame from a misplaced candlestick.

Kit stared at the black fog and she searched the windows in the hall for an exit that would not strand them on a balcony far too close to the blaze.

"Behind the throne."

She kicked off her other shoe, stumbled as he hauled her towards the hidden doors and they escaped into a smoke clogged hallway with another fire merrily eating the portrait of the king hung upon the far wall, black billowing from the door opposite, no escape.

The shoe in her hand served as an adequate projectile to break the glass of the window looking out on the back gardens of the palace. She stepped through the broken glass first, ensuring that no one was there waiting for the prince to emerge. There wasn't, but instead of following her through, he came at her back and lifted her from her feet, carrying her and her unwieldy train free of the palace walls and to the railing that overlooked the tree lined paths of the estate. Her cries to be let down went unheeded, and it wasn't until he settled her on the low stone wall that he let her go, knelt at her side and lifted her bare feet from the ground.

He hissed, and she knew better than to look.

The pain of glass slicing into her feet hadn't registered when she took the few steps outside, but now that she was motionless, the ache was worse than just the soreness from her shoes.

Kit pulled the dagger from his hip, not a showy knife like the sword he'd worn the first ball. This was a true weapon that could be turned to deadly purpose if needed, but instead he set the edge of the blade to her skirt and began tearing strips from the supple material and laying his liberated prizes across her lap as she stared down at him. When he finished, he handed her the knife, a prince acknowledging a soldier's commitment even as he went back to examining her feet, fingers pushing on the gashes and plucking out the embedded shards of glass while she kept watch around them.

Guards came rushing from the side of the palace, skidding to a halt on the tiles where Kit knelt with Eli above him. He turned his head to them, and Eli continued her sweeping stare around the estate, looking for whoever had set the fires. There was no chance that the painting had caught light on its own.

"Was anyone injured?" Kit's voice sounded strained, but he kept to his task, binding Eli's feet in silk, never looking at the men flanking him.

The response hesitated, and Eli looked at the man, wondering why he would pause so. The soldier's gaze was not on his prince but on her, and she remembered too late the mask covering her face, hiding her person from those who would guess her name.

The soldier answered before she could speak to relieve him of his doubt. "No, Sir. Everyone is out of the palace, and the king has been taken to safety. The fires are being managed, but the ballroom suffered great damage as did the hall towards the residential wing of the palace. Whoever set the fires…Sir, we think they were after you."

"Of course they were. They failed. Find them before they try again."

What an asinine comment to make. Who else would the fires have been meant for? That Kit responded with so little decorum proved he was under no illusions as to the attempts on his life, and that he had no patience left for those thinking him oblivious to the trials his life proved.

The men milled for a moment more before scurrying off, obeying his commands. Eli motioned for two of the soldiers to stay with them, and they frowned at a courtesan ordering them about. Kit's fingers pulled the mask from her face, though he gentled the touch when her hair pulled with the removal, a brief flash of apology in his eyes at the rough treatment though it was quickly overcome by the strain of their circumstances.

Her men obeyed her instructions more readily at her reveal, none commenting on her dress or daring ask after her motives before the prince. They did not know him the way Eli once had. She nodded, and the two joined her guard while the others dispersed.

She'd have to see a healer, and the longer he touched her feet, the more the pain spread. She doubted she'd be able to walk after much more time, but she wasn't going to be a girl in front of her men.

"Have the rooms within the palace been compromised?"

"I don't know, Captain."

She nodded, and Kit stood. Without ceremony or hesitation, despite the protest that slipped past her lips when she realized his intent, he lifted her into his arms and strode off towards the barracks.

The men followed behind them, and Eli held her tongue. She'd let him have his moment of authority.

At the door to her quarters, he turned and stared at her soldiers, her body still cradled gently by his strength, held more tightly to pass through the opening into her rooms. "What's your name?"

She smiled as best she could at the young soldier, the man hesitant before his prince for the first time.

"Khary, my lord."

Kit nodded. "With me, Khary." He motioned for the other man to guard the door.

His orders were obeyed, and Kit entered her haven with Khary close on his heels.

The door closed behind them. Kit paused long enough to tell the soldier to strip before carrying Eli to her small bed, the scent of damp earth and creeping vines suffusing her rooms. He laid her down on the mattress, not bothering to lower the blankets or tuck her in before he turned back to the main room and pulled the curtain she used as a substitute door down between her view and himself.

Muffled words reached her.

"Keep watch over the captain."

That did not sound confident, the order. It did not have the ring of authority her price's command usually merited. And yet footsteps sounded, and a soft "yes sir" answered.

She heard her door close and the lock turn. Two knocks and the sentry outside her room signaled his departure and she was left with a boy in the other room and her unable to get out of her damn dress.

She growled when Khary…

"Kit?"

"Keep your voice down, Captain."

He'd changed from his court clothes into the soldier's rundown uniform. The man had been in his night garb and simply thrown a jacket on top when the alarm sounded. Now Kit wore the striped sleep pants and green coat, chest bare beneath the unbuttoned linen.

"Did you send my man to die?"

"I hope not." He slid into her room, scratching at the stiff fabric of the coat before stripping it quickly from his shoulders, unconcerned with his modesty though perhaps he didn't realize his actions as such. "I sent him to act in my stead and spread word to the loyal to double the perimeter sweeps, especially near my rooms. He'll be guarded till morning when the deceit will be realized, but by then, if the assassin seeks to strike again, he'll find a trained soldier and a contingent of guards within the royal chambers and be caught in the act."

"And if the assassin, if there is an assassin and this wasn't some amateur on the attack, isn't fooled by your deceit?"

"Then he'll face you, and me. The odds are not in his favor."

"I can't walk. The odds are decidedly in his favor."

He stared at her, and she was glad that the leafy vines over her windows blocked most of the faint torch light from passing troops that would have revealed yet another blush across her cheeks.

He hung the coat over the chair in the corner, cracked his neck with a turn of his head, shook out his arms and stretched the kinks in his back. She watched, unable to tear her eyes from his bare chest, the faint lines of old scars she'd seen him receive, had doctored while in the field, bloody and bruised and still his friend. Sweet Night, she missed him as a friend, she missed that subtle intimacy that had been between them. Twice she'd rebuffed his affections, and she didn't know how to get him to look at her in the same light again.

He kicked off the low boots he was wearing. Apparently Khary hadn't been wearing socks upon rushing to his prince's defense. She never realized that feet could be so engaging, or that the man before her had such finely formed toes. That was a lie. She'd noticed everything about him over the centuries, but it was easier to forget when she was not near him all the time and he was overwhelming when they were so closely confined together.

"Are you planning on sleeping in that corset?"

Her gaze snapped to his. Like her face, his was shadowed and unreadable to her.

She should say yes, that the corset was fine for a night's sleep. He'd hear the sarcasm and leave long enough for her to figure out some way of destroying the dress to get it off herself. "The seamstress sewed it onto me. I can't get it off by myself."

He didn't ask what she'd planned if he hadn't been there. He said nothing except to look at the knife in her lap and move carefully towards her.

Did he think she was afraid of him?

Or was it simply an unspoken offer to leave if she didn't want his help?

"I can't stand, Kit."

She meant to call him "prince," truly she did, but his name came first to her lips, and he didn't seem to mind her calling him in the personal while alone in her rooms.

"Where were you planning to cut the fabric to get the dress off?"

"Side seams but I don't think I can wield the knife well enough not to cut myself."

She watched his nod of understanding, her gaze held by the twisting shadows crossing his face.

"Raise your arms, Eli."

She obeyed.

He squatted before her, took the knife from her lap, and went to work on the seams of her gown. The right side gaped open, and she crossed her arms over her breasts to hold the dress to her. For the Dark's sake, he'd seen her nude before, but that had been during war, when it was not a personal moment, when he was not in her chambers and it was not after a dance and she was not desperate to bridge the gap between them.

His head tilted down. She watched his shoulders shake and prayed it was with effort to keep from looking at her, that it was still desire she would see in his gaze if she managed to catch it and not some other emotion.

She heard his breath, watched the knife rise between them, hover at the side of her hip where bodice and skirt met, before snicking at the fabric unsure of how to proceed.

"If I slit the side of your skirt, you can step out of it and you won't have to destroy the other seams."

She didn't remind him that she couldn't stand and that no matter how he cut the dress, the best she could manage was a roll from its confines.

She didn't think his words were asking for a response.

He made the slice from waist to knee, knee to foot, peeling back the edge of the dress to ensure it was cut through.

Her leg looked pale in the black of the room. She recovered the exposed skin, never have felt embarrassed at the baring of it in the past, never as vulnerable then as now.

His voice was heavy in the weight of the dark. "Bed clothes?"

She was of the forest. Even if she didn't live within her woods, she was of the forest, and the fact that she slept with blankets on her bed that had been washed and bleached of any natural feel to them did not mean she forewent all of her heritage. She refused to sleep in garments that kept her farther from nature than she belonged. Fine, she had a nightshirt, but she didn't want to wear it tonight. She wanted to sleep beneath her canopy of woven fabric vines and pretend they were leaves cocooning her and feel his warm flesh at her back in the bed beside her.

He would never sleep with her.

So it shouldn't matter what she wanted.

"Top drawer, my lord."

"Not 'Kit' anymore?"

"Do you welcome the name then?"

"You turned from me, Captain."

She hadn't! She'd been told to stay away, and that obedience was the only option if she wanted to remain within the city walls and have any chance of seeing him.

"Nothing? Nothing to say to that?"

Anything she said would betray the command and that command would be questioned and she did not want to see Marius in trouble over it, knowing his feelings mirrored hers and that was part of the cause of his decree to remain aloof.

"I am Darkness, Kit. You're of the city, of the light. I—" she searched for a lie he might believe, "I didn't want you infected by the magic that was consuming me after the war."

"And now?" He stood, the blade pressed to his side, the hilt clenched tight in his fist while he stared down at her. "You came to the ball in a dress that begged the court to look and take notice and you said my name, not my given name, not my title, but the name only those closest to me use, and only in private, in the middle of the ballroom before hundreds of people. The story will spread that an unknown woman took that liberty with the heir to the kingdom and the best you can offer is that the magic inherent within you, that saved my people, is the reason for a hundred years of evasion but you chose tonight to repeal that lie?"

Damn it all, no, that wasn't what she was saying, and he knew it too. And how dare he call her bluff!

Rationally, her staying away and her using his name had little in common, but he was riding the edge of his enforced solitude, and she was desperate for the return of his company. A desire that had been denied, a companionship forgotten for a lifetime, broken by a name that was a plea for more than either of them knew how to voice.

The glass in the bathroom shattered and she grabbed the knife from his hand without thought. She threw the weapon at the door to the privy, using the magic in her to ensure that the blade flew strong enough to break through the wood and into the heart of whoever was on the other side of the portal.

A thump, and then silence. Guards began screaming in the courtyard, rushing to find the broken glass they'd heard, afraid to touch her door and alert any watchers to the significance of what was held within her rooms.

She stared at him standing before her, his hands supporting her bare waist where she stood to make her attack. Her feet were cushioned by the remnants of her dress fallen to the ground before her.

He stared back at her, his breathing harsh in the dark, as labored as hers. His words were a whisper in the dark. "You didn't give a reason, Ella."

Her answer was as quiet. "Because I am your soldier, Kit. And I am too close to you."

"You're my shield."

"Yes." She let the silence build between them. "What happens when you push me out of the way because your shield is meant to take a blow that you try to spare her from?"

"I wouldn't."

"No?"

"No." He stepped forward, closing the small gap between them, his heat wrapping around her, his chest pressed to hers, a delicious rub of flesh to flesh that was forbidden by his culture and as natural as breath to hers.

It would be so easy to rise on her toes and press her mouth to his, touch her lips to his and breathe in his air as he took hers.

She didn't remember raising her arm to wrap around his neck, nor him bending to lift her once more into his arms, carry her the scant step back to her mattress.

He laid her on the bed, and she stared up into the darkness that surrounded them and prayed the night lasted a few more minutes.

"It's the captain's room! The window is broken in the captain's room!" "Prince!" "Captain?" "Are you all right?" "Are you injured?"

Fists pounded on her doors, threatening to break the wood that gave her sanctuary.

He pulled the blankets over her body, tucking the covers around her for modesty's sake and retreated to the kitchen, though she thought his eyes did not leave her in the move.

She sat slowly on the side of the bed.

Her head was bowed when the guards swarmed her chambers and rushed to her bathing room.

"Well thrown, Captain." "Well done."

He stood in the doorway surrounded by guards who congratulated her on killing the assassin as a healer was called for and room was made for her feet to be tended.

Kit held her gaze until the guards ushered him from her quarters and she did not call to stop him leaving.

IV
The New Year

THE PALACE COURT was abuzz with anticipation for the Fire Night Celebration.

Every year, as regular as the Prince's Ball, was Fire Night, the celebration of the Longest Day.

Vellim Oncwihgt.

Torches burned from sunset to sunrise, helping the sun to shine all twenty-eight hours of the day.

She preferred Rashel Noie. The Day of Night. As a worshipper of the Darkness, it made sense that her kin was more attuned to the shortest day of the year.

But that didn't matter for this celebration, and as Eli walked through the torch lit paths of the palace gardens, long shadows cast across the tiled way, she knew it would not be a celebration for her this night.

Her father had come.

She felt the call to the dark trees at the end of the yard and answered.

No breeches or skirts. No boots to protect bare feet or bands to pull back fly away hair.

For the walk, she wore a simple robe, the material flowing around her form in black waves as she passed the fountains and the flowers and made her way to the one place not lit from within by fiery light. Her knives and swords remained in her rooms, a note, in case she lost.

"You've no voice among us to gainsay our contracts or the acceptance of them. We've been engaged to kill. We will honor the binding unlike you who betrayed everything to forego it."

"I betrayed nothing. The Dark—"

"Hold your tongue, Uustrama.*"*

Shit-eater.

Outcast.

She knew the name well. "How much to rescind the bargain?"

"More than a city spawn could barter."

Eli looked at the man who bore the title of Echisolos, her title, her father. Night's blood, he hated her, had always hated her, but now it was a darker, more violent hate in his heart.

"Name the price, old man."

His smile was bright in the pitch of night, white teeth snapping at her from his place hidden in the trees. Did he think he could tempt her to step foot on the forbidden paths of her homeland? Did he truly think her so dim as to risk all for his insults? "Your life."

"You can try to take it."

Her feet had ached, the glass slashes tender and standing in her boots nearly unbearable. But she'd stood straight on the road and looked out at the man who had sent his assassin to her room to kill her prince and met his eyes squarely. She would have killed him that night. She was numb enough to have killed her father who so callously wished her dead without a hint of regret. He'd said it wasn't the time. He'd said he'd call when he wished to end her humiliation. He'd said he would even offer her soul to the Darkness to be washed clean of her sins when he slit her throat.

Five months ago, and he called on the one day of the year the Night was least likely to answer Its servant's call.

Skill on the battlefield was already proven between her father and herself. They'd fought so many times over the years that both knew the strengths of the other. She was the stronger swordsman of the two. Of poisons, her father was a master and she but a novice. She could kill a man with a simple brush of her fingers to a pulse point along a wrist or arm, with a kiss to lips. He could spear a fly's wing with a knife thrown from two hundred yards away, an impossible feat he mastered. No, they would not fight with weapons this day, this night, but with the Darkness Itself.

She did not fear his magic. He should fear hers.

All must die.

A blessing and a curse, she knew. Death was sometimes a mercy, and sometimes a penance.

All walls must fall.

There would be nothing between their magic but the flesh they were born in; and the flesh would be the first to perish when their magic flowed.

For five months, she'd waited and resigned herself to having to kill the man who sired her.

And now, come the time, she didn't think she was ready, didn't think she could kill him despite the disgust in his gaze.

NO WORDS WERE spoken.

The Elichi and his witnesses approached her from the darkened tree line, circled her where she stood in the center of the path, the middle ground between palace and wood. He stood at the apex, directly before her, and she met his stare, unwilling to be the first to look away. There was a glimmer of fear as he looked at her, subtle, hidden beneath his hate. Did he think her easy prey? She hadn't weakened within the walls. She might have met him with a limp those months ago, but she hadn't weakened here with her prince beyond the trees' shelter.

He turned his back to her, and it was his steps that faltered though he tried hard not to show it.

He stripped.

She followed.

Two of the three watchers came forward to take his robe, the knives strapped to his calves and forearms. There was a reverence to the motions and she watched those who were her people as they ignored her. It took her a moment to realize it didn't hurt, to stand ignored amongst her kin. She'd spent more than half of her life in the city behind her. She retreated to the woods at the edge of the palace, throughout the kingdom, found a sort of peace within their dark shade, but she did not pine for the boughs of the trees; she did not let herself pine and felt no sadness at the realization.

The third witness came to her, a woman with eyes old as time itself.

Eli knew this face, the deep lines that marred forehead and made crow's feet at the corners of ancient eyes. The keeper of her people's history, the one who gave voice to the happenings within the wood, the Watcher of Souls. Quir. Annara had held Eli for her first scream in the world. This grandmother who had never claimed her yet stood witness today.

"Unto the death."

Yes, Eli already knew how the match between father and child would end.

Annara pulled threads of Darkness into her hands, met the cloth of Eli's robe at the shoulders, shredded the fabric with her magic, leaving Eli bare, as bare as the man before her, to the gazes of the witnesses around them.

The witch did not repeat her decree, and the new Elichi did not ask for the rules of the match, drawing shadows into his hands, twisting, writhing shadows, living shadows looking to tear flesh, taste the substance of blood which wraith was forbidden, into his hands before the Quir was safely out of the line of battle.

Eli watched the birthing of his ghostly creatures. Their arms wrapping around her father, petting and caressing him as their master while he drew more magic to him.

The creatures merged and grew, misted and solidified, lost their human appearances and manifested claws. Some broke free from her father's control, skipped playfully away down the darkened paths in the guise of shadow children, cackling instead of laughing, teeth bared in a snarl rather than an innocent grin. They raced towards the music of the festival drifting lazily on the wind. They raced towards the revelry that their malformed intent would destroy. It took less than a thought to send the phantoms back to the Void. But it was her magic that laid the creatures to rest, and his that lost control of more and more even as he rallied those beneath his thrall to attack.

He gathered the shades to him.

He gathered as much of the Darkness as he could control and command to him, and she knew.

Eli knew that even with their claws and with their teeth and with the madness he imbued them with, a thought would send the creatures into the Night, scampering away from her. She didn't need to call shadow to her spirit. She was the Shadow, the Elichisolos, the Mistress of the Final Midnight. The title was earned, yes, but she was born to it first, a mantel that she was always fated to assume. The thought did not bring her comfort. Knowing that Death had been her companion since her first breath did not soothe her soul for the lives she'd taken over the years or the life before her held in her hands.

For his life was hers, it was just a matter of when she'd take it.

Unto the death.

But perhaps she need not deal the final blow. Perhaps it was not a physical death that was required.

She took a step forward and the shadows swarmed towards her, thrown by his power, called by hers.

They formed a shield around her, whispering to her nightmares, watching her as she turned those violent, deadly scenes, to dreams of star lit fields with lovers running through tall grasses, shadows filled with glee racing for the peace she created rather than twisted with her father's magic. Their whispers faltered, changed, begged. She met the wraiths' gazes, turned towards them and beckoned until the swarm around her calmed to her touch, forgetting her father who was their master in favor of her commands.

She sent them back to the darkness, followed them into the Void and offered them shelter within the Nothing. Tiny hands devoid of sharp nails took hers as she led the shades into the ether, built them homes from blocks of Night dark brick, showed them fields in a forever twilight where they could dance and play.

Not all Darkness was an ending.

They whispered Queen, and she begged friend instead. They bowed, and she pet their heads in her passing. She opened a portal and walked through, stepped from the Dark to land a foot before the man intent on killing her. Not a single mark scarred her from his attack.

His eyes widened, and he stepped away, the emotionless mask of his face breaking with a flash of horror, hand raised to ward her off.

Eli followed, ignored the hand upraised, and cupped his cheek. Her touch brought with it easy access to his mind, allowed her to slip into his subconscious, into his dreams hidden deep inside, to his memories of a little girl who stared at the leaves swaying overhead and who danced to their rustling in the wind. She terrified him even then, his little girl, not his, the Darkness', with her leaf green eyes open wide as she listened to the Night only the priests were meant to hear.

She dipped deeper into his memories, the first time he brought her to the practice ring, handed her a sparring stick and she whirled the thin pole in the air with a speed and skill he'd yet to master. Eli had been terrified that day when she knocked her father to his back, knowing that she'd done what he'd asked of her, not knowing why he was angry over the accomplishment. She'd been seven years old.

The day she was born, he stood at the side of the bed holding her mother's hand while the Quir swaddled Eli in fresh cloths. The Watcher said that the little girl was a daughter of Echi, but he refused to hold his child. Cast was not determined at birth, yet there she was, Assassin claimed, and not even able to feed herself. The Priestosolos, her mother, wept. Her father denied paternity but was chosen to watch over the babe regardless.

She touched the memories he held and changed them.

Her arms wrapped around him when he collapsed, lowering them both to the ground where she rocked him, and his eyes looked into the past and remembered something new. She weaved midnight dreams of peace and comfort, a smiling baby without that odd awareness in her eye, a child who skipped at his side and danced with other children, not just the wind. Eli replaced the girl she had been, the woman she was, with something softer, something sweeter, something more to what he thought a child should be, and finally, with a feather-light touch, she made the woman in his memory die, her soul flowing back into the Darkness, never to trouble him again, at peace as he could now be at her passing.

"It is done. She has killed the memory of herself. She is dead to him. The challenge is fulfilled." The soft words echoed in the clearing. The old woman's voice proclaiming the outcome for the other witnesses to acknowledge.

Eli laid her father on the grass carpeted ground, folded his hands over his chest as he breathed easily, lost in his dreams until sunrise.

She turned to the ancient gaze staring at her, took the hand offered to help her rise.

Die aran. Little trickster. Red Fox. This woman had named her that, once upon a time. She had been the only woman to ever claim Eli as something than *other*.

"Thank you, Grandmother."

Tears beaded in the old woman's eyes, a strange fatality staring back at Eli. "Know that I wanted this."

Eli opened her mouth to question what the Watcher meant, but the spell struck too quickly, bowing her spine so that she was forced to fall away from the old woman who seemed to grow in a cloud of darkness, the lovely amber eyes of Eli's childhood turned bright red, an illusion but strong enough that she reached for a weapon she didn't have, fought the clothing of the Darkness around her the witch sent to attack.

A flash of metal sailed over Eli's head and pierced the gray fog looming over her. The dull wet thump of metal piercing flesh was loud in the silence of the clearing.

Eli scrambled to her feet, trying to scream to tell her guards to hold their fire, tripping over the ground as another arrow flew past her and her gaze followed the shaft to watch the fletching disappear into the darkness and the body hidden within the shadow began to fall.

"Stop!"

The soldiers continued to run towards her, three with swords drawn, one with bow at the ready, their heads on a constant swivel, watching the trees for any threat that might emerge.

She crawled over the soft earth to the quickly dissipating veil. Someone kept whispering "no," like the chant might forestall the inevitable fate. And it was inevitable. The first arrow had pierced Annara's stomach, the second a lung. If Eli were a healer, perhaps she might have saved the woman, but even healers could not bring back someone on the wrong side of the Night.

Annara brushed her bloody fingers against Eli's cheek, and Eli grasped the frail bones, so very frail in her hand, ignoring the tears in her eyes as she met the once more golden gaze of her grandmother, the warmth of magic that surrounded her in peace, clothed her from the eyes of the world, dimmed at Death's coming. "Iisfor—" The woman's fingers dropped from Eli's.

"Are you hale, Captain?" "Is she dead, Ma'am?" "She was attacking."

Eli bent her head over the Watcher, closed the dead eyes staring at her.

"She was attacking, Eli?"

She couldn't look at her prince as her tears fell and she held the one woman who had shown her kindness as a child, lying dead now in her arms.

V

ELI DIDN'T KNOW how long she knelt cradling Annara in her arms. Boots shuffled by and she knew the soldiers were keeping watch even as they left her to mourn in private. They, who didn't know why she cried, didn't understand tears for one of the woods, respected that need for silence, kept their distance from her, not like her prince who knelt before her, blocking most of the men's view of her face even if she hadn't asked for that courtesy. Her prince, who had not said two words to her since he left her room so long ago, offered his presence, his warmth, for her comfort.

The sun began its ascent, and she choked back her sobs, needed to move, to, to…

"Who was she, Ella?"

Ella.

He called her Ella when he forgot he was angry with her, when he forgot he wasn't supposed to grow close to her. The name was a comfort for her, a balm.

Whatever distance was between them, in moments, quiet like this, she was still Ella, and that thought brought fresh tears to her eyes, wanting that lost connection returned between them. She didn't ask for forgiveness. She didn't ask for his friendship. She didn't think he'd answer if she did. "The Quir. The Watcher of Souls."

His hand rose, stopped before he could touch her, dropped back to his side. "Who was she to you, my lady?"

She looked up to meet his gaze, holding tighter to the dead woman in her arms though she wanted the living man to take Annara's place, to hold when she felt the world shaking around her.

He looked over her shoulder before she could respond, and, with a small nod, two soldiers came to their side, kneeling for their prince's wishes. "You will treat the woman with the respect due her. Laurel boughs to line the cart, a shroud over her face. Bring her to the edge of the Dienobo and leave the cart to the Children of the Wood. They'll take care of their own once you're gone."

"Sir." There was a small hesitation in the soldier's voice, but it quickly yielded to their prince's command, unquestioning.

She waited until the men took her grandmother from her arms, a reverence she did not think they understood in their actions that she appreciated. She could not ask it though, how they knew. How he knew. "You're too knowledgeable about our customs, Prince." She could not look at him as she said the words. He knew a great deal about her culture, had even before she came into his service. He was dangerous, and he was compassionate, and she'd broken the bond between them not once but twice and her tears were for that above all else. The tears that squeezed from the corners of her eyes were for the man who knelt before her, who saw her, who hated her.

He did not respond to her statement. "I've heard the name, Ella."

Yet when he said her name like that, she doubted what she knew of him.

He reached for her, brushed the small droplet from her cheek, ignoring the shuffling of the few remaining soldiers sent to guard their prince and their captain. "*Watcher of Souls*. She is called as a witness to great happenings, exiles, executions, births and deaths. Why was she with you?"

An execution, though she didn't say as much to him. He didn't need to know that Eli'd come to kill her father or stopped for the affection Kit bore his own. She was an assassin; she needed to be strong. But here she was, crying, and he didn't seem to mind that weakness.

A flash of his hand, a shuffled half approach then retreat. The guards left, and she was alone with Kit kneeling on the ground. When the last soldier was past the hedgerow, he surged forward, and she flinched expecting an attack, and sobbed when his arms wrapped around her.

How he knew she needed—

Why he remained with her—

"Just a little longer, please Kit, just a few minutes more."

His lips brushed against her forehead, his chin coming to rest on top of her head as he obliged her, holding her without question or comment. And somehow, somehow that small brush of comfort when his lips touched her skin, soothed her world more than any tear or hug could.

HE STOOD, CAREFULLY drawing her to her feet with him. Her arms remained wrapped around his neck, and he made no move to dislodge her, brushing back her loose hair from her cheeks, thumbs wiping the trails of tears from her face. "However long you need me to hold you, love, I will, but Father will send more guards sooner than later, and I won't be able to hold you then."

By his gods and hers. Sweet Darkness, he'd called her *love* and she didn't care what else he said to her, what rules were demanded of her. Whatever he wanted, she would do, just to hear his claim once more.

Propriety be damned.

He took advantage, or she took advantage, of that strict chivalry, keeping her arm around his waist as he ushered her back to her rooms and the relative privacy of them.

Word must have spread before them for no one approached or stopped them as they entered the barracks and he opened the door for her to precede him into her sanctuary.

Eli stopped in the doorway between her small kitchen and the bedroom beyond. "Will you stay?"

"Yes."

That he lied to offer her comfort meant much to her, her prince who spoke as close to the truth as he could. She couldn't recount a single time that he'd deceived her, even with a half-truth.

The lock of her door turned. Her spine stiffened when his heat pressed to her back, his hand a gentle warmth on her arm. "For as long as you need me, Ella."

She stepped into her bedroom. The lilacs she'd placed in a vase on her nightstand calmed some of the pain in her soul. He moved around her, and she didn't look at what he was doing in her bathroom, her eyes closed as though she could hide from the truth a little while longer that way.

His fingers were gentle against her cheek when he tilted her face to him, the wet cloth in his sand wiping Annara's blood away. It was strange, the comfort she took from his touch, skin to skin with her. He hesitated for a moment, his fingertips shifting against her throat in indecision before he pushed the cloth away from her shoulder to wipe at the blood soaking lower against her flesh.

When had she—? She'd been naked, hadn't she—? That last, brief caress of magic against her skin, a final gift from her grandmother and Eli hadn't even noticed, wasn't sure she could look down at the gown clothing her, not without crying, without tearing it away.

"Shh, love, let it go for a moment."

His hands moved to hers, untangled her fingers from the black robe. He bent his head and her heart stuttered at the press of his forehead to her skin. He kept his eyes on the tie of the robe when he raised his hands to her shoulders and let them linger there as he went back to undressing her.

She shivered beneath his touch as the robe parted. His hands trembled when he retrieved the cloth he'd dropped on the side table and went back to washing the blood from her body. Eli watched his face. How many times had she watched his face, the total concentration he put into his motions, losing himself to duty? She didn't think he saw her as a person during the war. She was a body that fought at his side. This was different. And this was more. And his fingers trailed where the wet cloth went, soothing her skin in its wake.

He was not the only one trembling when she dropped her arms and the cloth fell to the floor leaving her bare. He followed, wiping the blood from her hips, her thighs, cupping her waist to steady her as he washed her feet.

The cloth was left on the ground when he rose. His hands trailed over the back of her legs, her hips, settled at her waist to pull her into his arms. Night, it was the most comfortable thing to allow herself to be held. She buried her face in his neck and pretended he didn't notice the damp of her tears soaking into his clothing.

He lifted her in his arms, holding her close as chills chased down her spine. Kit settled her on the bed, helped her slide beneath the sheets, sheets she hadn't been sure she'd see again. Her fingers clasped the dark linen beneath her chin though she followed him with a turn of her head when he moved to her toilet and she heard water running in the sink beyond her view. She'd yet to replace the door with its dagger sized hole through the wood, watching as he washed his face in her sink, stripped the shirt he wore over his head to wash what blood covered him from his flesh.

She watched him dry his hands as he stepped from the bathroom, his shirt hung over the hook on the door, an odd blue-black covering for the hole in the wood.

"Will you stay for a while more?" So soft, her words, spoken on a sigh she wasn't sure she meant him to hear, didn't know what response she wanted most.

He pulled his boots from his feet slid beneath the sheets at her back.

She expected him to lie there, a subtle heat to warm her, but he reached over her bare waist and turned her from facing away from him until they were eye to eye. When he leaned back, she moved with him, pulled until her cheek rested on his bare chest, pressed to the steady beat of his heart. That pulse sped at the feel of her skin against his, and she wondered if he felt the matching race in her body.

He didn't ask her to speak, to tell him what had happened, why elves were in his city, in his palace gardens. She wasn't sure she owed him the explanation regardless. He wrapped his arm around her back, tangled his other hand with hers draped over his chest.

"The Elichisolos came for me."

"But you're the," he paused. "Did you know her?"

"Him."

"But she—"

"She," her chest rattled in a breath at the thought of the Quir, "was the Watcher. The Elichi—he's my father, Kit." He stiffened beneath her, the hand running along her spine stilled and she felt his body prepare to move, to her defense? She didn't know. She pressed closer to his heat, holding him to her, absurdly pleased that he would react so strongly in her defense.

"He would have killed you?"

If only his anger on her behalf could ease the ache in her heart. "Families are not the same within the woods as without. The cock and womb that breed a child are not truly the family they are raised with. We find our caste young in life. Our parents are those who walk the same path as we do."

"He should have been a father to you then."

"He didn't like being overshadowed."

She waited for some response, not knowing what it would be, only that it would come. He would judge her now, the elves who were her family, the life she had lived, how utterly calm she accepted her father's threat to her.

His hand resumed its march up her spine, fingertips tapping until she relaxed, and he relaxed with her.

"The king wonders if I'll ever manage the same in regards to him."

He startled a chuckle from her, and that eased the last tension in her limbs. "I have missed you," *my prince*.

For a moment, he said nothing, did nothing, laid as still as a board beneath her. He tangled his fingers in her hair, tugged lightly. "I wasn't the one who refused to speak to you; who ran away at the merest sighting."

"I know."

He didn't ask her why, and she tensed in the waiting for the question though he continued to hold her without cease. "Tell me of the Quir. She attacked you. I watched her shadows swarm around you. Her eyes glowed, and you fell back. What were we supposed to think?" He asked knowing she would have thought the same thing in his place. He'd acted as a warrior, a leader protecting his people. He stroked her hair, his fingers tangling in her curls. "I didn't call for the attack, Eli, but only because the men fired before I could give the command. They saw their captain unprotected and acted to defend her."

A truth she wished didn't hurt as much as it filled her with pride. Her breath shuddered in her lungs. "She knew, Kit. She said she chose this path before the arrow struck." Eli tilted her head to meet his gaze as he stared down at her. "She watched things from this time and times to come and times long past. She knew that coming here, casting her spell, would kill her. I think it was what she wanted."

"Why do that to you though? Did she hate you that much to make you the instrument of her death?"

Annara chose Eli. The Quir chose who would hold her in her final moments, and honored Eli as such. For so long, Eli had forgotten the old woman who had been the closest kin she'd had within the wood. In truth, she barely knew Annara. Not even two hundred when she saved Kit's life. Barely enough time to form relationships, especially with her position as Elichisolos. But Eli had always felt affection for the woman, and the death was enough of a catalyst to allow her to mourn all those things she'd buried over the centuries, the life she lost, the un-family she had, the ones who might have called her friend, the man who held her now. "She was blood. My father's mother. The closest thing I had to one growing up." She sniffed back the tears threatening to fall again, disentangled her hand from Kit's so she could wipe the wet from his chest though he said nothing to spare her pride. Her lips twitched against his skin, and he shifted, grunted, ticklish, her prince. "She spared me from having to take the Elichi's life."

He stiffened beneath her, his hand stilling at her back. "Would that have been so bad?"

She reached for the hand she'd dropped, wanting the feel of that small joining between them. "He is her son, Kit."

He did not say she was the Quir's granddaughter and her claim to the woman's protection as important as her father's. He didn't say it, but he held her closer and she took comfort from that.

"Why call you out now, though? It's been centuries."

"The assassin at the last ball."

Kit groaned, and Eli found herself smiling again at his response. "I didn't ask. I can't believe I let it go so easily."

She didn't mention that he'd had other things on his mind. She rather liked that he'd been distracted by her enough to forget to ask after his, no, he should never be that distracted.

Eli pinched his side, and he yelped, only her arms around him holding them together.

"What was that for?"

"You being an idiot."

He mumbled something that sounded suspiciously like he was blaming her, but she could feel the smile of his lips against her forehead and didn't want to ruin that.

"I can't," she waited, letting him choose his words without hers to influence him. "I can't do this again, Ella."

Her eyes squeezed closed. She'd expected the conversation sooner. She'd expected to find a note pinned to her door telling her to pack her things and be gone by the next sunrise. Sweet Night, at least if he'd pushed her away *then* she wouldn't have heard him call her "love," wouldn't have felt that not-kiss against her forehead. If she wrapped her arms and legs around him, held him tighter, he couldn't leave. She was the one who had been so adamant about letting him go. His gods and hers must be laughing down at her now.

"I can't keep looking for you and watch you pull away. I won't." But his arms didn't loosen around her, and she met his gaze when he lifted her chin to force the issue. "Do not leave me again. Swear you won't leave me again."

"Yes" was on her tongue. Gods, she wanted to say yes so badly that she ached with it. But she was his soldier, his guardian, had sworn that she would protect him first and foremost. She would be called away for something or other over and over throughout their lives. It was inevitable. She didn't want to break the promise he asked of her and she would have to if she made her vow. "I want nothing more than to agree, Kit…"

The "but" hung heave in the air between them.

He did not hide the anger in his face, in his words. His hands clenched tighter where he held her, chin and side, forcing her to hold his stare. "Tell me why then, damnit. Tell me why you won't."

"I swore to protect you, Kit. I swore that vow first. I must leave you and I cannot—"

He smiled at her, and it was so at odds with her words, what she thought his response should be, that she stumbled to a halt. "You won't agree because you'll leave me for duty's sake?"

"Unwillingly, Kit, but I—"

"Duty is different, Ella. Duty will take us across nations and into politics and out the storm on the other side." His fingers stroked over her cheek, brushed over her lips in a feather light caress. "Don't leave me again. It was easier when you ran on horseback. At least I knew I could chase you and had a chance of catching up when you grew tired. There's no chasing a zombie, nothing there to reclaim."

She liked when he chased her, desired it even. "I thought you would have cornered me far sooner than you did."

"Had I known you would have been amenable, I would have."

She let her eyes drop closed, enjoying the steady rise and fall of his chest beneath her cheek, the ease with which he held her. "I won't leave if it can be helped."

"I will chase you if you do."

She smiled, unable to help herself from pressing her lips to the warm flesh over his heart, the first time she'd broken his vow of propriety, spurred by the kiss he'd given her.

He tensed beneath her, and she smiled at the shudder that worked through him.

She managed not to whisper words of a feeling she shouldn't have for him, relaxing in his embrace enough that sleep claimed her before her sense failed and she took what she'd denied all those years ago.

He stayed at her side the night through.

VI

The Four Hundredth and Eighty-Seventh Ball

SHE WOKE TO his arm curved over her waist, their fingers tangled together with her back against his chest. Her dreams had been pleasant, which she didn't trust. Whenever she dreamed something lovely, all hell broke loose within hours of her waking. She'd resigned herself to the phenomenon long ago.

It caused her to pull his arm tighter around her, his soft grunt of compliance uttered with a smile felt by the lips pressed to the nape of her neck. He blew a warm puff of air against her throat, made her jerk at the sensation, the spot sensitive despite her adamant refusal of being ticklish.

The knock on the door had him reaching beneath the pillow for the dagger she stashed there when they slept. His motions were sleep-slow where she reacted on instinct, the blade in her hand before he had a chance to grab the weapon.

"Captain. It's nearing sunset. You said to wake you then."

Blasted soldiers who never failed to obey a damned command. The man's punctuality ruined her little sojourn with the man she loved and…

Merciful Darkness.

She loved him.

She'd known she loved him, but it was the first time the thought nearly escaped her lips, was not hidden behind layers of duty and propriety and damn walls.

She clenched his fingers tighter, and he pulled her into his arms, letting his warmth comfort her for whatever reason she needed.

How easy would it be to say how she felt? How she'd felt for a long, long time?

He'd laugh to know the truth, and after he was done laughing, he'd likely thank her for her honesty and get down on one blasted knee and propose or do something worse like pull her into the middle of the training yard, or, Darkness be kind, the middle of the ballroom, and kiss her, not the brief press of lips to her skin he perpetrated subconsciously, but something passionate, fiery, claiming.

She might even take the ring he handed her.

She'd certainly kiss him back.

Her people didn't do that sort of thing, the rings and ceremonies. If people chose to spend some time together, then that was well and good, but not expected to last a lifetime, not like Kit's people who married forever. Which should frighten her, or disgust her, the idea of living with one man for the rest of her life, but she was almost desperate for it so long as that man was Kit.

"I'm awake, Lieutenant, thank you."

"Yes, m'lady. Should I see to the prince then?"

Said prince stiffened at her back, unused to being overlooked even when he purposely moved in shadow.

"Give him a little longer. He's not required until the first bell of the evening."

"Yes, Sir."

Kit pinched her side, the rub of his fingers over the mark too soothing to make the rebuke count. "The first bell of the evening? That's barely long enough to return to my rooms let alone dress."

She rolled in his arms, pressing her hand to his cheek now that she faced him. "Long enough."

She'd taken to wearing his shirt when he slept with her, preserving his modesty, she said, though the truth was she just liked feeling wrapped in his scent.

He never complained, not when she used the excuse of his bare chest to wrap herself around him—so that her prince didn't catch a chill, of course.

She brushed her fingers against the downturn of his lips, having heard of his valet's exploits over the past years. "You need to buy me time to dress myself. I don't have a man to help with the task."

"I'd dismiss the toad if I could. He's forever critiquing my color of choice."

"You look regal in black." Her hands smoothed over his shoulders, pretending to settle an imagined jacket across his frame. "But perhaps, just this once," he smiled at her and she smiled back, "you might try, perhaps, a green jacket. That's just a thought though."

He laughed at her, with her, and she fisted her hands in his hair, moving quickly to stop him from leaning down to kiss her, or pulling him away before she chose to lean up and take the choice from him. She gentled her hold, but he remained smiling at her, and she turned her face away to hide the color in her cheeks. He didn't pull back, and she didn't release him from her grasp.

"Is your dress here?"

"Maybe I won't be wearing a dress this year but will be back in uniform."

He chuckled, his hand rucking up her shirt as he stroked her back, his fingers finding the edge of flesh beyond the hemline of the linen, the scar he never failed to touch that wrapped her side to the front of her stomach. She looked up into his eyes, and he stared down at her.

"What style gown should I look for?"

"I don't know." The blush deepened on her cheeks, more so at his touch rather than ideas about her dress. "Amarice won't tell me for fear of her design being stolen before the ball."

"Amarice knows it's not the gown that draws the eye, my Captain."

"Most of your court would disagree, my Prince."

"Only the women, and that's because they're too jealous to look beyond the gown to the stunning elf wearing it."

She snorted, not sure she should believe his flattery, hating that she did.

Darkness how she loved him.

"Go, before the soldier returns spouting tales of you not being where you're supposed to be and causing a panic in the palace."

"One time—"

"Is too many when your life is on the line."

"I'm just a man."

"With a prophecy hanging over your head. One more year, Kit, and you're free."

"Or I'm dead."

No one knew why the fate of the city would be decided on his five hundred and eighteenth birthday, and there had never been anything to truly suggest that his life was the life of his country, but she protected, and it was the only reason she was welcome to remain with him, at least in the king's perspective, the guards, the city.

There had been three attempts on his life in the past three years.

The last less than a month ago.

She'd heard rumors that soldiers were hiding on the edges of the Dienobo, but she couldn't enter the forest for pain of death, and soldiers meant nothing without a leader, and no one had claimed that role yet.

"Go on, Kit. Three nights, and then you're free again."

"Will you come hunting this year?"

"No."

"You don't have to go in the woods, just stay at the camp."

"Like a little woman left behind to cook what her brave knight brings back to the fire?" She batted her lashes at him like the simpering fools he would dance with that evening.

He smiled. "You've been spending too much time listening to the maids in that dress shop of yours."

"You have your rituals, Kit. Let me have mine."

She spent the two weeks of his camping trip sharpening weapons and envisioning the day when she could hunt in the forests once more, practicing with her bow which she rarely used, arrow after arrow into a target until she could hit the heart or an eye a hundred yards off. She spent the time meditating, speaking to the Darkness that went un-worshiped within the halls of the palace, her small shrine dedicated at the far edge of the gardens, surrounded by trees which felt like the home she'd left so long ago. "Go."

He brushed his hand down her cheek, mimicking her motions, and then sat up, untangling himself from the sheets pulled around them and leaving her bed while she watched. He didn't ask for his shirt back, pulling his coat over his bare arms and lacing the front without regard for his unclothed chest. Men should always forego undershirts, or they should if she had say in the matter, and by men she truly just meant her prince, though there were fine specimens working in the barracks and garrison around her.

She didn't want to compromise any of *their* sensibilities though.

"How much time will you need?"

"An hour, maybe an hour and a half."

"I can stall for that long."

She kicked the sheet from her legs and he extended a hand to help her stand from the bed. His arms wrapped around her waist, and she leaned into his embrace, taking a final moment of comfort from him before pulling away and shooing him in the process. Outside her window the sun was just beginning to set, barely twilight but there were enough shadows that she pulled them to her and wrapped him in their embrace. "You'll find your room unseen."

"You don't have to use your magic for me. You know that, don't you?"

She wanted to, and so she did. "It keeps me in practice."

He argued against it every time, but he didn't shiver in revulsion or pull away from her when she drew the Darkness to them. He'd never pulled away from her, even when that Darkness was riding her so fiercely in the field after battle. For that alone, he held her heart.

He nodded at her trained response, and then he let her go, slipped from her door and into the sunset.

She returned to her bedroom, drew the long robe around her shoulders and the sleeves over her arms.

She gave him a moment to walk away before she followed after him, turned left from the palace, and into the city as he made his way to the back stairs which led to the private suites of the king and heir, and she to a dress shop whose front door was crammed with people hoping to catch a glimpse of her gown.

She was wearing green for this night. A green so pale as to be white until the light caught on the fabric and graced it with a bit of color. Her skin glowed against the lighter colors, or so the seamstress said.

If he wore the jacket tonight, he would match her in appearance. The thought made her smile and she stretched her arms over her head to help the seamstress settle the garment over her body.

CHAPTER THREE

The Four Hundredth and Eighty-Seventh Ball

HE KEPT HIS gaze resolutely forward, ignoring the whispers and the looks of the gathered crowd. Most of the women stared at him. Most of the men were turned nearly as one to the far corner of the ballroom and the goddess standing there. Kit was acutely aware of her presence, even if he'd only gotten the barest of glimpses of her so far, the white-green of her gown a fresh shade in the sea of blues and purples of the gathering, so last season, he thought he heard muttered by some mademoiselle or another as he passed by.

This new game between them made the balls a little less interminable. Seventeen years she guarded him on the dance floor as one of the fawning masses, and he danced with her to keep her from killing the nobles who would have dared for her hand when she stepped into the room.

She'd told him the name of the dressmaker when he'd asked, but only after he swore not to go looking for the woman.

Not that it was hard to find the most sought-after seamstress in the city, though most of the women in the trade benefitted from the novelty of the lady's creativity and Eli's vision in wearing the creations.

He held to his promise though, never searched out the seamstress, never begged for the information on what Eli's gown would look like beforehand. He allowed for the surprise of the night as she requested. And in the end, it didn't matter what dress she wore, or mask covered her face, he knew her, would always know her.

The masks were equally stunning, and equally mysterious. Jacques, having been commissioned for some time as the premier artist in the city, was only too happy to lend his skill in disguising the Lady of the ball. The mask maker spared no expense in his designs, though the same were always elegantly understated, a nod to the wearer herself. Kit sent the man due payment, hid the cost from his captain, though she looked at him oddly when her payment was refunded without cause from the man. Either way, the masks succeeded in covering her face just enough to obscure her identity while inducing a delicateness to the leather that suggested a light breeze or a daring hand might manage to pull the supple piece away without much effort. No one had yet to test the theory, and Kit doubted she'd allow them to succeed if they worked up the nerve.

She'd stopped him the one time he tried.

He smiled at the thought.

She was first at the ball, checking alcoves and corridors for any guests who were less cordial than not. The last ball she found a rabid trio of ogres behind the throne waiting to attack. Kit's father hadn't called the spectacle off despite the threat. The ogres had been questioned, and Kit had danced three nights away. The beautiful masked woman had only been in attendance for the third day, though he'd felt her eyes on him, watching for any other dangers throughout the course of the ball.

And when the dancing ended, the musicians taking a moment to rest while guests filed from the hall, she waited in the corner until every last person was gone, noble, servant, and guard, for Kit to claim a dance with her beyond the sight of those who watched his every move.

No king, no guards, no one but Kit and Eli, and the necessary orchestra. She didn't remove her mask, and he never said a word of recognition. The orchestra played without comment, and it was nearly enough for Kit. Enough, at least, to get through the three days of holding everyone but the one he wanted in his arms.

The sixteenth year she'd worn a gown that had no back at all and caught at her throat, barely managed to cover her modesty at the dimples of her spine where it wrapped around her. Apparently, the mistress-dressmaker had insisted Eli come for fittings for the gown, for which his captain maintained her disgust.

Seventeen years.

For as long as they'd been together, the centuries and so forth, these seventeen years had felt brand new and sparkly, not just from the sequins that sometimes decorated the fabrics that flowed around her form.

Kit kept his gaze forward as he walked down the aisle formed for him down the center of the dance floor, one hand at the hilt of his sword on his hip, the other crossed over his chest as custom dictated. Thousands of candles burned merrily in their sconces above his head, chandeliers glinting gold in the bright yellow light. The filigreed walls caught the sheen. Molten scenes of men and women in court attire, turned towards the dais and the throne atop it, carved into the walls over centuries of time, shadowed by their living descendants. Fabric shifted and moved in a sea of bodies, never still, and he walked down the aisle to present himself to the king.

A tepid spring breeze wafted into the room from the opened glass doors, balconies filled with as many people as were on the parquet floors. Fresh blossoms, still too new, fighting the impending frost that was common for this time of year, filled the trees and bushes, their scent overpowering the myriad perfumes cloying in the air.

He took a breath of the world beyond the golden throng, of nature, of the woman it reminded him of, and continued his approach to his father.

He managed not to touch the silver ring sitting securely in his breast pocket.

He reached the dais and stopped, bowed as a son should to his lord and king. There was the customary round of applause and then the orchestra struck up a lively quadrille and the ball was begun.

Kit was pulled into the first set, two ladies in sapphire and amethyst colored gowns flocked around him. At least one, if not both, managed to step on his toes, and his eyes locked on the floor trying to anticipate the next wrong step and save himself a broken foot. It kept his gaze securely away from the corner he most wanted to look at.

If he was lucky, he could steal a dance with her in the midst of the festivities, one only, that the denizens of his hell were willing to allow him with an unknown member of their flock.

He usually escaped among the gardens for at least an hour of the night. A moment where his back needn't be stiff with protocol or his lips twisted into its painful smile. Sometimes she found him out among the rows of cultivated plants. An aisle away, a path over, never close enough to share an improper word, but there, with him, all the same.

A baroness he'd danced with many times over the years slipped her arm into his before he could beg leave for a drink.

She danced, and he followed where her steps led him.

Kit didn't know if he managed to look at all graceful, but he tried, truly he did.

He argued that "trying" and "caring" were separate things when his father commented in one of the rare moments when Kit was allowed to sit out a dance.

His father was staring at Eli, though Kit doubted the king recognized the captain without breeches and a cambric shirt on. That Leon asked after the mystery woman every night of the ball made Kit smile, at least until Leon realized it likely meant the woman shouldn't be in attendance and threatened to have guards escort her from the property if her identity couldn't be discovered. Kit's assurances that the woman was a welcomed guest fell on deaf ears, but as his father didn't know any of the guards by name, and Kit did, they tended to follow his orders over the king's.

"Well dance with the tart then and get her out of here. Good gods, have you ever seen a dress like that?"

Kit couldn't very well ignore a direct command to look at the gown in question. So light a green, a blade of glass half buried by snow, yet there was something similar in coloring to his own jacket that said they were nearly a pair together. Surprisingly modest, considering her previous costumes, the neckline was a heart, just hinting at the bosom it concealed, and the skirt was long and, if not full, then pleasantly filled so that it flowed in a thick wave to the floor. The fabric itself looked to have been woven of thin straps together to form the bodice, and it was a surprisingly elegant effect garnered from such a pedestrian technique. At least, that was his thought until she turned to accept a glass of punch from some such noble or other and he caught sight of the back of the gown. The lengths of fabric that had combined to form the front were loose in their weaving along her spine, highlighting the smooth expanse of skin, the ridges of a thin frame well-toned, crisscrossing in layers though doing nothing to hide the flesh it covered. The vast majority of her back was bare, shadowed by wisps of fabric that was as much enticement as it was denial to the eye.

Her scars were invisible. Magic likely blocking their appearance to the mortal eye, yet he could trace the marks even with them being blocked from his sight, knowing them in a way he shouldn't. Somehow, the fabric straps of the gown followed those trails of struggle and triumph, a thing of beauty and a thing of pain.

"Are you going to dance or just stare, boy? Get out there and get her out of your system for another year."

He jerked back towards his father, looking the older man in the eye. "If you know she's the same woman, why allow her entrance time and again?"

Leon met Kit's stare, a sad smile on his face, a knowledge he shouldn't have discerned and that Kit had failed to hide well enough. "Because you smile when you look at her, Kit, and in the end, I want you to smile, son." He looked out over the crowd, the chatter of couples standing on the edges of the dance floor, the gaiety of forced laughter where a group pretended to be ignoring the royalty on the stage and failing miserably in the attempt. He turned his gaze back to Kit, held the stare between them. "I know that you think of these balls as a duty, and they are, that's true. But I want you to find someone to love, or at least like, and that girl there," he sighed, shook his head. "You have not smiled at another woman like you do her since you were barely one hundred."

"One hundred and thirty."

"What?"

"Nothing, Father."

The king waved his hand, dismissing Kit's remark. "She's pretty enough, and there's spirit in her, if her clothing is any indication of the lady beneath the gown."

"So you would approve of her as my choice?" Kit held his breath, not sure he should read so far into his father's words.

"No, but I would approve of an introduction, and the potential for a more suitable courtship than whatever game it is you play at these balls."

Kit laughed, unable to help smiling at the scowl on his father's face, the brief flare of hope in his chest. He caught the answering mischief in his father's gaze, an expression so seldom seen that Kit nearly asked if the old man was feeling well, not having witnessed the particular look in many, many years, not since his mother died.

The king tsked, and Kit sank deeper into his chair. "You know who she is."

The gleam in his father's eye suggested any dissembling on Kit's part would be met by some contrived punishment. He was too old to be sent to bed without supper, but the king might well require adding more open court sessions to Kit's schedule and that Kit could do without. "Yes."

"You won't tell me who though."

Half turned on his seat, leaning closer to his father, Kit met the king's stare. "I will not."

The implacable face before him did not change. "A king knows when to yield, Christophe."

"And when to stand his ground, Father."

The older man leaned back in his chair, a half-smile turning the corner of his lips. It was rare, so rare, that he and Kit had discussions not revolving around some issue with the country or the constant threat to Kit's life or his lack of an heir should the worst occur. Every other time they'd spoken of women it had been with an eye towards what Leon was expecting, not what Kit desired. "Is she unsuitable? Is that why she remains encased in mystery?"

"Quite suitable." If she weren't an elf and he weren't her peoples' sworn enemy. But Leon had accepted the woman as a member of the guard, and barely seemed to notice that she wasn't, strictly speaking, one of his citizens. It wasn't like she had pointed ears or anything absurd like that. "When she's ready, she'll take the mask from her face. I won't force it any sooner than she wishes." Of course, in a year, he'd be free of his curse, and in thirteen, she'd be free to return to the forest.

Leon shifted in his throne, staring at the dance floor rather than meeting Kit's gaze. "A king—"

"Is in charge of his own destiny. Yes, I know that too," Leon smiled, relaxing in his seat and turning to Kit once more. His father looked old. Deepened lines formed crows' feet at the corners of ice blue eyes. The king's sharp intelligence still shone brightly, but since forever, Kit remembered the near constant sadness lurking in their depths.

"A king attacks when it is necessary, shows mercy if he is able, upholds the law when he must, and bows before no man but the woman—" Kit trailed off, but his father's gaze sharpened on him even though he didn't finish the saying.

"He loves."

As a child, Queen Ata had finished the lesson with words of love, tempering Leon's authority with a softer lilt. His mother was as fierce as any; ruthless in a way Leon couldn't be when protecting his child. She tempered that love with rules and doctrines, but Kit never doubted it, even as he never doubted his father's devotion, though a colder one than hers.

Leon loved Ata; Kit knew that better than most. After her death, the king suffered greatly, and even Kit had been unable to console the man. Women came courting his father, and the king refused them all.

Kit understood not loving another. He understood too that a throne was not meant for love. But he'd fallen long ago, and he wasn't some passive prince willing to sacrifice his own heart for his people. He'd protect them with everything he was, but he wasn't going to be told who to marry.

He'd waited four hundred plus years to make the choice for himself.

He'd wait one or seventeen or seven hundred more for Eli.

Perhaps, if he had a chance to steal a moment with her tonight, he wouldn't have to wait at all.

"Ach," the king waved a hand before Kit's face, drawing the prince from his thoughts and to the present. Leon sat back in his chair, as near a slouch as Kit had ever seen. When he waved a hand this time, Kit took it for the dismissal it clearly was. "Dance with her then, boy. I'm tired of watching the two of you circle around each other every night. She pretends not to want you, you pretend your one obligatory dance is obligatory." Kit allowed the small smile to cross his lips at his father's assessment. "See to her and be done with it," the last he said in a grumble, "until tomorrow, I suppose."

"Thank you, Father."

The old man inclined his head, and Kit rose from his chair, his reprieve ended in favor of joining the dancing partner he desired. He made his way to her from the dais, watched her back straighten at his approach though she was faced away from him.

His captain's spine was not the only one to straighten at Kit's appearance. "Marius, I didn't think you were on duty this evening."

"That you consider this lovely event a duty, my Prince, is a tragedy."

Kit laughed, the droll tone of his commander's voice suggesting it truly was the tragedy Kit would name the ball.

The commander's forced smile hardened, eyes darkening when they met Kit's, no hint of sarcasm or enjoyment in his expression if one knew better than to look below the surface. "I was just telling this lovely lady that there has been a report of brigands outside of Undcrest. Scouts suggest they're not trolls as we had thought, but human mercenaries brought from outside our fair continent."

That other countries were after Kit's demise was not news. That those countries didn't share a border with his, well, that wasn't news either. That the mercenaries had hidden themselves among his people long enough to gather troops without being found or stomped out, that was different altogether.

Kit's smile was brittle as he stepped closer to Eli's back, his hand outstretched to pull her into the small group they were forming, barely a breath away from the bare skin revealed by her gown. The music and conversations around them were enough concealment for their words, but he lowered his voice all the same. "And your suggestion in dealing with said invaders, Commander?"

"A small scouting party, to confirm the rumors. Three men, easy to slip through a guard and capture the leader of the band, get answers from him if they're quiet enough." Her hands were held lightly in front of her chest, a giddy woman in conversation with the prince. But giddiness was not usually represented in the straining muscles of a woman ready to attack, the tension that fairly vibrated from her into the surrounding aura she emitted, drawing people in as much as it pushed them away.

She glanced from the commander, a quick look to catch his eye, the frigid ice of her Darkness made her pupils extend in star-like patterns throughout her iris, breaking the green of her eyes.

She wanted the fight.

He could blame it on the life she'd lived before him, that she was a dedicant of the Final Midnight, that she was the best at infiltration. No one expected a woman be a killer, and she was brutally efficient, which he appreciated on a military level. But he was there when she returned from the Darkness, knew the toll it took on her soul, just as he knew she wouldn't run from the battle ahead.

"When will you leave?"

Marius replied. "Horses are being prepared even now. They've set Abroath to fire. The miller was lost but the villagers managed to save the rest of the houses before they were destroyed."

Kit looked between the two soldiers, this conversation likely repeated for the second time for his benefit alone. "They're outside of the walls?"

"Abroath has only wood to shield them, no stones as the forest is closer than the quarry."

"They've no protection besides a fence?" His voice rose with the incredulity, saved from attracting the attention of the other guests only by Eli's flippant laugh that grated on his nerves.

The partiers looked away from Kit's revel, returned to their own.

"They've us." She met his gaze quickly, fast enough that he saw the feral gleam in her eye, justice riding on swift hooves.

His hand settled against her back, pulling her into his side as dancers swelled around them, a country dance, taking up more space than the dance floor allowed. She relaxed into his touch, and he prayed no one noticed the liberty he took, even if it was a guise for those around them. "When will you return?" He whispered the words in her ear, leaning close enough to play the besotted male to her shining damsel.

She looked away from him, the red stain to her cheeks covering for her non-existent blush. Oh, he could make her blush, true enough, but not now, not under these circumstances. Her response was a demure soprano, blending in with the lighthearted tones of the women around them. "When it's done."

"We'll organize the armies while—"

"No." This from Marius who leaned closer, his smile dropping out of place for a moment before the mask resettled. "There's enough fear that war is coming."

Not a rumor bandied around the palace but something the peasants knew and feared. Kit clenched his teeth, knew the expression on his face was more snarl than smile. "Is it? I seem not to have heard such news."

They'd kept this from him, the possibility of war. Did they think him so weak that they needed to hide the potential?

But of course not. This wasn't war in the traditional sense, was it? This was something else, something personal, an attack on him, the final shadowed master stepping into the light.

There're been three attacks on his life in as many years.

Only one year left before the prophecy was complete and his country was safe from desolation.

His enemies were desperate now.

"It was always likely to come to this, Kit. The closer you came to your majority," Marius shook his head. "Not majority, you're already an adult. Your—"

"The prophecy. The closer I came to fulfilling the prophecy." The word left a bitter taste on his tongue.

"We've been preparing for years, Kit. It's all just been called to a head since the first reports of attack came in. Our soldiers are ready to be called to duty with a moment's notice, but no standing army yet, to keep panic at bay."

"Because panic leads to death."

Kit let his eyes close, head bowed.

All this, all this fighting and preparation and death because some witch atop the city walls said that a child born in the spring of the blooded moon, a child as dark as a king's legacy and as light as a mother's love, would be the life or death of his world, would crumble the walls into nothing and the people into ash and stone if he died before his five hundredth and eighteenth year.

Five hundred and eighteen. The number was arbitrary. At least, Kit had found no reason otherwise for such an age, and still he held his breath with his people, hoping he survived.

"So I'm to pretend nothing is wrong and go hunting as normal."

"Yes, and I'll be hunting too."

He turned his head to his captain, held her dark gaze with his. There were words on his tongue, wanting to be said, silenced because of uncertainty. She hunted at Death's side. And he was hunted by the same.

The ring in his breast pocket was heavy, was barely felt.

Marius clapped his hands, his face lighting with a sickeningly sweet smile, drawing Kit's attention, Eli's, back to the commander. "A dance first, to forestall suspicions."

"Marius—"

"Commander—"

Marius kept the grin in place, speaking between his teeth. "Your father is motioning for you to get on the floor, Kit. If you don't dance with the girl, he'll question it. And if he questions it, you'll be stuck within the palace until war comes full out and we'll lose all chance of stopping it before it starts." He met Kit's gaze, pain, bitterness, chasing the manic look from the man's eyes. "If I thought I could whisk her away without obeying his commands, I would." He took a last step forward that put his shoulder to Kit's, leaned in so he could whisper to the prince alone, below what even Eli with her elfin ears could hear. "And if I thought you'd let her go without pining for her the whole of the hunt, I would. Take the dance, Prince; tell her you love her."

Panic filled Kit. His head snapping up, staring at the man before him, Eli tensing at his side preparing for an attack that wouldn't come. He managed to keep his words calm, even affected a bored, indifferent tone that Marius shook his head at. "How long have you known?"

Eli frowned. "Known what?"

"Ask me after your dance, my prince."

A nod, for he didn't trust his voice not to give him away, and Kit took Eli's hand in his, pulled her into his arms, smiling to the man he cut off even as he spun them into the center of the floor and away from grasping hands, women reaching for him, men for his captain.

Her hand settled into his, and he was tempted to wrap his other arm around her waist and draw her closer than propriety allowed, feel the touch of her silk clad legs against him. He held her gaze as the music played around them, but he couldn't smile looking in her eyes.

She didn't smile up at him.

He spun her to the music, and she dropped her skirt in her free hand so that her fingers brushed against his side, a subtle, gentle movement easily missed if one wasn't watching for it, improper yes, but allowed in the turns of the dance. He stepped closer to her, just a breath between them, not touching and yet so very close to it. Her hands lifted to his shoulders and he raised her into the air for a twirl.

He bowed when the music ended, and she sank into a delicate curtsy.

"Come back."

She nodded.

"Be safe."

"And you."

She rose, and he aided in her escape by pulling the first lady he could into the next dance, the court smile back on his lips as he ignored the urge to turn and watch her flee the crowded room to a fate unsure for both.

DAWN WAS LIGHTENING the sky when he finally returned to his rooms, his eyes gritty with lack of sleep and mind weighed down with the knowledge of the soldiers already on notice that they might soon be recalled to active duty, how many swords and bows and arrows and instruments of war had already been gathered in preparation for the fighting to come.

He pulled the ties at his throat, loosening his jacket so that he could undress and find what little sleep he could before the next night of dancing and planning occurred.

Kit took the ring from his pocket and strung the silver band on the chain around his neck.

She'd return.

She'd return, and he'd be here to greet her.

He refused to believe anything else.

He'd ask her then. He would wait until then.

The ring settled against his chest, the cool metal warmed by his skin, warmth he could pretend was from her when he closed his eyes and slept.

Book Three

CHAPTER ONE

I

After the Four Hundredth and Eighty-Seventh Ball

"NO WORD YET, though that's to be expected. I've sent the runner back, and the next exchange of soldiers will arrive on the morrow for their turn in the fields."

"Lovely that we could use the excuse of hunting to gather our soldiers and drill with them for a few days." Kit was sure his commander didn't miss the sarcasm in his voice.

"Like you wanted to be out here hunting without your captain with you."

Neither spoke of the fact that said captain never went hunting with them regardless.

"She's likely following whatever trail there is to follow by this point. No other reports of attacks. She must have succeeded at least in her initial assignment."

"The fact that she assigns herself without approval is the issue."

"True enough. I'll let you tell her that, Kit, it'll probably go over better from you." The general sighed, "And technically, I did assign her, my Prince."

Kit snorted, remembering the truth of the man's words, and Kit's own part in not dissuading his captain from going. He snorted because he knew that if he did say aught in disapproval of her actions, she was like as not to skewer him as she was to skewer Marius, though she might regret the deed if it was him, where she probably wouldn't stop at just one blade for his General. "Her temper's gotten better."

"Certainly, my lord." Marius laughed, and Kit joined in the small relief, grateful that for a moment they didn't have to think of whatever fight lay before them.

His horse shuffled, and Kit patted the beast's pale neck, promising that they would ride soon enough. The first exchange of soldiers had gone well. The barriers the court magician had erected held strong against any who was not wearing a signet from the court. None could find the camp but Kit and his men. It was a safe place to plan for a war. And it was a sound area to gather an army behind the prying eyes of enemy camps.

"We should get some hunting done. More mouths to feed come sunset tonight."

"True enough, Kit." Marius hauled hard on his reigns, turning his horse about to head for the woods and away from the plateau they found themselves scouting on. "First kill gets to watch the other skin the catch."

"Just the one or them all?"

"All."

"You're on, General. I won't be doing the work tonight."

"Not like last time, you mean?"

The older man urged his horse into a gallop, roaring as he sped away from Kit, signaling the conversation at a close.

Kit watched his friend ride into the tree covered terrain, followed quickly behind. He drew his bow from his shoulder and angled the quiver at his hip for an easier draw as his horse flew over the ground trying to catch its partner. He whooped when he overtook Marius and the hunt was on.

"GO ON, MARIUS. It's not like I'm in any danger here. We've got patrols everywhere." He smiled at his commander. "These trails have been my home for years now."

"Your idea of home and mine are very different, Kit."

Kit laughed at the other man's words, enjoying the cool breeze against his sun warmed face. He looked forward to these hunting excursions, the few days of the year when he was allowed outside of the palace walls, beyond the bounds of petitioners and commoners and nobles. Even if his solitude was intruded upon by soldiers preparing for war, he still appreciated the beauty of the forest around him, appreciated being a soldier, or a hunter, or something other than a prince, even if his military theory was what led men to listen to him when planning for the eventual attack. He was simply a man here, a soldier preparing to survive, hoping to survive, and this was just land. That no one had ever attacked him in the woods hadn't escaped his notice. Whether it was religion that disallowed the Dienobolos from attacking within their homeland, or if they thought it an unfair advantage to kill him in their forests, he'd never feared them here within their world.

He wished Eli could share that with him, but her exile was his fault, he regretted the cause, but not that she was with him because of it. Keeping her from the woods kept her with him for a while longer, and he didn't regret that.

Four men dead by her hand. Four hundred years as recompense. She'd saved his life at the cost of her peoples.

He loved her for more than that.

But she wasn't here, and he couldn't afford the distraction of wondering after her, not even when he felt relatively safe within her once homeland.

Besides, there was a bet to collect on, and other concerns to consider that took precedence.

"That rabbit won't skin itself, General. Get to work."

Rabbit stew would feed two, three men at most. The deer would provide good venison for many more. But Marius' triumph in the hunt didn't negate his loss in the bet.

Stew and steak for the evening meal. It would all be eaten that night, unless others had met with success in the woods that day as well.

The stew was a favorite of Kit's. He was already looking forward to the meal, especially as he wasn't preparing it himself. He could well imagine the smell of the rich broth set to boiling on the fire. The scent was in the air.

"Stop salivating. I'm liable to spit in the pot just to irk you."

A grumbling Marius was nothing new, and Kit smiled over at his companion. He pulled the ropes with their dangling meat from his saddle, tossing the rodents to the general who drew his horse to a halt, waiting to catch. The man held Kit's stare, his gaze firmly saying what he thought of Kit's need to go off alone, bet or not, safety or not.

"I just need a moment to myself, Marius. There are enough people within calling distance if I should need anyone. Just a moment alone, and I'll be back."

His mother would frown at Kit's insistence to disregard his guardian's remarks. *As prince, you are a model for your people. If you refuse to follow a command, why should they? You must be beyond the mundane desires of the gentry, even the noblemen. You are prince and must always accede to the wisdom granted you, even by another's decisions.*

Yes, he was a prince, but his mother died before she could talk about the rigors of war or the isolation of nobility. He loved her, knew his father loved her, but his mother had taken being queen much more seriously than his father had, at least while she was alive. Kit missed her, but he missed the childhood he'd been told not to expect.

If he had children with Eli—

Best not to think thoughts like that.

He gripped the reins in his hands a little tighter.

He'd managed not to touch the ring at his throat, not to draw attention to it. Marius would have a fit if he saw it. Marius would know who it was for.

No. Best not to think of that.

"I'll have them save you some stew then, yes?"

Kit laughed, knowing the soldier who had spent his youth training Kit, was Kit's closet friend besides the woman not given entry into the wood, would give Kit a moment because Marius was always looking out for him and what Kit needed.

A moment was a need.

"Thank you, my friend. If I miss out, it's my own fault. If one refuses to be on time for good stew, then he doesn't deserve the reward of a bowl."

Marius laughed, hunching over his pommel while he turned his head to meet Kit's gaze. It was not that amusing as a comment, and both men knew better than to truly seek humor in their situations. The general sobered. "Your word?"

Kit ignored the hesitation in the man's voice, the concern. "My word. No ill will if you eat up my hard-won spoils without me."

The general did not ask again, did not require Kit to promise to be careful. The attempted levity was promise enough. "I'll hold you to that."

The stolid response made Kit's lips curl, a half-smile not worn for court pressing his mouth.

The commander wheeled his horse around, preparing to return back to their campsite. He would halt the raising of the protective spells around their encampment until Kit returned. "Don't be too long. You won't enjoy me coming to find you."

"Don't lie, Marius. You'd send the others while you stayed warm and full with my rabbit."

"Probably true. Don't go far. The elves aren't on the attack yet, but once they learn about the mercenaries, that might change. Best to keep your eyes open."

"Yes, sir." Kit saluted the man, mock formality aside, he honored the words and the intent behind them.

Marius only wanted Kit's safety.

Kit understood that. "I'll hunt out any trouble."

"Don't you dare, Kit."

He smiled at the other man, "I definitely meant to think about saying *won't* hunt out trouble."

"Amusing. I should beat you."

"You can either have rabbit stew, or put me on the list for disciplinary actions, but you can't have both."

"You can be a real prick sometimes, Kit."

"Blame my father, I learned from him."

"It's not your father you remind me of."

Kit pretended not to hear the comment or react to the image of his captain that it conjured.

With a kick, knowing the commander wasn't waiting for a response, Kit pushed his horse into a hard gallop, pulling away from the camp and the soldiers settled down within the space. He bent low over the horse's neck, urging Oberon faster, feeling the bunch and release of muscles as his mount ran free across the open valley surrounding by forest on all sides.

It was a wonderful space, nothing manmade or stone entombed within the woods or their lands. Here the dells were of untended grass rather than rows of crops set to feed a people. Whatever the elves ate, they didn't farm the land to do it. These fields had never been touched by farmers' hands. And it was a blessing that Kit wouldn't deny, and his heart took full advantage of. The more he hunted the deep forest paths, the more he questioned what Eli had been thinking to ever risk leaving them behind.

Breath ragged, both man and beast, they slowed at the edge of a stream, just inside the border or wood and glade. Oberon knew these paths after the many years of carrying Kit through the trees. He had no trouble following the water to more spacious pools with their crisp water to drink. Kit dismounted and left his horse graze while he washed his face in the cool stream.

Oberon's hesitation to drink drew his gaze to the water, the hint of red tinting the trickling flow. He cupped a handful and raised the offering to his nose, sniffing at the iron scented liquid in his hand. There was blood coming from somewhere upstream, perhaps an injured animal, gods forbid it be a human or elf.

He should not look alone.

And yet he rose regardless, inching along the bank, hoping that he spotted whatever was hiding before it or they spotted him.

The male faced away from Kit, though the five others with him were hardened men, each with blood still wet upon their faces, black clothes meant to help them hide in the trees as they sought out the prince and his men.

"We get the prince. We gut the prince. The walls fall, and our lord takes command. It is a simple enough order to obey."

Was it possible they hid from the elves as well? Did the woodland folk not care that even more peoples were inhabiting their domain than normal? Had they finally chosen a side in this war that was coming?

"This guttersnipe didn't tell us nothing 'bout where the prince is."

The man who responded had only one good eye, the other carved away by a scar reaching from hairline to lip. He sharpened a curved blade in his lap, ignoring the body strung up in a tree and the man who still played with the corpse. "Well you shouldn't have killed him then until he did."

"He said ill about my mother."

"Your mother was a cantankerous whore who deserved all the ill names piled upon her."

"Well yeah, but no one else but me's allowed to say that."

This area was supposed to be clear of the mercenaries. Kit's patrols went through this area every morning and ensured that it was so.

He racked his memory trying to recall a patrol not returned, a soldier lost and not back at the camp. Had he miscounted before the raising of the wards one night? Was he so poor a leader as to have lost one of his own men?

Had he sent men out to die and not even noticed they didn't return?

Oberon grunted and kicked at the ground.

The mercenaries rose as one, turned to the stream and the bushes that hid Kit, that blocked the sight of the horse but not the beast's sounds. The torturer turned the quickest, his eyes glowed in the dark, a mad light in their depths, no humanity left within him. He wiped his blade along his leg, the red smear standing stark against his pants for a moment before the blood soaked into his clothes.

Kit held his breath, didn't dare make a move.

The brute stepped closer. Wind stroked over the leaves, blew them across Kit's face. His bow was strapped to his saddle horn. His sword likewise with his horse. The knife at his side would not do much to protect him from the four advancing towards him.

"KIT! Run!"

An arrow whizzed past his face, finding its mark with a wet thump in a mercenary behind him.

He did not hesitate to obey the command, taking the distraction and his savior's aid to fling himself away from the enemy and towards his horse. Kit managed to vault into the saddle, kicking Oberon into the deeper woods and towards the camp where his men could take the bastards chasing him and he could reach safety.

Damnit. He should have been more careful.

A trio of his guardsmen fell in around him, close on his tail as they raced through the forests.

"They're hunting the prince." Kit knew better than to name himself as the target. His men would as well. He did not think the bastards giving chase knew his face, or at least prayed that they didn't. Luck tended to be a fickle bitch.

Rinauld motioned to split up; Kit following him while the other two went in the opposite direction. Yes, best not to head towards the camp lest it become compromised.

Get out of the woods. Get Kit out of the woods.

But men had already died for him, and the thought of fleeing sat uneasy in his stomach.

Not that the choice was going to matter.

He heard the arrow whizzing before the pain punched through his shoulder. The agony was not instant like Kit thought it would be. He managed to turn his head down and stare at the arrowhead that had punched to his chest, even raised his right hand to touch the blood coated metal tip before the burn began and he had to hunch over his horse, praying he didn't fall from his seat. His left arm was numb. The bow he'd been holding fell from his fingers and he heard the crunch a few moments later as following hoofs broke the wood apart. His horse was slowing, and the world was blinking around him.

Rinauld looked back, nearly turned to come to his aid.

"Ride, you bastard! Get the fuck to safety!" Kit managed to yell the command even as he was overtaken by the bandits. If they knew he was the prince, he was dead anyways. If they thought he was just another soldier, if they thought that, perhaps, Rinauld had gotten away and Kit would know to where, he might live another day. He hadn't seen the body of the poor sod they'd killed. Kit was intelligent enough to know that it couldn't have been pretty if the man was dead, but he, Kit, wouldn't die.

The conviction would have sounded better to his ears if the world wasn't going gray and the ground wasn't rising up to meet him.

He hit the earth and could only think that he was lucky Oberon didn't trample him, that the other horses milling around didn't trample him as his consciousness fled and he was lost to sense.

HE WOKE TO the feel of hard wood beneath him, jumbled by the rough turn of wagon wheels over uneven terrain. Kit managed to keep his eyes closed, listening carefully to the sounds around him, counting the different breathing patters of three men, no doubt a driver somewhere up ahead. His arm was on fire, the numbness having worn away to prove that the nerves in his flesh hadn't been destroyed.

He cracked his eyes open enough to look at his surroundings. The small cart boated barely enough seating room for the four of them sharing the space. It was covered, which he didn't know if that was a plus or not given the number of men around him and the condition he was in. If the damn space had been left open, he would have had a better chance of tossing one of his opponents over the side, but he would fight on. The one nearest him had a knife. If he was quick enough, he could grab and kill the bastard before the others knew what was going on. The entire idea that he might be quick enough was a sham. With his arm as bad off as it was, already wheezing with the pain, Kit knew he was no match, but he wasn't going to go to his torture without at least taking one of them with him.

As far as decisions went, it was not his wisest. It was not his worst either, which was the sadder truth.

The cart lurched.

He threw himself to the side at the first guard.

Pain rampaged through his body. He grit his teeth when his good hand closed around the hilt of the knife and he managed to pry it free of his opponent's grip.

A pair of arms circled him from behind, locked beneath his jaw and around his head.

His air grew short.

Kit plunged the knife down.

At least one of them was dead with him.

II

WOOD POPPED IN a fireplace. It might have been a grate for all Kit knew, but he could smell the charring, the almost homey scent of warm fall afternoons curled in the den after a long court session with his father. A glass of brandy at his side, a book on his lap, papers ruffling in the heat of the room. Even the quiet of his library was undisturbed but for the hiss and sizzle of the flame. Soon Eli would come to join him, as she always did, bringing with her a snack, remembering his luncheon even when he forgot, was too busy for it. She'd wait till the king left before coming. He'd even share whatever morsel she brought

His lip quirked at the thought as he reached to the side table for his glass of amber salvation.

The fire burned through his body, eating at his flesh rather than the wood.

Kit's eye opened, memory surging in, panic and pain quick to follow. The arrow in his shoulder. The attack of the kidnappers, torturers more like. He pulled on his wrists, biting his lip at the agony of his pierced flesh, the drag of rope against his skin. At least the arrow had been removed, though he wasn't sure that was a mercy yet. Unlikely, given the circumstances.

He yanked at his right arm, hoping brute strength would accomplish his freedom when he could feel the strength of the rope used to bind him, the lack of slack for movement, the tear of his skin around the harsh weave of his bindings. His legs too were tied, boots gone so that his ankles felt the burn same as his wrists while he struggled.

"You're awake. How marvelous. I don't particularly enjoy having to wake up my dear guests. I do find a water bath to be refreshing, but the odor of mildewed flesh and cloth becomes quite intolerable after a time, don't you think?"

It took everything he had not to thrash in his chair, not to turn and try and pinpoint where the voice was coming from, scream out at having been caught in the first place. He panted there, in his seat, waiting for the inevitable, unwilling to hasten the moment of its arrival by searching for the male coming near him. Teeth grit, he replied in the same tepid, congenial tone of his presumed torturer: "I apologize for my rudeness, but it seems I am quite unable to rise."

The bastard laughed, a courtier's laugh, fake and pleasant and hiding the demon beneath. "You are too kind, my dear man, but do not worry over your inabilities. I assure you, they will not matter long." Wood scraped over hard stone. "Before we begin," a small man, glasses perched atop his nose, eyes smiling as he stared down at Kit, cheeks a merry red as though he were glad to be at his task, set a chair in front of Kit's.

Kit's grip tightened on the armrests as the man took a seat before him, legs bent to cross the left over the right, arms loosely folded in his lap.

"Could I interest you in a drink? Water perhaps? Or I believe I can rustle up a good liquor if you prefer? I do so believe that these sorts of matters require at least the basics of etiquette to remain civil lest we revert to our baser instincts and accomplish nothing at our task."

"Civil? I'm not sure I understand your meaning, sir."

"Yes. Exactly; precisely so. Sir. We shall keep to etiquette and thus proceed accordingly."

"Proceed at what?" Honestly, if the bastard wouldn't say it, Kit would. The male was playing with him and Kit found he would prefer knives or whips or whatnot than this charade presented as normality.

"Why, I should very much like to know where his Royal Highness, Christophe de L'Avigne is hiding. Would you be so kind as to tell me where I might find him?"

"I imagine his palace is a good start."

The male tsked, his smile slipping for a moment and a hard glint coming to his eye. The glasses slipped and beneath the frame was revealed the demon eating away at the soul of the man, if there had ever been a soul to begin with.

Ah gods, if Kit believed, now was the time to pray.

"My dear man, the Prince has been hunting for the past weeks as is his yearly wont to do. He has yet to return home. We know this, as we have managed to close all highways to his escape from these lovely woods. His hidey hole has yet to be discovered, and as such, we know he is here. You," the male leaned forward, slapping Kit's thigh as though long acquaintances reunited over old tales, "were a member of my good lord's party, and privy to his location."

"I was not."

"You would begin your lies already?"

The fingers dug into his flesh, all that separated the man's nails from Kit's skin a layer of buckskin too thin in Kit's opinion.

Civility is for kings and pawns. There are times that a prince must not be civil to defend his people.

His mother had taught him that too.

He doubted this was what she had had in mind during that lesson.

Kit managed his best court smile, the one that dared those who desired a dance to come and ask a barely leashed male riding the killing edge. He was feared on a battlefield, vengeance and control. His control was fraying, and he had no other way to attack bound as he was. "Fuck you." He was cordial, in his response, holding the man's gaze, refraining from spitting on the little shit.

The cherub sat back, the smile slipping from his face entirely, eyes going dead not even pretending at congeniality any longer. "I had hoped we could avoid profanity."

"I apologize for having given you the impression that I was a gentleman."

"How kind of you to correct my assumption."

"Indeed."

Kit flinched when the man drew a knife from beneath his coat sleeve, flinched, but did not look away, daring the bastard to put the blade to use.

The steel glinted in the faint flickering of the fire somewhere behind Kit's shoulder. He watched the man nod to someone at his back, though the inquisitor remained focused on Kit. There was a rustling of metal, a crash and sizzle and screech. His interrogator leaned forward, lowered himself slowly to his knees between Kit's bound legs. He touched the hem of Kit's breeches, slipped the tip of the blade between skin and cloth, and cut. Kit's pants parted easily beneath the edge of the knife, slit from ankle to knee, knee to pelvis, the process repeated on the other leg. Hands followed the revealed trail of flesh, catching Kit's breath in his throat. The cloth was pushed off his legs. The knife returned, and Kit held his breath as the inseam of his pants was cut to his waist on either side of his groin, baring him fully to the man's view but for his underclothes. Those, the man left for a moment, moving to Kit's shirt, sleeves then torso so it too could be removed.

"Yes, quite nice." A slap against Kit's stomach, barely a tap but enough that had Kit's held breath expelled in a rush, a growl rising in its place, and the male laughed before pressing the knife to the covered jewels protected by small cloths. "Shall we see what a soldier keeps under his clothes, boys?"

Kit turned his gaze to the wall over the man's head, letting the ass do as he would, calming his breathing, internalizing the ache from his shoulder, the pain that would no doubt follow soon enough.

They didn't know they had their prize.

He just had to stay alive until his men found him.

Give enough to entice them into keeping his heart beating one day more.

The knife nicked his groin. He bit the inside of his cheek to keep from making a sound.

"Impressive, even when flaccid. Lovely boys, don't you think?"

A muted murmur of assent was the response to the man's question. So they weren't all male-lovers then. Kit didn't think that would save him much if they turned his body against him. Damn. The nervous laughter tickled the back of his throat, threatened to release. He'd spent a life alone hoping for the chance to sleep with one woman, obeyed the godsdamned protocol that a prince was supposed to adhere to, never touch, never taste, and this was how it was going to end for him, never knowing her embrace, not even a kiss.

One of the kidnappers stepped around the side of his chair, handed the gentleman a whip, and stepped back out of sight. The turning of metal over in the fire grate sounded harsh in the room.

"Do forgive me, my good man. I did not catch your name."

Kit didn't respond.

A pink tongue slipped between the man's lips, wetting the red flesh. He breathed in, whistling at Kit's silence. "It is a simple question." He ran the whip between his hands, shaking his head at the feel, snapping his fingers for the guard to return and bring with him a pair of heavy gloves, hold the whip while the inquisitor covered his delicate flesh.

Kit watched, fingers tensing on the arms of the chair.

"Much better. Ah yes, your name. What is it?"

"Go to hell."

The pain was not what he had imagined, searing as it streaked across his chest and upper thigh, a thin line that radiated agony that faded quickly enough into gentle throbbing. The first strike hadn't broken skin.

It was worse than the strike of a blade on a battlefield. He knew what that wound felt like.

"Would you like to try again?"

"Cousar du pouwn liqfiat."

The last curse had barely fallen from his lips before the whip slashed twice in quick succession, a line down his right side, the second across his abdomen, layering along his elbows.

Eli had taught him that one night when her guards came to rouse her for evening patrols and he'd nearly been caught in her room. *You are pig shit.*

"I do not speak the woodland tongue, boy, but I am quite sure that *that* was no name you just spoke."

Kit's lack of response resulted in an equally brutal assault of the whip, still not breaking skin, still a painful agony he'd not known before in his life. The fifth mark wrapped over his shoulder, slashed across the open wound of the arrow's piercing. It brought a shrill cry to Kit's lips, barely held back.

The man pulled a kerchief from his breast pocket, wiped his dry brow and let the slip of cloth drop to the floor. Kit followed its descent, missed the raising of the man's arm, the ensuing strike unanticipated, all the harsher because of it. This time his torturer did not stop at five strikes or at marking Kit's flesh in red lines. Blood blossomed across his chest, ran in rivulets down the ridges of his abdominals, quickly joined by more lines as the beating continued, grew fiercer. Kit lost count around twenty-two, tipped his head back as the leather strap came closer and closer to his face, wrapping his neck on occasion but never striking his cheeks or eyes or cock. The man was an expert in wielding the weapon, a true master of his trade. That did not make the bearing of the abuse easier and told only that Kit's agony would last for a long time.

Every third strike, the man asked for Kit's name. And Kit held his tongue, teeth clenched against even a scream at his abuse.

"What is your name!"

The whip slashed a line from his wounded shoulder across the meat of his stomach to the head of his prick.

Kit screamed with the wound, the blood painting his body red now.

"Kit. Kit...kitkitkiii—"

He gasped out his name, sobbed it really, ashamed he could not withstand more than he already had.

He sat in his chair shaking, hunched forward as far as he could, trying to protect his abused body from any more.

"That wasn't so hard."

The man was out of breath, which was at least a small victory for Kit, knowing he had made the male work for Kit's response.

"See what being reasonable can bring?"

The rope binding his right wrist was released, the snick of a knife cutting through the cord, thumping boots moving to his left side. There were at least three men in this stone walled prison room. If he managed to pull the one freeing him over his body as protection, he might manage to take out the other guard and leave him facing just his tormentor and the whip which he was determined to withstand now.

The knife appeared at his left side. Kit moved fast enough to relieve the male of his weapon, claim it as his own. He forgot his legs were bound as well. If his ankles were free he might have managed to free himself, but his ankles were bound, and he fell over the body he pulled over his shoulder, the chair fell on top of him, and the whip master laughed while Kit struggled to breathe at the agony filling him. He refused to release the knife in his hand. Lying prone on the ground, his arm outstretched before him, the male on top of him stood and stepped on his right shoulder. There was a pop and then there was pain and Kit's fingers spasmed their grip on the blade before releasing, both arms useless now, one dislocated, the other unhealed from the arrow of a day before.

"Get him back in the chair. And get it ready."

Kit yelled, and he thrashed, and he screamed, and he fought, and it was all useless as they bound him back to his seat, lacing ropes now over his chest and biceps as well as thighs and calves, binding him tighter than before. He screamed, and he yelled, and he thrashed within his bonds while one giant of a man grabbed his wrist and turned it over, baring his palm to the room, his fingers closed tight in a fist. A second man joined the first, pulling Kit's fingers open, holding him as still as possible while the whip master exchanged his first implement for a cross shaped brand, red hot from the fire. Kit's eyes widened at the implication, and he yelled and screamed and cursed them all as the bright poker came closer and closer to his skin, burning him just from the heat alone before it touched his flesh in the center of his palm, held until the sizzling stopped while he continued to scream. And it was a scream. He couldn't help it. Perhaps, if Kit had been given time to prepare himself, he might have held his tongue, refrained from making a sound at the pain, but he was a prince. He'd been beaten in the lists during training practice. Beaten on the field of battle and walked away from that. But this was nothing like those times. He had no frame of reference for this agony. And it overcame him.

He revived to the splash of icy water down his body, nearly passed out again when the cold touched his burned palm.

He didn't know how long he'd been unconscious, but he didn't think long given that the man before him was still holding a red brand in his gloved hands.

Kit's other hand was quickly dried from his dousing and pried opcn.

His eyes widened, unbelieving and yet not shocked they would maim both of his hands so.

"So you don't forget the lesson, little boy."

The poker came down across his skin, as intense and agonizing as the first time.

He panted through it, met his tormentor's stare with a snarl and baring of teeth.

"Good show, old boy, but not enough. Tip him."

The goons turned his chair over, flipping it to its back, letting him fall onto the flagstone floor, his head striking the ground, spots dancing before his eyes at the crash. His hands clenched into fists unthinking. The raw wounds were agony, searing through his brain, shortening his breath. That pain was not enough to distract him from the hands now grabbing his right foot, the heat coming closer to his skin.

He screamed for them.

He screamed at the agony as they burned the bottoms of his feet, no chance of him running if he were set free, no chance of him grabbing for a weapon if one was left within his reach.

They hadn't asked him a question. *Dear gods*, ask him a bloody question.

He'd tell them whatever they wanted. Over the river, through the woods, across the stream, back again, he didn't care. Find the camp. Let him go. Stop the burning, please, stop.

He blinked, and the world shifted reformed around him from the dark nothing his moment's reprieve of unconsciousness granted. Black stones rose above him into eternity. He couldn't see the top of the dungeon they were holding him in. This was no temporary shelter. This place of pain and evil was something that had stood for a long while. The stones of the building were blackened from years of fires left to burn out and smoke.

He blinked, but his focus frayed all the more until the glow of the fire just beyond him caught his attention, was all he could see, blocked as a shadow passed before it, replaced a dying brand back into the flame. Kit watched the fires churn, smelled the remnants of skin burning away. His skin, from his hands and feet, burning away from the brand whose scar he would forever bear now. He blinked, but his eyes remained closed.

"Throw him in a cell. We'll continue after supper. Venison, yes?"

Don't yield, Prince. Never yield.

He wouldn't. He wouldn't yield. He'd promised; he'd promised his mother; he'd promised Eli. Hadn't he?

The bindings around his body were cut; his arms were pulled above his head and he felt the pain as his right shoulder popped back into place and the wound at the left opened and bled freely once more. He was dragged to a cell, left lying on the cold, unclean floor. He didn't make a sound.

The world faded away.

III

HE LOST TRACK of time or stopped counting the days and hours and tortures he endured.

Master Simeon came every day.

Kit liked to think of the man's arrival as morning, his only contemplation on the world beyond the gray black walls of his prison, his hell. The sun didn't touch this dungeon he was relegated to. Night came when Simeon left, and the guards opened his cell door and the doors of the few other prisoners within this wretched place, leaving him alone to their tender mercies. He'd screamed himself hoarse the first week. It had taken another before his throat was too swollen to make a sound above a whimper, not that he didn't try. That he could still feel the pain in his body, the beatings, the rapes, the pokers and the whips, broke him. Shouldn't he feel nothing after a time? Shouldn't he become numb?

In point of fact, the torture master was genius, never letting Kit adjust to a particular style before a new implement was added to his torment. Wounds healed, and then were reopened in new ways. His chest was covered in scars, his thighs and arms. Kit didn't want to consider what his back looked like.

The fire was the worst. Before his body was too weak to fight, those first days when he'd still had hopes of surviving this, being rescued quickly, he'd tried to escape. Feet and hands burned, hung from a hook in the ceiling, they'd left him there while they went upstairs for a midday meal.

His shoulder aching from being popped back into place without a chance to heal, the other burning from its wound, he'd managed to wrap the chains around his wrist, pull himself up, hoping to find a rafter high above to hide upon, out of reach of his tormentors. The other prisoners yelled for Simeon. Simeon came running before Kit had managed more than a few feet off the ground. That was the first night the other poor sods given a reprieve from their torture by his presence were allowed into his cell. Honestly, he should have expected the rape. And he had, the master had no boundaries and if it would hurt, then he would use it against Kit.

They'd pissed on him when his body was too broken to perform or use anymore, when their bodies were wrung dry. Cuts and bruises and worse remained when consciousness found him at the end of a bucket of water the next morning. It took three buckets to clean him to Simeon's liking, the second and third salt water to ensure he did not enjoy their ministrations. He grew used to the salt and sting.

Day by day he lost himself to the agony. He found himself laughing when they would chain him in the center of the dungeon for morning washings. Laughing, when the fire was stoked, and the red pokers removed to renew the burns on hands and feet, see what raised skin looked like on chest and thigh and groin. Laughing, when the knives and the whips danced before his vision. He cried at the agony of it, screamed and cried like a boy and not a man.

And he laughed.

When was it exactly that he could no longer recall where his camp was?

At some point, all directions, all knowledge of the prince's camp fled his broken mind. He should know. There was something he was supposed to remember and know but for the life of him he couldn't recall it and they kept asking, day after day, and he had no answer to give them so he laughed because laughing made him cry and Master Simeon wanted him broken and he was broke.

Kit...

The memory of her voice would flit through his mind. Her voice. He didn't know who she was anymore. He should probably know who she was, who he was.

Kit.

Yes, that's what Master Simeon called him. That was his name.

Kit.

The master had a bucket of coals spread over the floor. He was lifted on chains, hung above the hot embers.

Master asked where the prince was.

Here, here; I'm here, Kit screamed.

Master said he wanted the truth or he would make Kit burn.

Kit cried as he was lowered to the coals.

Master smiled and let the chains drop and kit could not hold his own weight against his pain and fell to the burning floor.

kit screamed when the fire burned into his already blackened skin.

The kit begged the master please no more.

Master said to answer, and he would stop hurting the kit.

The kit screamed at the blisters forming on his flesh.

Master had a bucket of water poured over him, but the coals still burned where they stuck to his skin. Not his face or hair; must not let his hair burn or the brain would burn too. That's what the Master told his minions who poured more water over the kit to put the fire finally out and he laid in the hissing coals because he could not move, dared not move, hoped no movement would kill him.

The bad men held the kit down in the night.

The coals hurt worse than the bad men.

The bad men said his flesh was warmed by the coals. Bad men were too timid to touch the red embers and bring them to the kit to warm him for their use.

The kit stared at the cell bars. Tears slipped over his cheeks. He stopped trying not to cry.

THE KIT COULD not move from his cell. Bad men, Master's men, dragged him from his prison. Bad men dropped him on the floor. The kit stared at the door bad men left through.

The kit was alone for the first time since the Master came.

Kit…

It hurt to make his fingers move, pull him over the stone floor. The burns made him weak, but he was alone and he needed to find the voice in his head. He had to find it now before the voice was gone and the Master returned.

"You have had him for a month and he's told you nothing! What do I pay you for?"

The door opened to the Shouting Man.

Bad men swarmed around Shouting Man, rushed down the stairs and pulled the long knife the kit scrabbled for from him. Bad men beat him. Kicked him and beat him and the kit curled on the ground and could barely see through swollen eyes the dark stone around him.

Shouting Man grabbed the kit's hair. Shouting Man pulled the kit's head back and then dropped the kit to the ground. The kit sobbed. Help me, uncle, the kit tried to say. But the words would not come, and the kit watched his uncle stand back and kick out and there was a snap in the kit's torso and pain speared through him, fresh pain that stole his breath and his whimpers and sobs and the darkness returned.

Uncle shouted, and Master bowed and pleaded.

Master smiled red and Master fell in front of the kit. Master's eyes stared into the kit's. Master got to die, but not the kit.

Warm came from Master and flowed over the kit's numb fingers and down the kit's flesh and turned his skin pink in the dark night of the dungeon.

"The new torturer will be here at dawn. If the rat doesn't speak then, kill him. There are enough soldiers trapped in these woods to capture and use who will be of more use. We've only a weak before *Losfidalia Quantir Forseith.* He must die before the gods return. The walls must fall so I might rein."

Bad men agreed.

The kit was left where he lay.

Uncle Shouting Man left through the door and slammed it closed.

Kit shivered on the floor.

Only one more day, and they would let him die.

There was something he was supposed to remember, someone he couldn't remember. He couldn't remember himself. That must be it.

Kit.

CHAPTER TWO

I

FOR A MOMENT, only a moment, she felt him, felt the pain and agony of his soul reaching out for hers. In the Darkness of her dreams, she felt him, a brief brush of his mind against her own, drawing her north, north beyond the woods to a place of stone and darkness and men swarming a room bound round with metal bars.

Eli woke from the vision, bolted from her bedroll in the prince's camp and barely found the slop bucket before her stomach heaved and she fought to get control of herself. She needed to speak to the General. She could find Kit. She could find their prince.

THE MAN WAS discussing strategy at a table in his tent, sleepless as he'd been for the past month since their prince had vanished, been captured.

"A tower. Where is there a tower dungeon? They're holding him there."

Marius looked at her, his eyes glazed from exhaustion, incomprehension shining in his gaze.

"Kit's there, in a tower dungeon. We need to find him now."

"There are no towers around here, Eli. The closet one is Kravn's Keep. Kravn has been in contact with the king. There has been no sighting of the prince near him. For the gods' sake, Eli. Kravn is Kit's uncle. He's been searching as hard as we have for our prince."

"I am telling you, Marius, General, he is there. Kravn is lying."

"He is the King's brother."

"Fuck the king's brother and fuck the king. I'm telling you Kit is there."

She knew. She could feel it in her soul. She could feel him, snatches of moments throughout their lives, moments of heartache, of pain, of fear, but always him. Always when he needed her or when she needed a brief moment of knowing he was alive and somewhere in the world with him.

She'd known since the moment he danced with her nearly four hundred years ago. She might have denied the binding between them, done her best to deny it and break it, and ignore it, but it was there, and every day he was missing, a piece of her died knowing he was out there alone and she couldn't find him.

But she knew where he was now.

Her heart was struggling to beat. Her breaths were labored in her chest. Her limbs felt numb and swollen yet physically there was nothing wrong with her. She felt nothing within her flesh to account for her weakness, yet she was weak, and death was dogging her steps and if she could feel the devil chasing her, he must already be at Kit's side. There was no time left. She knew her prince was standing on the threshold and if he was not saved soon, he would not be saved. Not soon. Soon was too long from now.

"I beg you, Marius. Listen to me. He will die by sunset if we do not rescue him now."

"Out."

The other members of the General's command fled at the anger in Marius' voice.

She watched his careful movements as he placed his palms flat on the table between them, staring down at the map on his desk instead of looking at her.

"You have never trusted me and I—"

"How did you get through the patrols to meet us here?"

She stilled. Her breath, her heart, her mind, stilled at his question. He did not know who she was, who she had been before that night on the road after the ball with the prince. Kit would never have told her secret, but this commander was not an idiot, was not dumb nor ignorant but a force to be reckoned with at all times, on the battlefield and in the strategy tent.

He knew she was of the woods, hadn't questioned that she was an elf, well, had but never let that question dictate to him. He knew she couldn't enter the wood and he could guess why.

But Kit would never have told him who she was, no matter what, the choice was hers.

"Three hundred and some years ago, when you were still earning your place under my command, word reached me that a new Elichi had been chosen for the woodland realm. Rumor said that the previous Priest of the Sword was young, in her prime, not expected to fall for a lifetime or longer and yet less than a hundred years into her rein, she was replaced in her position. Eli. Elichi. It is not a name so much as a title."

"The title means nothing. It is the skill that grants the title that is the prize."

"How did you get through the patrols, Eli? We are ringed round and cornered here. There is no way through or past without meeting the full force of the army sent to cage us, without braving the woods denied you. This was a well-planned attack. This is a coup. The only reason our enemies have yet to take the city is that they believe the prince still alive in our guard and are searching for him. They have not realized their prize is within their grasp and has been for a month or more. But you were not here when the patrols began. You do not hunt these woods or any other and never have. Yet he was captured, and you came on swift wings, but there was no breaking of the ring around us. How did you get through the patrols, Elichi?"

"I am no longer that person. Three hundred years ago the title was stripped from me. I am not that title any longer."

"You were of the forest. Four men died by your hand. The banishment stands for four hundred years and it has not been that many. Yet you are here, and the patrols remain unhindered. How did you find us?"

"The woods were not guarded but by those who name them home."

"You killed four men, four of your own men, to save my prince once before. How many did you kill to come to his aid now?"

"They are not my people any longer."

"How many?" He slammed his fist on the table, and she did not understand this anger he had at her presence.

"Why does it matter?"

"Because I cannot find him, yet here you are saying you can and I do not know that I can trust you with my heart!"

And there it was, the truth she had known for a lifetime or more, and that she did not think her prince realized. She'd given in to that truth, obeyed it, knowing her claim was as valid, more so, than this man's, but she hadn't said that, and Kit had suffered, and was suffering now. She'd spent nearly a hundred years as a shadow, so this man could love her prince and her prince could find another because she was nothing to her own people, would never be enough in the view of his.

But the general and she loved the same man. And, by the Darkness that Covers the World, she prayed the prince loved her more than his friend she shared this tent with.

She would give the only answer a man as in love as herself would accept. "Yours is not the only heart that will fail without him."

He met her gaze with tears in his eyes. To see a man so overcome ate at her soul. It was a reason she made a terrible priestess under her mother's rule. She hated the pain of a wounded heart, would rather destroy that sorrow than rebuild it. She was a killer and made no excuse for her life choices, but she loved too, and that was nearly unforgivable. Her life changed the moment she met Kit, yielded to the need to be near him, to know him. She did not regret that choice.

"I ensured no one of the woods died by my hand in coming for you. They won't kill within their borders, not even the prince they want dead more than any other. It's why you've been safe hunting these woods all these years. They don't kill, but they won't stop anyone else from doing the deed within their woods."

"They would kill you."

"Yes. If they caught me, I would be the exception."

"They did not see you."

"Exiled from the forest does not mean I am no longer a child of it. The Darkness protects its own."

He held her stare, unyielding. She clenched her fingers into a fist, determined not to beat the man for his time in answering, time they did not have to waste. "You are certain in what you've seen?"

"I am certain. On my heart: he is in the tower."

The man leaned over the table between them, his hands dark against the vellum of the map spread out before him. "Then we get him out."

II

SHE DID NOT know the king's brother. The man had never been introduced to her, and she had never bothered to introduce herself to the nobles of the court who were not her prince's direct compatriots. What did she care of others? That her heart beat only for him, even if she hated the admittance of the sentiment, was all that truly concerned her.

But the man who stood before her, graying hair, and stone-gray eyes, so similar to his nephews, would never be mistaken for anything but nobility. She did not need the ring on his finger nor the announcement of his personal guard to tell her who he was. His harsh appraisal, the leering grin he sent her way as he stared at her, meant nothing but another moment she was from her Kit's side. He laughed, and she stood straight and unbowed before him, letting his idiocy give her time to decide the best way in which to kill him. A knife was too quick for someone so foul.

She might love the king, just a little. The king was part of the man she loved, and so she could not hate him entirely. But this man, if man could describe the type of demon he was, was no family to her, and she had no mercy for him, not for what he'd ordered done to his own nephew, even unknowingly. He'd ordered it done to anyone caught for his greed. He was worse than foul.

"A female. Are you mad?" He turned to look at the men standing at her back.

Dressed in the uniforms of mercenaries they'd killed to reach the keep, the general and the prince's guard did not react to the criticism.

"You asked for the best, and we have delivered her into your keeping."

Kravn, that was the name of this evil, sneered at her and her men. "Kill them all. We'll do the job ourselves." He raised a hand to call his servants forward, men oozing from the hall to circle her and her guards.

"A demonstration, perhaps, my lord?" She did not drop the hood from her head, though tilted her face enough that she could meet the man's eyes.

"Blood will make a lady sick."

"I am no lady."

She moved faster than he could follow. If she so desired, she could likely kill all of those in this tower before they knew she was attacking. It might not be quick enough to stop one of them from slitting her prince's throat, from slitting hers at the same time. Better, instead, to wait, and to fight after Kit was safely away.

So she moved and grabbed the guard at the bastard's back, pulling him against her chest and backing towards her men, dragging him with her. Her knife drew a thin line of blood at his throat, and she smiled at the scent of iron wine in the air.

Her victim clutched at her arm pinning him, and she ignored the scrabbling of his fingers against her.

How long had it been since she used the magic inherent to her people to take a life? How long since she had hunted for the evil that sought to hide in the Dark's embrace?

She'd grown complacent within the borders of the city. She'd called shadows, and fought battles, but she'd foresworn her vow to the Master of the Final Midnight. She was the hand that ushered man to the Darkness.

She could love, for she loved Kit. She could heal, and she'd healed for Kit. But a healer's gifts could be turned dark so easily. Pinch a nerve in the arm, and the hand would go numb. Leave the vein closed and the flesh would bloat with blood unable to return to the heart. So easy, to crush bone housed within the thin covering of skin, watch said skin sag without a skeleton to hold it erect.

She leaned in to her victim's throat, her words carrying easily in the room. "If it is any consolation, I will kill you when I am done with you. But until then, know agony." A thought was all it took for his arm to shatter, bone snapping through skin at her will. No, not enough though, not nearly enough for the thoughts she read in this man's mind, the vision of the broken body in the cell below that had not suffered like this but had suffered worse in so many ways.

"*Qui forlcrum domini galrustion.*"

Know the agony he knows.

She forced the memories of Kit's torture to this man's mind, that which this man had inflicted she returned to him tenfold, and when he screamed himself hoarse, she willed his arm gone, and the flesh unraveled, and blood and bone dissolved beneath her will, exposed only for a moment to the watching eyes of the men around her before the limb was eaten by the Darkness of the night that her kind called God, that her people worshipped as That Which Covered the World and was Inescapable.

Eli let the male drop from her grasp, slitting his throat as he fell forward to writhe on the ground at her feet in his last moments before Death claimed him. The Darkness consumed him, leaving no flesh, no ash, no blood or remembrance of the body that once had been behind. Only the clothing, untouched by her magic and her fury.

For so long she had kept a leash on this side of herself, enjoying her life in Kit's court, a life of blood and death and the battle and dance of swords, but pure, untainted by the magic of her mother's court. She was the Elichi. She was the Daughter of the Darkness, the Priestess of Final Midnight, the only female to earn the title as the ruthless killer who was Justice to those deserving of a harsh end, Mercy to those who begged a quick death.

She hadn't forgotten this side of herself.

Kit hadn't shied from it when they were at war and she fought to save his life and her own. He'd held her when she fought back the madness trying to claim her.

Kit had renamed her.

A title is not a name, he'd said.

It was not a name, no, but it was who she was, and it was so much more than just a nightmare told to scare little city dwellers into sleeping through the night.

She was Eli.

The men at her back grasped at their swords, ready to draw them against her.

She fought back the Darkness, because she wasn't vengeance here, she wasn't justice.

She was the captain of Kit's guard. She was here for the man she loved, the man who was dying in the dungeon below her feet.

Today she was not the Dark's Mistress, and she could not let the demands which once consumed her do the same now.

She fought the darkness, and it was Marius, standing at her back, who placed his hand against her shoulder, gave her a touchstone to cling to. Hers. These men were hers. They would fight for her, and she would fight for them.

She took a breath, sent waves of whispering dreams of happier times to her men, soothing them like their mothers would, rocked to sleep in warm embraces.

The men of the keep, she wrapped in fear so that they would remember who and what she was, and they would give her what she wanted, even if they didn't realize she wasn't there for his death.

"You're from the woods."

Her smile was hollow, pulled at her skin grown too tight to her bones. She was not herself, flooded by the power that was her birthright and her damnation. If she was lost to it now, he would die, her prince would die, and she would die with him. Her death did not frighten her as much as losing him did. For a moment, for a breath, she broke apart, lost herself to the power swirling within her veins, to the rage at the injustice it sought to fight. For a moment, she was not herself but who she once was, and then Marius' hand tightened, and her mind was her own again.

The king's uncle bowed to her; bowed to her power and her terror.

"Where is he?"

But she knew the answer. Down the stairs, beyond the door. He waited for her. He did not know she was here, but he was waiting, and she'd come.

The traitor pointed at the door behind her, and she turned to face her men standing terrified guard at her back. They were afraid of her. The acrid scent of sweat filled the air, fists gripped swords like they had a chance of stopping her at her zenith. She felt the surge of dark approval in her veins at their terror and had to fight hard against it.

She could kill them all. It would be easy. A thought, a whisper, a touch as innocuous as a brush of fingers against a closed fist and they would die, screaming in agony, and she could walk free.

But there would be no coming back from the killing edge. There would be no hope for her if she took all these lives, some unclaimed by the Darkness, some worth saving under the Night's Eye.

If she gave in, she would be nothing more than a vessel of the Black, and she did not know if she would remember to spare Kit if she was consumed.

Marius stood strong, stood before her, met her gaze to bring her back to their place amidst the demons in this hellhole. Oh, she could see the terror there. He might have offered his touch to ground her, but it was a weak thing. He was trusting her with his heart, and he didn't know if that trust was misplaced, and until she saw Kit, saved Kit, she didn't know that she could get enough control of herself not to be a threat to the men she had adopted as her family. She knew there was madness in her gaze, but Marius held her stare, and nodded, leaving the way free to her approach, her descent.

She blinked her eyes, let the tear fall and knew he watched that last vestige of humanity she claimed as her own dry on her skin before she opened the door and descended into the madness she would either raise her heart from, or die within.

No one stopped her from closing the door at her back.

THE FIRE IN the grate was banked. Its heat barely enough to suffuse the small fireplace, let alone the room beyond. Cell doors lined one side of the space. All but one was empty, the men within standing at the bars, staring as she descended into their domain. She kept her gaze on them, stalking from the stairs to stand before their cages and gauging the hearts of the men within.

"All shall die." Her voice held the Dark power still riding her hard. It took a single touch of her hand against theirs before they fell to their separate floors and writhed there. "Tenfold times tenfold. You could have been free, but you stayed to torture him because it was not you who suffered. Tenfold times tenfold. The price is weak for what you have done."

But she didn't have time to exact greater retribution than that.

Not vengeance.

Vengeance was for the weak; those who needed to clean their souls by the shredding of their persecutors.

No, this was Retribution.

Payment in kind.

A thought froze their vocal chords, silenced their screams so they were denied even that small outlet of escape from their suffering.

Her gaze fell on the one she'd come for, and she would not be distracted from him any longer.

Carefully, for he flinched at the slightest sound, she made her way to the center of the chamber and her prince lying naked there. He did not shiver nor look to her. There was not a place unmarked on his body, bruises and bleeding covered him, blackened his eyes and burned his arms and chest.

"Kit."

She knelt at his side, but he made no sound but to drag in a breath that rasped and barely supplied him with air. The cloak she wore was warm, meant to cover him while they subdued the keep and brought him to safety. Her cloak was meant to give him comfort, but if she covered him with the heavy cotton lined with fur, the weight would bury him. Skin and bones. Gone was the graceful prince she'd known, the soldier, the warrior, the dancer, her comfort. Left was only a corpse kept breathing by a will likely broken to basic thought, too afraid to die and yet begging for the sweet release all the same.

A sob tore from her throat, her hands hesitating over his skin, afraid even to brush aside the cinders clinging to burns layering his flesh. "Kit."

He eyes fluttered, barely able to open beneath the bruising that swelled them closed.

His lips parted but no sound emerged.

Still, she read the words he spoke in silence.

"I know you."

"Yes. I'm here. I'm here, Kit. I'm here."

His hand rose from the ground, not far, barely enough to notice, but it rose, and she reached for him, lifting his swollen fingers, his burned palm, to her cheek, burying the fury at his torture deep inside so that he would not feel the cold wash of her rage, would not flinch away from her.

"Ella." His fingers curled against her cheek, brushing her skin with his knuckles. He smiled at her, a brief upturn of lips cracked and bleeding. "Love—"

If she hadn't been holding his hand, it would have fallen to the cold stone floor the moment the last of his breath left his lungs. She pulled him closer, felt the stopping of her own heart as he died before her and she was powerless to save him.

No, not powerless, not yet.

She channeled the despair in her spirit, the Dark power of destruction that her mother used as the greatest healer of the Dienobolos.

She was her father's daughter, she knew that, but she'd done her mother's will from time to time. She could heal him.

Please gods, Merciful Darkness, just once, she needed her strength and her magic to respond to her will as it was meant to, as she desired because she could not lose him, not yet, not now, not when she had only just found him, when there was too much left unsaid between them, too much left undone. She held his hand to her heart and pressed her hand to his, formed the circle between dead and living and breathed into it, willing her life to be his, their souls to finish the binding between them.

The world shuddered.

Not the dungeon, not the ground at her feet, but the world in total, that which was her home and beyond the woods she'd grown up in. The world shuddered, and died, expelled a breath that was held deep within the bowels of the earth and shattered. Or would have shattered, for her breath filled his lungs, and his heart beat a painful staccato within his chest and the world steadied, reformed to his life beat, held together for a moment more.

Sweet Night.

It was not the walls that would fall if he died. Not just the walls within which he lived and was meant to rule. Why had his gods made him the fate of the world? How could no one have ever guessed at that truth? He was far more precious and far more important than any had known, and she did not have the skill to hold him to this life for very long.

A thought opened the door to the dungeon, brought Marius to the stone steps to look down upon the hell his prince was forced to live in.

She could hear the fighting, the battle waged above.

Marius would have guarded the door for her retreat, for his prince's retreat.

Brave man, to stand and face her after her demonstration above. Likely no other had been willing to take the post.

"We need a healer. He won't last much longer, and I cannot carry him from here alone."

The commander nodded, rushing from the doorway to her side, Kit's side. The man did not know where to lift, no place free of pain on Kit's body, their movements bound to cause more agony than spare any. Still, they managed to raise their prince, his arms slung about their shoulders.

Eli looked to the stairs, expecting their enemy to walk through the door and block their path. But it was not their enemy she saw, and the guards who defended their retreat nodded to her, fear in their gazes, yes, but respect too.

They managed to get Kit up the stairs.

At the top, the commander passed Kit to another soldier, taking post to get them from the building.

She knew the moment Kit returned to consciousness, the moment he tensed against her hold on him, prepared himself for whatever new torment awaited him. "We're getting you out of here, love. Stay with us now, we're getting you out of here."

"ELF!"

She turned at the call, looking at the stairway leading to the upper levels of the keep and the raging bastard whose sword even then pierced the belly of one of her men, her ally, her friend. She turned to the call, and Kit turned with her.

She did not expect him to know who the man was. That Kit was aware enough to tense, for a rage as dark as her own to pour out from his spirit, was a terrifying thought, not that it was undeserved, but that she was infecting him with her own Darkness. In the moment it took her to think the thought, he lurched from her grip, overbalanced and she had to scramble to keep him from tumbling to the floor. He hung limp from her side, choking on blood that welled past his lips, the purple around his ribs enough to know that the broken bones had finally caught an organ and pierced through. She should have been more careful, known better than to stop and turn. He coughed, and smiled, and she looked to see Kravn fall from his perch on the stairs, tumble over the banister and land on the ground of the main floor, the knife Kit'd thrown piercing the man's heart.

The fighting stopped for a moment; the mercenaries' leader dead on the floor.

Eli thought that perhaps they would disperse, they would be free to leave with the master dead.

A cry split the castle, and the fighters yelled to augment the bellow, renewing their attack for the spirit of their dead leader.

"We need to get out of here."

Marius must have heard her over the din, sword slicing into the torso of his opponent, clearing a space for them to escape into, rush the main doors and into the waiting dawn of the day beyond.

She helped her partner lift Kit into the cart they'd brought with them, climbed in after her prince and shifted until she could rest his head in her lap, keep him within her arms while they fled.

Her soldiers filed out, the men rushing from the keep, Marius the last to leave, supervising the retreat.

She must have known, deep in her soul, that one of them would not leave this place alive. He must have known that the better option would be to save her life at the cost of his own.

He stood in the castle doorway, his men mounting their horses, preparing to flee, the remainder of their guard already ranged in the forest as escort for them all. Marius stood in the doorway, and turned back to the keep, closing the portal behind him, remaining to stall whatever men still lived so they had a chance to escape.

"NO!"

But her word was mistaken, and the driver of the cart snapped the reins and the horses flew forward, into the woods, away from this terror, towards a hoped-for safety.

There were mercenaries in the woods, still blocking their path.

They needed a healer, or he would not make the journey from this place.

His breathing stuttered, his eyes opened wide with his panicked, strangled breath. She pressed her hand to his sternum, felt the Black of her magic rush down her arms in flowing vines, weave from her flesh to his and bolster what little strength remained within him.

"Get us to the woods!"

"They'll kill us, my lady."

"I'm your fucking captain! Get us to the godsdamned woods and I will get us past their patrols. We need the Priestosolos. She's the only hope he has."

"The elves will kill us same as the mercs!"

"Leave them to me."

She matched her breathing to his, forced her spirit into his flesh, his body to yield to her will. She held him to his flesh, refused to let him die though death must have been a relief to all that he had suffered. She kept him alive, and spread before her a plea for sanctuary, a call for aid, her magic spiraling into the roots below the wheels of the cart, the branches reaching far into the woods, the forest answering her plea as they barreled deeper into the trees.

Called by a priestess of the wood. Begged by a priestess of the wood. Summoned by a priestess of the wood.

Her once people met them at the boundary of glade and forest, rode herd on her guards and spirited them along the hidden paths to the center of the Priestosolos' territory and the greatest healer in this realm. She kept her hand to his heart, let her tears fall unheeded down her cheeks as the beating beneath her palm stuttered and pleaded to stop.

They raced through the woods, and she knew her once brethren gathered close not for his protection, but to ensure that she did not escape what justice was owed. They raced to salvation and doom.

Merciful Night, let them see his life is what keeps ours from dying. Do not let him die. Do not let us die.

III

THE ELVES SWARMED them when the cart came to a stop in the center of the wood. Eoa, the Mother Tree, as large around as a house and taller than ten stories, rose in the center of the grove, the beacon of the Dienobolos and their worship. From the trees surrounding the mother wood, Eli's people stood with bows pointed to the ground, safe within their flying homes, guarded by the branches and leaves the rooms were built into.

No one moved, not her brethren, nor the guards.

"*Isto fortuis rad'lichoi eist.*"

Her mother walked from the hewn doors of the great tree, the oak having been hollowed out over the centuries to form the Temple to the Darkness all elves worshiped. The High Priestess would not forgive Eli's betrayal. Already she called all arrows to be turned upon Eli in the cart. The Dienobolos would not miss when they let the bolts fly. Eli would die with the shaft of an arrow through her heart if her mother were merciful. But her mother had called for imprisonment first, and it would not be a quick death she faced.

By the breaking of her exile, returning to the wood, Eli accepted the death sentence she'd earned herself. She'd called for sanctuary though, and once invoked, in the Darkness' name, her mother and her brethren were bound to offer respite until words were broken amongst the elves and those seeking refuge.

"She has invoked Sanctuary, Priestosolos."

Eli did not know the man who walked boldly towards her mother. Once, upon a time, Eli had been so bold too.

Priesto, a Priest of the Dark. *Solos*, the highest amongst men.

From the moment of her birth, Eli knew her mother only as the High Priestess. The woman who bore her showed the same love and devotion to all her people, blood bound or not. When Eli achieved the rank of Elichisolos, it was her mother who made the offering to the Darkness, bound Eli to the Wood and summoned the Night to fill Eli with Its power. That Eli chose to offer death, a warrior and not priest or healer, to the Night, deepened the rift between them, but it was still the only day she remembered feeling her mother's pride in her, and she'd betrayed that by saving this prince. Twice over now.

Her mother was not just priestess, though it was the greatest of her titles.

It was not the priestess that Eli sought to invoke within these woods.

"Lieasolos, I invoke Sanctuary for these men and their prince. I beg the Darkness for Healing as we have too long misunderstood the—"

She would have finished her tale, told her mother that it was not the walls that would fall if Kit died but all the world. She would have spoken the words and offered her truth as proof of them, but her heart lurched within her chest, a painful contraction that staggered her, bent her over her prince as his breath expelled and once more the ground began to shake.

Had she the strength to look about her in that moment, she would have noted the trees quaking to their roots, branches tumbling to the ground without wind or rain to cause the fall. Eoa screamed, a harsh sound of twisting wood and burning forest though no fire swept through the grove.

No, Eli did not look about her and see the destruction of his death. What Darkness was granted to her, what little skill her mother had imparted in healing, Eli poured into his ravaged flesh, held the wisp of spirit not yet flown from his body to this world, used it to reel in the soul of the man she loved, even knowing how desperately pained and willing to die he was.

Her heart beat.

Air filled his lungs.

The tremors of the earth stilled, and she wept for her strength was spent, the Darkness that was her birthright and earned by strength of arms, was light within her, leaving her empty. She could not hold him if he fled his body again. If she could not hold him to her, then she would follow, and be glad for the obliging.

She trembled at his side, not having realized she'd fallen in his plight, unable to even hold him with the weakness in her flesh.

"Please, Lieasolos," her words slurred against her tongue, eyes trying to focus on her mother now in the cart beside her, ancient hands placed to the prince's chest in what Eli feared was a ministration of death. "It is not the walls that will fall."

IV

ELI WOKE IN the clutch of a nest, her body cocooned within the warm embrace of branches piled high with blankets and hot stones. The gentle hand caressing her forehead soothed her, calmed her, tempted her to burrow back into the warm embrace of slumber and forget the world around her.

Her eyes opened wide, staring at the woman sitting at her side, the woman staring back.

"Did you know, when you spared him all those years ago, the truth of his life?" Her mother spoke in their native tongue, a language Eli expected to hear only curses in before she died, yet this was a simple question asked with an unassuming tone.

"No, Priestosolos."

The priestess' fingers moved to Eli's throat, testing the strong pulse beating there though the ache remained deep in Eli's chest, not all from Death waiting too close to claim her, *him*.

"Did you bond him, knowing we would not kill you once we learned his death would kill the world?"

She had not meant to bond him at all. Knowing her death would mean his in the end offered no comfort to her. She'd felt his suffering when she'd taken stupid risks over the years, faced Death and survived to tell the tale and he'd waited for her return, never knowing how close his end came at her hands. Had she known what bonding to him would mean, had she known that she'd committed the act without thought or knowledge of how it was done, she would have reversed it post haste. Was it too late to do so now? If anyone knew how it was undone, it would be the High Priestess; and if Eli begged mercy from the Dark, the

Night might answer kindly and allow her life to be severed without the loss of his. "I offer my life in payment for the ones I've taken. I beg only that you separate the bond you speak of. Let him live, Priestosolos, I beg it of you and the Darkness that Claims us all."

"You did not answer my question, child."

"I bound to him the night the brethren attacked, Priestosolos."

"And when did you learn that his death heralded the death of us all?"

"When he died in my arms in the dungeon they held him in." The anger and bitterness and self-hatred were clear in her voice. The man she loved, the man she had given everything up for, had only grown more and more enamored of over the years, had died, not once, but twice in her arms and she was too late to save him. No, that was not precisely true. She hated herself because he should never have known such suffering.

Tears slipped from the corners of her eyes.

She swiped at them, closing herself to emotion as befit the position she once held within the Dienobolos. She would not shame herself or them by crying over fate's fickle ways.

"Can you sever the bond between us? Can you spare him from the taking of my life? Whatever I must do, I offer it to you in payment, but I beg you," how desperately she wanted to plead to her mother but spoke only to the priest instead, "I beg you, do not make him suffer further."

The Priestosolos stared at Eli, a gentle hand making idle circles on Eli's chest as she laid on her back in her bower. The hand stilled over her heart, the longest finger tapping out the rhythm that coursed blood through Eli's body, life into her. "There is a way to do what you ask, to sever the claim your heart has laid on him. This I could do for you."

Eli looked away from her mother, stared into the limbs of branches above her head that created a second floor. Many times as a child she'd run through the massive tree, trailing her fingers over the burrowed nests within its thick trunk. She sang to the injured or the ill that remained within the wooden nests as they were treated by her mother, the healers within the order of *Liaea*.

So many aspects of the darkness: the priests who prayed to the night, to *Pirie* in the Darkness; the healers worshipping the *Liaea*, the inner blackness of the body never to touch the sun. *Echi*, Master of the Final Midnight, the End of All Things, harbinger, guardian. *Rouchim*, the gatherer, the nurturer, Lady of the Earth, Keeper of Secrets; *Ashet*, the laborer, the sentinel, Lord of the Forge, Harnesser of the Light. All aspects of the One Darkness, all housed here, within Eoa, the temple that stretched into the Eve.

She could have offered herself to the *Liaea*, used the darkness to heal, or help or forge or honor, but she'd chosen *Echi*, been the Master's Darkness come to Man, and now that darkness betrayed the life she wished most to save.

She heard the 'but,' in her mother's voice. Her death would not be so simple as the breaking of a bond. Though exiled from the wood, she'd been a daughter of it still, worshipping the stars in the heavens that illuminated the Night, gave It shape and soul. Priestosolos could break the bond between Kit and Eli, but Eli would lose the Night as her guardian in the sundering.

"No, Daughter."

Eli blinked away the moisture in her eyes, turning her head once more to the woman at her side.

"You are, and will always be, a child of the Night. Your soul was anointed by the Darkness and that can never be turned away. I can break your bond to the boy—"

"Prince. He is no boy, has not been for many years."

Her mother nodded. "—the prince. It would be a simple thing to turn your heart from the beating of his. But I cannot turn his heart from yours, Iisforsos."

Iisforsos.

First to Walk Among the Stars.

Eli's brow furrowed. "I do not understand."

"Let us see to your prince, and then I will explain."

"Priest—"

"Come, Daughter, we've spent enough time here. Your prince is beginning to spiral again."

She'd forgotten that the *Lieasolos*, once ascribed to a healing, was bound into the being she worked with. Her mother would know every tortured breath Kit took, each stuttered beat of his heart. Eli tried to ignore her own bonding to the man. It was hard enough to imagine giving him up, but she would make the sacrifice gladly, even if, as her mother said, his heart was bound to hers. Rather he should live, and she die. His life was all she wanted for him.

Eli struggled to free herself from the tangle of blankets surrounding her. The nest was warm, but it did not help the chill chasing down her spine. She missed having him at her back, knowing he was there when she slept, or would come at the rise of the night. She missed his hand extended to help her rise when dawn chased the black from the sky.

The hand she took now was cold in comparison, old where his was once young and supple. Would his hands be the same ever again? She knew the burns that covered his flesh.

She missed the smile when he met her gaze in the morning, missed the returning of it on her own lips.

"Come."

Eli walked at the high priestess' side down the winding path that climbed the inner walls of the tree trunk. The bed she'd been given was on the fifth spiral so the descent took time, though the silence between them was calm and peaceful.

Still, her heart beat faster the nearer they drew to the main floor. She dared not look over the railing as she would have to step to her mother's right hand to do so. She did not deserve to walk in such a place. But the closer they drew to the temple proper, the greater the pull of his misery became.

"You put him on the altar?"

His blood would awaken the Darkness. He was not a disciple of the woods. He could not make the same offering, suffer the same acceptance as she or her mother or any other of the Dienobolos made.

Eli made to push past the high priestess, very nearly succeeding in getting around her mother and to the aisle leading to the dais before the breath was stolen from her lungs and she dropped to the floor, choking as she tried to breathe but no oxygen came to her.

The Priest passed her, and air returned.

Eli gasped in great lungfuls, coughing though all she wanted was to sprint to Kit's side, protect him from whatever the Priestosolos would do. She managed a strangled "Please," but her mother did not turn back to her, continued down the path into the darkened Sanctuary and the secrets held within.

She fought to her feet.

Eli pulled herself along the rows of pews, sobbing at the blackness beyond the portal. It would not matter if they saw her tears. She would die in this place either with his last breath or when her life was taken for returning before her exile was complete. Let them see why she chose the man on the slab over them; let her heart make their hatred wane or grow, she didn't care.

The few who lingered within the pews made no move to help or hinder her. They did not turn their heads to her sobs, stumbling along after the High Priestess to the sanctuary and the Dark beyond.

Eli lurched through the doorway. Her hands broke her fall on the hard wood flooring, scraped and bled into the grain.

Only once before had she been in this room. Her eyes had been bound, her wrists tied above her head. Five strikes of the whip, one for each aspect of the Night. But she came as a supplicant of the Echi, and suffered five more for the Master's pleasure. Through the wounds, the Darkness found her; her blood drawn and offered to the Black. She walked from the temple bloodied but alive. It took her fourteen days to see through the void and for light to pierce her eyes, make her more than the wrathless Judgment of the Echi, give her back part of the humanity her offering to the Dark obscured.

She had not seen the interior of this sanctum then.

She did not look now, her attention focused on the robed men and women around the body lying so still on the stone center of the temple.

"Elichi—" The priest, healer, who spoke turned the attention of the others Eli's way.

She was weak. She could not fight with the strength and speed with which she was accustomed. That did not stop her from attacking the three who made towards her. Triplets in robe and power. The Darkness did not call for the sacrifice of their lives.

Eli screamed, flipped one of the elves over her shoulder, another she felled with a short jab to his groin.

Kit thrashed on the slab, seizing while she fought, and her mother joined with the other priests to surround him, those battling Eli subduing her only as her breath floundered once more, this time do to the man dying atop the table, and not the magic of the Priest.

"NO!"

A wave of magic pulsed from her, moving those gathered around her love away, keeping their hands which could do so much damage from his flesh. She would not let them hurt him. She had begged for sanctuary.

Her legs collapsed beneath her. The three ignored the hand she raised in warding against them. They knew as she did that she did not have the strength to attack again. She crumbled to the wood, her forehead touching the smooth grains, begging, but she did not know if it was to the Dark or to priests she plead.

The healers came no further, and she managed to lift her head enough to watch them flood back to the slab and press their hands against Kit's flesh as they had been before she came before them.

"Elichi," this time her name broke through her emotions, settled her in the room with the healers working to stabilize a body broken beyond what it could endure. "Help us save him."

The Priestosolos held Eli's gaze, the Darkness eclipsing the white of her eyes as she bent her will to saving the prince.

Save him.

Yes, she could save him, Eli would save him.

But she did not know how. She knew how to grant Mercy, send them into the Darkness. She did not know how to bring them out.

Her mother's power encompassed her, soothed her. Frayed nerves were sewn together, helping her find her center, react with more than just emotion.

She rose on unsteady legs, clutching at her chest though the pain was nearly gone.

"Here, Elichi."

Eli was directed to the head of the altar, urged onto its cold stone top. The robed priests gently lifted Kit's head from the slab, her crossed legs a cradle to rest him in. She could not stop herself from stroking over his face, brushing back the matted strands of hair from his forehead. What energy she had went into soothing him, the tears that fell from her eyes onto his face were inconsequential and she brushed them against his skin, the boiling force of magic within her held in each small drop, eased into his body with her touch.

She knew the moment the next seizure came, felt the tensing in his muscles as though they were her own.

Her mother was silent.

Eli didn't know what to do.

The Darkness that had so long been her shadow, her accomplice each time she took up a sword or brought an assailant to their knees, rose up in her, overwhelmed her, reached to destroy and she wrangled the power into a loving caress, stroked into his brow, his arms, his chest, all that she could reach of him, ending the spasms before they began. His breath came no easier, his ribs still broken, his burns still weeping, but he did not thrash, and she prayed that that was enough, that keeping him calm would allow those with her to work their will on the body before her.

She immersed herself in the Darkness.

Her eyes grew blind but for the glow of stars. She could no longer feel him where he laid against her. If she had a body, she did not know it, and it did not matter as she channeled the Night to the seeking hands reaching for her, her soul a conduit as she opened herself to Infinity and lost herself to the Eve.

V

SHE FLOATED THERE, in the nexus of power and energy that surrounded her like a womb, reformed her, sheltered her. There was a reason she was not meant to remain in its warmth. Something, no, someone needed her to return, but the Night was so dark, and the Darkness so complete, that there was nothing to follow to reach that questing something calling her.

She did not want to leave regardless.

The pull was not so great here in the void. She could ignore its tickling presence in the back of her mind if she so chose to do so.

But the Dark began to lighten, the cocoon she had woven about herself to dissolve beneath the fingers peeling apart the wispy layers of the night. No matter how hard she tried, she could not repair the damage, could not stop the spread of sunshine into her bower. It burned her, where it touched, and she scrambled back from its bright embrace, desperately trying to hide, not wanting to return to the OverWorld, enjoying the safety of the Eternity she rested in.

The nagging tug in the back of her mind grew stronger, pulled harder. Her fingers dug into the nest around her and passed through the thick branches like they were a mirage and she was waking from the dream. She cried as she was pulled away, but away she went, and her tears were not enough to hold her to the Night. Warmth covered her cheeks, patted gently, and she opened her eyes to the blinding light she had thought to escape in the Dark. There was too much, and she could not see, but the Dark did not come to rescue her, and she was held tight in solid arms, a heart beating against her ear. She was a daughter of the End, and yet the new day claimed her and she could not get loose.

"Thank the Darkness."

She blinked, and the world focused around her, the last of the Night fading from her eyes. Torches were burning, flicking in and out of her sight as people moved, a great many people, more than there had been, than she remembered when, where, what had happened? Why was she here? Where had she gone?

Her throat was dry, lips parched. "Moth … Priestosolos?"

The older elf smiled down at her, and she could not remember why it was odd for the woman to be doing so. A hand stroked again over her cheek, brushed back knotted strands of hair from her forehead. The woman sang, whispered, hummed softly. There was a reason to fear this woman, but she did not know what it was or why. "Welcome home, Iisforsos."

Was that her name? She could not recall. But the woman, Mother, looked at her with love, with compassion. She must know.

"Calm, Daughter. Hush now. Rest."

There was someone she was supposed to find, something she was supposed to do, to save.

"Rest, Iisforsos. Rest." The command echoed around her, the dark power of her Mother's magic soothed her thoughts, blanketed everything but for the need to sleep, to let go.

Her eyes closed.

Whatever Iisforsos wanted, needed, she would worry about in the morning. It meant nothing within the warm embrace of the arms around her.

CHAPTER THREE

I

SOME NIGHTS HE woke in a cold sweat, unable to recall what visions had danced through his head while he slept. Some nights he didn't wake, and those were worse, having to relive a hell his waking thoughts couldn't remember but for the phantom pains in his body, lingering even after the sun rose. And they weren't all phantom pains. Most remained with him, aching, unhealed, healing but not quite whole yet. His ribs were the worst, they made sitting in bed an agony, rising and walking and breathing nearly impossible. But remaining abed did little to aid him in feeling whole, feeling competent.

His hands clenched, the skin tight, the muscles aching. Scars covered his palms, marks from a branding iron he remembered in his subconscious, remembered the pain of, but couldn't think back upon. Even staring at the scars made his stomach clench. He started most days hunched over a bowl, his supper, or lunch, whatever food he'd managed to choke down the day before revisiting him. That he was sick made him angry. That he couldn't keep down a meal, that he couldn't stand the thought of being touched or seen, after nearly twelve months, made him nauseous and the process started all over again. He laughed, because he refused to cry any longer. He had no tears left regardless. He didn't remember if he'd cried during his torture. It seemed like a good enough bet that he had. He thought he remembered laughing, for the sound now had a hint of the madness he had grown used to some time ago.

The first time he woke, the first time he stirred from the coma his body slept in, there had been no one with him to calm his shaking, the horrors of his dreams. So weak, he'd barely managed to reach the chamber pot in time for the bile in his belly to spew out. He hadn't been able to get back in his bed. That he knew it was his bed astounded him. He'd cried then, at being home, not knowing how he returned, that no one was there with him. But death shouldn't hurt this badly, so he knew he was still alive, and that was worse.

He refused a manservant, not wanting anyone to witness the sweat that coated his body, nor the scars that he would always bear. The ones on his soul, invisible to the world, were the worst. Every look he received, whether knowing or not of what he'd suffered, he shied from, felt the pity for his survival in their gazes.

A coward would end it. Or was it cowardly to seek such an out in oblivion?

He could do it. If he killed himself, the walls would still stand. The prophecy had come and passed. His life meant nothing to the survival of the city now. The walls were their own again, his death would not crumble them. Five hundred and seventeen, nearly eighteen.

Survive the trials of the year.

No one else had attacked to take his life since his return from Kravn's Keep, from the Dienobo. There could be nothing worse than what he'd suffered already.

Two more months and the year would be over.

If nothing else, he could wait the two more months before he killed himself, just to be safe.

He did not want to wait, and that was the problem.

Perhaps the prophecy wasn't fulfilled then.

The niggling doubt that his life was still the fate of the world was what kept the knife hidden beneath his pillow, sheathed instead of bloodied.

"BOY, ARE YOU paying attention? The minister asked what you thought of the plans?"

Plans? What plans?

Kit had been sitting in meeting after meeting, hands gripping the armrests of his chair to keep him upright, focusing on every breath he took as pain swamped him. Was it too much to ask to be allowed to curl into a ball and rest for a little while? Not that he ever really rested, but he wanted one night spent without the memories battering his subconscious mind. Almost it would be better to face them head on, but if they were this bad in his sleep, he did not want to know what they would be like awake.

"Apologies, Father, Lord Minister, I fear I am not myself. If you would leave the plans with—"

He didn't know if he had a secretary. Marius had always been his right hand, despite his position as a soldier and not politician. Kit didn't really know all that many of the nobles, and those he did were little more than passing acquaintances, met from balls he despised or court sessions where they were too busy arguing politics to whisper more than the less than jovial greetings they meted out. Kit didn't even know if it would be appropriate to request one of those simpering fools as his impromptu man of letters.

"Of course, your highness," Minister Grouel smiled. The expression was the same one Kit had received from his tutors when he was still in nappies, condescension masked with required fondness for the heir of an empire. "I'll have everything sent to your rooms for your perusal. We are in no rush."

Which meant that if Kit didn't get through the paperwork by tomorrow night at the latest, all hell would break loose and it would be on Kit's shoulders. Just another thing to weigh on his soul.

"Son, are you alright?"

The king leaned over his throne, his hand reaching towards Kit's clutching at the armrests.

He'd thought the wheezing he heard was simply a bird caught behind the great chairs, or a servant in need of a glass of water. That the sound was coming from him hadn't crossed his mind, and yet, the attention now drawn to it, Kit found himself struggling to draw in a breath, beads of sweat dotting his forehead as he fought not to crumple in his chair. To be proven so weak before ministers and nobles and his father… The thought did nothing to relieve the burgeoning panic in Kit's breast.

He heard someone calling for a physician, a healer, guards to help him back to his chambers. Hands wrapped around his arms, lifting him from the chair and pulling him through the halls of the palace. He knew he was being carried, but his mind focused only on his chest, the feel of a whip breaking skin, a boot to his side and the sickening crunch of connection with his flesh.

Panic attacks had never plagued him.

Yes, after the war he'd been lost in his own head for a time, but not like this, not thrown back into the misery so completely, so unable to separate the past from reality as he was now.

Kit pulled from his guards' arms when they reached his room, stumbling away from them and to the open balcony doors, begging for air, sweet, fresh air, far away from the plague of flagstone walls and a black ceiling that stretched into an eternity he couldn't escape.

No one followed him onto the small ledge. No one spoke to him, or if they did, he did not hear them.

He closed his eyes, soaking in the sun on his face, the warmth and the smell of nature even if he was still in a building too far removed from the glorious earth and the freedom of the tree shadowed paths.

His shoulders bowed over the railing, back bent, relieving some of the pressure on his chest. He shuddered with the hidden memories that were beginning to spill over into his daytime. If they continued, his father would find him unfit to rule.

Gods, but wouldn't that be perfect.

He snorted at the thought.

A lifetime spent learning how to run a country only to be barred from the job because by learning how to rule the country, he'd been placed on the wanted list of everyone else in the world.

And yet, being denied the kingdom, being forced to abdicate before he even took the thrown might well be what he wanted most. To live, freely, without complications, without the responsibility of a hundred thousand people depending on him for safety and security. He could work in the foundry. He'd done it once. Hard labor, yes, but he'd been good at it; the work had made him feel like he'd accomplished something at the end of the day. Worse case, he could sell his sword arm. So the idea of actually battling set his stomach to twisting, but he could do it, if he needed to. He'd spent nearly two hundred years embroiled in blood. No one would question a soldier's scars. He could kill again. He could get away from the palace and the walls and the destiny that had had him kidnapped and tortured, that had called for his death and he'd been too cowardly simply give in to and die. If he'd just told the master…

Master…

The kit…

His knees buckled, and he fell to the stone of his balcony, one hand clenched round his middle while the other supported him as his stomach purged of the fig he'd eaten for lunch. He'd gotten good at moving food around on his plate to appear as though he finished a meal though nothing stayed down.

He should be happy he survived.

He would have been happy, but his life had come at the price of hers. He could live with the insanity if she was at his side. Fool woman had taken him to the Woods. Fool woman, she should have gotten herself out and left him to die for Fate's sake.

He wanted Marius to stand next to him on the balcony, his calm presence a balm to Kit's rioting emotions.

He wanted Eli at his left, her hand in his, the quiet acceptance she'd excelled at. She'd laugh at his thoughts, at his planned escape, telling him he was a fool for the consideration. But she wasn't here. And Marius wasn't here.

He was alone, a prince to a kingdom who pitied him, and he couldn't fault their opinion as he pitied himself just as much.

He couldn't meet his father's gaze for fear of seeing the same emotion reflected back at him, worse: shame. But it wasn't his father's shame he feared most, not when he looked in a mirror and could not escape the same in his own eyes.

He pushed himself to his feet, turned away from the sky and trees outside, retreated to the hard mattress that was his prison and salvation both. Easier to dream about his horrors than live knowing everyone else imagined their own version for him.

His chest hurt.

His limbs were weak.

He laid down in the bed and closed his eyes.

He hadn't told the master who he was, what the bastard wanted to know. No, that wasn't true. The master hadn't believed him. He lived because the man was a fool, and Kit was pathetic.

II

"THERE WILL BE a ball for your birthday next month. We will celebrate your life, Christophe, your strength in surviving what you have, the fulfillment of the prophecy, the salvation of our City."

"I will not be in attendance."

No one said anything about the rasp in his voice that wouldn't heal. He'd healed as much as he was able now. The healers came every week. Reported to the king that his body was nearly whole. His ribs no longer ached, burnt muscles had miraculously regrown and he'd lost no range of motion despite the damage he'd suffered. The men whispered, when they thought he wasn't listening, that the woodland physicians were miracle workers. They'd healed him, their enemy.

Kit hated the elves with the same passion he hated the memory of his uncle, the loss of Marius, the men who even now rotted in the king's dungeon, held prisoner after attacking the capital trying to find Kit, never knowing he'd fled unwillingly to the forest and beyond their reach. Of course, Kit hadn't heard of their capture until his father's vengeance had been wreaked upon the men. Funny, but he had no pity for the bastards, even if they'd never shown a moment's torment to him.

"You will most certainly be in attendance, Kit. You must show the people that you are whole, that you are my heir and you have overcome what was done to you. It will be the greatest celebration we've ever had for you. It will put all other balls to shame."

"I have hated this tradition since the day I turned thirty and women began throwing themselves at me to catch a prince. These balls have never been about celebrating me."

"This one will be—"

"Father," Kit met the king's gaze, forcing himself not to flinch away from the desperation in the man's eyes. "Have I not suffered enough? I beg you, do not do this to me."

"Tradition—"

"Please, Father."

The old man stared at Kit, and Kit did not shirk away from the hard gaze.

The first ninety-nine balls had been unbearable. She'd been there the hundredth and for the following three hundred plus excruciating experiences. Even when she was silent, ignoring him, knowing she was near, somewhere near, had made getting through the three days manageable. And the past seventeen years when they had fled to each other in the Dark of the night between dances had been magical. This last year, the ring—

Simeon had taken the chain from Kit's throat. He'd taken the ring and thrown it in the fire, the ring Kit wore until he could deliver it to his elf, his captain.

It was the only time Kit had willingly braved the flames.

There was a circle branded into the palm of his right hand, stark against the cross that discolored the rest of his skin.

The master had still taken the ring from him. Kit hadn't asked if it had been found in the ruins of the tower after his father's men destroyed the place upon Kit's survival. No one would have known to look for it anyways.

He looked in his lap, unable to hold his father's gaze any longer, staring at his clenched hands instead.

She wouldn't be his salvation at this ball.

He had no one to turn to.

Surely his father could understand that he could not be around that many people. He no longer had the constitution for it.

"I cannot cancel the ball now, boy. The announcement has already spread. The Arqueanmen have already replied that they will be in attendance, their princess with them. Quiofol has similarly pledged to come. Even the Dienobolos have promised to send representatives to augment our new peace treaty with them."

Yes, a peace treaty that Kit wanted to shred, not caring that he lived by their grace when they'd killed the only woman he ever loved.

Dear gods.

Dear gods, letting the thought invade him reignited every pain he'd suffered, not yet even one year old. And she was the worse pain of all.

"I cannot do this."

"Kit—"

No, he did not want to hear his father's pleas.

He fled the throne room, their court sessions over for the day. He no longer needed to be in his father's presence, and perhaps that was the best way to survive this newest torture. For he knew, no matter how much he might protest, no matter how desperate he was to escape, he would attend the ball as his father wished because his father was king, and he was prince, and he was nothing if not dutiful.

But he refused to be complicit in his suffering, at least, he refused to plan or discuss his torment.

Kit did not stop at his room.

His guards knew better than to follow him. Barely four months since the healers pronounced him whole and he spent the better part of his days in the lists, the only peace he had when he swung a sword or released an arrow. His soldiers made the fighting worthwhile, never shirking their duty to provide a good battle for him. He knocked them down faster than they could swing at him. The anger and pain in his soul gave him strength. If he didn't worship his gods, he would have thought the Darkness had claimed him as its own, so great was the terror and destruction he sought to work. But he never hurt his men, took special care to train only, never unleash the full fury in his soul.

This was not a day for the lists.

The emotion had been riding him hard for the last few weeks, an emotion he didn't have a name for, something between abject depression and mindless need. He didn't know what it meant, but the sword wasn't enough now, and he needed to run.

He came to the stables, not waiting for a groom to saddle his horse before he led the stallion from the stall and jumped onto the beast's back. More and more lately, he'd taken to riding the poor beast without a saddle, not wanting to take the time or explain where he was going to any groom or soldier sent to stalk him. He needed to move, and Oberon had never unseated Kit, always a steady mount to ride on.

"Fly, boy."

The horse responded to the command with a giddy hitch, sidestepping once before finding the path and sprinting down the lane. Hooves clacked over the bricked road, but Oberon had no trouble navigating the terrain, not even a slip on the slick surface. Kit should have waited to let the beast loose until they were beyond the city walls, but the moment the horse galloped, the thoughts deserted him for the feel of the wind in his face, hair whipping around his head. Shouts echoed at his back, but he ignored them, knowing the guards sent as his escort would follow his trail eventually, find him wherever the horse's head took him.

He closed his eyes, hands buried in the horse's mane, knees tight around the flanks, bent low over the neck. Kit tipped his face forward, hiding from the sunlight along the path. As much as he hated the elves, he found a quiet peace beneath the overhanging branches of the trees, the leaves that hushed the sounds of the world around him.

How long it took to get to the woods, he didn't know, but he didn't open his eyes until his horse's hooves no longer clicked over the road but clomped mutedly on thick ground beginning to burst with spring grasses.

An early ripening of the earth.

Spring come early, summer burns, the leaves will fall beneath a blanket of snow.

What Kit recalled of the past year was a mellow winter and a mild sun during Vellim and V'roshar. This winter would not be so easy to bear if the adage held true. There would be snow and cold and more like than not the harvest would suffer from the heat of the summer sun.

He would not regret the heat of this day, nor the advent of the spring as he sat up on Oberon's back and watched the woods close in around them.

The horse picked his path with care, winding through trees, snuffling at the few remaining patches of snow lightening the ground. Were they close enough to the Woodland realm that elves were watching him through the trees? Would said same elves hold true, let him pass unmolested through their forest? He almost hoped they wouldn't. The two knives he carried would hold against a sword. He'd gotten rather good with the short blades, good enough that he'd made Eli—

He didn't finish the thought. Every time he thought of her, he forcibly changed subjects. It was hard enough to bare her absence without seeing a reminder of her in his every action.

"*Even the Dienobolos have promised to send representatives,*" he mocked his father's words.

Yes, send the elves to the palace walls, cage them in the glum of sandstone and marble boxes. No peace would come from the visit. No elf would take comfort in the cold sterility of the castle.

Yes, of course not including her, she was always the bloody exception to the rule.

He argued with his subconscious, letting the tirade consume him.

A river of thoughts, memories he'd forced down for nigh unto fifteen months now, almost a full year, of commanding himself not to think of the woman he lost.

But she was there, in the turn of Oberon's head, like the beast was looking in the shadows for her slight presence to call him towards. The birds sang overhead, and he expected to hear her shrill whistle scaring them off any moment. A branch touched his shoulder when he didn't duck far enough to avoid the caress, and he reached behind him, trying to bring her closer, take her hand in his own to hold as they rode.

She'd hated the palace walls as much as any elf.

Her windows were always wide open within her rooms, the fresh scent of all her plants encompassing the space. She pretended she was in her homeland, and he had taken the same comfort within her nest as she had.

He'd refused to return to her rooms once he woke from the coma.

He refused to allow them to be cleaned and reassigned.

During the war, she'd foregone a tent on the battlefield, preferring to spend the nights beneath the stars even when the weather was harsh, and the enemy was too close to their lines for comfort. She'd slept in his bed when she needed the comfort of his arms to draw her back from the Darkness, and he'd come to her for the same. It had been natural to spend a night in a lake with her and no walls to confine them.

No wonder then that no matter where he went he felt her presence like a ghost around him.

And he wanted a lake right now. If he couldn't have her, he wanted the memory of a lake where he could pretend she was there holding him while he slowly sank under the water.

The temptation to simply breathe in the wet would be too great though.

Oberon shied, shuffling on the path, rearing so that only the tight grip of Kit's legs around its middle kept him seated.

Kit clenched his hands in the mane as he stared over the horse's head at the cloaked figure before him. Small, which Kit knew meant little in determining gender, but he still pegged the sprite as female. Elves were often more delicate of frame than their human cousins. "Have you come to tell me to leave your forest?"

The hood swayed left then right.

"No, then?"

A nod this time.

Kit laughed, a harsh sound that broke the silence around him. "Was there something you needed, or are you content to silently stare at me?"

He sat atop his mount, his hands sweating where they were buried in the horse's mane, prepared to reach for his knives if he needed to, force the beast to run if the woman proved violent towards him, if others should appear.

A gloved hand emerged from the billows of her cloak, waving him towards her. He caught a glimpse of light clothing, not enough to tell if she wore breeches or skirts as she turned away, expecting him to follow. He found he wanted to. How strange. He didn't mind this invasion of his solitude.

Oberon walked forward, quickly catching up with her smaller steps. The beast nuzzled her hood, and her hand rose to keep the dark green weave atop her head. Black strands blew in the slight wind, jostled free from his horse's ministrations. For a moment, the pit in his soul had filled, thinking that, perhaps, somehow, she'd survived whatever death her people had prescribed for her. But he did not recognize her black hair, and she could not be the woman he hoped for.

Her hand stroked over Oberon's neck while they walked.

She made no complaint that he did not dismount to walk beside her or offer her his seat. Her stride never changed though to him they walked for hours. His eyes drifted closed and blinked slowly open, the healed body still not at the same stamina as Kit had once been. Her hand moved to his thigh, patting him as gently as she did the horse, afraid he was as skittish. The thought made him smile.

It was in a fog that his horse stopped. Not a visible fog, but one that had clouded over Kit's eyes, cast the world as part of a dreamscape, one he did not wish to remove himself from.

She supported him as he dismounted, her arm moving to circle his waist while his legs adjusted to bearing his weight once more. Where she led him, he followed. The longer they walked between the tightly spaced trees, the more he leaned on her, felt her leaning on him. It would be pleasant to draw her into his arms for a while, sleep in a bower of leaves and pretend that the arms around him cared, weren't pushing him back to a palace and the life of a prince who wished to be something simpler. An archer, perhaps. "Or a cloth weaver."

Had he spoken aloud? He couldn't tell, and he didn't care but that didn't stop his lips from quirking at the words.

He smiled at the woman. If she noticed, she gave no sign and it didn't truly matter, not when she pulled at his shirt and deftly stripped him of his boots then pants.

Funny, but she stripped him and he made no move to stop her. He didn't feel scarred standing so bared. Mayhap the advent of the hood kept him from noticing her gaze along the fading lines across his torso and back. They were white now, though the skin still stretched and pulled with his every movement.

She pressed her palm to his chest, the mark over his left side where the arrow had left its scar. Her fingers brushed over the mark, ran the ridges of it, brushed like she could smooth the scar away.

She did not touch him as his healers did. It must be the gloves she wore that made her bold, her touch less intrusive against his skin. He should require all those seeking to caress his flesh to wear gloves so that he could not feel the trembling of shock from their fingers, nor the bareness of soft caresses over harsh weal.

He should care that he stood before a stranger naked as he hadn't been since he was born. He refused to think on the other times he'd been as naked as now.

Her touch was not for his flesh though. He had the impression that she stared through him, looked deeper, beneath his skin to what remnants of his soul remained. Words lingered on his tongue, wanting to tell her it was gone, long gone with the woman who it belonged to, but he held his tongue, let her touch the outer shell of what remained of the man within.

He could not understand the words that fell from her lips. The voice that spoke them though were far too similar, the alto as deep as another voice he remembered, another hurt he wished could be forgotten.

He trembled, the spell around him breaking the longer she touched him, clearing the fog as his mind fought to break free of memory and comfort.

Her hood tilted back, too deep for him to see the eyes he thought tried to catch his.

She stepped away.

He sighed, let the fog engulf him once more.

A tilt of her head, and he looked towards the pool lingering in the shade of a small grove. It was only natural for Kit to take the hand that she extended towards him, let her lead him to the water, the silence of the forest soothing.

She released him at the shallows, stepped away like she was afraid he would pull her in with him though the thought had not occurred before then, and made him laugh to see her retreat. If a faceless woman could smile, she did so, and he found himself smiling with her.

He stepped into the water, expecting to feel the winter cold biting at his toes, but it was warm, as warm as a nice bath at the palace, more soothing in its lack of confines.

Smooth stone was beneath his feet, not mud. This basin was not an idle pond deep in the woods as he'd thought. Should he leave? Was this a sacred sight of the Dienobolos? He found he didn't care.

The deeper he walked into the pool, the more the fog closed in around his mind, and the clearer his dreams became. Even knowing he was enchanted, he felt no fear at the magic and let it work its will on him. He looked over his shoulder, and she nodded again, permission or acceptance, an emissary of the forest or a child of its people, he took her word and relaxed within the warmth.

Kit dunked his head beneath the water, sluicing the liquid from his face when he remerged. He slicked his hair back along his scalp, blinking back the droplets weighing down his eyelashes.

He turned to watch her lift now bare fingers to the clasp at her throat, pull back the hood of her cape, draw the heavy weight aside and lay it on the ground at her feet. She settled in her skirt along the material, the light coloring in stark contrast to the deep greens of the forest around them. Had her feet always been bare, toes digging into the dirt at the edges of the cape? She blushed at his observation, and he grinned, stepping to the side of the pool, close enough to where she sat that a simple stretch allowed him to shift the hem of her cape over her feet to keep her warm. He squeezed her toes, and she wriggled beneath his touch.

"I miss your eyes most, Eli."

She smiled at him, waved him away and back into the pool where the winter chill couldn't touch him.

"Are you going to remain there?"

Her lips grinned wider, eyes sparkling in his imagination where the vision existed.

"I miss your voice."

But she did not speak to relieve that ache.

"Come with me."

Her smile turned sad. The glimmer in her eye was not that of the light's reflection but of moisture beading at the corner, a blink sending the shimmering tear down her cheek.

If he reached for her, he could wipe the small droplet from her face, brush away the second and third tears slipping down her porcelain skin.

He remained still, not touching her as she did not touch him.

She shook her head no.

He did not ask her why.

Kit stepped back into the deeper waters, dropping her gaze to search for a natural seat in the small pond, sinking into the steaming bath until the warmth covered his shoulders and he leaned his head against a soft piece of earth. He closed his eyes to her vision, would have covered his ears with his hands if she spoke, no longer wanting to see the vision, no longer wanting to be caught in a fantasy he could not have.

His skin pruned.

The leaf distilled sunlight waned over his head

Birds chirped in their green bowers. A deer or a fox scampered in the underbrush, disturbing the silence that had lingered around him.

The fog in his mind began to clear.

He opened his eyes and he was alone in the pool.

He should worry that he'd wandered onto some sacred spring of the Dienobolos. Perhaps, if he did not long so dearly for death, he might have been more concerned.

Kit slipped from the steaming water to retrieve his clothes, folded neatly in a pile beyond the pool's edge. A bath sheet was draped carefully over a low hanging branch at his boots' side.

He dried. He dressed. He followed the darkened path through the trees, a path he didn't remember but for the hand leading him though he followed it ably enough now.

His horse snorted at the other end of the tunnel and whinnied when Kit finally appeared. The beast lowered himself to the ground, no vaulting onto the animal's back this time. Kit patted the stallion's head, and once more gave the roan its lead to return them to the palace.

Soldiers stirred on the roadside when he emerged from the trees. They looked as unconcerned as he felt, though they formed up around him quickly enough. Not a one dared to tell him he was a fool or that he was inconsiderate for having run off so uncaringly. Marius would have made the comment and then taken Kit to the lists the next morning to hammer the point home. Kit couldn't bring himself to care if he worried the men or not. He wanted to wallow in the mellow of the pool for a moment longer, let himself be distracted from all that laid before him, the ball, his father, the elves and his fate, remember the vision in the trees, not the truth of his life.

They reached the city gate as the sun set.

No one stopped him from leaving his horse with the groom and moving towards the palace without the entourage which had followed him.

Kit ascended the stairs to the great hall, followed it to the family dining room and his father waiting within.

The doors opened. The doors closed. Leon stood, a hand raised no doubt to berate Kit, but Kit spoke first, ignoring tradition to have his say.

"This will be the last ball, Father. At the end of the three nights, you will choose a bride for me. I will wed her. I will bed her. You'll have an heir you don't pity and are not afraid of," *and I'll be free of this life you wish me to live*. The last he did not speak aloud, though it hung heavy in the air all the same.

His father made to reply, and Kit raised a hand to stop him, unfinished with his ultimatum.

"We both know I am no longer fit, Father."

Poor Leon, poor Kit, for the king did not dispute the words, sank slowly into his chair to which Kit came and knelt at his side.

"Surely you have thought the same over this past year."

"You are a prince." Which neither confirmed nor denied the truth of Kit's declaration.

Kit snorted but there was no humor in the sound. "I am a damaged prince. Who would want me to become a king someday?"

"Kit—"

Just his name.

His father said only his name, and Kit heard the pain and torment in the old man's voice, the tragedy weighing the sovereign down. He knew what Kit had suffered. Someone had told him that Kit might never be the man he was before. There was an acceptance of Kit's words in that single name that Kit had not expected to ever hear.

And he was profoundly grateful for his father's compassion.

"You will remain? You will aid whoever is to become king after me?"

Not a command. A plea from a parent losing his only child.

"You would want me to?"

"Always, Christophe. You are my son."

Kit swallowed, fought the closing of his throat and the despair at having no place to go regardless. "For as long as I can." *Until I can stand it no more.*

III

The Four Hundredth and Eighty-Eight Ball

The First Night

HE REFUSED TO wear the red.

Kit didn't care if red was his father's chosen court color, or that blue went well with his eyes, or that gold would make the black of his hair all that more vibrant. He refused any and all colors of doublets the costumiers brought him, maintaining that he would wear the black already in his wardrobe and that they could waste their fripperies on the other nobles in attendance.

"But at least let us embellish it," they pled, and he stared back at them, unmoved until he was left alone with his severely cut jacket and the black breeches and boots to finish the ensemble.

He'd consented to having his boots shined to a bright sheen, accepted the circlet they'd demanded he wear.

His father wore a gold crown, as befit the ruling monarch. Kit wore silver, and rarely at that.

Never before had he worn the circlet for the ball, and yet his father insisted, and Kit couldn't find a good enough reason to argue against the demand.

So he wore the damn crown, and even consented to a the heavy silver chain, jewels of black onyx set between the small detailed crests of his ancestors: a bull, one leg raised as it prepared to charge for his greatest grandfather Euridone who gathered the first plains men into one village during a snowstorm; a griffin cradling a maiden in its arms for Marcel, the king who offered his life to the gods in payment for his people's survival from famine. His father bore the crest of a noble steed, he who unto the world opened, for Leon had established the roads, built over the crumbling foundations of what once was and opened trade to the westerners and those across the wide sea.

He touched the emblem of the wolf prowling in the woods.

His uncle's sigil – the man still honored as kin though the sight made Kit choke.

Once, when Kit was young, he'd asked the bastard why Kravn chose a lone wolf as his emblem, and his uncle had said it was to remember that he was not a king, that he roamed alone, but a wolf was always meant to be pack, and someday would return to Leon's side as such.

Kit's hand curled around the state chain. It took all he had not to rip the jewels from his throat, take sword and slice against the damned silver and onyx until it was no more.

He did not have a sigil on the chain.

His father threatened to denote Kit as the phoenix.

Kit forced his hand to open and let the heavy metal fall back against his chest, the black of his silk jacket all that kept the jewelry from touching his skin.

Three days, and he would have a bride. There would be a wedding. He would bed the poor lass. He would breed an heir. He wished only that the path of his life did not feel as dim as it did when he thought of what laid before him.

At the very least, he swore that he would protect whatever seed sprang from him. There would be no curse placed upon its head. No god would claim his child. Kit would not let them.

"The Arqueanmen are sending their princess. You would be heir to two thrones.

"Ignobis of the Quiofol is coming himself and bringing with him twelve of his virgin brides, all said to love dancing more than anything else. You would have the choice among them, which to

take as your own. He's even offered one as a mistress to cement the binding of our two nations together as one.

Words spoken over the course of weeks trying to decide whom Kit would prefer as wife, to get anything resembling interest to spark in Kit's eye. His father had spoken of every woman who would attend, and Kit had sat and listened without care, because he truly didn't.

"The Priestosolos is coming herself to the ball, Christophe. The Piestosolos! She never leaves the woods, and she's bringing three Daughters with her. Well, of course, we'll choose one of the elves. We do owe them for everything and—"

Ah yes, a debt to be repaid for the murder of one of their own and his attempted murder over the course of his life. But, yes, let's reward them for saving a broken soul.

"You said you would marry whomever I chose."

Yes, and except for the irrational anger in his heart, he didn't regret granting his father that power. And at least an elf might know where she was buried, would be able to show him to the grave where he could lie on the ground and be close to her even as he was husband to another of her kind.

Kit adjusted the cuffs of his coat, the silly frilled shirt that peaked from the edges of the black, a dark grey, different enough to lend some color to his dress, if grey could be considered a color. The leather belt wrapped twice around his hips, the first loop tight, woven through the hoops at his waist, the second loop looser, able to bear the weight of the ceremonial sword he buckled to his left side. The scabbard was ceremonial. The sword was edged, a thin steel, lighter than the blade with the elaborately gilded hilt that was unwieldy where this blade was uncompromising. He hadn't worn that formal blade since he nearly died with it in his hand, and it'd taken a girl to save his life. He smiled at that thought, that he should wear a real weapon lest he chase after some other pool fool wise enough to run to the woods away from him. The smile died, because he would not be chasing the woman he wanted.

At least he'd be able to protect himself without her aid.

How many times had she leaned in his doorway, ready to escort him to the ball, or to a formal event, and said the same to him?

He'd worn the green jacket for her. She'd insisted only the once, and he'd done it, and then his world had ended.

The green was still in his wardrobe. When the healers left, and his frame was bone and flesh and his father commissioned a new set of clothes for him, he hadn't let them take that one coat that he would never wear but couldn't abide losing.

He turned from the sight, back to his bed and his weapons laid atop the mattress.

A dagger at his hip, gilded sheath to adhere to the strictures of the ball, one in his boot that no one need known about. A final glance in the mirror at his pale face and his sweat beaded forehead.

Who would have thought that a prince could look so sick of a dance?

With a dignity he didn't feel, he stepped from his room to the flitty laughter of noble women walking through the halls just past the royal apartments on their way to the ballroom or the banquet room or some other such room opened for the masses for these three interminable days. He followed sedately enough behind the guards posted outside his room, so that he couldn't run? Or there to protect him from the women who would conveniently get lost at the edge of dawn and seek a way to entangle him in wedlock without his choice? As his father had said, the choice was already made, now was just a matter of actually taking his vows. Three hundred and eighty-seven years and he'd had her in his arms, had the ring in his pocket, and he'd been too late. Three hundred and eighty-eight years, and he'd missed his chance. If an heir wasn't expected of him, he would go to his death never having touched a woman in a carnal light, been happy to have found her on the other side of the void, pure for her.

His breath hitched.

But then, he wasn't really *pure* anymore, was he? Not after…

This was all too soon, and his heart was hammering, and his palms were sweating through the gloves he tugged on when he left his chambers.

Losing himself in the darkness of his mind, he'd done it once, found his way back from it once, could do it again if he needed to. He could be whatever his father demanded of him. All he had to give up was the man he was, become an *it* once again. The kit, not—

"My prince?"

He'd stopped walking, and now one of the soldiers was holding his arm, standing far too close.

"Apologies. I was lost in my thoughts."

Could they hear the lie? That it wasn't thoughts of the ball that he was lost in but darker, crueler remembrances?

"Are you ready to continue, my lord?"

It's "Your Highness." He was not a lord. He was higher than a lord. And all he wanted was to just be a man, not a count or a duke or a sir or a lord, just a man, a baker or a soldier or a tailor might be nice.

He didn't tell the guard that though. With a small nod of his head, a "Yes, please," he motioned for the men to precede him, followed them to the royal entrance to the ballroom, waves of sound, musicians tuning their instruments, gossips tittering away waiting for him to arrive, buffeted the small space he stood in as he waited for the steward to announce him and for his hell to begin. He adjusted his gloves. The left hand curled over the hilt of his sword, the right was stiff against his thigh.

The crowd quieted at his fanfare and the steward gave Kit a nod before walking out onto the balcony and announcing Kit's name. His guards lined the stairway. Kit stepped out and bowed.

"PRINCESS AURORA, IT is my greatest honor to introduce you to my son, Christophe."

"Might I have this dance, your highness?"

The slight woman looked nervously to her escort for confirmation before nodding her head and taking Kit's extended hand. She was as unhappy to be here as was he. That made him feel lighter about the whole of the situation, though he doubted his jaded response would please his father.

They danced well together to a reel and then a Gavotte. He managed to coax a smile to her pale lips when he stumbled and bumped into a preening man who kept staring at the princess with a mix of disdain and desire. Anytime the man's gaze caught Aurora's, she blanched, and Kit took issue with his partner's distress.

When the waltz began, she graciously took his hand, though there were others ready to take his place, her place, by that point. He obliged the slight girl, for she was slight and young, even by her people's years, too young to be considered a woman yet.

"You will not marry me, will you, Prince?"

He smiled at her frankness, finding something to like about the woman she would become. "No, your Highness."

"There are shadows in your eyes, shadows that hide much sorrow."

He spun her, not knowing how to respond.

"I cannot lift those shadows for you. I'm not sure I should try, though I would be a friend, if you needed one."

"I have a plethora of friends gathered round, your highness."

"Not the type of friend many of these women would be." Her gaze snaked to the people around them, reptilian in movement, a product of her heritage. Kit had not had many dealings with the dragons before, their country rather closed though his father had ridden to meetings with them over the years. Too dangerous for Kit to go, of course, but the woman before him did not appear dangerous, and her smile was a softer thing than what many of the courtesans wore.

"You are too young to be so wise, Princess."

She smiled at him, though her eyes darkened with acknowledgment. Not many must see the truth of the woman they met.

Kit wondered if all dragons were the same.

"The flesh is young, yes." He met her mahogany gaze, so dark within the candlelight of the ballroom. "The soul is far older indeed."

He could not tell if it was a rebuke or simple statement of fact. "Forgive me, my lady." He bowed his head while he held her in his arms, this ancient soul in the body of a youth. It put him to shame, having thought her but a girl, and for that he apologized and had the feeling she knew it.

"Nothing to forgive, Prince. Your soul is much different than the body you bear too."

"Too true, your highness." Too true.

The song ended, and he bowed again, ensuring that his was the motion of deepest respect, that those around him recognized that whoever this princess was, she was to be most honored.

She smiled demurely back at him, allowing him to lead her to her guardians standing along one wall of the great chamber. "I will be gone in the morning, though I would not insult you or your father by my leave taking."

His father would say she was too young, and the slight would be easily forgiven as such.

"No insult in the slightest."

Indeed, his father might approve that the youth left early and was not saddened when she failed to catch herself a prince. Of course, she was not an elf, and had no chance regardless.

Still, Kit found the woman pleasant and would be sad to see this ancient young princess leave.

They would have been a poor match, this girl with a woman's eyes and a woman's secrets. Too much swirled in the coffee gaze, hinting at the power and love she held or would hold for another someday. He did not want to come between that, wouldn't.

She extended a hand and he kissed the back of her white glove, pressed his forehead to the fabric as a sign of admiration to her.

"Thank you, Prince. I had not thought to find any joy here." Her fingers touched his jaw, turning his gaze to meet hers. "The Gods…they say all things return in time. Perhaps your time is come, young one."

He smiled at the term, even as her guards shifted steps, wondering at the exchange, unsure how he would take it. "I do not believe in the gods, my lady. They've brought me only sorrow."

"A pity, for they have believed in you, and a wiser choice they could not have made."

"LORD IGNOBIS, PLEASE, please, bring your fair maidens here to meet the prince."

King Leon waved at a hulky giant of a man, his head at least two taller than Kit's own tall build.

Staring up at the man craned Kit's neck back. Ignobis, skin sunburned a dark red, hair shaved short to his round head, stepped before the king and took up nearly the entire dais with his bulk.

Kit had not been made to feel small in—

Few sought to overpower him, and yet this man did so with nothing but his size. It was unnerving and brought back far too many memories. Kit's breath held in his chest even as he bowed to the man before him.

A gaggle of women stood behind the man, guarded by as many giants each. Ignobis kept his wives pristine, in body and mind, or so it seemed. Not a one of them took their eyes from the floor to look at Kit when the lord started listing off names. They stood still, unmoving, like they were afraid of drawing the noble's attention even as they knew they must have it.

Did they think it would be a mercy to be Kit's bride rather than their husbands?

Still untouched.

The thought flitted across his mind, and Kit looked again at these cowering, browbeaten women and felt pity stir in his breast for them. Even if they were not now at the hands of their husband, Kit saw the marks of long horror in their sallow skin and sullen faces. Whatever life they held with the man who claimed them, it was not a merciful one, and stirred memories far too dark in Kit's mind.

"Go, go, you must dance with them."

His father laughed when Ignobis stepped aside and opened the way for Kit to reach the women. Kit could not tell one sunken face from another. He did not wish to dance with any of them. He did not want them to know he had nothing but sorrow to heap upon them nor only pity for their plight.

He extended his hand, and the women stepped aside, the slowest left to join him for the first dance.

A quadrille, minuet, Loure and Gigue, Bourrée, Gavotte and Musette and the orchestra called for a brief pause and Ignobis claimed his brides saying there were three more nights to choose during.

Pearl clung to Kit's arm when her husband came to retrieve her. She looked over Kit's shoulder at the line of her sisters he'd yet to partner with, Ruby and Sapphire, Topaz and Garnet, begging them to save her from her master's touch. Kit held her hand until Ignobis pulled her sharply away and it would have caused a scene to hold any longer.

Her sister wives followed slowly behind her retreating form. None fought against the demands of their husband.

"I am sorry."

Diamond stopped and looked at him.

He thought she might speak, might beg, might curse, but she said nothing, her eyes dead as she turned back to her sisters and followed the lordling from the room to wherever he was staying within the palace for the ball.

Kit could not save just one or two of them. He wasn't sure he would turn out any better than their bastard husband when he wed regardless. With a fervent prayer to the gods that the women wouldn't suffer, he returned to his seat beside his father's throne and watched the brightly dressed men and women of the court dance and gossip while he waited for his next partner to arrive.

IN HER FACE he saw the woman he loved grown older, grown wiser, and he hated it.

The Priestosolos walked steadily up the steps of the dais, and inclined her head at the king, her gaze raking Kit without caution, beyond protocol. He met her steely eyes and forced himself not to snarl at the strongest elf of the Dienobolos. His hands clenched on the armrests of his chair.

"You've healed well, Prince Christophe. I'm glad to see my talents were not wasted on you."

He clenched his teeth, knowing he should state his gratitude for her healing, knowing that any words that left his mouth would curse the woman before him.

"And what talents they are, Priestosolos. You honor us with your presence. It is because of you and your skill that we are here at all."

Her gaze broke from Kit's and she looked at his father with a gentle smile turning her lips at the compliment. They exchanged pleasantries, his father's rasping tenor mellowed against her soft mezzo. With his eyes closed, Kit could almost pretend that the woman was any other person speaking with his father than the one who had placed a bounty on his head the moment he was born, and who'd killed her own daughter for the saving of his life.

Because that's who Eli was, wasn't it? She was the daughter of the Priestosolos. Not the daughter in the way the three women cloaked in black were Daughters of the Wood, but by flesh and blood and heart. And didn't the realization make sense? Eli's coldness, the strength of her spirit to withstand the life of an assassin with compassion intact? The knowledge that she'd never hid, and he'd never asked for before

And this woman who was priest and healer had still had not hesitated to order an infant killed, her own daughter murdered.

And the three fake Daughters at her back were here to be his bride, and his father was content with the choice. Kit should be grateful it wasn't the bitch himself he was being pledged to.

"Come forward."

The three women answered their priestess' command, stepping away from the crowd and to the edge of the dais, never taking the steps up, always remaining below Kit and his father and their mistress. They pulled their dark hoods down, revealing hair the color of corn spun silk, a red as dark as blood, and one as dark as a moonless night. Their faces were masked, golden ovals obscuring any question of bone structure beneath, a mesh over the eyes so that he could not see the color behind the disguise. All three wore gowns as dark as the Darkness they worshipped, draping gowns that reached to the floor, covering them from head to toe, their hands gloved, their throats shadowed. They were of similar shapes, all of a height. And they were here to wed him, and he had to fight not to flinch from their appearance.

He dismissed the blond and redhead out of hand, not knowing why his gaze was drawn to the raven-haired elf, ignoring the shiver of memory, not wanting to remember that day in the woods, the dream of a dead woman.

Kit had the impression that she was studying him as much as he studied her, though he could tell nothing with the mask over her face.

She was, if he was honest, perhaps not as well-endowed as her sisters. The black of her dress clung with more ceremony to her slenderer curves, the hint of muscles beneath. Not a daughter of Pirie then. Perhaps this sister walked the forests, worshipped the aspect Ashet and the fields and furrows between the tress. He would be amused if he thought the Priestosolos would dare to send a sentinel of Echi as a bride for him. Already one of the Assassin's brethren had died for him. He would find no comfort in another of their ilk.

The one he stared at shifted, her head bowing slightly at his continued appraisal.

That it was noted was not lost on him.

He subjected each of the other two to the same perusal, remembering not to turn his gaze back to her lest his unmasked face give him away.

Silence broke him from his thoughts, his head turning to his father and the priestess to meet their stare.

"Ask them to dance, son."

The conductor motioned for a recess.

"The first set after the break is yours, my ladies."

Not a one answered him, a nod, and then they moved into the crowd, the black of their dresses setting them apart from the colorful menagerie of the guests around them.

"You did not listen to a word I said to the priest."

"Did I need to?" He met his father's gaze. "You said the choice was made, Father. I assumed my input was not further required. Or did I miss a question directed at me whilst you spoke with," he bit his tongue, "the priestess?"

The older man flushed red in anger but recovered quickly enough. The blush could be put down to the color of his coat though Kit doubted anyone had seen the man's face. "Perhaps you would be interested to know that your future bride is bound in silence until the stroke of midnight on the third night of the ball?"

"Not really."

Leon sputtered, his hand gripping Kit's shoulder with a strength Kit found impressive given that he thought his father little more than a politician. "For the gods' sake, Kit. Try! I do not want you to suffer in whatever marriage you would have."

"I would not have one."

"You swore—"

"So choose, Father. I don't care. If the witches would prefer their silence, then I have no qualms with it. The dance floor is no place for discussion anyways."

"Kit…if you prefer the Princess Aurora or one of Ignoblis' offerings, I would not stop you from picking them. I would have you pleased, my son."

He could not tell his father that his son was dead inside. The son they'd brought back from the woods, carted in a coma through the trees, from a dark tower, was nothing more than a ghost of the man he'd once been. Oh yes, he knew others suffered harsher fates than himself. He knew it was only a sense of entitlement that made him think he deserved to be treated with more care, as better than any other man out there. He didn't even know if the man he'd come upon in the forest before his capture had been recovered, recognized and buried and hailed a hero for all that he suffered. Was it bad to comfort himself with the thought that perhaps the poor fool had not suffered as long as Kit? He hoped it was so at least. And in the end, it meant nothing, and he had no response for his father but silence.

"The musicians return, and I am to dance, my king." Kit bowed, crossing his arm over his chest in the formal way a courtier would acknowledge their king. He bowed and did not look at his father's face as he descended the dais and extended his hand, not caring which of the black robed women accepted the offering, just that someone accepted, and he could pretend, for a moment, that it was another black dressed woman who swayed in his arms.

HE KNEW HE danced with all three of them. Vaguely, he remembered the change in songs, the change in grips clutching at his hand as they twirled around the ballroom. He bowed, his partner changed, and he remained on the dance floor, refusing to return to his father's side, preferring to lose himself to the dancers whom he hated.

Silks pressed against his legs, reds and blues and golds, and he let the hordes pull him into their masses, sticking out in his black, always visible, always known as different amidst the colors. He smiled politely to each partner. He even managed a few pleasant, rather trite, remarks. Yes, the weather was indeed very mild for this time of year. No, he didn't think the frosts would return to ruin the spring blooms. Indeed, he hoped the adages were false and that the coming winter was not too harsh. Practically a year away, and still they talked of winter and weather and colors and carriages. Nothing pertinent, inane chatter, not a mind among those who found their way to his arms.

He caught his father looking at him once, motioning to return to the thrones. He ignored the command and spun away, spun until his feet ached and beyond.

The bells chimed thrice, and the band played a final waltz, and Kit begged his leave of the peacock colored woman in his arms, smiling as he fled the ballroom in advance of the guests.

His guards could not catch him as he moved through the halls. They needn't have feared. He found his way to his rooms easily enough, locked the door at his back when he entered and shrugged out of his doublet, the gray shirt beneath sticking to his skin with sweat.

He ripped the cloth away, leaving it a puddled mess on his floor, kicking his boots off quickly after, the stockings covering his feet.

He stood at his balcony, bare-chested and barefoot, breathing shallowly of the crisp air, the sun too far away from dawn.

Those invited to stay in the palace for the length of the ball would rise late the next morning. Breakfast would be another affair of mind-numbing conversation and rhapsodic smiles aimed at him. Almost he looked forward to it, just to see if the elves would be uncovered or if they would retain their masks throughout their stay, dancing or not.

Like the elf standing in the courtyard below his balcony, leaning lightly against the rail to the garden.

He could not pick out her hair from the night around her.

The black harpy then.

What was it about her that drew him so, that he fought against the wanting of?

He found a white shirt in his wardrobe and slipped the silk over his head. He didn't bother with the ties at his throat or tucking the excess into his breeches. He didn't bother with stockings or boots, slipping through the small door that, upon a day, would lead to a second set of rooms for his wife and his children. He'd used the escape often as a child, never since he reached his majority though, always keeping the locks turned so that they could not be used against him either. The locks were on his side of the door. He slipped through the rooms and down the far stairwell, found his feet eating up the ground, arms pumping at his sides, running across the stones, running to the woman on the terrace, stumbling to a halt before the glass doors to the outside.

She hadn't moved from her position except to tilt her head back, her long black tresses hanging down her spine in curling waves, blowing lightly in the breeze.

He remembered.

He remembered finding a similar woman escaping the harsh confines of a crowded ballroom and seeking sanctuary in a place silent from the noise above stairs. Another woman, and another ball, another life long ago.

But this was not that woman.

And he was not that boy.

The knife was in his hand before she had a chance to draw another breath. Not the elf standing in the garden. No, this was not that elf, who found him in the dark and who he reserved the majority of his hate for.

He did not hesitate to push the Priestosolos against the wall, covering her mouth to stall whatever words she sought to speak to him, any cry for help she might utter. She'd found him silently enough; she could die the same.

"I could kill you, and it would be an easy thing, not only in deed but in thought." His voice whispered in the still of the night, no one there to listen to him but the woman he held captive. "I would have gladly died to spare her life. This body would have gladly died, would not have cared what became of it so long as she lived, but you saved it. You saved me when you'd been trying to kill me from childhood. Was it that your assassin failed to kill me all those years ago? Or was it that she stayed and that is what you couldn't stand most, that she stayed with me and you lost a disciple and thought to punish me with this half-life while taking hers? And now you think I will be your tool, married to your spawn without a thought or care of my own?" He shifted closer to her, ignored the shaking in his hand as he shifted his free fingers to her dark hair, felt the supple softness of her skin beneath his fingers, tangled himself against her scalp and yanked, relishing the hiss of pain as she arced into his knife and drew a line of blood across her throat. "Which one do you not care to lose, priestess? Which one will you sacrifice to my hate?"

"You do not hate us."

He smiled, a cold, cruel smile that he pressed to her cheek, his words a whisper over her flesh. "Only you. Are you so willing to trust that my hate won't run cold enough to take my revenge on your Daughters?"

"You do not hate my daughter."

"You have no daughter, bitch." He released her, stepping back, eyes scanning the hall, noticing that the gold masked woman now stared at the window where he stood with his knife, barefoot and his shirt gaping at his throat, frantic and wild and without anywhere or anyone to run to.

A younger him would have been horrified.

When he woke in the morning, after a night of fitful sleeping with memories of his actions to rouse him, he would be horrified.

Now, now he opened the door, ignoring the elf panting in the hallway and crossed the distance between himself and her successor.

He held the knife between them, the blade pointed towards the ground, dripping red rubies onto the broken stone path.

She gripped his wrist, steadying his hand.

With a calm grace, she turned the blade towards her chest, stepping into the point, enough to pierce the black of her dress, bare the pale flesh beneath as the edge cut the lace of her gown and stained her skin with her mother's red.

They stood there, staring at each other while he imagined another woman's eyes and the black covered pools of the present begged him to forget.

"Will the debt be paid?" *If I kill you... Will I find peace if I take your life for the one you destroyed?*

Her gloved fingers left his wrist, brushed over his lips in a gentle caress, akin to the first tasting of a fine wine. It was only natural to purse said flesh and press against her thumb.

Her chest rose and fell faster, and he pulled the knife away in fear of piercing her pale, pale skin.

He replaced the knife in its sheath at his hip, turned and walked away, into the hallway, past the woman still standing there, watching, up the stairs and down the hall to his rooms, ignoring the commotion of his guards as they tried to figure out how he sped past them. He waited for them to unlock his door before slipping into his darkened rooms and closing himself away.

He sank against the wood, sank to the floor and wrapped his arms around his upraised knees, ignoring the way his sword dug into his side, and the dagger slipped loose from his hip.

Kit leaned his head against his knees and closed his eyes.

What had he done?

Why did he care?

IV

The Four Hundredth and Eighty-Eight Ball

The Second Night

HE PLEAD EXHAUSTION to escape brunch the next morning.

The ladies of the court were excused from other activities as they went about the arduous process of preparing themselves for the festivities of the night to come. The men went on a short hunt through the manicured lawns of the estate.

No one expected him to join in that, the memories that it might conjure for him.

That they thought him so fragile would have made him growl or laugh, he wasn't sure, seeing as it was likely true regardless.

He slipped from his rooms and the expression on his face must have been adequate to convince his guards to let him be, wander as he would without their presence guarding him. One thing to be grateful for, he supposed, though there were few places left to explore within the palace grounds not invaded by some such frivolity or other. Women laughed and cackled in the parlors while they discussed dresses and which color it seemed Kit preferred since he'd dance with it so many times the night before. He only knew what they discussed because the screaming denials of pink and peach reached his ears and he investigated before he realized what it was the women were discussing.

The older gentlemen, not out on the hunt, took up residence in the library, stealing Kit's solace that he might have found among the many volumes of books housed within the wooden shelves.

The ballroom was abuzz with servants resetting candles and polishing windows and sweeping the floor.

The kitchens were too terrifying to imagine as Kit got as close to the stairs as he dared before the clanking and sizzling of pots and pans made him hurry away.

Soldiers were in the lists.

The duelists were all otherwise engaged for the day and their space occupied by dancing instructors anyways.

Kit stopped to breathe.

He hadn't felt at home in the palace since he returned bedridden. Likely before that too. The only place that felt like home to him was a heart no longer beating, no matter how much the midnight beauty made him ache inside.

Only one place remained touched by her influence.

Careful that no one saw him, he slipped from the palace steps towards the barracks, stopping at every sound lest someone should come towards him. He was undisturbed as he reached her rooms and slipped behind the unlocked door to her space. The leaves of her plants were vibrant against the sand-dun of the walls. Someone had watered her garden, cared for it even though she wasn't here. He walked through the plants, brushing aside leaves, fingers lingering over the waxy green stalks and brightly blooming spring blossoms towards her bedroom, the area she'd cordoned off with a drapery, a private place he'd found as much sanctuary in as she.

The sheets on her bed looked fresh changed, turned back as though she could slip beneath them at the end of any day. There was something of the forest here, deeper than just the flowery scent of fresh blooms, fresh turned earth, grass after a storm, leaves burning in the autumn fall.

He stripped his vest from his shoulders, unbuttoned the clasps of his shirt from his throat.

Kit hung the garments over the back of an old chair in one corner. He settled his boots beneath the seat and tread carefully over the wooden floors, warm compared to the rug covered stones of his room. He hesitated before pulling back the covers and slipping between the sheets.

Did it disrespect her memory to lay in her bed absent her consent? Did he have it in him to care?

Strands of fabric wove a canopy over his head, the green vines growing out of velvets and laces and whatever other fabrics she'd scavenged to make the covering. Bunched fabrics resembling flowers were pinned to the mess, dipping towards the bed as though truly alive and she was the sun they reached for.

He blinked, staring up at the lime and fern and mint colored ropes above him. He blinked, and it took him longer to open his eyes when a shaft of sunlight pierced through the shade and landed against his face, warming his chilled body though he had the blankets pulled around him.

It was easy enough to draw one of the pillows beside him, wrap his arms across the soft fabric and pretend that he held something firmer, just as lush but in a different way, that the heat of a body was beside him and not this heat warmed mound of feathers and cloth. His father would be shocked to know Kit knew what it was like to hold a woman not his wife in his arms. But he'd been on a battlefield, and he hadn't wanted to hold another soldier when she came to him and asked and offered comfort.

He nuzzled the curve of neck in his arms, imagined the rise and fall of a chest against him, the pound of a heart against his fingertips.

We are not at war, Kit.

No, not on a battlefield, but always at war. This was just inside him now, hidden behind the flesh he bore.

She offered no more words inside his head.

Her silent, black haired sister sat beside him, the full-face mask gone and only a piece of gold mesh covering her eyes remained. She took his hand from the pillow, lifting his arm aside so she could remove the piece of fluff from his dream, replace it with her own warm body. Her head burrowed beneath his chin, into his chest, lips a soft caress against his skin as she turned her face to the side and wrapped an arm around his waist and he wrapped her in his embrace.

She smelled like her sister, all earth and twilight, the edges of the dark.

He breathed her in and gave himself to sleep.

HE SMILED AT the press of lips to his, the breath of wind across his face as he woke slowly to a setting sun.

How long had it been since he'd slept more than an hour or two at a time?

He replaced the pillow at the head of the bed, straightened the bedclothes when he stood, replacing the room to what it had been before he disturbed the dead. His fingers brushed along the top of the chair when he donned his clothing, slipped back into his boots.

The room looked untouched.

He wondered how many times he could sleep between her sheets before his scent overpowered hers and he lost that last touch of her in his life.

Would his wife mind that he spent his nights in a dead girl's rooms?

His lips twitched into a smile. He truly didn't care what some elf thought of him. He almost hoped that Eli'd left a curse on the place, that any of her sisters who dared enter the dwelling would incur some blasted stomach ache or night terrors of spiders biting at their skin.

He wished her plants a fine evening before he closed the door and left, fingers trembling over the latch now that he had committed himself to departure. Gods, how he wanted to stay and dared not remain a moment longer.

A GUARD MET him at the steps of the palace, looking him over for any injuries as the man hustled Kit to his chambers and a valet, uncalled for and unwelcomed, forced Kit to a bath, laying out clothing for him to wear despite Kit's protests that he could manage on his own.

At least the fool left him his blacks, and Kit slipped into the more loosely tailored coat over a white silk shirt and slacks that fell in neat pleats down his legs. He did not wear boots with the ensemble, slipping his feet into equally black half shoes that did nothing to detract from the hem of his garments.

He felt a fool in the clothing but had seen enough men sporting the attire the night before to know it was the fashion.

He refused to think on how he'd acquired a set of the garments for himself, who had been close enough to measure him, the implied touching that must have occurred as such.

TONIGHT WAS LESS formal.

He entered with a group of gentleman similarly aged, managing a few insipid conversations with them before they split to allow him to make the first bow before the king and step aside as they each took turns at subservience.

Aurora was, as promised, absent from the proceedings.

He noted this without his father's regard, quietly grateful that the lady had managed an escape he himself was forbidden.

The five wives of Ignobis he hadn't managed a dance with the night before returned for the second night of the ball, the other women absent from the proceedings. He took one dance with each lady and watched as they were hurried from the hall in the aftermath. It seemed the good lord didn't want Kit forming any attachments with the offered brides.

The sisters of the Dienobolos were in attendance, though only the flaxen haired lady and her ginger counterpart approached him for a dance. Tonight, their faces were covered in half masks dripping with silken veils to cover their cheeks and lips. Flashes of what they might look like behind the shadows tried to draw his eye, but he danced unseeing.

Their priestess was absent from the ball altogether.

Other dancers approached him after he'd done his duty by those guests given status for the event. Subtler gowns, gowns that draped rather than billowed, pressed against Kit during waltzes and reels. He could feel his partners' legs touching his own when they spun too close to him. As he recalled, he'd noticed a similar phenomenon the night prior with the elfin dresses of the Dienobolos. It appeared that if nothing else, the ladies of the wood were changing fashion, and the women of the ball were all too keen to change to suit the trend.

It mattered little to Kit what they wore or didn't wear for a dance.

Kit did not pretend enjoyment in the act this night.

He danced, as was expected of a prince, paid the proper courtesies and adoring glances.

Through it all, he wore a smile that was as fake as many of the jewels on these proper ladies' necks. No one called him on it, but everyone knew. That he was displeased was not new to the proceedings. Had he been cheery, likely the patrons would have been terrified and blubbered, wondering what new ailment afflicted their prince.

At the first break in music, he excused himself from the ballroom and made his way to the great hall where tonight's feast had been assembled. He took a glass of wine and a sweetmeat for himself, pleading introductions when he was begged to sit with this table or that. He managed a quiet moment in the hall, long enough to guzzle the red and swallow the sausage before a flock of young lasses exited the ballroom and he fled in the opposite direction of their approaching coven.

He found himself in a quiet music room, stopping the minstrel from plucking on his instrument with a raised hand. "You're dismissed, please."

The poor man fled Kit like he was Hades come to collect his soul.

If only Kit could flee as easily, he would not feel such a weight on his shoulders.

He sighed when the musician rushed past him and he locked the doors upon the man's exit, managing a small sigh in relief that he had found a haven to escape to.

Kit moved to take a seat on one of the lush couches of the room, wide enough to serve as a bed should he manage to stay hidden away long enough for silence to fill the halls.

He noticed her then, sitting in the corner, her hands folded in her lap, unconcerned with his presence or his subsequent dismissal of her entertainment. His fingers clenched over the edge of the couch. "My apologies, my lady. I had thought I was alone."

The troubadour hadn't looked at the woman to alert Kit to her presence, hadn't hesitated in leaving his audience behind at Kit's demand.

She didn't appear to mind the quiet.

Perhaps she was as desperate for solitude as he.

"And I apologize for last evening."

She nodded her head, and he caught sight of her lips behind the gauze, a delicate pink that contrasted sweetly with her moonlight skin.

"Would you remove your mask?"

She shook her head, though he had the impression that she smiled at his request, despite denying it.

"Your priestess is not in attendance tonight." He did not expect an answer and was rewarded with her silence and what he felt was her stare. "I should like to extend my regrets to her for my actions previously."

The woman stood.

He'd not heard her name.

In truth, he didn't remember any of the three elves being introduced beyond title of Daughter.

He'd meant to ask Eli if that was there way, that they were called by their titles and stations rather than given a name to be known by. Did all "daughters," in turn serve Pirie? Eli had called the ones who attacked them by name, hadn't she? He'd not thought to look up the words she'd used back then, and now the words slipped through his memory without remembrance.

She approached him as she would a wounded animal, coming at him from the front, allowing him ample time to move aside, to keep her in his direct vision. It was habit that had him turning at an angle to her approach, allowing his peripheral to catch anything that might be at his back, attacking in tandem with her.

She stopped at his maneuver.

He did not apologize for it.

She extended both hands, her palms towards the arched ceiling overhead, clear of weapons. With a soft swish of her gown, she sat on the edge of his couch, turned so that her back was in the corner and she could watch him as he watched her. Her hands remained in her lap for him to see.

He recognized the motion as a request to join her.

He obliged, not taking his gaze from her masked face as he circled the back of the couch and sat against the opposite end, spine equally pressed into the meeting corner of cushions.

She made no other movements for long moments, allowing him to stare, and he sat wondering if she stared in turn. Slowly, so as not to startle him, she reached down to the edges of her skirts.

He tensed, waiting for a knife to slip into her hand and the lunge that would plunge the blade between his ribs. Would he seek to stop her if she attacked? He did owe her a debt of blood as he had cut her mistress the night before.

Her fabrics rustled, and there was a soft thump onto the carpeting, followed quickly by a second equally soft thud. She replaced her hand on the arm of the chair, moved the other to the back, and lifted herself enough to curl her legs beneath her bottom, settle her skirts around her calves so he could not see her covered feet, if elves wore stockings that is.

He glanced quickly at the shoes, expecting leaves and twigs bound together.

That wasn't fair, he knew that. Eli'd worn the same shoes as any other lady of the court. He had no right to think this woman would be different, and yet he thought it all the same.

Her shoes were as black as her gown, as black as the starless night beyond the castle walls. The crystal caught the light and refracted it, sparkling in the dimming candle flickers from chandeliers set to burn for too long. Remarkable shoes. Impossible shoes.

He held her gaze as he bent to lift one in his hand, bent close enough that her gown brushed against his arm and chest as he leaned into her and brought the slipper to his eyes to examine.

"Incredible."

He turned the slipper over between his fingers. Weightless, nigh lacking in any tactile sensation at all. It was like holding a piece of the Darkness given shape and form to suit the whim of the wearer but ready to return to its true nature at the flick of a hand.

"Best not to show these to any of the other women, my lady. Your dresses they might manage to emulate, but we've no magic such as this to call on for fair maidens to trample."

Her head tipped back, and he had the impression she laughed with him. Back and tilted to the left. Another elf had similarly sat before.

He turned his eyes back to the shoe and the safety it represented. "Will you take vengeance against me if I close my eyes and took my gaze from you?" He looked at her long enough to watch the shake of her head, the hand that rose and begged him to lean back in what comfort he could find.

"Should I trust you?" He imagined another woman sitting across from him, a grin stretching her lips wide as she replied that he had before, why not once more? But it had taken many years for that other woman to gain his trust, and he was no longer that boy.

She leaned forward slowly, stopping when he tensed, shifting further when he relaxed at her approach. He raised a hand whether in warding or benediction he didn't know, but she took the gesture as her own, caught his fingers between hers. The white glove he wore pulled smoothly from his flesh. The grip she had on him did not allow for him to clench his fingers and pull away. He vibrated, the deer before the huntsman, and watched the black of her gloves melt away with the will of her magic.

She brushed her bare thumb across the back of his hand, the scars on his knuckles from fist fights in the barracks, a hard jab with unprotected skin. He sucked in a breath when she pressed too deeply against the still tender flesh from his most recent bout in the lists, but he did not stop her, and she did not pull away despite his discomfort. She stroked over the length of his fingers pulled from their fist with her gentle ministrations. He didn't offer any resistance when she turned his hand over and stared at the horror of his palm.

Kit turned his head aside, not wanting to see her reaction to the destruction that was his skin. The mottled skin was red and raised, extra padding that still ached and pulled with every flex of his fingers. She traced the edges of the cross, the way the longest beam extended to the base of his heart finger, over the crest of his wrist. The ring in the center of the design was a deeper red than the surrounding skin, highlighted in its exaggerated precision. This she traced with extra care, lingering over the mark though she, nor anyone, could know what it was from. That did not stop her touch from having more compassion when she stroked it. Maybe her magic gave her a knowledge he hoped to hide.

He flinched at the press of her nail into the skin. It brought his gaze back to hers, the mesh covered eyes that bored into him despite his inability to see them.

Yes, he still had feeling in his hands.

Yes, it was likely a product of her people's healing.

"Should I trust you?" The question slipped from his lips a second time, and he caught the straightening of her shoulders, the hitch in her breath.

Was she nervous to be so interrogated? Was there something she wished to hide? Were memories crowding her the same as they crowded around him?

Her face tipped back to his hand, and he looked down to where she still held him. She traced the ring once more, slashed from left to right across his palm, two dots piercing the upper portion of the design. She wrote "yes," across his palm, and he smiled for she'd written the same many years ago when he'd asked after a letter in her barracks and the marks so different than his own alphabet.

Not her. This was not that woman.

He pulled his hand away and stood. She fell forward a half step into the space he vacated, barely catching her balance along the edge of the couch. He clenched his hands at his sides to keep from reaching out to steady her. "Apologies." Kit just managed to bite back the stammer of his words, his need to run from the room. "Excuse me."

Kit walked past her, walked around the couch so he was not tempted to sit again at her side, walked to the door and unlocked it, pulled it open, slipped from the room.

It took all his will not to look back at her as the door closed behind him. He leaned back against the painted wood, not knowing what it was he truly wanted to do. One hand was clenched and pressed against one gold leafed panel, the other remained curled about the handle itching to turn.

What was the matter with him?

What spell were the elves weaving this time?

What if his father chose the blond or the scarlet woman over the girl with the black hair?

It was so much darker than black though. Would it be as soft to the touch as the night sky to a child's dreams? Could he trust it, her, if it was?

Surely the king would recognize the difference between the woman and choose the staid witch over her sisters. Surely, he knew his son would feel most kinship with a witch as dour as himself.

The sound that broke from his lips was half sob and half chuckle.

Mayhap it would be easier to bear if his father chose either of the other women over the one the last living part of his soul wanted to betray his memories for.

V
The Four Hundredth and Eighty-Eight Ball
The Third Day

"KIT?"

The knocking at his door roused him from the light doze he'd been enjoying in the chair he'd pulled out to his balcony. He stretched slowly, working the kinks from his spine and arms, knowing that his father would not be pleased to be kept waiting while Kit dallied.

He stumbled over to his clothing from the night before, evidence that no servant had come to him yet this day, and the king was here to ring in the new dawn that Kit had hoped to sleep through. He kicked the boots and suit towards his wardrobe, the only effort he was willing to make this early and grabbed the robe slung over the end of his unslept in bed.

He opened the door, knowing better than to try and block his father from entering his rooms though Kit refused entry to the king's guards.

He was no threat to the man. Hells, if the king died, Kit would be stuck ruling a land he desperately hoped would supplant him the moment anyone offered him a throne. For that alone, he'd protect his father with his life, willingly done, even.

"Can I help you, father?" He kept his tone modestly contrite, expecting a tongue lashing over his disappearance the evening before, for not having attended whatever meetings he'd missed this morning.

The king moved through Kit's bedroom, ignoring Kit's question, touching the silks of Kit's unrumpled bed, the curtains that Kit refused to draw closed for fear of the walls closing around him. Ancient fingers glided over the waxed surface of Kit's dining table, the covers of the books and papers strewn over the wood, refuting the main use of the piece of furniture. Leon walked to the balcony and stood staring at the chair set there until Kit joined him in the doorway, waiting.

"I'm tired, boy."

Was he meant to respond to the statement? If so, Kit didn't know how.

"I'm tired of ruling, of these balls, of the endless stream of grievances and petitions that shuffle through my doors daily. I'm tired of looking at my only child and seeing a ghost of the man he once was."

He met his father's gaze as the man sat in Kit's chair.

"When you were a child, I had to set three guards around your room, two at the door and one at the window. No matter how many times I told you of the danger, you still climbed down the trellis and found a way to touch the earth and the trees of our lands. If you'd known how to ride, no doubt you'd've flown all the way to the woods and the demons who wanted you dead within them." He smiled tiredly. "Thank the gods you learned control before taking to the saddle.

"I had the trellis removed once. That didn't stop you from trying to climb down the walls with your tiny hands gripping at tiny cracks between stones. Thankfully your guards were watching you so closely, too afraid to distract you from your task, but ready to catch you should you fall.

"You were never afraid of the fall, Kit. You lived. Even when your mother died, you never wasted a day.

"Then you came back with that woman from the forest, and there was a darkness to you I'd not known before. I saw it in the way you looked at her; knew something she'd done had hurt you to your core and you were fighting your way back to yourself. And you returned, boy, you did. You came back stronger than you'd been. You smiled and talked. There was a lightness to your steps every time she was around. And she was safe, treating you only as her prince, a soldier's job to protect and defend.

"But it wasn't that, was it? She was as charmed by you as you were by her. And I was too blind to see what it meant." He sat forward in the seat, reaching for Kit's hand. When had the king's hand grown so old, lost their strength? Poor man to seek in his son the will he'd long lost. Poor father to find out too late the son was as bad off. Kit clutched the hand holding his, offering what comfort he could, knowing it likely wouldn't matter in the end. "If she'd returned with you, after everything that had happened, would you have come back to me? Would you have found your way from the darkness?"

He answered the only way he could: "The Darkness is all consuming, Father. It takes us all in the end."

His father sat back in the chair, dropped Kit's hand from his grasp, eyes searching Kit's face for what Kit didn't know. "You will never love anyone the way you loved your Captain. You will marry for duty. If I died today, you would rule for the same reason. But you would remain this shell you've become." He stood slowly from the sunken chair. "Is there no way to bring you back?"

"One, but the gods do not return the dead to the living world."

He had not meant to say the words. His father longed as heartily for his lost love as did Kit. It was cruel to remind the man of the same.

"If I could release you from this life, Kit, know that I would."

The king squeezed Kit's shoulder, the motion of a man to another man, not blood to blood, father to son. It must be easier to consider Kit as other than child. Gods knew Kit found it easier to forget that the man he served was also his father.

Knowing that his life counted only for the benefit of the kingdom was not a comforting thought.

It was not precisely true, but he'd not had a childhood like the peasants and courtiers. When he was young… But he'd never really been young.

The old man shuffled to the balustrade, leaned over the hard marble to stare at the patio below. A few couples ranged the walkways to the gardens, some in deeply improper poses when they thought they could not be spied by anyone else. Kit watched the smirk on his father's face, bereft of the condemnation that he expected to see at the display. "The blonde seems most voluptuous, but those damned dresses conceal too much."

Kit joined the king at the rail, settling so that his back was to the gardens, leaning against the stone and tilting his head up to the cloudless sky. Dawn was chilly this morning, and the robe did little to keep the bite of the wind from his flesh.

He did not say anything in response to his father's words.

"The redhead seems spirited, or at the very least she seems to enjoy the dance which will serve her well in our court. She would likely demand you continue to throw balls, son, just to make you waltz." An unhappy thought, though the king had likely meant it as a jest. "Not her though, is it boy? There's only the one who calls to you, and even she you would deny if I allowed it."

Wise man, to know how desperately Kit wished he could.

The king touched his shoulder, and Kit turned in kind, facing the gardens below and the few people who had spotted them from below. Leon waved, and Kit followed suit, regal to a fault.

The king stepped back from the rail, into the shade of the palace walls, beyond the sight of the people staring.

Kit didn't care enough to hide, wondered who else might have seen him at his midnight wonderings on the balcony. No one had said aught to him as of yet. "Which one would you choose for me, Father? Which elf shall I take to bride?"

"Give me something, Kit." The hands were stronger now as the pulled at Kit's arm, forced him to face his father and the desperation on the man's face. "I would see you happy in this marriage. I would have it bring you a measure of peace if it might. Which of those women would heal you? Give me something to help you, boy!"

"But I am healed, Father."

"Christophe—"

He pulled away from the man, jerked out of his hold and stared back out over the gardens, deserted now that a repast had been rung, the echoes of the bels still lingering in the air calling those awake to the dining tables.

"Kit…it is not a betrayal to find what joy you can, despite the love you have lost."

No, it wasn't a betrayal. The betrayal came long ago when that love was never taken, and now yearned for another without consideration of it having vanished. "The blond."

"But—"

"You asked my opinion, and I have given it. Do not ask more of me." Kit could not mask the bitterness in his voice, nor did he try to hide the pain in his expression when he turned back to the man and watched his father flinch away.

Give him the light. Keep him from the dark. He would not be reminded of the woman he missed, or the devil come to taunt him with the wanting.

"As you wish, son."

Kit did not move as his father left him alone on the balcony. The door to his rooms closed quietly, and he bowed his head, wanting only to escape, not knowing where he would run to.

He wondered how far he could ride before the sun set.

He wondered what he could escape, and what would catch him if he fled.

A last ride, and then he'd accept his fate.

VI

THE STABLE HAND yawned at Kit's approach but managed a tired smile. He handed Kit gloves before walking away to bring Oberon from the stalls.

Kit waited patiently, soothed by the ritual he thwarted as often as embraced. He adjusted the fingers of his left hand, rubbed his palm over his thigh. There was a scuff on his riding boot, not that he cared, but he bent over, scraped at the mark while he waited for the white horse to be saddled and brought to him.

He looked up at the clomping of hooves, the mare and his stallion dancing around each other.

He looked over his shoulder at the woman walking towards him, legs encased in tan breeches, a billowing shirt of black rippling around her with her steps. She wore her full mask, and a hood, hiding what color hair she had beneath it, though he knew by her steady lope it was not his glass slippered lady from last night before but one of her sisters.

The groom left Oberon at Kit's side, brought the mare to the woman and helped her to mount.

Kit said nothing, and she was obviously silent with her spelled voice and would not expect conversation as such.

She nudged her horse forward and he followed.

They moved well together, he accepted her lead as they walked slowly through the city. She stopped in the square, her face moving to the buildings and the shops, the merchants just beginning to bring their wares to their stalls for the day. Her head paused while turned to the baker, Cinta's fresh cinnamon and ground clove rolls filling the air as the man left his shop to lay a tray of fresh pastries on his table. Kit found his eyes drawn to the delicacies as well, nudged his horse over and smiled at the man, the grateful stare in return for a life saved so long ago.

He requested two of the treats, which the baker supplied readily enough, waving off Kit's offered coin in exchange. Kit smiled for the male and insisted on the payment.

She watched him return to her side, her mare sidling beside Oberon while Kit handed her the cinnamon roll to eat.

He watched the way her hand lifted delicately to remove a small panel over her lips, the mask still held in place to shield her.

Red lips like berries growing on the vines in the groves of the palace.

He rode with the sun-kissed lady, his offered choice of an hour earlier.

She nodded, and he thought that it was with more understanding than thanks or recognition. Perhaps it was a trait of the elves to pick at their partner's thoughts. He had the impression that she rolled her eyes at him, the quick turn and shake of her head all he had to read her by. But she didn't deny his thoughts, and he sat his horse without condemnation, absurdly content that she might know his mind, and not expect aught else from him because of it.

Once more they kicked their horses into an easy walk, reaching the walls of the city and the path beyond. She kept her mare to an easy trot, and he followed her lead, wondering where she would take him if he said nothing to gainsay her. They turned towards the wooded path. Branches soon obscured the sun, forming an arch over their heads as they passed onto the forest road.

Beyond sight of the city watch, beneath the dark trees of her homeland, she removed the hood over her head, pulled the pins holding her braid to her crown so that the long yellow tail flowed down her back. She swayed on her mount, moving naturally with the horse's rhythm, her hair following the motion. The braid swinging like a pendulum, entrancing him, stealing his focus. To think that so simple a thing could hypnotize him. Yet even knowing he was being drawn into her spell, he did nothing to stop it. He would see what she wished him to see and would not fight her.

They moved from the path into the woods. He recognized the trees only so much as to say that they could have been the same trees he'd ridden through the month prior in search of a ghost deep in the depths. Her mount wove smoothly through the thickets, and his followed without pause.

He leaned back in his seat, ignoring the discomfort of the saddle to lay prone on the horse's back, stare at the thick leaves above him.

One said green blade drifted down from the canopy on a light breeze.

Kit opened his hand, reaching up to catch the delicate leaf. Even here in the twilight of the woods, there were so many colors of green in one single shaft of life. Whirls of yellow, lines of forest pine, veins of something closer to black, and all so bright in the darkness. He watched the way the branches swayed and listened to the whispering of waving foliage. No wonder the elves found such sanctuary beneath the trees.

His horse stopped, and Kit drew himself back into his seat.

She held his horse's reins, dropped when he reclined along the beast. He hadn't heard her dismount, but now she stared up at him from the depths of her mask, and he waited for whatever she would have of him. She led the stallion further down the path, walking at his side while he rode. Where they passed, it was like only he left an imprint on the world, her presence one with the wood around them.

He ducked beneath a low hanging branch and beyond was a wide circle surrounding a central tree. He felt a vague sense of recognition, of panic, but it passed soon enough, or perhaps his apathy just held sway within his breast.

The rustling around him drew his gaze to the canopy, his eyes taking in the homes built within the giant trees, rope bridges connecting them to each other, the men and women lining the walks and staring as intently down at him as he stared up at them. He could not tell their expressions, too far away to make out smiles or frowns, what their whispered words might be saying about him. They didn't matter, in the end, when the Priestosolos emerged from the great tree in the center of the clearing, and even the wind stopped whistling through the wood at her approach.

She stopped on the last step to her tree, her hands spread wide, head tilted to the boughs and the people there. "Blood has been spilled, and blood has been paid." Surely if she had told them of his attack, he would not be so easily allowed entrance into their homeland? But he could see the mark of his knife still fresh upon her throat and wondered if her people knew the true meaning behind it. "The Darkness demands that any who make the sacrifice be admitted to our grove if they seek our shelter. Are there any among you who would gainsay this man the right to be here?"

"*Qui forsome slobec mistaf?*" What offering has been made?

Kit could not see the speaker, nor tell if the voice was male or female. He stiffened at the challenge of the tone, could guess well enough their meaning. Asked the same question himself, though remained silent, unwilling, even in his suicidal thoughts, to condemn himself.

The priestess motioned, and his guide raised her hand in support to help him dismount. His hesitation was not remarked upon, and her hand did not waver, but it took him longer to meet whatever fate awaited him than he thought it would.

Now that the time had come he was afraid.

His boots thumped into the carpet of grass, bending the delicate blades beneath his tread. A breath of wind swept before him, creating a path to the center of the glade and he did not need his guide's hand to tell him to follow where the breeze led him. He found it easier to look at the priest as he moved, and she held his stare until he was before her.

A second gold masked woman appeared at his other side, her presence making itself known out of the corner of his eye. They caged him, and he wondered if the black-haired elf was at his back waiting to catch him if he turned to run.

"Kneel, Prince."

No, he did not think he—but hands grabbed at his arms and pushed him to the ground. His knees struck the earth harder than he thought they meant for him to fall, but their grips did not loosen about him. They held him tighter, and he did not fight when they pulled his arms roughly behind his back to hold him still.

The priestess drew a knife from beneath the sleeves of her robes. The garment flowed with her as she descended the stair and crossed the distance to where he waited. She stood before him and pressed the point of the knife beneath his chin, the tip just grazing the node of his Adam's apple.

He met her gaze for a moment, seeing the same aloof disinterest he felt swirling in his own blood. With a small smile, he tipped his head back, eyes closed as he waited to feel the knife pierce him.

The tear of cloth parted by the knife jerked him away from visions of his death, enough that he struggled to understand what was happening and did not fight the women who stripped his shirt from his shoulders, bared his scars to this world of elf and Night. They caught him quickly enough when he flinched and tried to draw away, pulling at his arms to restrain him, knees pressed tight to his back, so he was forced to bend awkwardly and rely on them for his balance, his shame bare for all those who wished him dead to see.

"Blood has been spilled so that ours would not. Blood has been paid and is honored. Will anyone speak against him?"

What in the gods' names was going on?

Around him the whispering of the wind, the gentle melody of tinkling leaf-fall and feathering-grass stilled. No voice was raised in question or protest and he did not know what to do.

She bent towards him, her eyes holding his, concerned, if he had to guess, though why she should care he didn't know. "You came expecting to die. You do not carry a sword or shield. You walk calmly into our ranks and would give your life without struggle," she tilted her head and it was far too similar to Eli for his comfort or his sanity. "Why, Prince?"

His lips parted in a grim parody of a smile, one that did not try to hide the ache he harbored within. "The struggle is to live, my lady. Death seems a relief." His whispered words did not move beyond her hearing, but they still seemed too loud to his ears. He could not regret the speaking of his darkest secret, not here where the Darkness knew all things.

She reached and took his chin in her hand, the knife in her other still held threateningly enough. The warmth of her flesh surprised him, though he didn't know why. He thought she would be as cold as he was, but she was flesh and blood and life. She looked over his shoulder and he watched her nod.

The silence reigned.

The knees against his back fell away, allowed the exaggerated arc of his spine to relax. He found it did nothing to relieve the unsteady beating of his heart nor the rasp of his breath before his enemies.

"Not enemies. Enemies no more."

He did not trust his voice to gainsay her, not that he thought she would allow the words with her power.

She lifted her knife once more, and he closed his eyes, unwilling to watch. If the blade made a sound he did not hear it as it sliced into skin. There was no pain though the scent of iron filled the air between them and he wondered at the lack of feeling to his wound.

He blinked, and she handed the blade to the woman on his left. A bead of blood welled on the pad of her thumb, staining her pale flesh red.

She knelt before him and his heartbeat sped faster, and he stared at the darkness swirling in her eyes.

With tender slowness, she pressed the drop of blood to the skin over his heart.

"For the Iisforsos. You are accepted among us."

His head tilted, eyes widening at the gesture, not knowing the name.

She walked around him, and he turned as much as he was able with his guardians holding him, to follow her movements.

He needn't have strained, for he tensed when her hands settled against his bare shoulders from behind to hold him in place.

His fingers clenched and unclenched, and then it began.

Elf after elf stepped forward, the rustling in the branches signally their descent to the earth to reach him. Each blooded their finger on the knife in his guide's hand, each pressed a mark across his chest. Each accepted him for the Iisforsos and he wondered that he did not know this name they committed him to.

He watched as best he could the lines they formed across his skin in blood. Along his collarbones, down his sternum, tracing over his ribs, dipping along the bones of his hips and pelvis. Each touch made words gather along his tongue, brought him closer to the edge of asking why, what was the point, when would he die, but his lips remained sealed, and he knelt receiving the bloody tribute bestowed upon him.

And finally relaxed into whatever inevitability awaited him.

It took a lifetime, and it took no time at all. Old faces and young, men and women, children and grandparents, they all came and they all marked him. His arms were released, and bloody prints pressed over his biceps, traced his fingers. She hummed behind him, and he realized that her tune held him captive, was as part of the spell her people were weaving as the blood they painted him with.

The elves did not return to their homes after touching him. Far worse, they gathered around him, their presence sometimes ten deep in spaces as they waited and watched him and his chance of escape diminished with everybody that closed in the space until only a single alley remained for those left to walk through and press their blood to his skin.

"Ashasolos." High Servant of the Forge.

The male stepped forward, arms heavily muscled from hard labor, face burned from the sun, and yet with a peace to his countenance that Kit envied for this was a man content with himself. He stepped forward, and knelt as the priestess had knelt, pierced his thumb as the woman had pierced hers, braced a hand on Kit's shoulder, and placed a blood print to Kit's forehead. The man smiled at the mark, his hands covering the woman's at Kit's neck, and leaned forward, pressing his lips to Kit's though there was nothing sexual about the embrace, soothing, compassionate instead.

"For Iis, you are welcomed by Ashet."

The man stood and took his place at the front of the wall of souls surrounding Kit.

"Chimsolos." Earth's Venerated Lady.

The woman who stepped from the crowd had once approached Kit already, the first time with a young child in her arms. The infant had wailed at the pricking of a finger, but calmed upon touching Kit's skin, the gentle soothing cluck of the lady's tongue.

He had not noticed that the Nurturer had not made her own mark against his flesh.

Now the woman knelt as her brother had a moment before, pierced her finger and drew a line from his lower lip to the tip of his chin. Her lips were soft where the man's had been strong. She kissed him with as little passion, and yet as much heady acceptance.

"For Iis, you are welcomed by Rouchim."

Kit touched his tongue to the wetness when she stood away, tasted iron in his mouth but did not flinch from the tang.

"Elichisolos." Master of the Final Midnight.

He tensed as the assassin stepped from the crowd.

The man was shorter than Eli had been.

Kit had hoped—

For a moment Kit had hoped that all of this was just a ritual; that at the end of everything, she would be the one to walk from the crowd and mark him as her own. How foolish of him to pray for something he knew would not occur. He closed his eyes, not wanting to look at this man who had, in all likelihood, been tasked with taking his predecessor's life.

The male pressed his thumb to Kit's temple and dragged his finger across Kit's closed lids from one side of his face to the other.

This kiss held none of the heart or warmth of the others, but neither did it bestow aggression. It was, and so Kit accepted it, knowing that the touch, granted in such a way, was significant as it did not foretell his death for a moment longer. Kit blinked his eyes opened, stared into the face that was so familiar to him and alien at the same time. The eyes, the assassin had Eli's eyes, and Kit jerked away at the meeting of his lost love's father.

"For Iis, you are welcomed by Echi."

Kit shuddered at the benediction, and though the tone was static, the words themselves were filled with acceptance.

The high priestess released Kit's shoulders and it took him a moment to realize that he was no longer held by the women who brought him to this place. He remained rooted to the ground, though he watched the Pristosolos as she knelt once more before him.

"Lieasolos." The Healer.

She raised the knife again, but instead of her thumb, this time she pierced her palm, letting the blood well in her cupped hand. When the red made a small pool against her flesh, she handed the knife to her Daughter at his side and met his gaze once more. She gripped his shoulder, leaned into his body, and placed her palm over the first mark she'd made against his chest.

A high wind whipped through the trees overhead, leaves fluttering to the ground in the gale.

She did not look away, and he found himself unable to, pelted with the soft green hail.

When the storm quieted, when the silence reigned once more, she leaned forward and kissed his blooded lips.

"For Iis, you are welcomed by Liaea." This she said to him and to the crowd around them, gathered to witness this moment, which he still did not understand and was unsure that he desired the knowledge. "You are one of us now. You are worthy of her, though perhaps it was we who had to prove we were worthy of you as well." The High Priestess, the High Healer, smiled gently at him, bent forward and kissed his brow.

She stood, and he looked up at her from his place on his knees. "Marked by blood, bound by blood, we welcome our brother to the woods."

He flinched at the sudden cacophony around him, men and women cheering as he was helped to his feet and the priestess took his hands in hers, a final kiss to each of his scarred palms.

Her fingers lingered over the ring, and her eye caught his, and he wondered what it was she saw in his gaze, what the odd gleam in hers meant.

She leaned close, careful not to smear the still wet marks on his skin though the breeze had done much in drying the blood covering him. "She is waiting for you at your ball, fair prince. Go to her and find the peace you're looking for."

Go to her…

Yes, he would go to the woman he was fated now to marry. Accepted into the fold because he was to be bound to one of their own. Forgiven the blood debt against him because his father had signed a godsdamned peace treaty with these elves and his was the flesh that would fulfill the promise of that contract. Accepted for he had paid dearly for that debt and would remember the marks on his skin for his life.

He wanted to rage. He wanted to snarl.

How dare she mark him! How dare she not take his life!

He'd come fully expecting, fully prepared to die. That he was being denied by yet another party infuriated him. That he was being bound by another party to a fate beyond his choosing broke him. He had counted on the Dienobolos refusing to part with one of their Daughters in marriage to a city dweller. He had counted on the fast tempers and tempered cruelty to end him before the day came where he took one of theirs again as his own.

They failed him.

Gentle hands turned him away from the Mother Tree, turned him towards his horse and his exit from this accursed grove.

His fists clenched, wanting to lash out, strike, destroy. He was 'of the forest' now; if he killed one of these people, they would be bound to kill him in turn.

Just one. Just kill one of them and he would be free.

And yet the faces surrounding him smiled, and some smiled with a hint of sadness in their eyes, some with joy, most with a wary mix of acceptance and trepidation, but no pity. They'd been the ones to see him broken when he first emerged from the tower. They'd known the worst of what was done to him. But they didn't pity him, and he didn't see hate in their stares.

His fingers unclenched. His eyes closed, and he let himself be led away.

His shirt was in tatters, but it was all he had and the hands leading him helped him into the ruined linen. Oberon was led to him, and he climbed blindly up into the saddle, eyes unfocused as he gave the horse its head.

"Wash the blood away, Prince. Your people would not understand our ritual, and the sign will not need to be read by my Daughter for her to know you've been accepted."

He turned in his saddle to look at the woman standing before the open doorway to the tree temple. His horse moved restlessly beneath him, and Kit nodded once, not knowing how to respond, before leaving the forest far behind him.

The woods thinned into distinctive paths. He didn't bother to direct his mount, the animal seemingly knowing which road to take to return to the city.

For a time, Oberon followed a stream, the merry trickling of the water grated on Kit's nerves, but he stopped, as he had been commanded, and dismounted. He stripped his shirt from his shoulders. Dried flakes of blood drifted from his skin and settled in the trickling water. He watched as the red washed away in the current, knelt, and lifted handfuls of the sun warmed water to his chest, his face. He used a rock rubbed smooth beneath the stream to rinse the red smears from him. Kit dunked his whole head in the cold, clearing the fog from his mind, returning to his unwanted reality.

He washed his skin until his distorted reflection ran clear in the water.

The midday sun dried his flesh quickly enough.

He dressed and mounted and found his way back to the road and the city beyond, exhaustion weighing heavily upon him as he left his horse with the grooms and made his way to his chambers. No one stopped him, no one seemed to wonder at his absence or question his dazed look.

At the stroke of midnight, she would stand before him and he would take the mask from her face. He would have a bride, and she would have for a husband a broken man lost to memories of a love he'd never truly known.

He wished the elves had killed him

He wept that they had not.

VII

The Four Hundredth and Eighty-Eight Ball

The Final Night

HE WOKE TO the shuffling creep of his valet trying to be silent while preparing Kit's clothing for the evening. The poor man flinched when Kit sat up in the bed, but said nothing, not even to direct Kit to the bathroom where the tub was already filled with steaming water, bergamot soap waiting on the cloth at the side. He shut the door so that he would have privacy while he bathed and so that he could undress without prying eyes. Even his servants still sought to sneak glances of him, their eyes misting over when they saw his scars. He was more worried that they might see specks of dried blood coloring his flesh than anything else.

He stripped and stared at himself in the long mirror against the wall of the room. Nothing different about him that he could see, nothing to denote his woodland adventures, no mark to call the elf to him. At least he had some muscle tone back. His ribs were still pronounced but not so much as to be obscene. Dark bruises colored the skin beneath his eyes, but he'd always looked tired, or so his father told him. His hair hadn't grown past his ears, but the barbers kept it well shaped. Besides the multitude of scars covering him, he looked like any other poor soldier. Only he bathed in a pool with scented oils and dressed in velvets and satins and had someone else polish his boots every morning.

His hands clenched, short nails biting into his palms. Yes, he could feel the pressure, might even consider it pain, but it was dulled. He could feel her tracing symbols against his palm, but most of what he felt came from memories of what he'd grabbed or scratched or rubbed before.

Kit climbed into the tub, sitting back in the marble bath so that only his head was above the water resting on a folded towel left for that purpose. He stared at the ceiling, the painting of Atha cradling an infant in her arms. The infant had Kit's face, and the goddess looked like his mother, or at least that's what he'd been told when he asked after the models.

He sat in the small pool until the sun touched the horizon and the water turned cold to the touch.

Dried, a towel wrapped around his waist, he unlocked the door and moved towards his bed, the candles adding light to the quickly fading sun beyond his windows.

"Your father requested it, sire."

Kit touched the green brocade on his bed, gold leaves sewn onto the fabric with the closures buttoned down his chest. How appropriate.

"It's fine."

The man tarried, unsure whether to offer assistance or leave as was Kit's usual preference.

Honestly, Kit didn't know what he wanted either.

"How long till the bells ring to signal the start of the ball?"

"Two hours, sire."

He let the towel drop to the floor and picked at the undergarments laid beside his attire for the night. "Find me in two hours then."

"Yes, m'lord."

Kit pulled the small clothes over his legs, breeches, shirt and boots. The jacket he slung over his arm, unwilling to put the coat on before he had to. The moment the velvet covered him, he would have no choice but to acknowledge what would happen when the clock struck the darkest hour.

His guards came to attention, readying to form ranks around him. "I'm heading to the barracks."

He did not tell them why, and they did not ask, but at least they knew well enough not to follow him down the side stairs and across the way to the training yard. The soldiers there stopped to nod at him, looking to one another to see why he was upon the sands. When he ignored them, they returned to their drills, though he felt their gaze lingering on his back as he went to Eli's rooms and let himself through the door. Carefully, he closed the panel behind him, pushed the lock into place, hung his coat on a hook in the closet and closed that door too before he turned back to the room and its greenery.

It took him less than ten minutes.

It took Kit less than ten minutes to smash every vase, every pot, cover the flooring in thick dirt, broken leaves, torn roots so destroyed they could not be transplanted, never be saved. He flung the chairs against the walls, shattering the legs into broken timber. The vine canopy he yanked and pulled till it fluttered in tatters from its rails. He trampled dirt onto the bedspread, used his knife to cut the mattress and pillows and pull the white feather stuffing out to mix with the destruction on the ground.

Ten minutes, and what was left of her presence was destroyed and nothing felt soothed in his soul.

He'd not broken the windows. The bathroom remained intact. Opening her wardrobe had seemed too personal, and he didn't want to touch her clothing, see his shirts that had found their way into her closet, her scent mingling with his.

He fell to his knees in the dirt, his hands curled together, fingers stroking the brown that coated him, and sobbed.

Kit sobbed, and it went against everything a man should be, should ever do.

And he didn't give a rat's ass.

The door opened and closed slowly. No more thumping of swords or clanging of steel outside the small space. Poor fool, whoever had been sent to see what commotion he was causing.

But it wasn't a male's tread that crossed over the broken pots and shards of ceramic to come to his side. Her hand settled against the back of his neck and he wondered how she'd managed to find him, and why she'd been the one to come looking.

He did not struggle when she led him to stand and walked with him to the bathing chambers. Her hands pushed him against the cream painted stucco beside the wash sink. She took his dirt smudged fingers in her own, her black gloves such a contrast against his flesh. Her head shook, and he had the impression that she was looking at his face from behind her mask, but he could not see her eyes with the gauze covering them.

No, that wasn't true. He could see the moon white skin of her face, but her eyes themselves were pools of black, no white within them, no iris he could discern. Blind, he thought, but she touched him with such surety that she had to have her sight. The dark pools of her eyes were as black as her hair, blacker, if he had to guess.

She did not stop him when he cupped her masked cheek in his stained palm. "So beautiful, your Darkness."

The gold was smooth beneath his touch as she turned her head, pressed the fake lips to his skin in an imitation of a kiss.

She stopped only to pull her gloves off before taking his hands once more, turning the faucet so that the water warmed, and she could wash the dirt from his flesh. He caught her when she tried to pull away, but she looked at him with those void-dark eyes and he let her go only so far as the small cabinet against the opposite wall, pulling out a cloth and returning to the running water, dampening the cotton before reaching to wash the dirt from his face and neck. Her fingers opened the ties of his shirt, trailed over his skin while he leaned his head back, allowing her access to whatever she wished to touch.

With a gentleness born of a healer's touch, she stripped his shirt from him.

He watched those midnight eyes as she looked over his chest, her fingers passing a breath above his scars.

She trembled, and he realized she shed silent tears for him.

"Did you not look your fill that day in the woods?"

Her face tipped up to his. Her eyes widened at his understanding.

He should hate her for taking Eli's face, for making him dream for even a moment that he was with the woman he lost. But he had nothing in him with which to care, and his father's choice of wife would not matter as she was the only one left to have.

Her hands shook, but she turned back to her task and stroked the cloth over his skin. A droplet ran from his collarbone down his chest. She pressed her hand to his flesh, her bare hand to his stomach, her calluses and scars pressing against his, stopping the drop from falling any further down his torso.

There was a different sort of tremble to her limbs now, an answering quake in his own body that wanted to respond.

She met his gaze when he reached to touch her hair, curl the black silken strands between his fingers, step closer into her body, the towel forgotten between them.

A knock sounded beyond the small room at the door to the apartments.

Instinct had him pushing her behind him, using his body as her shield though the door was locked, and no one tried to force their way into the room.

It took two swallows before his voice was steady enough to respond with a gruff "What?" The terse word was the best he could manage.

"You said to find you at the bells, my lord. They are about to start ringing and I—"

Kit heard the hesitation in the young voice.

His valet broke the spell her soft touch had woven over him.

That she thought to magic him into having feelings for her made his head hurt with anger and the longing made that anger burn all the brighter.

He was afraid. He was afraid that it was not her magic that wrapped him in desire, but some small spark of life that remained and desired to thrive in her presence.

She tugged his arm, turned him back to her and it was all he could do to maintain the anger in his thoughts, the sneer on his face.

He would not be swayed by the tears gathering in her black eyes.

She tried to push him back against the wall, but he would not budge. The spell binding her voice prevented her from even uttering a sound of displeasure, for which he was grateful, not having wanted to hear her tears or her frustration. That didn't stop her though, the hand she pressed once more to his bare chest slapping against his skin, succeeding in pushing him away from her for a moment in time.

He growled; bared his teeth like some feral animal that hunted the woods. Maybe she would understand his threat better if he emulated some kin of hers, wild, untamed.

Or not, since she stepped closer and he met the unanswered response in her gaze.

How he used to love inciting a similar reaction in her once-sister. Watching Eli react to some brazen remark had been one of the greatest highlights of his day.

She shook her head, so similar to his Captain, that he felt the ache more keenly. Now he felt her magic, a distinct thing from what feelings had woven around them a minute before. Her magic surrounded him, pulled cloth from the darkness and wrapped him in its embrace. The softest of silks fit tailor made to his skin. He could feel the heat of her hand through the shirt she dressed him in, pristine by her grace.

When she drew her hand back, he longed. He longed for the heat of her to return.

This time he went when she pulled him, retreating over the dirt strewn floors that slowly cleaned as he passed, broken pots reforming, soil lifting in the air to fill them, leaves ripped apart reknit and found their homes in their vases once more. Even the canopy over the bed reformed, though the wispy strands with flowers on them were left where they fell, like some artful seduction which the destruction had revealed. Feathers floated back into the bedding and ripped cloth received neat, invisible stitches to put them back together.

Did she expect gratitude for repairing what his sorrow had broken?

To be sure, the apology for the mess stuck in his throat.

He stopped before the door, his mouth open to speak what words he didn't know. She pressed her fingers to his lips, stilled his apology, his gratitude.

The elf stepped against the wall, out of sight of the door and the servant standing sentinel outside.

Kit pulled his jacket from the closet, finally tearing his gaze from hers though he felt her watching his every move. He made to sling the coat on, but her hands stopped him once more, helped him once more, smoothing his shoulders, resettling the closures at his throat and down his chest. She leaned into him, and he rested his chin atop her head, his arms wrapped around her waist to keep her close.

The valet knocked again, and Kit disentangled himself gently from his elf. He cupped her gold covered cheeks, stared into the dark pools of her eyes, and turned back to the door. He did not look back in his exit.

VIII

KIT LEFT HER there with a flourish, snapping his fingers to hurry his poor valet along, allow her a chance to leave without witnesses to her presence. It was one thing for a man, even a prince, to sweep a woman away, but another entirely for a woman to approach a man.

He was used to it, used to having to protect his companion when they did not realize the danger themselves. Eli had never cared what others thought of her actions. It must be an elf mentality.

His valet pulled him to a stop outside the ballroom, grumbling about dirt stains and scuffed shoes and how had Kit managed it all in the space of two hours. Kit was almost amused by the endless chatter, the harangue, distracted from the ball by this young boy and the dark elf.

Unfortunately, the distraction did not last nearly long enough, and Kit remembered why tonight was both relief and devastation all too soon.

Today was in truth the day of his birth. The fanfare for his introduction would be the grandest of the three days. All those who had gathered for this final night would sink low in curtsies and bows and he would walk down the center of the aisle they made for him and take his seat on his father's throne. Leon would absent himself, as it was Kit's right to rule someday, so let him feel the weight of said power on a less grandiose scale.

But beyond the introductions, this was the least formal night of them all. For once Kit took his seat, and with his father gone, no one held to the strict dictates of society for Kit himself would have it so.

Most of the attendees had formed their clicks and had established partners for dances well in advance of the musicians striking up the first notes of whatever song they chose to perform. Everyone had their partners, and Kit smiled at the ladies designated to beg him for a dance, though usually he could rest, not expected to take every hand offered to him on this last of days.

He wondered how this year would be different, at what point his father would appear and make the announcement that everyone had waited for for centuries: that Kit had found a wife, and one of the dancers would someday be queen.

There had been a time, in the early years, when Kit was young and he pretended that there was a chance of him choosing someone he loved, that Kit would stumble upon his father during a rehearsal, standing with a mug or whatever he was drinking before an empty room rousing the ghosts of his court to cheers at Kit's bride. Often, Eli had been with Kit for the performance, and they had sat in the library long after the king had left listing off the qualities that seemed most important for a prince's bride. Everything from the ability to call birds to her side with the notes of a song, to being able to spin straw out of gold, or was it straw into gold? It was more amusing still to leave the invented lists on the king's desk or somewhere where a courtier might see it and the ensuing panic it would cause. Leon would stomp red faced through the palace. And inevitably a woman would attend the year later with a live bird leashed to her gown or a ball of thread dyed the crispest of golds. The woman with the thread had tried to tether Kit with it. Eli had disavowed the tradition after that. Leon too had kept his musings silent in the aftermath.

Kit shook his head, clearing the memories from before his eyes. Gods, but why didn't the thought hurt as much as before? He did not want to let go of the pain.

Trumpets sounded. The nattering of the ballroom grew quiet and footmen pushed the doors open. His valet stepped aside, and Kit stepped forward.

He kept his hands at the small of his back and walked with his eyes trained on the noble steed above the throne. He walked up the stairs to the dais, turned and watched the ranks of men and women sink low in their formal attire to honor their prince, a man they likely knew very little about beyond rumors and gossip. They rose, and he bowed in return, gratitude for their obeisance. He rose, and the musicians went into a lively quadrille. He sat on the throne and watched the colors of the various ball gowns swirl around him.

Ignobis was absent, his brides with him. No black dressed Daughters of the Dienobolos waited in the throngs of people to steal a final dance. His father had not sought him out to tell Kit which bride would step through the doors at midnight. Kit wouldn't tell the older man that the elves had decided without input from the king.

Kit stared at the doors through which he'd entered, stared unseeing at the gilded arches, hands loosely clenched on the arms of his chair. The room blurred with memory, with wishes.

The third night of the ball.

She'd walked in late, as she had every evening prior. Her gown was black, and yet beautiful in its austerity. The dress had been fitted beneath her breasts, the creamy swells of her flesh much too prominent for the fashion of his people, but she hadn't cared. A single emerald stone had sat in the hollow of her throat, bringing color to her auburn hair and bright green eyes. There had been mischief around her, and when she'd moved, and her dress had revealed the shape of her legs behind the fabric, the courtiers had flinched back in horror and he'd been fascinated by the strength of self it would take to ignore all the looks and whispers that surrounded her entrance. She'd worn the same dress all three nights. All three nights, she somehow looked more elegant than the last.

Kit smiled at the woman bowing before his father's throne. She trembled, and he wondered how long he'd kept her waiting for him to notice her. So Kit stood in recompense and extended his hand, led the young girl into the reel, even managed to smile at her timid attempt at conversation with him.

She had been silent the first night of the dance, weaving among the patrons without pause, searching. He had wondered what it was she was looking for, had had to ask. When he stopped before her, she had run into him, not even knowing he was there, perhaps knowing but who could say. "Would you dance with me?" And she hadn't refused.

Her fingers had been cold in his, and he'd taken a tighter grip on her hand, not to hold her to him, but to share his warmth. It was the first time her head had tilted to the side and he had smiled for her. He slipped her arm into his, led her from the dance floor to the table and the champagne waiting.

The glasses were not his intent, and he pulled her to the chairs set along the far wall, held her hands in his, rubbing them gently until they warmed in his grip. "There's nothing to be worried about here, no nerves to give in to." He had stroked her thumb with his, "It's just a dance, my lady."

"Is it not far more than that, my prince?"

"Not tonight."

He accepted the glass of wine thrust into his hand by an overzealous father flouting the virtues of his daughter in the red dress. Yes, of course she was well mannered and had all the courtly graces, dancing, embroidery, song. Kit refrained from asking if the woman knew how to wield a sword or had ever travelled the wild paths of the forest.

Wouldn't it be nice to breathe in the fresh scent of flowers in the garden?

So, Kit had obliged and extended his arm and escorted the young woman to the gardens. He doubted there were assassins waiting in the hedgerow, but the girl never looked at the greenery or the roses fighting for an early bloom in this false spring. Her eyes remained on his face, and Kit fought hard to ignore the sycophantic light in her eyes.

He watched her staring at the blackened gardens beyond the lit torches of the patio. The snow had melted during the afternoon but had left the paths muddied and no one dared the pebbled roads to explore the plants just waking from their winter hibernation. "They are lovely in the spring."

She looked quickly at him from the corner of her eye, never fully taking her gaze from what shadow hid behind the glass. "They are so manicured. What of nature remains to them?"

"I have never thought of it before."

"You city folk, ever fearing the untamed trees. Do the deer run freely through the woods? Have you ever found a shadowed path to linger among?"

"No, my lady, but I have no guide to show me the way."

She smiled and turned her face away, and he wondered if he should ask her if she would be willing to serve such a purpose the next day. A minuet was struck by the orchestra, and Kit looked once more for her hand in the dance. The moment of hesitation which had threatened the night before was gone, and she accepted his touch, her hands warmer today though still cool. "We shall have to find you a glass of brandy."

"Whatever for?"

"To warm you."

"There are other ways to do the same." And her eyes had glinted at him with mischief and he had followed her onto the dance floor, no longer leading but being led.

Three sets he dedicated to her, always coming back throughout the night. Her cheeks grew pink and the green of her eyes darkened with something more than just pleasure in the dance and he wondered what she would say if he asked her to stay.

Kit begged a moment to himself, laughing as he stumbled up the steps, perhaps too many sips of champagne himself this night. Were not men meant to go to their marriages drunk? Not noble men, of a surety.

He was not nearly drunk enough, regardless, and even as he leaned his head back against the throne, the room shifted into focus and steadied about him, waiting.

The gilded clock at the top of the staircase struck the final bell of midnight.

The musicians stood from their seats to riotous applause and Kit turned with his Ella to the performers, raising his glass in salute, letting her hand go so that she might clap as well.

It took him a moment to realize that she was not clapping at his side, that the brief touch of her fingers to his cheek had not been in accidental play but in barest farewell. He turned enough so that he could watch her pushing through the crowd and to the servants' entrance. A white clad maid nearly fell in her haste to make way for the lady rushing past.

Kit blinked, blinked again, and then did not hesitate to follow rushing to reach her retreating form.

The crowd made room for him, hustling to get out of the barreling way of their prince, many unsure of what the emergency was but unwilling to risk facing the expression on Kit's face if they waylaid him.

He reached the courtyard of the palace in time to see her rushing across the grand circular drive to the waiting carriages, no, horses stabled in the yard. She stumbled once, and he called for her to stop, resuming his chase as she kicked off her shoe and reached the stallions in the paddock.

Her horse reared when he grabbed the reins, but she held her seat. Kit did not deny that he was impressed with her skill even as he fell away and she set her heels to the horse's flanks and through the palace gates.

Surely, she knew he would follow?

He blinked the room back into focus, back into the present and the silence that had fallen in the grand space. Nearly as one, the nobles and courtiers had turned to face the staircase and for a moment he was frightened to look up and see which woman stood at its peak.

The gold of her mask had been replaced with a white lace that concealed nothing of her identity even as it hid her from the rest of the crowd, wrapped her in a veil he was privy to see beyond. Her black tresses hung freely about her shoulders, diamond shards woven into the strands, catching the light from the thousands of candles in the chandeliers. There were no straps to her gown, her shoulders bared for the first time since her entrance to the ball. The white of her dress was only a few shades paler than her skin, the faint blush lending a rosy glow to her moonlit flesh. And the gown itself, beyond its striking color, the way it sparkled as though woven with crystals, was unlike anything anyone had worn before. The bodice lifted her breasts while maintaining the slim lines of her figure. Pearls and jewels formed the neckline, emphasized the gentle curve of material over her bosom, highlighted the gold chain that stroked her throat with a lover's caress before slipping into the delicate amount of cleavage she revealed. The skirt, from where it billowed out below her sternum in soft waves of nearly sheer white, shifted and moved with her every breath, settling like a cloud on the ground, waiting only for a wind to blow her away. If she danced, when she danced, her partner would fall into the dream with her.

She looked a ghost, standing in the middle of the hall.

She looked a princess awaiting her prince.

Her hand trembled as she reached for the rail and walked slowly down the stairs to the dance floor. A breath was inhaled, and Kit could not tell if it was his alone or if the watchers breathed with him. She stepped onto the dance floor, and a hundred eyes watched her walk the same path he had walked before to meet him at the throne.

It was self-preservation that kept him seated. His legs would have shaken; he might well have fallen on his knees, ready to worship at this woman in white's feet, the silent flash of light before the darkness claimed a soul, the peace that led the spirit into the night.

A clock chimed somewhere within the silent palace. That it was heard was testament to the shock of the people gathered within the ballroom.

The great bells in the tower began to ring.

He counted one and stood. At the second he moved down the steps of the dais and stood upon the wooden floor at the third strike. His stride was measured, not long, not fast, just a pretty dance to be performed for the gathered assemblage as he moved to meet her in the center of the floor, each having crossed the space in silence. She slipped into a shallow curtsy at the fifth toll. Kit bowed for the sixth.

His hand rose, and she dipped her head in demure acceptance as he settled her comfortably in his arms for the waltz. The first strains of the violin were hesitant, unwilling to break the spell even as they gained confidence and the prince, and his princess danced across the hall.

He spun her to the peal of a bass bell, having lost count of what number tolled.

The orchestra let the last chord of the song ring throughout the hall, broken only by the final tenor chime far overhead.

He pulled her into his chest, buried his face in her hair. She leaned against him and her tears wet the lace of her mask, shattered against the green of his jacket.

"Eli—" He raised his hands to cup her cheeks, look at her beloved face and the changes wrought within it: the hair that was no longer a mix of mahoganies and scarlet, the eyes without their ring of green. He wiped wet drops from her cheeks, not removing the mask from her, allowing her a moment more of her secrets. "I don't understand."

She trembled in his arms. Her hands gripped his shoulders, staring at his throat rather than meeting his gaze, a first for her, for him, he was certain.

"I don't understand."

Chapter Four

She slipped from his arms, fled the question in his gaze, the hope and the despair that she'd put there and that he'd endured because she had not been at his side.

With a knowledge born of centuries of living within these walls, she slipped from the ballroom and down the steps of the palace and into the night beyond.

He would follow her. He always followed her. And when he caught her, she would cry, and she would plead because for three days she'd been locked in silence and watched him suffer and she did not know of any way to relieve the pain she'd caused him. Her heart beat with that pain. Her soul ached at the sorrow that bled from his pores.

She ran, stumbling when her slipper caught in the grass and she gasped as her grace deserted her and she watched the ground come reaching up to catch her.

Strong hands closed around her waist, pulled her into a body that wrapped around her and took the brunt of her fall. She landed at his side, spared the harsh impact by his chivalry while he fought to catch his breath beside her. She reached without thought, the darkness that flowed through her veins coming easily to her command, spearing into his body and banishing the pain of a bashed elbow and bruised spine. His back arced beneath her, her magic filling him and soothing him and more intense than she'd meant it to be. The Blackness fled with a thought and he sank slowly back onto the cold earth, breathing easier at the least.

She met his grey eyes staring up at her, unable to speak until he took the mask from her face, terrified he might not give her a chance to explain.

"Are you a ghost then?"

She shook her head.

"Then have I died and finally found you?" His fingers curled into her hair, pulling at the tresses, teasing her with the gentle tug. He shifted and touched the mask beneath her eyes and she was grateful for the dark of the moon that hid the blush she couldn't control, hid the changes in her appearance that she hated because she was not the woman he once knew, not anymore. "I'm not the same person either."

She blinked her eyes open, not having realized she'd closed them to his soft caress.

He brushed the lace once more, slipped his fingers beneath the soft edge and peeled the damp fabric from her skin.

"I don't understand."

She understood too much.

With a desire heightened by centuries of denial, she bent the few inches between them and claimed the kiss stolen from her by her brethren three hundred and eighty-eight years ago. She kissed him, and the Darkness answered her desire with a roaring rush of pleasure that consumed her, billowed out from her in great waves, caught him up in the maelstrom and bound them tighter into one being. Her heart did not just beat with him but was the same; his breath was hers, his flesh was a second skin and as sensitive as her own physical self. She was his memories as he was hers, her year spent as apprentice, trying to learn control of the dark power that she'd welcomed into her body to save his life, fighting to regain enough control that she was not swept away by the Night. The dreams he woke from, memories buried within his subconscious of pain upon pain, scars that bled against his psyche and echoed into his waking world. Months of relearning to breathe while his ribs healed, and his lungs remembered that a deep breath didn't have to hurt. The pity in the eyes of the soldiers who had been there at his rescue, seen what had been done to the body. The pity from his king who saw only a broken son and could not reconcile the man who was and the one he had become. He brushed against the pain of her heart reaching for him only to be blocked by his conviction she was dead, the number of times her mother and the other elves stopped her from running to him, burned her letters, caged her in a cell surrounded by light that not even the Darkness filling her could overwhelm.

She leaned back first, looking down into eyes that she ached to stare into for whatever eternity waited for her. "I tried. I tried so hard to come to you. I begged her to send word, that you were dying from the not knowing, the pain worse than whatever tortures you'd suffered."

"I would not have believed anything but you standing before me." He brushed back the dark hair from her face, fallen forward around them at their kiss. "How? I thought she killed you."

"No. No, she said that the debt had been forgiven, only three lives bound my exile, the last was by your hand."

"But that's—"

"Her word is law, Kit. She said it and it was believed." She paused, answered his first question. How was she here now, if not then? "I woke in the temple and you were gone. You'd been gone for days. My mother sent you away with your guards, her healing as complete as she could manage, the body needing rest while the soul healed or fled. No one knew how to bring you back, and I was caught in the Void, unable to help even had I wanted." She did not resist touching his face, tracing the faint lines of magic that decorated his skin, the blessing of her mother and the other high priests of the Dienobolos. She laid her hand over his heart, felt the power of the Priestosolos that marked him.

It was an accident, that she let the surge of her magic fill her hand and flow into him. It was an accident, but she did not regret overwhelming her mother's binding and claiming him as hers alone.

"When I woke, the last of the light left me. My hair was black as the void, my eyes; my skin paled as a child of the Midnight must be pale. No matter if I sat in the light for hours, or chased the sun for days, it was like the bright rays could not touch me.

"I was so angry, Kit. I was so angry and so scared and any emotion, every emotion, threatened the little sanity I retained." She could not meet his gaze, afraid to see fear in them, disgust at what she'd become. "They were right to keep me locked away. And when I rose from the madness, I did not think you would want me any longer, had already let me go—"

"Never." He shifted and shifted again when she tried to pull away, holding her closer. "I will never let you go."

"I'm not the girl you knew."

"I'm not that man either."

He did not say that without her he was a shell. He did not need to say the words for she'd seen the truth when acting out her mother's final game, final test. That he'd threatened the priestess made her smile, enjoying that he'd loved her enough to avenge her against the highest-ranking member of the Dienobolos.

"You never used to blush this much."

"I blushed," she could not help the small smile that came to her lips at his remark. "My skin just did not show it."

"It suits you, fair lady."

She did not fight his lead this time, allowing him to roll her to her back, smiling at the green stains that would rub into her dress with every kiss he gave her.

This one was a softer thing, born of joy and content, not laced with despair that the first might be the last as well. He kissed her, and her eyes closed, head tipping back as her staid prince, so proper for so very long, lost the battle she'd hoped to force him past all those years ago, so many times over the years.

He breathed against the pulse at her throat. "Your mother," he hesitated, and she did not know where his thoughts had turned. "She said I was accepted. That I was for Iisforsos."

"The First to Touch the Stars. The first to walk amongst the Void and return with Its power, Its servant in this world."

He brushed the ridge of her brow, the corner of her eye, swept her lashed when she closed her lids to let him touch. "You. She accepted me for you." His fingers were soft when they traced the swell of her lower lip. "Iisforsos."

Yes, that was what she was called. A new title for a new time just as she had come before him once bearing a different guise. But that was not what she wished him to call her. "That is not my name, Prince."

He rose over her, rose to stare down in her eyes. She wrapped her arms around his neck, holding him tight, waiting for long forgotten memories to emerge and to see the response she had once sought to deny.

He smiled, his weight and his warmth settling over her. "Then what is your name, my love?"

"Ella. Just Ella."

"No."

She frowned up at him, trying to read the deeper emotion within the smile in his eyes.

"Not 'Just Ella.'" He held her chin steady, leaned towards her until his lips brushed hers with his words. "My Ella. Always my Ella."

"My Prince. My Kit."

And it was true.

EPILOGUE

WHEN THE SPRING rains ended, there was a wedding.

It was not a small affair, as a prince's wedding cannot be small.

Nobles and knights, ladies fair and frail, all came for the final ball that the king would throw in honor of his son.

The streets of the city were filled with peasants and soldiers, with elves who left their wooden homes to visit those made of stone. There was smiling and crying, laughter and arguments and it was good and natural, and, in the end, it was a type of magic, all the men and women and children gathered together in celebration.

In the month before the wedding, the prince and his captain rode through the city, rode the length and breadth of their kingdom. He spoke of the people, and she spoke of the land, and where they went they were received and they were accepted.

It is said that where the fair captain tread, health came. The sick healed. The old felt young again.

And where the prince followed, wisdom flowed. Men and women flocked to him for his counsel and his compassion.

The gates of the palace were thrown open for three days of feasting, and for three days there were no peasants or princes. Everyone danced and wined and dined as though they were equals sharing in their rulers' joy.

On the third night, as was tradition, the prince entered the ballroom and walked to his father's throne to sit upon the dais where he would someday rule.

He did not walk alone.

They sat on chairs pressed together, the prince and his captain, elegant, regal, and beloved of each other.

Prince Christophe de L'Avigne took his vows before a priest of Atha, his mother's patron goddess, the goddess closest to his father's heart. He took his vows before the Priestosolos of the Dienobolos and offered his prayers to the Darkness. His captain held his hands, kneeling at his side to repeat the words back to him, binding the woods and the city into one, the gods of the light, and the Darkness combined.

It is said that she wore a dress as dark as midnight, studded with diamonds that sparkled in the light of the candles set to flame around her, that she brought with her the calming shadows of the woods and the quiet peace of a restful night. For her crown, a simple silver circlet bound up her dark locks, a jewel dripping atop her forehead, elegant, a thing of nature and of man.

The priest twined their wrists with a rope of ivy.

The priestess draped their shoulders with cloaks of fine wool woven barely a stone's throw from the palace steps in the city surrounded by stonewalls.

When the ceremony was over, and the multitudes held their breath to watch, it was the kiss shared, so pure and so sweet, filled with longing and with love, the love of lifetimes, that bound the two, bound the pain and the suffering and the salvation into one being, and promised a bright future.

AND OF COURSE, THE CHARMING PRINCE AND HIS ASSASSIN PRINCESS LIVED…

...for now...

For the next installment in the
NEVERLANDS SAGA look for:

About the Author

Andi Lawrencovna lives in a small town in Northeast Ohio where she was born and raised. After completing her Masters in Creative Writing, she decided that it was time to let a little fantasy rule her life for a while. *The Never Lands* were born out of a frustration with happily-ever-afters, and a burning desire for the same.

For more information on Andi Lawrencovna and
The Never Lands :

www.AndiLawrencovna.com

ABOUT THE COVER DESIGNER

JULIE NICHOLLS IS an English woman living in a small town in Bulgaria with her husband and two fur babies. Her love of creating artwork has been with her all of her life. When she was a child, she drew and painted constantly and only after leaving school did she have to put it all on the back burner while she worked. Julie was born way too early to study Photoshop in college, but if it had been invented then, she would have fallen in love with it immediately. It's her primary tool for creating artwork, together with a few other essentials.

She creates book covers, banners, icons, and promotional advertisements for authors to use for their websites and books.

You can find her on Facebook at "Covers by Julie" and "Mirishka's Artwork," or for more information on Julie and her work, visit:

WWW.JULIENICHOLLS.COM